BEC MCMASTER

YOU ONLY LOVE TWICE

LONDON STEAMPUNK
THE BLUE BLOOD CONSPIRACY

ALSO AVAILABLE BY BEC McMASTER

YOU ONLY LOVE TWICE
THE BLUE BLOOD CONSPIRACY, BOOK THREE

With the clock ticking down, the Company of Rogues must find a deadly killer and stop them from assassinating the Queen... before London burns.

First rule of espionage: don't ever fall in love with your target.

Five years ago, Gemma Townsend learned the hard way what happens when you break this rule. She lost everything. Her mentor's trust. The man she loved. And almost her life. Love is a weakness she can never afford again.

When offered a chance at redemption, the seductive spy is determined to complete her assigned task: to track down a dangerous assassin known as the Chameleon, a mysterious killer sent after the queen, whose identity seems to constantly change.

But as her investigation leads Gemma into a trap, she's rescued by a shadowy figure she thought was dead—the double agent who once stole her heart.

A man with few memories, all Obsidian knows is Gemma betrayed him, and he wants revenge. But one kiss ignites the unextinguished passion between them, and he can't bring himself to kill her.

Can Obsidian ever trust her again? Or is history doomed to repeat itself? Because it soon becomes clear the Chameleon might be closer than either of them realized... and this time Gemma is in the line of fire.

CHAPTER ONE

"We need to send the Duke of Malloryn a message...."

The word's echoed in Obsidian's ears as he slipped along the edge of a roof, stalking his quarry. Fog swirled around his boots, tendrils curling away from his cloak like the tentacles of an octopus. Ahead of him, a pale figure vanished over the next gable, completely unaware of the danger that stalked him.

This was Langley's first mission.

Too bad it would also be his last.

The young *dhampir* operative had been newly transformed only a year ago, the *elixir vitae* changing him from a blue blood afflicted with the craving virus into a more evolved creature. Faster than a blue blood, stronger, and practically invincible, the *dhampir* were what blue bloods were always meant to become.

Langley paused at the edge of the gutter, sinking to his haunches to survey the street below. He flexed his right fingers, as if nervous. Probably was. This assassination had been requested by the Master himself; the man who ruled

Obsidian and his fellow *dhampir*. The others worshipped the master, though Obsidian felt nothing.

Emotions sucked like a black hole within him, bleeding him dry. He remembered nothing.

He felt nothing.

He was nothing.

"I am a weapon," he whispered to himself by rote. "Forged out of the flames themselves."

Obsidian melted into the shadows, pressing his back to a chimney. Below him on the street, he could make out Langley's quarry.

The young woman wore a becoming dress of lavender that set off the pale cream of her skin, despite her dirty apron. She'd dyed her hair black since the last time he'd seen her five years ago, and swayed through the crowd with an innate sense of grace that drew the male gaze, no matter what role she played. One of the Duke of Malloryn's spies, she'd worn many names and faces over the years. She called herself Gemma now, though he'd known her as Hollis Beechworth.

Obsidian's hand slid to the knife at his side.

There. There was the hot press of emotion, flaming like a supernova through his veins. He didn't understand it. He knew her face. Could recall the night she tried to kill him all those years ago.

But nothing else.

Only this curious surge of hunger within him as the darkness in his soul suddenly reared its head the second he saw her.

He needed to know why Gemma—he refused to think of her as Hollis—pulled at him like this.

And he needed her alive if he was going to decipher what it all meant—just why he was so drawn to her.

"Have her killed," his master had commanded, *"Put her in a white gown, like something a debutante—or a thrall—would wear. Then shoot her straight through the heart. And leave her on Malloryn's doorstep."*

A message for the duke—their nemesis.

A mission for Langley, to prove his allegiance to the cause.

A pity Langley was never going to pass his test.

Obsidian let the fog mask his movements as he set out in search of his prey. The other *dhampir* had vanished, stepping off the rooftop and landing in the alley below. Obsidian stalked along the edge like a cat on the prowl, watching the young disciple slip along the alley.

Gemma made her way through the streets, tucking a strand of black hair behind her ear and flashing a wicked smile at a man who tripped over his feet when he saw her. In the murky London afternoon, that smile brightened the day. She would never be the most beautiful woman in the room, her chin a little too pointed to be classically handsome, and her pillow-shaped mouth too full for the current fashion, but she was eye-catching in a way no other woman could compete with. Vibrancy flowed through every inch of her body, and she made a man feel alive just looking at her. Every glance from those hot-lashed eyes seemed like she'd just thrown down a gauntlet; *try and take me.*

If you dare....

For a second Obsidian paused, his gaze drawn to her smile. Color vanished from his vision, the world bleeding into shades of black and white as the hunger roused within him, and his heart gave a shuddering pulse. He wanted to dare. He wanted his hands on her, his lips and teeth skating over that creamy skin. He wanted to slam her back against a wall and capture that lying little mouth and make a ruin of her prim gown. He'd never felt like this before—at least, as far as he could recall—and the reckless desire chafed at him.

Why her?

Why did his inner darkness stir whenever he thought of her?

Because she's mine, whispered the darkness within him.

Then she was gone, and Langley scurried to the edge of the alley, as if to make his move.

Obsidian stepped off the edge of the roof, gravity catching hold of him. He landed in the alley lightly, his knees bending to absorb the blow and the long edges of his great cloak flaring out around him like wings.

Langley spun around, relief flooding his expression when he saw whom it was. "Bloody hell, Obsidian. You nearly scared three years off my life."

"Apologies."

Obsidian straightened and strode toward him as Langley visibly relaxed. He barely knew the disciple. They were all merely cannon fodder, created for the Master's purposes from the ranks of Lord Balfour's former Falcons. Spies and assassins once, they served the same role now they were a little harder to kill, and far more bloodthirsty with the transition.

"Are you here to observe whether I pass my test or not?" Langley sneered a little. "The bitch might have eluded the other assassins sent to kill her, but I assure you I shall not fail."

That's right. This one thought highly of himself.

"No." Obsidian lunged forward, burying his blade right in the center of the other *dhampir's* chest. Langley never even saw it coming. Clamping a hand over the other *dhampir's* mouth to silence any sounds of the skirmish, he swung behind him, wrenching Langley's head up to reveal his vulnerable throat.

Langley struggled, his dark red-black blood gushing over Obsidian's gloves as he yanked his knife up until it met Langley's sternum. There were many things a *dhampir* could survive. You needed to cut out their heart to be absolutely certain the evolved craving virus wouldn't re-animate them.

A choking sound vibrated in Langley's throat as his flailing hand landed on Obsidian's arm. Struck him again. Finally clutched at his sleeve, as if to beg for mercy.

"Sshh," Obsidian whispered, drawing the other man back into his embrace. "It will all be over soon."

He made certain of it.

Langley's hand fell from his sleeve, his weight suddenly slumping against Obsidian as his knife macerated the other *dhampir's* heart. The breath wheezed out of Langley's lungs.

"My apologies," he whispered in the younger *dhampir's* ear as he lowered the body to the ground. "But Gemma Townsend is mine."

If anyone was going to kill her, it was going to be him.

The woman who called herself Gemma Townsend had the feeling she was being followed.

A curious incident, for she herself was following someone.

And yet, the familiar prickle of being watched itched the back of her neck, and all her senses were on high alert.

A spy being spied upon. That was the sort of jest that would have made her dearest friend, Baroness Schröder, laugh.

Yet now she was out in the field, she couldn't afford to.

"Where are you?" she whispered to herself, slipping through the thinning crowd of people as she glanced over her shoulder.

The dreary afternoon fog settled over the buildings like a mantle, people tucking up their collars as they hurried home. Horses' hooves clopped on the cobblestones, and a steam carriage veered past, hissing a lungful of smoke in her face as she stepped up onto the curb.

Dozens of people strode the streets, but as she surveyed them with a practiced eye she knew none of them had the vaguest interest in her. In her field of work, she could always spot a person's tells. It had become second nature over the years. Someone loitering—the way she was—or turning to survey a nearby window in sudden curiosity when their mark turned around. Usually a single person hovering just out of the line of sight, and weaving through the crowd, using them as cover.

Three men jostled past her on the sidewalk. Gemma tucked her basket of posies close to her skirts. She'd blackened a tooth, and her cheeks were stained with soot, her eyebrows thickened with the judicious use of powders. She'd hovered over a bowl of boiling water that morning so her sleek black hair dried into frizzy strands, and pinned it up haphazardly. Nobody glancing at her would take a second look; girls selling flowers were all through this section of Covent Garden.

The best way to be invisible was to play a common part in plain sight.

And yet, she was fairly certain someone had made her.

She scuttled on, trying to keep the Earl of Kylemore in view. At the corner of her eye, she thought she saw something, and glanced up as a flicker of movement vanished into the shadows on the nearest roof. Odd. Could have been a pigeon, she supposed, but—

There.

Right behind her.

A shape emerged from the fog and Gemma slipped the knife from her sleeve in a smooth movement, the hilt falling into her gloved palm like an old friend she knew well.

A hand snatched her elbow, jostling her in the crowd, and Gemma's fist curled around the knife as she moved to strike and—

Pulled the blow the second she recognized her assailant.

"We have a problem," the Duke of Malloryn muttered under his breath, his shadow falling across her.

Gemma gasped.

"You nearly had an immediate knife-shaped problem." She glanced into the duke's unexpressive face as he gripped her elbow in the middle of St. Martin's Lane. "What the hell are you doing? I almost stabbed you between the ribs. Have you not heard the rules of going undercover? Never sneak up on a fellow operative when they're on edge."

"I thought you saw me."

She peered behind her, that uncanny feeling still rippling along her skin. "I knew someone was watching me." Someone had been watching her for weeks now, she was certain of it. *Or maybe your nerves are just playing games with you?* "But I thought I caught a glimpse of them on the rooftops. Just shadows in the fog, I guess."

Malloryn stared into her face, reading her like an open book. A dangerously handsome man, it was his mind one had to be wary of. Thoughts ticked behind those chilling gray eyes, as if he could see right through her. "Are you completely recovered after that incident in the museum?"

Someone had tried to kill her.

And she swore another man had saved her life; she'd caught a glimpse of a tall, pale blur reflected behind her in the glass cabinet as she fainted from blood loss.

Malloryn wasn't talking about her health, however. "I'm fine." He'd been somewhat skeptical of her claims of being followed that day, but Gemma knew what she'd seen.

"Good. Come with me."

Ahead of her, the quarry she'd been pursuing all morning began arguing with an orange seller. The Earl of Kylemore was allegedly a member of the Sons of Gilead, a covert alliance of disgruntled lords from the Echelon who were hoping to overthrow the queen. Last month the SOG burned down three of the city's draining factories before most of them were either shot or caught by the Nighthawks who protected the city. A few had escaped, and though she suspected Kylemore wasn't highly placed within the SOG, she'd been hoping he'd be able to lead her to the men who were. It was time to round up the last scraps of the SOG and end them.

If Kylemore saw her here with Malloryn, she'd never get close to him again.

The only reason Malloryn would risk breaking her cover was if something insanely important had arisen.

Gemma shot Malloryn a saucy smile, not quite willing to destroy weeks of hard work. "Its a ha'penny a posy, if you're asking, milord."

Eyes glittering, he tugged a handful of coins from his purse and pressed them into her hand. "I'll take the lot."

Gemma blushed, accepting his arm and behaving like any flower girl who'd found herself propositioned on the street. "This had better be important," she warned as the Earl of Kylemore vanished.

"It is." Malloryn strolled with her toward the end of the street.

A steam hack was waiting there, though he hadn't brought his usual coach and four.

The door opened abruptly, revealing Herbert, the Duke of Malloryn's butler-slash-spy-slash-assassin, depending on which day of the week it was.

"Cheerio, Miss Townsend," Herbert said with a wink as he hopped out.

"Herbert," she greeted with a flirtatious shrug of the shoulder. "He's got you driving steam carriages now?"

"Got to keep my hand in," Herbert replied. "You never know when Malloryn's going to cast me to the curb, and then I'll still be able to feed my poor, misbegotten family."

"You don't have a family," Malloryn said, kicking the step down for her. He didn't so much as smile, and Gemma exchanged a long look with Herbert. Once upon a time Malloryn had owned a sense of humor, though she saw it eroding day by day, year by year.

Something had happened.

"Get in. Now."

Gemma got in. "Where are you taking me?"

"The Ivory Tower. I need you to take a look at a body."

CHAPTER TWO

"The Ivory Tower," Gemma breathed, peering through the windows as the carriage pulled up in the courtyard of the enormous marble-sheathed tower that stood where the remains of parliament had once lain.

It had been built during the despotic prince consort's reign, the founding stones laid years ago when he overthrew the king. When Princess Alexandra came of age, he'd forced her to marry him, promising to build a dynasty of power and might. The Echelon—the aristocratic blue blood lords who'd infected themselves with the craving virus—had become formidable and dangerous under the prince consort's rule, until three years ago when the humans, Nighthawks, and mechs banded together to overthrow the prince consort.

Now the queen ruled from the heights of the tower, though it was said she despised the signs of her former husband's excesses and often preferred to reside at the smaller keep of Windsor. The Echelon remained, but it was stripped of its previous power, and there were new rules to keep them in check.

"May I ask whose body I'm supposed to be looking at?"

"You'll see," Malloryn replied, as one of the Coldrush Guards who protected the tower jerked the back door open. The guard's hair was a pale blond, typical of his blue blood status.

Before the revolution, the craving virus remained the exclusive right of the aristocratic Echelon. It gave them enhanced senses, extended their lives, and increased their ability to heal until they were almost invulnerable. The blood lust was an unfortunate side effect, and the photosensitivity tended to inhibit their movements during the day—especially as they aged and their craving virus levels bloomed—but that mattered little to an entire social class who did most of their frolicking at night anyway.

While the Council of Dukes had once held the power to limit who received the blood rites—prominent sons of influential members of the Echelon mostly—accidents tended to occur when the craving virus was so proprietary and bloodletting was the prime means of a blue blood's diet.

Any "rogue" blue blood was offered one of three options; join the Nighthawks who patrolled the London streets and served as thief-takers and hunters; the Coldrush Guards who protected the Ivory Tower and the queen; or be executed.

Malloryn slipped out of the carriage impatiently.

Gemma followed.

"This way," he said, leading her toward the squat tower at the northern edge of the walled courtyard. Thorne Tower.

Oh, blast.

Home to traitors, political hostages, and those prisoners whose crimes were dangerous enough to warrant further questioning, Thorne Tower loomed over the courtyard like a watchful guardian. She was responsible for a good handful of its inmates.

"I know you enjoy holding all your cards close to your chest, but I'm about to expire from curiosity."

"We have a slight problem," Malloryn replied. "Jonathan Carlyle is dead."

"The Chameleon?" *Dead?* The man had been wanted for the murders of fifteen high-profile blue blood lords. He'd had the aristocratic Echelon on edge for years.

Nobody knew whom he worked for, though she and Malloryn suspected. Nobody knew why he'd killed the men and women he had. And for an assassin, he had a peculiar signature style unbecoming for the trade.

It was as if he'd wanted the world to know which deaths belonged to him.

Even as he'd spent years protesting his innocence once he'd been caught.

"Why is it a problem if Carlyle's dead?" Gemma's mind raced. "Half the Echelon will sleep better at night knowing he's no longer breathing. He tried to kill you too, if I recall."

"Tried." Malloryn gestured her through the main door to the tower, ignoring the pair of guards on duty. "He's not the first. And I'd like you to draw your own conclusions. You were the one who captured him. You know him best. I want your opinion on something."

Malloryn. Always as bloody oblique as he could be.

"Your Grace." One of the tower guards waited inside, wearing the proud livery of the Coldrush Guards. "I've kept the scene for you."

Malloryn hadn't yet viewed it? Hmm. This was rather disconcerting.

"Ah, Jamison. I've bought my secretary to take some notes for me." Malloryn gestured obscurely toward her. "Now, show me to his cell."

Secretary. She could work with that. Gemma immediately let herself fade into the background, hunching her shoulders a little and lowering her gaze. No sign of the flirtatious Gemma Townsend remained behind, and nobody watching would ever notice how much she could take in during such an act.

Thank God Malloryn had made her clean her face and strip off her rumpled overdress in the carriage.

Gemma followed him up the circular stairs leading to the prisoner wing, tugging her cape jacket neatly into place as she went and smoothing her rumpled skirts and hair. By the time they reached the top, she'd completely shed her flower girl persona, twisting her hair into a neat chignon.

"We found the first guard here," Jamison said as they turned the corner into the prison wing.

A body lay on the other side of the barred door. Jamison unlocked it, even as Gemma peered around him.

The guard on the floor wore the same uniform Jamison did. He had a pistol in his hand, and most of the left side of his face was missing. Whoever did this wanted it to look like a suicide.

Which meant they'd somehow managed to subdue the guard without alerting any others, kill him, then pose the body. Unusual.

"This door was locked?" Malloryn asked.

"Yes, your Grace."

"Nobody saw anything out of the ordinary?"

"Not a damned thing. It happened in the middle of the guard shift."

"And nobody heard anything?"

Jamison shifted uneasily as they stepped through the door to where they could get a better look at the body. "Some of us thought we heard something, but it occurred during parade training in the yard. Lots of yelling and horns. Lots of noise. Whoever did this timed it spectacularly well."

Hmm.

"Do you have regularly scheduled parades?" Malloryn asked.

"No. This was organized yesterday. The commander was displeased with the recent turnout of the guards, and thought we needed drilling."

Who? Gemma mouthed, prompting Malloryn to ask the questions she couldn't while she was supposed to play his subordinate.

"Who is he?" Malloryn asked, resting his hand on hilt of the cane-sword sheathed at his hip.

"Robert Kirkland. He's been an officer of the guards for nearly ten years. Good man." Jamison's voice roughened. "Or at least, he was."

Malloryn asked a few more questions, before looking impatient. "Show us the cell."

They moved along the hallway.

The iron-bound doors set into the stark stone walls were closed and locked down. Occasionally she heard people shifting behind them, but Thorne Tower was meant to break men. Not offer them a single luxury. Even light and sound was denied to them in the solitary wing.

Another body lay slumped in the hall.

"John Dunne," Jamison explained. "He's the warden. The curious thing is, he had keys upon him, but they were still in his pocket."

"Or maybe someone put them back?" Malloryn mused.

Gemma examined Dunne. Throat cut from behind, ear to ear, though that wouldn't kill him. The blood trickling from inside his ear showed where a thin poniard had been stabbed. That was the killing blow. Blue bloods could heal from almost anything short of decapitation or removal of the heart.

In this long, narrow tunnel, there was no way he couldn't have seen or heard his assailant coming. Which meant he knew the perpetrator.

Little pieces of the puzzle began to fit themselves together.

The next cell door lay ajar. Gemma's steps slowed.

"Who opened the door?" Malloryn asked.

"It was open when the guards made their rounds," Jamison explained. "That was the first sign something was wrong. We were coming from the other direction, so we didn't see Dunne or Kirkland until it was too late."

Gemma examined the door. The lock hadn't been tampered with. The keys hadn't been taken. Perhaps the killer had their own set of keys? A breathless sensation swept through her.

An inside job.

It had always been the first clue.

Three dead bodies.

Jonathan Carlyle.

She'd been working undercover in Lord Randall's house when his new footman—Carlyle—had murdered him.

She'd spent a year on the Chameleon's tail, trying to track him down. The second they got word Randall was the next target, she'd been sent in to stop it. Instead, the murder happened right in front of her.

From the forged reference they'd found on Randall's desk, Carlyle had previously been working for Lady

Harrenhall, the fourteenth victim. They couldn't tie him to any of the previous thirteen murders. It was as if Carlyle appeared out of nowhere, presumably killed Lady Harrenhall, and then moved on to Randall.

But the letter of reference, Gemma's eyewitness account, and confirmation of his previous employment with Lady Harrenhall were enough to condemn him. Case closed.

A sudden horrible suspicion swept through her, and she pushed inside the cell.

Jonathan Carlyle had spent years protesting his innocence. He couldn't remember shooting Lord Randall, and he'd managed to stick to his story the entire time they questioned him.

And now he was dead.

The three years since she'd captured him hadn't been kind. Carlyle lay on the floor, his thin body arranged carefully with his hands clasped over his chest and his eyes closed.

A flashback of Lady Harrenhall slammed through her mind, superimposed over Carlyle for a brief second. She'd been training her memory since she was four, and it was easy to recall the precise details.

Gemma circled the body. "A single bullet to the temple." From the blood spatter pattern on the wall, Carlyle had been standing in front of it. "He saw the killer enter. He faced him. He died."

No trained assassin would ever let down his guard long enough for another to draw a pistol and pull the trigger, and the Chameleon had been the best of the best.

How the hell had someone gotten the drop on him like this?

"Could you give us a moment alone to view the body?" Malloryn asked, though his tone left little doubt it was no question.

Jamison vanished.

"Well?"

She knelt by the body, careful not to touch it. "Inside job. Assailant had his own set of keys and knew the building, the guard roster, and forthcoming events. He chose his time well. Dunne knew him, and didn't protest when he saw him. Indeed, I suspect he was comfortable enough in our killer's presence that he voluntarily turned his back on him. Then our killer moved on and shot Kirkland before staging it to look like a suicide. I want to know if all the Coldrush Guards carry the same style of pistol."

"You don't suspect Kirkland?"

"He kills Carlyle, slits Dunne's throat, then walks all the way to the barred gate before shooting himself? Highly unlikely. And why kill himself?"

Gemma frowned. Why stage Kirkland's death to look like a suicide at all? The second the guards saw Dunne or Carlyle, they'd know this was a murder.

"None of this makes any sense," she muttered, her gaze turning to the playing card the corpse held in his rigid fingers. The posing of the body. The bullet hole to the head. The presence of the playing card.

A horrible suspicion lurched inside her chest.

Malloryn knelt on the other side of Carlyle and then used one of his daggers to turn over the card.

Gemma swallowed.

It was the King of Diamonds.

"Gemma?"

"This is the work of the Chameleon," she said breathlessly, though she'd *known* in some part of herself.

"Or as near to it as I can imagine. I'm sure it will be confirmed when you have the bullet retrieved."

There'd be a diamond etched into the outer casing of the bullet.

A calling card of sorts.

"As I suspected." His lips pressed firmly together, faint sign of inner turmoil. "Which brings us to a rather intriguing question: How did the Chameleon murder the Chameleon?"

CHAPTER
THREE

The ride back to the Company of Rogues' private safe house was quiet, leaving Gemma lost in her thoughts.

She couldn't help going over the Carlyle case in her mind, wondering if there'd been something she missed.

What she wouldn't give to be able to go back in time and question him most thoroughly. *Were you working alone?*

Or....

Did someone give you that bullet and insist you kill him?

Was the real Chameleon still out there?

Had he been laughing at her, all this time?

Was he cleaning up his mess?

What had happened today in that cell? Why now? Why had the Chameleon been quiet for the past three years? Or was it a copycat?

Malloryn himself stared out the window, his fingertips drumming a steady tap on the sill. It was as much a sign of agitation as she'd ever seen from him.

"What is it?" she asked.

They'd been working together for nearly fifteen years. She knew this man from the inside out.

"We long suspected the Chameleon worked for the prince consort. You captured him the day of the revolution. There's been not a single murder since then, and it seemed you had your man."

"I saw him kill Lord Randall with my own eyes."

"I'm not disputing your recollection." Their gazes met. "But why has it taken three years for someone to murder the Chameleon? We were no closer to getting a confession off him. Nothing else has changed. Except, of course, for recent events."

A couple of months ago, a disgruntled group of blue blood lords had begun plotting against the queen and the Council of Dukes who ruled the city.

A rogue *dhampir* agent named Zero had been found pulling their strings, and they'd been lucky to stop her before she fed dozens of people to her stable of vicious vampires.

An uneasy suspicion swirled through Gemma's midriff. "You think the Chameleon's murder has something to do with the current issues we're facing."

"Someone's pulling strings. Someone wants to cause chaos in the city, overthrow the queen, and destroy *me*. You heard what Zero said when we captured her." The enemy agent had been almost gleeful as she told Malloryn something was coming for him. "This is aimed at me. All of this. I have a vendetta with an unknown enemy. And now, suddenly the prince consort's most dangerous assassin is murdered in the same way he used to kill others? I cannot help but think it's connected."

"Blood and ashes, I hope not. We've barely recovered from last month when Lord Ulbricht and the Sons of Gilead tried to poison the Echelon's entire blood drinking supply with Black Vein."

"Anarchy doesn't rest."

"No, but I wouldn't have minded another week to recover," she said with a sigh.

London flashed past her sash window, pedestrians hurrying along through the foggy afternoon.

A dull roar began to churn beneath the hum of the carriage's steam engine; Gemma tilted her head intently, trying to make out the sound. On the footpath, a young governess grabbed her charge's hand and hurried him away. A butcher hastily yanked the door closed to his shop, and flipped the latch. A haberdashery yanked their blinds down as London began to stir.

"Down with the queen," someone roared.

"Take back what's ours!" another man yelled.

Her eyes met Malloryn's. "Oh, heck."

The duke tensed.

"It's probably a good thing we took the unmarked carriage." As one of the Council of Dukes who ruled the city, the embossed silver griffin symbol that was the House of Malloryn's personal sigil would have only inflamed the current situation.

"Might take the long way around, Your Grace." The tinny echo of Herbert's voice vibrated through the small speaking device installed in the carriage. It looked like any other hack on the streets, but Jack, the inventor who worked for Malloryn, had made improvements. *"Streets ahead look congested."*

A polite way of saying a riot was brewing.

The humans and mechs resented the long years they'd spent crushed beneath blue blood heels. The blue bloods who'd once done exactly as they pleased resented the new rules. The queen walked a knife edge of balance, trying to assuage all the races, and so far, it seemed she could please nobody.

One glimpse of a pasty face, and this entire section of London would go up as though someone had struck a match. Gemma had never hidden her face before, but there'd been reports in the paper of people being beaten because of how pale their complexions were. A couple of innocent humans had been torn apart last week in Hyde Park. The Nighthawks who patrolled the streets were pushed to the brink of their capacities, especially with their leader still recovering from an assassination attempt last month.

Whistles suddenly blew.

A dozen Nighthawks appeared out of nowhere, clad in the strict black leather uniforms that heralded them. Charged with keeping the streets quiet, they'd been dealing with unruly mobs all month since the last clash between rioters and Nighthawks turned deadly, and now trouble constantly brewed, like a storm on the horizon.

"Do you think it will ever end?" she asked quietly. "Do you think we can ever come back from this point?"

Could there ever truly be peace in London?

Malloryn reached past her to tug the curtains closed.

"There is always hope, Gemma. I spent the last fifteen years fighting for freedom from a despot who had all the power. We did it then. We can overcome our problems now. It will just take time."

She sighed.

"Frankly, I refuse to allow someone to destroy our fragile peace." Malloryn rapped on the carriage roof with his silver-handled cane, as if to prompt Herbert for speed. "Which is why we must stop whoever is trying to rouse these riots and set London aflame. I know it seems overwhelming, but take it one step at a time, Gemma. Today we deal with the Chameleon. Tomorrow we deal with the true enemy."

Home sweet home.

The Company of Rogues' new safe house was a nondescript townhouse in the middle of Marylebone. Malloryn's spy network was unparalleled, but he'd wanted a group who could deal with the current threat to the monarchy—the mysterious, as yet unnamed organization who'd been stirring up chaos in the past year with the intent of replacing the queen.

What he'd ended up with was the aptly named Company of Rogues.

COR had been formed several months ago from a random assortment of blue bloods, mechs, and verwulfen. Each member was a specialist in his or her field; Caleb Byrnes was the best tracker the Nighthawks had to offer; Ingrid Miller, now Ingrid *Byrnes*, had been a verwulfen bounty hunter; Liam Kincaid had a particular gift for mechwork; Ava McLaren was a crime scene investigator from the Nighthawks; Jack Fairchild worked downstairs in the laboratory, creating all manner of mechwork weapons to assist them in their endeavors; and Charlie Todd came from the rookeries of Whitechapel, where he was a jack-of-all trades. Thief. Roguish charmer. And what she suspected was a near-level genius, with his father's gift for tinkering with gadgets.

Which left herself, trained in the arts of espionage; Herbert, the most dangerous butler in London; the baroness, who ran COR in Malloryn's absence; and Malloryn at the head of them all, setting them into play like a master puppeteer.

Gemma trailed Malloryn up the stairs toward the training room, where the sounds of grunts and blows echoed.

Inside the room, Byrnes, Kincaid, and Charlie looked like they'd been busy beating the stuffing out of each other.

Byrnes appeared to have been doing most of the beating. Since his transformation into a *dhampir* two months ago, the color had begun to drain out of his skin and hair, thanks to the Fade, and while he'd been dangerously fast and lethal as a blue blood, now he was incomparable.

Kincaid, a newly infected blue blood with a mechanical arm, was still getting used to the changes to his body and his increased bloodlust. He and Charlie circled Byrnes, fists held up defensively, as Byrnes lashed out with a sudden high kick that almost took Charlie's head off his shoulders. Charlie ducked, slapping the blow aside, as Kincaid slammed his fists down on Byrnes's back.

Or where Byrnes had just been.

Byrnes spun low, sweeping Kincaid's feet out from under him, and then straightened abruptly, slamming the flat of his palm into Charlie's chest.

The pair of them hit the training mats, and Kincaid stayed there, cursing under his breath. Charlie flipped to his feet, his blue eyes twinkling as he noticed the pair of them in the door.

"Gemma. Malloryn." He winced. "Just in time to see Byrnes hand us a thrashing."

Byrnes scrubbed his mouth, showing no hint of surprise. No doubt he'd heard them coming up the stairs with his exquisite hearing. "You almost had me that one time."

"Once." Kincaid groaned, and found his feet with a flexibility he hadn't owned last month. There was no sign of the mechanical leg braces he'd once worn. "You were being generous."

"Where are the others?" Malloryn asked.

"Ava and Jack are in the laboratory downstairs, tinkering with Jack's next project," Charlie said promptly. "Ingrid's reading a book, and I'm not certain where the baroness is."

"Probably avoiding Malloryn," Byrnes muttered sotto voce.

"I beg your pardon?" Malloryn shot him a sharp look.

"Nothing." Innocent did not become Byrnes.

"Tsk, tsk," Gemma chided, filling the sudden tense silence in a rush. The duke was getting married within a week, and betting odds had reached fever pitch as to whether he was going to get the bride to the altar or not. But not all the Rogues were enjoying the lead-up to Malloryn's wedding. "If I were the ladies, I know where I'd be."

She waggled her eyebrows suggestively.

Everybody suddenly reached for their shirts.

"Herbert, can you fetch the baroness?" Malloryn threw over his shoulder. "Tell her to be in my study in five minutes, then send for tea."

"At once, sir." Herbert vanished.

"Perhaps you can solve a problem for us, Your Grace," Charlie called.

"Yes?"

"Let's say the three of us were discussing who the most dangerous rogue in the Company of Rogues is," Charlie said, with an impish smile as he hauled his shirt over his head. "Now Kincaid is a blue blood and Byrnes is *dhampir*, it's upset the ranking a little. We're trying to sort out who fits where."

Malloryn blinked. "Who fits where on what? A scale of which one of us is the Most Dangerous Rogue in the Company of Rogues?"

Men. Gemma rolled her eyes, though she couldn't help looking to Malloryn to see what his answer would be.

He abhorred wasting time, but she'd seen him start to warm to the rest of the Rogues in the past couple of months. Sometimes he needed a bit of lighthearted banter in his life.

"I already know the answer to that question," he replied, slapping the file he'd been carrying on the table. "I don't need to guess."

"My vote's for Byrnes," Charlie explained. "Presuming all goes wrong and Byrnes loses control of his inner *dhampir*, I think he's the most dangerous. He's faster than us now, and stronger. Impervious to most wounds."

"My vote"—Kincaid crossed his arms over his chest—"is you. You destroyed Charlie and me in the ring last month. Barely even broke a bloody sweat. I think you could handle Byrnes."

"The question isn't, can I handle him." Malloryn snorted. "If Byrnes ever slipped his leash, then I wouldn't go after him myself. It's a ridiculous assumption."

A Malloryn answer to a T.

"And you're all looking at this all wrong," Gemma added, unscrewing the lid on the flask of blood at her hip. "All three of you look at strength literally. You should be thinking of strengths *and* weaknesses. Vulnerabilities. You're asking who the most dangerous Rogue is; not who the strongest one is. So sorry, Kincaid, you're out of the running."

The man could probably lift a carriage by himself, and with his mech arm a single blow from him could smash ribs, but he was nowhere near the top of *her* list.

"Byrnes isn't, either. He has a ruthless edge Kincaid lacks, but we have a major trump card against him. If Byrnes gives in to his dark side, then Malloryn would send Ingrid in to bring him down," Gemma replied, sipping her blood. "Byrnes has three major weaknesses; his wife, sunlight, and the Black Vein serum. If you want to take him down without damage, you send in Ingrid to bring him to his knees. He's physically incapable of hurting his wife, and she'll have motivation enough to bring him down any way she can—except dead. If you want him dead, then you take a sniper dartgun and sit in wait where he'll least expect it, and use the serum against him. If you want to escape him, you'd better hope the sun is shining brightly, thanks to his newly acquired *dhampir* weaknesses."

Or you created an ultraviolet incandescent illuminator to use against him, but nobody technically needed to know about that—and Jack hadn't quite gotten the prototype she'd requested right yet.

Because Byrnes wasn't the only *dhampir* out there.

Just the only one who was working on their side.

"But where does everyone else fit?" Kincaid demanded.

Because the size of ones balls is important.

"Easy. From least dangerous to most dangerous; Ava, Jack, Kincaid, Charlie, Isabella, Byrnes, Ingrid, Herbert—for you're all forgetting dear Herbert—and then Malloryn at the top," she replied.

"Herbert?" Kincaid blurted. "The butler?"

"You think he's a *butler*?" Incredible. "That's why you're down at the bottom of the list. You'd be dead before you even noticed where the threat was coming from."

"Charlie's above me!" he protested.

"Charlie's had the benefit of learning how to fight under the Devil of Whitechapel," she said with a shrug. "I've seen him with a cutthroat razor. And he's faster than you. Besides, when you fight, you fight to put a man down. You're a pugilist at heart. Not a killer."

"Hence," Malloryn said with no small amount of amusement as she decimated them, "why Gemma is at the top of *my* list. If, for some godforsaken reason, the Company of Rogues start fighting among themselves, my money's on Gemma taking you all down."

The three of them turned to look at her.

She smiled sweetly and merely sipped her flask.

"So who wins between you and Malloryn?" Byrnes's eyes narrowed thoughtfully. "Hypothetically?"

"Malloryn."

"Gemma."

They spoke at the same time, and then looked at each other.

"You're right," Malloryn said to Kincaid. "I wiped the floor with both you and Charlie last month. Who do you think taught me to fight?" He gestured toward her in an extravagant hand wave. "Gemma has skills none of you can ever dream of owning. Myself included."

Which was a polite way of saying she'd spent most of her formative years training to be an assassin.

A small knot formed deep inside her. "And yet, you're my equal now in the ring."

"Tell me you haven't thought about how to take me down, if such a thing was required," he said dryly.

Have a plan to kill everyone in the room. It was the first thing Lord Balfour's Falcons had taught her as a little girl. She shrugged uneasily. Hard to break small habits. "You don't think I'm actually going to tell you how I'd go about it?"

Malloryn shared a small smile with her. "Worth a shot."

"And you don't think I presume you haven't worked out how to take me down in return? If the pair of us went to war, you win. When it comes to pulling the trigger on you, I hesitate. You don't."

Trained as an assassin or not.

She'd never truly had the gift for killing.

Especially not friends.

"I seem to recall a different story."

"Five years ago," she said pointedly, knowing he was stirring up the past to put her on edge. Malloryn simply couldn't help playing games; but she could play them too. "You're a far more ruthless man than you ever were, Auvry. Now? I think you'd pull that trigger now."

Malloryn looked vaguely uncomfortable.

"What happened five years ago?" Charlie asked.

Gemma screwed the lid back on her flask and sucked in a small breath as she steadied her sudden nerves. *Russia happened.* "Malloryn didn't pull the trigger. He let me live."

And then he saved my life.

"You two were on opposing sides?"

Every face in the room suddenly sharpened at Charlie's question.

"No." Her voice didn't so much as quaver as she looked up and met the duke's eyes. "I was working for Malloryn, I just wasn't following orders. I decided to protect a target he wanted dead."

"An enemy agent who was about to fracture my plans to tear down an entire alliance."

Her lips pressed together.

Dmitri was more than that to me.

But it was all a lie.

And so, she didn't argue.

"Malloryn had one shot at him, but he couldn't pull the trigger because I was between them. You say I let love ruin me, but you used to have a heart too, Auvry. It was the only weakness you potentially had. Now? I think you'd take that shot." She'd seen the darkness stirring in him throughout the revolution, and the lengths he'd gone to in order to defeat Lord Balfour and ruin the prince consort.

The man that came out on the other side wasn't the same one who'd gone into that fight. "So if it comes down to Malloryn and me? King takes queen," she conceded.

"You might be surprised," Malloryn replied tautly, the pinched expression about his nose showing how closely her arrow had struck.

"It's a good thing we'll never have to find out," she replied, gracing the room with a false smile. "Problem solved?"

"Well, I'm convinced," Byrnes replied, scratching his jaw. "As cold as my blood runs at times, it's a little unnerving to watch the pair of you debate murder over a flask of blood as if you're discussing the weather."

Kincaid scowled. "Agreed."

Charlie shrugged.

"It's the important questions in life," she replied, and finally gave in to the urge to roll her eyes.

"Now... do you think we can discuss actual business?" Malloryn demanded. "As enlightening as this little discussion was, the Company of Rogues has a new problem. Someone has just murdered the most dangerous assassin that's ever graced the Echelon in the exact same way he used to murder others. We know how he was killed. We don't know how his killer got in. Or who it is."

He slapped the file against his thigh.

"And... I have a credible report stating his next target is the queen."

Gemma looked at him sharply. Playing his cards close to his chest, indeed. "It is?"

No wonder he'd been out of sorts.

CHAPTER FOUR

"They called him the Chameleon," Malloryn explained, once all the Rogues—besides Ava and Jack—had assembled in his study. "A master of disguise who could kill any target, no matter how high profile or guarded. He was an assassin who plagued the Echelon in the years before the revolution, and he was caught the day the prince consort was overthrown. Or so we thought."

"Intriguing statement," Byrnes mused, his glacial eyes lighting up with glee. "*Or so we thought.*"

Gemma settled into her usual armchair between Baroness Schröder and Charlie. "Of course *you'd* be interested."

Byrnes smiled a devious smile. He never could resist a challenging case. "It's been a boring month. Malloryn's had me confined to the house while we waited to see how my transformation would affect me."

For years blue bloods had feared the Fade—the end stage of the craving virus, when all the color drained out of their skin and hair and they began to transform into a bloodthirsty vampire that would slaughter anything and everything that moved. However, the Company of Rogues had recently discovered there was one other course of transmutation for a blue blood. Using the *elixir vitae*, a closely guarded secret serum, blue bloods could become *dhampir* instead. As fast as a vampire, with the same weakness to sunlight, but retaining their mental faculties.

"Tell me more about this Chameleon," Byrnes purred.

"Fifteen assassinations over the course of five years," Malloryn replied, tossing a file across the polished mahogany table toward Byrnes. "Gemma? You know the facts best."

"His most high-profile kill was Lady Harrenhall," Gemma said, pushing to her feet and standing next to Malloryn, "and several of his previous assassinations happened to be the prince consort's enemies. His last kill, Lord Randall, was the one anomaly to the pattern. Randall was a trusted cousin of the prince consort who was working on his behalf to forge an alliance with the blue bloods of the Russian court. They played golf together. He was murdered the same day of the revolution and his killer apprehended on the spot, though he refused to confess and claimed he had no recollection of killing Randall."

"You believe this Chameleon worked for the prince consort?" Ingrid asked.

"We suspect he had to be connected to the prince consort in some way, as there are too many coincidental deaths among the prince consort's enemies."

"He?" Byrnes asked, pouring a brandy for Ingrid. "If you don't know who it is, then how can you presume?"

"Because we have several witnesses and every single one of them describes a different man. Old, young, bearded, clean-shaven, brown hair, blond, tall, short.... He was a master of disguise. There is no distinguishing characteristic beyond his calling cards; the King of

Diamonds card is usually planted on the victim's body; a diamond is engraved on the casing of the bullet used to kill; and there's nowhere he can't get into, no one he can't kill."

"He wants to be known," Charlie mused.

"He's proud of his work," Byrnes added.

"And the man you thought was the Chameleon?" Ingrid mused, sipping her brandy. "I presume there's a reason we're discussing this case now."

The baroness rounded the table toward the opaque projector at the far end and removed one of the caps so the screen on the wall at the opposite end of the table suddenly lit up.

"As Malloryn said, we thought we'd captured him three years ago," the baroness said. The projector flashed as she slid a small slide into place, and a photograph of a man with a neatly trimmed mustache flashed up on the wall.

Malloryn stared at the image. "Jonathan Carlyle. The man we thought to be the Chameleon. Carlyle was serving as Lord Randall's footman—a new posting for him—when he put a pistol to Carlyle's head and pulled the trigger. Gemma brought him in. Since then, he's been locked away in Thorne Tower and the queen's best questioners have been working on him to discover whom he worked for. For three years he's pled his innocence, and he seemingly couldn't remember being in the room at the time of Carlyle's murder. He stuck with this story regardless of what was done to him, and I've seen dangerous men break under less. He simply couldn't remember anything beyond his lordship sending him to fetch brandy. He didn't know why he did it. He claimed to like Lord Randall, who'd given him a position that gave him the ability to send money home to his elderly mother. He felt like he owed Randall a debt, and he used to sob when Randall was mentioned. It's always bothered me because we could never understand how such a limp handkerchief of a man like Carlyle ever managed to carve a swathe through half the Echelon."

"Interesting," Byrnes said, leaning forward. "A man with no reason to murder a blue blood pulls the trigger, but can't remember why. I'd say I wanted the Randall case, but I'm fairly certain there's more to it. You said the Chameleon was murdered."

"This morning, Carlyle's cell door was discovered unlocked. Someone put a bullet through his forehead in a move seemingly reminiscent of the Chameleon. He had a playing card in his hand—a King of Diamonds."

"You think the real Chameleon is still out there, and you misjudged."

"I don't know what I believe," Malloryn countered, glancing her way.

Gemma ground her teeth together. She'd been the witness who saw Carlyle standing over the body of Lord Randall. Yet it wasn't the first time she'd failed a mission spectacularly.

You didn't fail. You saw him.

Behind closed lids, she called to mind the image of Jonathan Carlyle slipping into Lord Randall's parlor and pouring him a glass of bloodied brandy, which his lordship took. The second Randall lifted it to his lips, Carlyle removed the linen cloth on the tray in his hand, revealing a pistol.

He'd put the muzzle to Randall's forehead and pulled the trigger before she could even cry a warning.

"I saw it happen," she burst out, unable to tolerate Malloryn's pointed silence. "I was undercover as Randall's secretary at the time, trying to stop the Chameleon before he completed his mission."

Byrnes tapped his fingers on the edge of his chair. "If Gemma saw Carlyle pull the trigger, and yet someone else killed Carlyle, then we have two Chameleons."

"Possibly. Or perhaps Carlyle was a scapegoat. Perhaps the real Chameleon knew we were closing in and wanted to throw us off the trail?"

"Could it have been blackmail?" Charlie asked. "Perhaps the real Chameleon forced Carlyle to kill Randall?"

"Why did he not remember killing him then?" Ingrid asked.

Gemma seethed. If it was true, then the Chameleon had known she was on his trail and had deliberately fooled her. "You said there was a credible threat against the queen?"

Malloryn withdrew a playing card from within his waistcoat and held it out to her.

A single bullet hole was drilled through the center of the card.

He turned the card around, revealing the suit.

"Queen of Diamonds," she whispered.

"Someone pinned this to my front door with a knife, then put a bullet in it. It happened just before lunch, and woke me."

Gemma's breath came a little faster. "He wanted you to know he was coming for her."

"Indeed."

She was convinced, as nothing else could have convinced her. The Chameleon had spent years playing games with Malloryn. Every death had been a mockery. A *catch me if you can*. And then she'd finally done it, and the murders stopped, and she'd had no reason to doubt the Chameleon's identity. "This is him. He's back. And he's definitely after the queen."

But where had he been for three years?

"Find him," Malloryn instructed. "I need to return to the Tower and put security protocols into place."

"He'll be on the inside already," she whispered.

"I know."

Their eyes met.

"If he kills the queen, then London goes up in flames," Malloryn said in a dangerously soft voice, and suddenly Gemma knew the stakes were higher than they'd ever been. "We cannot afford to fail."

No matter what.

But who the hell was the real Chameleon?

And where had he been?

CHAPTER FIVE

"Where the hell is Langley?" Ghost demanded, standing on the docks that led to the Core—the secret heart of their London operations.

Where you'll never find him, Obsidian thought, though he didn't dare meet his brother's searing blue eyes.

The leader of the *dhampir* paced along the train platform deep in Undertown, where their base was hidden. Ghost stood almost an inch taller than him, his hair an unruly shock of white, his brows and eyelashes bleached to match. He didn't dare go aboveground for fear he'd send people screaming at the sight of his pale, pale skin; a certain sign of the Fade.

But then, Ghost generally preferred to avoid most humans anyway, unless he was thirsty.

"You sent Langley after a dangerous target," Silas replied. He was another of the original *dhampir* who'd been created by Dr. Erasmus Cremorne at Falkirk Asylum. There'd been seven of them that survived the initial experiment, their bond forged through blood, pain, and finally fire, when they'd banded together to break out. "What'd you expect?"

"Success." Ghost clasped his gloved hands behind his back. "This makes two of our acolytes dead by the hands of one of the Company of Rogues. The Master won't appreciate our failure. And Langley was good. I trained him myself. This makes no sense."

"Clearly your new batch of *dhampir* aren't as good as you think they are," Obsidian murmured. "Or you underestimated Miss Townsend."

The same way he once had.

Never again.

"Do you want *me* to take care of it?" Silas asked. "Why not send your best?"

Obsidian's gut muscles locked. He kept all expression off his face, however, and merely stared at the old train platform beneath his feet.

Silas was the one *dhampir* he actually gave a damn about anymore.

If he considered anyone a brother, it was Silas.

Killing him would be... difficult.

Could he do it? Was Miss Townsend's life worth the price of the one man he still considered a brother?

No. Surely not.

But there was that slither of darkness within him, a whisper of demand and ownership. *Mine.* The mere thought of someone else putting their hands on Gemma made the craving rise within him, as if his darker half was trying to tell him something.

What the hell was wrong with him?

What had she done to him?

"Why not send two of the acolytes?" he countered. Ghost stiffened, as if considering both options, and Obsidian realized he needed to sell his suggestion. "This is plainly a larger task than one can handle alone, but I hardly think Silas needs to stir himself. Send two. Give them a week, at least, to watch Miss Townsend's movements before they make an attempt. Perhaps Langley rushed the job?"

"Perhaps I should send *you*?" Ghost's voice grew dangerously soft. "If we're speaking of my best...."

"I thought you wanted me watching the Ivory Tower? You've been praising your new Falcon recruits. Surely they can handle a simple assassination?" Pain bloomed within him, stabbing through his brain. Easy. This felt like a trap, though he had nothing to prove. He'd burned Gemma from his memories years ago.

Which is why you're killing those sent to hunt her.

Ghost and Silas exchanged a glance.

"You are," Ghost finally said. "I want you to get me inside the tower."

"I'm working on it." He'd been patiently mapping the keep's strengths and weaknesses for weeks now. The queen lived there, high in her gilded tower, thinking herself safe from the world.

Obsidian didn't truly care whether the queen lived or died, but the Master had given strict instructions.

The queen needed to die a bloody death.

London needed to burn.

And the Duke of Malloryn needed to watch it all happen.

"Then work harder," Ghost threatened. "I need a way inside the Ivory Tower before the queen's birthday ball."

"My apologies. It's not as though there are several legions of Coldrush Guards to avoid, a good legion of metaljacket automatons one mustn't wake, and a wall that's impossible to climb—even for me."

"Are you being sarcastic?"

"Would I dare?"

They stared at each other. *Careful. Brother.* Obsidian gave Ghost a thin, faintly edged smile. Frustration edged within him. Ghost ruled the *dhampir*. He always had, but ever since he and Dr. Richter managed to make a breakthrough with the *elixir vitae* and learned to create new *dhampir*, Ghost had become insufferably demanding.

I am not one of your sycophantic underlings. And if you think I'm going to kiss your boots, then you should perhaps think again.

"It's that straight fuckin' face of his," Silas said, bursting into the silence as he slammed a hand down on Obsidian's shoulder, squeezing lightly in warning. "Can never tell when he's makin' mock, but Obsidian knows how important this is. He'll get us in. Ain't nowhere he can't get into if he's half a mind. You know that. Just needs time."

Ghost's eyes narrowed. "You're dismissed. You have three days to get inside the tower and out again. I need the transmitter placed at the very top. And I think you're overdue a visit to Dr. Richter. I'll have him schedule a reconditioning appointment for you."

"You're too kind. But I'll need all my faculties for the task ahead of me." Visits to Dr. Richter's always helped ease the headaches that plagued him, but the cost was several days rest. Obsidian couldn't afford to lose consciousness for so long. Not with the target on Miss Townsend's back. He bowed his head as he stepped backward. "I'll work on the tower."

Ghost turned to Silas. "Send two of the new class after Miss Townsend. They have a week to deliver her body to Malloryn's doorstep. I want him distracted, his attention turned away from the tower, while we plan how to get at the queen."

"Consider it done," Silas replied.

"And how goes Project: Chameleon?" Ghost murmured under his breath to Silas, as Obsidian turned toward the narrow stairs that led from Undertown up to the streets of Bethnal Green.

His ears pricked up.

"You could say... it's been resurrected," Silas replied.

"Good. That should catch Malloryn's attention."

Even with his back turned, Obsidian could hear the smile in his brother's voice. Taking the stairs two at a time, he threw himself into the climb, his thoughts churning.

The situation with Miss Townsend wouldn't end with Ghost's defeat.

No matter how many *dhampir* Obsidian killed, Ghost would keep sending them until she was dead, and it made the muscle in Obsidian's jaw tense.

She was *his*.

His target.

His to kill.

She'd betrayed him in Russia. He remembered that, though his memory was patchy. He also remembered the taste of her mouth, though he refused to think about those thoughts at all.

He needed to get this Gemma situation under control. Find out why he couldn't kill her. Find out why he couldn't stay away from her.

But first, he needed to ensure his fellow *dhampir* never got their hands upon her. He'd managed to give himself time. A week before they made their move. Which meant he had a week to burn her out of his system for good.

How the hell was he going to lure her into the open?

He couldn't break into Malloryn's not-so-secret townhouse and steal her out of her bed, as the rest of the Company of Rogues was on the defense following his recent break-in and the last thing he needed was to draw attention to the act.

Somehow he had to get his hands on her and finish this, before Ghost did.

And that was when he realized just how to get her out of the safe house.

"We've got another potential Chameleon target," Baroness Schröder said, striding into the breakfast room.

Gemma almost spilled her cup of tea as the baroness slapped the file on the table. She jerked it toward her. "Another? I thought he was going after the queen?"

Inside the file was a King of Diamonds card with a bullet hole right through the center.

"Leo Barrons received this late last night," the baroness said.

"The Duke of Caine's heir?" she asked, looking up in surprise. Barrons served as Caine's proxy on the Council of Dukes and remained firm friends with Malloryn. Indeed, he was possibly the only person Malloryn truly considered a friend these days. "Does Malloryn know?"

Isabella poured herself a cup of tea. "Yes. Herbert said Malloryn sent a servant with the card this morning. He couldn't make an appearance himself. Apparently he's having his final fitting for the wedding this morning. But he'll be here at eleven, and he wants you ready."

Hell. Chameleon or not, that had been carelessly done of her.

Gemma circled the table, setting her own tea down, and hugged Isabella from behind. "You know Malloryn cares nothing for Miss Hamilton. This is merely a result of the girl outplaying him. Her reputation is ruined and if Malloryn doesn't marry her then so is his."

After all, the girl's dress had been torn and her throat bloodied when she'd thrown herself at Malloryn in the garden of some blue blood's ball. Two seconds later, half the Echelon came walking around the hedge, and the girl claimed he'd proposed. As a proponent of the Thrall Bill, in which he'd argued for tighter laws concerning what a blue blood could and could not do with his contracted thrall, Malloryn could hardly refuse.

It was clear she'd been with some blue blood.

If Malloryn had denied her, he'd have been considered a hypocrite, and any sort of political sway he'd managed to build behind the bill would have vanished.

Isabella reached up to squeeze her hand before politely disengaging. "Thank you. I don't know what I'd do without you."

"Give him time to deal with this wedding fiasco, and then...."

"I don't need time." Isabella pushed away from her and dumped two sugar cubes into her tea. "He called off our arrangement weeks ago. Said it wasn't fair to either of us. I suspect he meant me."

Gemma stared at her friend helplessly. "I never knew you had such intense feelings for him."

"I don't," Isabella replied sharply. "I knew what I was getting myself into when I seduced him. Malloryn doesn't own a heart. There was no point trying to capture it."

But he'd captured hers.

Gemma could see it written all over the other woman.

With her own experience in heartbreak, she ached to see someone else desperately trying to gather their shattered decorum and put the pieces of their heart together.

"What are you doing tomorrow night?" she asked.

Isabella's dark eyes flickered to hers. "I haven't any plans. Why?"

"Come with me. You and I shall have a night at the theatre together. We'll laugh and drink far too much champagne, and maybe engage in a little casual flirtation." Somehow she managed a saucy smile. "Who knows? Perhaps the both of us will find a distraction for the night? My bed's been empty for far too long."

Isabella's eyes lit up, then she sighed. "I suspect you're going to be too busy with this Chameleon business. Malloryn wants you working on Barrons. He's setting things into play at the tower to protect the queen himself."

"Shall we postpone it then?" Gemma lifted her cup of tea to Isabella's. "The second I capture the Chameleon, we'll celebrate. No gentlemen allowed. Perhaps we could invite Ingrid and Ava?"

Instantly Isabella's face shuttered. "As much as I enjoy their company, they're both sickeningly happy at the moment. I don't think I could stand to hear any more talk of weddings right now, and if matters go the way I suspect they will, Miss McLaren will be wearing a ring on her finger in no time."

Most likely a correct assumption. Gemma deliberately chinked her porcelain cup against Isabella's. "Just you and me then. We'll drink to broken hearts and set out to break a few of our own. Now. Brief me on the Barrons situation."

She'd taken the bait.

Obsidian strolled through the misty shadows around the Duchess of Casavian's manor, watching as the curvaceous figure moved through the windows. He'd recognize Gemma anywhere; nobody else quite managed that seductive sway, with the flirtatious lift of her shoulder and the tilt of her chin.

He could vaguely remember seeing her for the first time across the ballroom of the Winter Palace five years ago.

Blond curls had been draped elegantly over one of her pale shoulders, and her gown had been the color of blood on snow. She moved like a woman well aware of her body, all honeyed smiles and swaying hips as she rested her hand on the Duke of Malloryn's arm, surveying the ballroom before her. Elegant, graceful, and sensual. The cut of her gown hugged those rounded breasts, with a thin scrap of lace not quite hiding her cleavage. Everything about her was a tease. No man could resist. Even him.

And when their eyes met....

A breathtaking moment had shaken him, where the world had dropped away around him, his heart feeling like it stopped, quite literally, in his chest.

With the memory came the lash of pain. Obsidian sucked in a sharp breath, bracing himself for the harsh file over his nerves.

Do you still love her? Dr. Richter whispered in his ear as he connected the reconditioning machine to the steam-driven generator.

Nyet, he'd replied, his body flinching as Richter flicked the switch and the generator began to hum. He knew this pain far too well, and his muscles clenched as he began to anticipate it.

Ghost took up the positive and negative clamps. *The bitch betrayed you. She tried to burn you alive and then protested her innocence, thinking we'd fall for that. We shall burn her from your mind. By the time I'm done, you'll never willingly think of her again.*

Please, he'd begged, needing to drive the ache of her from his heart.

The reconditioning had succeeded far better than he'd have ever hoped.

He couldn't think of Gemma without feeling the answering echo of pain anymore.

He could barely remember their time together.

Just the whisper of poison from her lips as she lied to him with her touch and her smile. The kiss of heat on his skin as he woke to find the bed hangings on fire and "Hollis" nowhere to be seen.

In the window before him, Gemma reached for the lantern on the stark outline of what he presumed was a chest of drawers. Second window from the end of the house, third floor.

Skoro moya yadovitaya lyubov....

Soon.

Gemma leaned forward to blow the lantern out, and light fled from the room, plunging it into merely another darkened square in the stucco brickwork.

Sensing a shadow moving on the rooftop next to Casavian manor, Obsidian faded into the overgrown hedge across the street like a wraith.

Moonlight refracted off pale hair on the rooftop. Just a brief flicker before the shadow vanished, but Obsidian knew who it was.

Caleb Byrnes, the COR agent who'd been transformed into a *dhampir* by Zero. Though newly made, Byrnes represented a threat, because he alone could potentially match Obsidian if it came down to a fight between them.

He'd gotten her out of the COR house.

Now he had to separate her from the rest of Malloryn's agents.

The sensation of being watched was back.

Gemma gathered her skirts as she climbed the steps to the British Museum at Barrons's side, her gaze darting here and there, and the small briefcase she carried banging against the side of her leg.

This was where a pale man had tried to kill her almost two months ago, leaving her bleeding and begging on the floor.

This was where a second man had saved her, though she'd caught only a glimpse of him in the reflection of one of the glass cases.

For a moment she'd thought she'd seen a ghost from the past, but it had to have been her mind playing tricks on her.

Dmitri had died in Russia, according to all Malloryn's reports.

And yet, what were the chances two "pale men" had been sighted right when the city seemed overrun with these cursed *dhampir*.

Gemma couldn't suppress her nerves. Barrons had been invited to a lecture on the White Court. The Imperial Family of the White Court were considered the world's first blue bloods, and she and Malloryn had bandied about theories they were actually *dhampir*, for Dr. Cremorne's research indicated as such when he had discovered how to create the *elixir vitae* from some ancient Tibetan documents.

A lecture on *dhampir* origins in the exact place where one had attacked her?

Surely it had to be mere coincidence.

Either that, or the Chameleon was amusing himself at her expense.

"This way," Barrons said, catching sight of the group of tweed lingering in the foyer.

"I wasn't aware you had an interest in the origins of the craving virus."

Barrons strode at her side like a leonine creature stalking his own personal savannah. "It's a recent interest of mine. Malloryn asked me to do a little research."

He had? Gemma hurried along at Barrons's side, reverting to her meek secretary persona.

"What do you want me to do?" Barrons asked.

"Nothing out of the usual. Attend the lecture, talk with the other scientists. I'll be in the background, keeping an eye out for any unusual activity. As soon as we arrive, I'll take a brief tour of the museum to check the security."

Also to make a survey of anyone loitering. She disliked Barrons being so openly public, but he'd refused to stay at home. Her life would be so much easier if men just listened to her.

As they walked up to the group of scientists standing in the lecture hall, a dozen sets of eyes locked on her in astonishment, as if they'd never seen a woman before.

One of the scientists took off his half-moon spectacles and began to polish them, as if he simply couldn't believe his eyes.

"Egad," Barrons whispered to her, "I have brought a specimen of the rare female variety of *homo sapiens* to attend. Some of these gentlemen have never seen one in its natural environment before."

"Very droll, my lord. This would be my cue to take a tour of the museum," she murmured under her breath. "Happy researching, Barrons. I do hope they don't bore you to tears. I'll see you when the lecture ends."

Barrons gave her an amused smile, and then turned to greet his fellow enthusiasts. Gemma pressed her fingers to the aural communicator tucked within her ear. "Subject's arrived at his destination. I'm going to make a sweep of the building. Have you got eyes on the main entrance?"

"Aye," Charlie replied, his voice giving a tinny echo through her earpiece. *"Nothing's going to get past me."*

"Thanks."

Malloryn hadn't been very happy about being forced to split the group's focus, but he'd conceded they couldn't take the threat to Barrons lightly.

She moved through the exhibits, her skirts swishing about her ankles. Light streamed into the pale marble rooms, and the air was dry and still. Gemma couldn't help feeling a pinch of nerves as she found herself in rooms filled with glass cases and exotic items on display.

She entered the Egyptian room, her heart starting to pick up its pace.

The museum remained still and musty around her. This was where she'd first felt Dmitri's ghost; the day the mysterious pale man stabbed her and she'd expected to die.

She hadn't died.

Instead, she'd woken up with her wound already pink and healing, and her craving virus levels skyrocketing in her blood.

A chill ran down her spine as she heard the swish of a light footstep behind her.

Just nerves, you fool. There's no one here.

And yet, she could feel all the hairs on her spine lifting.

Gemma took a breath. "Hullo?" she called, taking a cautious step forward. "Is anybody there?"

Silence.

The faintest shift of leather on the marble floors caught her ear. Gemma froze. She'd thought she was imagining things, but that was definitely the sound of someone else.

"*Gemma?*" Charlie muttered in her ear. "*What's wrong? I'm getting some... static interference....*"

"Keep your eyes on the target," she whispered, taking several more steps. Stillness radiated through the darkened room.

This was ridiculous.

You took a fright. It doesn't mean anything. The Chameleon isn't after you, after all.

But what if it wasn't the Chameleon?

Someone had been following her.

Someone had saved her life in this very room.

As if to prove her wrong, something small and round rolled across the floor. Gemma drew her pistol, spinning in that direction, her heart hammering in her chest. A child's marble bumped against the side of a case, and spun to a halt.

"Curse you, I know you're here. You healed me," she whispered, turning in slow circles, hunting for him. "I should have died but I didn't, and I couldn't understand why...."

A listening sense of silence this time.

"I know you're following me. What do you want from me?"

Nothing.

Nothing but silence.

"I want to see you," she suddenly demanded, her voice ringing out loud and sharp. "Damn you, show yourself!"

"*Gem...sha...*" Charlie's voice gave a high-pitched whine in her ear, and then shirred into unintelligible static.

Gemma whipped her earpiece free, wincing at the sound. What on earth was wrong with her communicator?

Movement shifted out of the corner of her eye. She spun around, her skirts whisking against her ankles.

Something sharp bit into her neck.

Gemma slapped a hand there, feeling the tiny dart that stuck out of her skin.

A man stepped out of the shadows. Gemma's breath caught in her throat as he took a step toward the light. First his shoe appeared, and then his slacks, and then hands gloved in black leather.

Broad shoulders. Pale, brown hair that brushed against his collar. And that breathtaking, oh-so-familiar face. A face that mimicked those she'd once seen on a painting of Lucifer's fall.

"Dmitri," she breathed, heat flooding from her extremities and centering in on her heart like some sort of protective mechanism. Her body was stiffening up, her legs losing all feeling. Hemlock. He'd used hemlock on her.

Everything flashed before her eyes. Saint Petersburg. Dancing under gilded lights. The taste of his mouth the first time she kissed him, her gloved hands sliding over his roughened cheeks.

The shock of the bullet ripping through her chest, and the icy plunge she'd taken into the river that literally stole her breath.

"You survived," she slurred, as her knees went out from under her.

The floor pitched toward her, but he was there. Strong hands caught her before she hit the floor, and he slung her up into his arms as her pistol clattered to the ground.

"Dmitri died," the man said in a toneless voice. "All that's left now is Obsidian."

And then the world vanished around her as everything went dark.

CHAPTER SIX

Five years ago...

The first thing Dmitri knew was the dry, pasty taste in his mouth.

Heat warmed his skin.

Light bloomed in the room.

His body felt heavy and hot, and as he couldn't sweat, his breath was coming in short, sharp pants as if he had to dispel the heat somehow. Pain screamed along his back as the heat burned him.

Rising up to a level of full awareness was difficult. His bones felt like lead. Dmitri finally managed to open his eyes, and what he saw made his heart stop dead in his chest.

The curtains on the bed were on fire, flames licking at a blanket thrown haphazardly across the end of the bed. Smoke choked the air, and he could see flames eating at the doorframe. His bed was empty, only the vague indentation of a woman's body lingering in the sheets revealing his mind wasn't playing tricks on him. He hadn't been alone when he fell asleep.

"Holl-is?" he tried to yell.

Nothing. No sign of her.

Panic roused him as nothing else could. Dmitri coughed and spluttered as he dragged himself off the bed, his heavy body still fighting him.

He staggered toward the wall, the muscles in his thighs shaking, as if they could barely handle the weight of him. His arms were blistered, and the pain nearly drove him to his knees.

Smoke thickened the air, driving him low. Dmitri choked as his lungs found no oxygen. He had no clue where the window was. Fire bloomed between him and the door.

How the hell was he supposed to get out?

Where was Hollis?

The last he knew she'd been in his arms, her naked skin pressed against his as they lay there content. A single stolen moment with his Master's enemy before they could be found. They'd both known the risks, but he hadn't been able to stop himself from capturing her mouth for a kiss that night. Hadn't been able to turn her away as the long-suppressed passion that burned between them flared to life.

"Obsidian?" someone yelled.

Silas. His head turned in the direction of his brother-by-blood's voice. "Here!"

A dark shape loomed out of the shadows, Silas emerging from under a sodden blanket. "Ruttin' hell." He draped the blanket over Dmitri. "What in the blazes happened here?"

A sudden roaring whoosh burst over them, a fireball blooming in the air as the flickering flames found the overhanging canopy of the bed.

"We need to get out of here now!"

His head still swam, mouth sticky. All he could see was smoke swimming around him, burning down his throat.

"This way!" A hard body shoved him toward the right.

The steaming blanket Silas draped over his shoulders tore the blistered skin from his arm and back, but at least it provided some protection from the flames.

A chill guided him toward the window, the cold air outside. He tried to get the latch open, but Silas grabbed his arm.

"No time," Silas gasped.

They both went through the glass. Slamming into the snow outside, he rolled onto his back and gasped. The shock of intense cold on his naked flesh, following so swiftly on the heels of the raging heat, broke the last vestiges of the drugged hold on his body.

"What the hell happened?" Silas shoved to his feet, throwing the blanket at Dmitri to sling around his waist.

He didn't know.

Dmitri glanced up at the burning room, pushing to his feet. Why was his mouth so dry? What was that taste? The last thing he could recall was Hollis giving him the glass of blooded wine before she smiled at him and began to tug at the laces tying her nightgown together.

He'd drained the cup dry.

You drank the wine.

You lay with her....

And then you slept....

A sleep so deep, he'd barely felt the bed catch fire.

Horror sent him reeling. Ghost had warned him not to compromise himself when it became clear the game he'd been playing with her was deeper than they'd both intended.

Dmitri had been working for Lord Balfour to form the prospects of an alliance between the Russian Blood Court and the English prince consort, and she'd been working for the Duke of Malloryn to destroy it. He'd never been entirely certain if she'd known of his loyalties. With his Russian heritage and his accent, he could pass for one of the court, and nobody knew he worked for Balfour.

But she'd been pointed out to him as a target by Ghost.

"Malloryn's 'cousin,'" Ghost had laughed. *"Or at least, that's what he's telling everybody. Ostensibly here to assist in the diplomatic efforts by pursuing an English-Russian marriage alliance, though Balfour's warned us Malloryn wants to destroy any prospect of a treaty and the girl's his spy. A former Falcon of Balfour's, if you can believe it. Malloryn's hinted he'd like to marry the girl off, and half the court is salivating. Not for marriage, of course. It would dilute their precious bloodlines. But she's got them exactly where she wants them. She's a beauty. They're all baying after her, but for some reason she seems to have singled out Sergey Grigoriev, which means Malloryn wants something from Sergey. Your mission is to distract her. Keep her away from Sergey. And find out what she's after."*

"How, precisely, would you like me to do that?"

The question was not without merit.

"Seduce her. Become her friend. Kill her. I don't care. Just keep her away from Sergey, and keep it quiet. We don't want to draw Malloryn's attention. Balfour considers him a pup, bested by his betters, but I'm not convinced. There's a certain kind of rage in his eyes whenever he looks at Balfour. I've seen hate like that before, and it's dangerous."

"Seduction's not my style," he'd said coolly. No. For him, the kiss of a knife to a throat was as close as he got. They all had their skills.

"She's already rebuffed Silas. So you'll have to learn."

But with Hollis, it had been easier than he'd ever expected. The second he laid eyes upon her, he'd known he'd wanted her. He'd done his duty; intercepting her for a dance before she could make her way across the ballroom to Sergey. She'd glanced over his shoulder the entire time, eyes tracking Sergey, until he made her laugh and she'd finally looked at him as if she saw *him*.

"See something you like?" he'd asked.

"I don't know," she'd responded, as she swayed in his arms. *"I haven't yet made up my mind."*

The smoke in his lungs still choked him as he stared up at the burning manor. People were streaming from the main doors, spilling out onto the snow in alarm.

"What happened?" Silas asked, lifting his head and spitting on the snow.

Dmitri couldn't find the words to answer.

There was no other explanation he could imagine.

The woman he'd given his heart to had tried to kill him.

Now....

The warm bundle in his arms stirred.

Obsidian strode up the circular staircase within the abandoned manor he'd found on the outskirts of London, heading for the observatory. His head ached, driven into the past by Gemma's presence, though all he could truly remember were flames.

Flames and treachery.

She tried to kill you. Now you can return the favor.

A hand brushed against his chest, Gemma's head lolling to the side as she groaned. He needed to get her locked away before she could awaken completely.

Mably House had once been home to the Dukes of Vickers before the previous duke betrayed the prince consort, his entire line blighted and stripped of everything but the clothes on their back. Someone had tried to burn the manor, but it had been crafted of solid stone and though most of the house lay in ruins, the east wing had fared a little better.

Nobody came here anymore.

The gates were painted black and soldered shut.

Mably House represented the death of a Great House, and nobody dared stir the ghosts that lurked within. Any trespassers knew they invited harsh penalties, and so most tended to avoid the place.

Except for him.

"Dmitri?" Gemma whispered, in his arms.

He could just make out the pillow-shape of her lips and see the faint rise of the lush curves spilling out of her bodice. Fingertips grazed his shirt as if to test if it were really him as her dark lashes fluttered against her pale cheeks.

"Dmitri is dead," he whispered, pausing to juggle her in his arms as he drew another syringe from his belt. "You killed him, you lying little bitch. Do you remember?"

Eyes the color of a field of cornflowers tried to focus upon him, her pupils forming tiny little pinpricks. "You... shot me."

For a second he almost saw something else. Smoke curling from a pistol as Hollis's eyes widened and she tumbled backward off a bridge.

"I have no recollection of that."

Sharp nails dug into his forearm. "Well, I do."

She began to struggle, and he injected her with enough of the laudanum-hemlock injection to send her blissfully under again.

The observatory loomed ahead of him, lit by a single glass pane in the roof. Starlight gilded the slate floor in a silvery glow.

Laying her to rest on the heavy marble slab in the middle of the room, he brushed a strand of dyed black hair off her cheek, unable to help himself. Her fingers lay curled into her palms, her head splayed to the side and the faint cleft in her chin shadowed beneath her lush mouth. For a second, Obsidian's heart gave a pulsing twist in his chest, the darker half of his nature whispering through his veins, urging him to kiss her.

He reared back, his hand going to the knife at his side. He should never have brought her here. He should have simply put the blade through her black heart; and yet the second she'd slumped into his arms, he'd wanted more.

He'd wanted to look into her eyes as he asked her, *"Why?"*

This was madness.

But his knuckles strained white on the knife, and he turned and took two swift steps away from her, cursing his resolve under his breath. Obsidian paced the observatory, scrubbing at his mouth.

Killing her would be only too kind for what she'd done to him.

But again he saw that smoking pistol and her accusing eyes. *"You shot me."*

A sharp stabbing pain sliced through his brain, like a pickax to the skull. He'd never remembered that before, but it felt as though her words brought a shiver of memory to the surface, like a leviathan surfacing from the depths of the ocean.

All he'd ever had of her was the sight of her laughing and fluttering her eyelashes at Sergey.

The teasing glint in her blue eyes as she played suitor against suitor, smiling mockingly at him the entire time she wove her way through the Russian court.

The kiss of flames against his skin.

The rasp of smoke in his throat.

And the taste of betrayal.

She was an enemy spy.

"She was an enemy spy," he whispered.

She deliberately seduced you, seeking to use you.

"She deliberately seduced you...." He couldn't say the rest.

She tried to kill you.

"She...."

He pressed the heel of his palm to his aching forehead. The fugue was coming, sweeping over him like a black tide. He had to get out of here before it overwhelmed him.

But...

Moonlight fell across her fallen figure, caressing the soft curve of her cheek. Gemma looked like a fairy-tale version of Sleeping Beauty, goose bumps pebbling her skin from the chill of the room.

She looked innocent.

And what had that flash of vision meant? Her words had unlocked something he'd not known was buried within him.

He needed to know what she meant about shooting her.

But not now. Not now.

Swinging his cloak off his shoulders, Obsidian draped it over her like a blanket. A blinding white light floated through his vision, blurring her face. The tingling started in his fingers.

He needed to get out of there before he fell.

Pushing away from her, Obsidian strode toward the scrolled gate that guarded the observatory and clanged it shut, the lock slamming into place.

It was only when he staggered down the stairs that the pain eased up a fraction.

And then the world vanished as he slammed to the floor.

CHAPTER SEVEN

Gemma woke to darkness.

For a second her heart pounded as she tried to gain her bearings. What had happened? Where was she? The last thing she remembered was—

She sat bolt upright as memory returned, her hands tangling in fur.

Blood and ashes.

Dmitri!

Gemma nearly fell off the hard bed she lay upon, and then froze. There was no sign of anyone else in the room. Indeed, she could barely see a foot in front of her face. A thin sliver of light cracked through a glass pane high in the roof, revealing a single star, but she suspected the cloud of smothering London smog dulled its light.

Night then.

But what was...? She picked at the thing beneath her, feeling out its soft shape. A fur-lined cloak. And not one of her own.

She'd spent the past month wondering if the face she'd glimpsed in her state of semiconsciousness had been real. He'd saved her life in the museum when one of his comrades tried to kill her, but when she'd woken she'd thought she'd imagined it.

And then she'd been so certain she was being followed. Everywhere she turned Gemma felt him hovering there, like a ghost that haunted her. A glimpse of a face she thought she recognized before it vanished in the crowd. Gemma had wondered if she was going mad, stricken by years of guilt and nightmares. She hadn't dared say anything when someone broke into the COR safe house and killed Zero before she and the Duke of Malloryn could question the *dhampir* woman.

It was him. It had to be him. I felt him in the house. But Gemma had long since learned Malloryn expected proof. And...

He died in Saint Petersburg. Dmitri died.

One of Malloryn's own spies had confirmed it, saying he'd seen the assassin enter a building just before it exploded.

She'd never dared believe otherwise.

Gemma pressed a hand to her chest, where the scar between her breasts remained. *He shot you. He's not the man you thought he was. So don't think this means anything other than danger for you.*

But why the hell had he locked her away in here?

Why hadn't he just killed her?

One wall of the room was crafted of steel bars, with an elegant scrolled effect to the iron. Gemma peered through the bars and then rattled them. Solid. Where the hell was she? An orangery? An observatory?

Her skirts scuttled over something dry and rasping on the slate floors. Gemma knelt, the objects crackling into dust in her palms. Leaves. Long-dead leaves. She patted her way up the building, following the trail of dry leaves and finding a gnarled vine that clung to the walls. Rough stone met her palms and the room held the dry, still air of a mausoleum. Her heart started ticking a little faster. What if he'd put her in a crypt?

Wherever they were, she didn't think it was very well-populated. She should have been able to hear something; even in the dead of night London was full of life and sound.

A brief tour of the room revealed it was round and scattered with pots of dead plants. The windows were covered with slim panels of some sort of metal, crafted so expertly there wasn't even a hint of a crack between them through which she could slip her fingernails. The roof soared far above her; though she suspected she might be able to climb the gnarled old vine attached to the wall, her head turned unerringly toward the scrolled iron of the bars caging her in.

When it came to escaping, she'd been in tighter scrapes than this.

And Gemma's rule was simple: take the easy option first.

A good thing she came prepared.

There was no sign of her weapons, lock-pick set, or any of the various other sundry items she carried about her person. He must have patted her down. Even the pins in her hair had vanished, leaving her hair tumbling precariously down her back.

Clever man.

He clearly knew what she was capable of.

Or thought he did.

Reaching down her dress, she tugged the bodice away from her breasts, revealing her corset. A thin slit gaped in between the under layer of the corset and the smooth silk of the exterior, through which she wriggled her finger.

Something hard and thin met her touch. There. Got it. Gemma began to tug, drawing the wire out of the seam.

Thin enough to use as a deadly garrote, when she bent it into shape and manipulated it, she found herself with a makeshift lock pick.

Not a sound whispered in the darkness of the hallway beyond.

Gemma knelt and inserted the wire in the lock. She couldn't see a damned thing, but that didn't matter.

Who would have ever guessed her blindfolded lessons as a child would ever come in handy?

"Thank you, Lord Balfour," she whispered into the night as the lock gave a satisfying click. It was the first time she'd ever been grateful for what he'd done to her as a child.

Victory. Gemma's lips curved dangerously.

She stilled, listening for any sound of alarm, but nothing moved in the darkness.

Had he left her here?

Time to find out.

It was not a crypt.

Gemma crept down a winding staircase, catching the odd glimpse of twinkling lights in the distance through the narrow gaps between the boarded-up windows. Close to London then. An enormous empty manor full of dust and dry leaves, and the smell of charred timber. She could barely breathe for the thrill of rushing blood through her veins.

Dmitri was here. Somewhere.

He had to be.

The staircase opened up into a wide hallway, the floors a ripple of shadow. Black and white marble tiles, she guessed, though chipped and pitted and scarred by signs of fire. Wallpaper hung in strips from the walls, and someone had slashed the paintings that still hung there, marring the aristocratic faces she caught a glimpse of.

She slipped into the massive foyer of the mansion, moonlight gleaming through the open panes of the door, reflecting back off the broken shards of glass that hung there. Inch by inch Gemma crept toward freedom, easing her weight forward onto her toes so the faint heel of her boot made no sound.

She was almost there when instinct lifted the hairs along the back of her neck.

"Going somewhere?"

Heart leaping into her throat, Gemma spun around, settling into a defensive stance as her gaze darted through the shadows.

She hadn't heard a damned thing.

A whisper of movement caught her attention. There. In the shadows by the staircase.

"Who are you?" she breathed.

Obsidian, he'd said. But he looked like her Dmitri, and she desperately, desperately needed to know the truth. Had it truly been him? Was her mind playing tricks on her?

The silver gleam of the moon marked a bar of light across the floor, separating the pair of them.

All she could see were shadows rippling as someone moved in the darkness. A mocking laugh breathed into the air. "You pretend not to know me?"

"Step into the light," she whispered, the drum of her heart hammering a pulsing rhythm upon her ribs.

"Why?"

"I want to see you."

Moonlight gleamed off the polished toe of his boots. She caught a glimpse of the wet shine of his leather breeches as the shadow stepped forward.

Gemma held her breath, taking a half step backward.

Light spilled over his tall frame and his sculpted face, delineating the fine arch of his nose and the harsh slash of his cheekbones. He'd always been dangerously handsome; his mouth a touch full, his eyebrows thick and intense, and a faint scar slashing across the corner of his mouth.

It was him.

It was truly him.

Sleeves rolled up to his elbows, revealing the muscled strength in his forearms. His hands were covered in the liquid-black of leather. A trim waistcoat fit him like a glove, nipped in to display that narrow waist, though it strained over the broad planes of his chest. He'd dyed his pale hair and brows brown, as if to try and blend into a crowd of humans, but this man would never be able to fade into the background of a crowd. Not with that face. Those cheekbones. She'd seen his face a thousand times in her dreams, but she'd never truly believed she'd see it in the flesh again.

Gemma's heart skipped a beat as Obsidian tilted his head slightly to the side in a move she'd seen a hundred times before. His hair brushed against his collar. An eyebrow arched mockingly, as if to say, *did you miss me?*

There was nothing of the man she'd loved in his cold, arctic gray eyes, but every inch of that gesture pulled at her heart.

"You died," she whispered.

The explosion that rocked the Winter Palace had killed him, according to all of Malloryn's reports.

"Apparently you didn't try hard enough."

A faint frown tugged her brows together, and then Gemma realized what he meant. "I didn't set the explosion. I thought that was your side!"

"Why the hell would we try to destroy the palace of the Tzarina who'd just signed our treaty?"

"Well, someone did. I wasn't even in the country anymore. I was aboard an airship, far to the west."

"Indeed."

She eased back another step, licking her lips nervously.

"Do you truly think you can outrun me?"

No. Gemma lifted her chin in a show of false bravado. "In these skirts and my favorite heeled boots? I doubt it. You've always been faster than I am, even in bare feet." Her options were rapidly narrowing. No weapons. Nowhere to hide. "The question is... do I have reason to run?"

"I don't know." His rough voice sounded dangerous. "You tell me."

"You've been following me."

He took another step through the bar of moonlight.

Gemma took a step back. "You killed that *dhampir* who attacked me in the museum."

"What *dhampir*?" The bastard was taunting her.

"And you healed me with your blood," she whispered. "Ava spent days trying to work out what was wrong with me and why my craving virus levels went through the roof then returned to normal. I knew. I knew deep in my heart what you were, and what you'd done. I barely caught a glimpse of your face, but I could feel you there."

"Very good, Gemma. You're almost there."

"What do you want from me?"

Silence.

A tense, prickling silence in which she could almost feel his gaze sliding over her body like a caress. For the first time, she saw hesitation within him. He didn't know himself.

She released a shuddering breath. "If you wanted me dead, then I would be dead. You've had more than enough chances."

"If I wanted you dead, you would be. All I would have had to do was stand aside."

Referring, no doubt, to the *dhampir* in the museum who'd tried to kill her.

"Perhaps I'm not that easy to kill."

"Perhaps."

Gemma tensed. "So what now?"

"Are you going to come quietly?"

She tipped her chin up. "What do you think?"

The faintest of smiles touched his mouth, but then she blinked and wondered if she'd imagined it.

"Loudly. Quietly. It doesn't matter. You will come in the end."

"Interesting choice of words."

His gaze flattened. "You're not escaping me, Miss Townsend."

We will just see about that. She turned and fled, fists pumping at her sides. Not toward the door, but the window beside it.

Gemma threw herself into a slide, plucking a shard of razor-sharp glass from the windowsill at the bottom. Pain slashed through her fingers and a part of her—the predator part—reared within her at the scent of blood, but she had no time to worry about it.

"You think a piece of glass is going to stop me?" He stalked toward her.

"My apologies," Gemma panted, raking the room for something else she could use as a weapon. "Someone very inconveniently removed all my weapons. I am reduced to this."

Flinging the shard toward Obsidian, she bolted for the dining room in the next room, her fingers wet with blood and the craving virus itching beneath her skin as it sought to heal her.

"Damn you, Gemma." Glass shattered against the wall. He must have smashed it aside.

She'd never beat him on flat ground.

Scrambling under the dining table, Gemma crawled across the floor, shoving chairs out of the way as she tried to flee.

A chair was wrenched from the table and shattered against the wall. Gemma kicked the one in front of her out of the way, and then did an abrupt about-turn in the direction she'd come as Obsidian launched himself toward her decoy.

Cursed skirts. Panting hard, she slipped as her knee trapped her skirt beneath her. Gemma shot forward, throwing herself into a roll as she came out from beneath the table. Lace ripped as she launched to her feet, but she sprinted back toward the foyer as a roar of rage bellowed behind her.

"You're not going to escape!"

"We'll see!"

She caught a glimpse of a dusty coat stand out of the corner of her eye and lashed out, throwing it behind her as she bolted past.

A hand locked around her arm before she'd taken three steps, and as he hauled her back toward him, Gemma spun, driving the flat of her palm up into his chin.

Obsidian's head snapped back, and she swept low, taking his feet out from under him. She turned to flee before he'd even hit the floor, but a hand snatched at her skirts and hauled her back. Staggering over the top of him, she went down in a crush of silk, struggling to kick free.

Curse her damned fashion sense. Why had she not worn one of her training outfits today?

A hand slammed between her shoulder blades, pinning her flat to the floor where she got a mouthful of dust. Coughing it out of her lungs, she felt herself being hauled to her feet, an iron shackle of a grip snagging her by the bustle.

Arms as strong as iron bands wrapped around her, hauling her up over his shoulder. Gemma kicked, but Obsidian drove her backward.

Her back slammed against the tabletop, the breath smashing out of her. Gemma cried out, trapping her legs around his thighs, but it was too late. Moonlight flashed off the flat of his blade as he drove it toward her throat—

And held it there.

Gemma froze, heart racing and her chest heaving.

The prick of the tip of the knife pressed against her carotid. Barely a whisper of a threat, but she took it seriously. She didn't dare move. Barely dared breathe.

"Not you." The words broke from her lips.

Not like this.

She captured his gaze, forcing him to look her in the eye. Her chin tipped up. Obsidian's hand curled around her throat, his weight leaning forward, which dragged her skirts up between them.

Look me in the eye and do it. She captured his hand, sliding hers over the iron grip on her throat. Holding it there. Feeling the hatred vibrating from him as the razor-sharp edge of the blade nicked her skin.

Adrenaline hammered through her veins. A certain kind of rush that seemed destructively intimate. The rich, coppery scent of her blood flavored the air, and she knew he smelled it too, for his lashes fluttered, his gaze dipping to her throat.

Suddenly, that restless feeling beneath her skin began to make sense. The hunger roused within her, the predator swimming to the surface. She saw the same stark need in his own eyes.

He was not immune to her.

Gemma squeezed his hand and arched her spine. As if drawn by a magnet, his gaze dropped lower, almost as silky as a caress as it shivered over the upthrust mounds of her breasts, his eyes bleeding to black as the hunger roused within him. Pressed as he was between her thighs, she felt the rising bulge of his cock and stilled again.

Barely three layers of clothing separated her skin from his.

Five years of betrayal and pain.

The skin between her breasts ached, as if the bullet wound there remained like an invisible wound. He'd done that to her. But in some deep, dark part of her, it didn't matter.

Three layers of clothing. Skin on skin. Obsidian's brows drew together, as if he sensed it too. He seemed just as confused by his reaction as she was.

A shocking thought occurred.

She stroked his hand again, and there it was. The flinch. A faint softening of his grip.

It took her breath.

Because she wasn't the only one trapped by need.

By the past.

She couldn't still the rush of thoughts through her head. She couldn't outrun him. Couldn't outfight him. But maybe she didn't need to?

Gemma's thighs locked around his narrow hips, and suddenly she could feel every inch of him pressed against her inner thigh.

"You can't kill me," she whispered. "Can you?"

Obsidian shoved away from her, driving the flat of his hand against his brow as if his head ached. He held the knife clenched in his fist and shot her a look of raw fury.

Slowly, she pushed upright from the table and slipped off its surface.

"I ought to," he said coldly. "I want to."

"What the hell does that mean?"

"You are mine," he breathed, his hair falling across his face. Every inch of his chest expanded, as if he fought to control some raging beast inside. "That's all you need to know right now."

Sheathing the knife, he turned and strode toward her.

Gemma backed away, tripping over the lip of the rug, but this time she knew trying to escape was pointless.

Obsidian hauled her over his shoulder, and she didn't fight him—didn't resist—as he turned toward the staircase, and her makeshift cell.

Because she knew she was never going to be able to escape him using force.

But maybe she didn't have to?

CHAPTER EIGHT

Obsidian found a lantern and a hessian sack, and hauled both of them up the stairs with her. The light hurt her eyes as he set her down inside the cell, but Gemma took the chance to study his face.

She didn't know what was going through his mind.

This man....

She didn't know this man.

There was no sign of the Dmitri she'd fallen in love with, the one with his gentle hands and the heated look in his eyes when he glanced at her. Obsidian, he'd called himself, and she realized then the man she'd loved had vanished.

Feeling bruised on the inside, Gemma forced her shoulders to square as this devilish stranger set the lantern aside and dragged the hessian sack forward with a clank. If he thought for one minute he was going to defeat her, then he really didn't know her that well. He might have taken all her knives—all her weapons—but he couldn't take her most dangerous ones.

And she'd already proven he wasn't invulnerable to her most precious asset: her sexuality.

"How did you get out?" He examined the lock before turning those dangerous eyes upon her.

"Magic."

Eyes narrowing, he swung the gate shut behind him. "Where is it?"

"Where is what?"

Hands caught her waist and spun her around. Gemma's hands slapped against the rough stone of the walls as he forced them there.

"Don't move," he growled.

"Or you'll what? Slam me on a table again?" Her voice grew rough. "I think if you wanted to hurt me, you'd have done it downstairs. You couldn't do it, could you? You couldn't bring yourself to harm me. No matter how cold the mask you wear, I know he's still there inside you somewhere."

"He?" His hands slid down the curve of her hips, and then up across her abdomen, searching for weapons, she presumed.

"The man I fell in love with in Saint Petersburg."

"That man never existed."

"*Liar.*"

"Consider him buried, Miss Townsend."

Gemma's heart gave a twisting clench in her chest. Seeing him alive had been a slap to the face. She'd buried him in her heart all those years ago when he'd shot her. Told herself a million times that what she'd felt for him was nothing more than a myth. He'd betrayed her. Lied to her. Pretended to be something he wasn't, which was somewhat of a mockery, for she'd been trying to do the same thing.

Trying.

She'd conjured something between them, only to discover it a lie, and the truth had shattered her.

And then he'd died when the Winter Palace exploded, and Gemma had known true agony, for despite his betrayal, knowing he was dead tore her wretched heart out of her chest all over again.

"Not buried, Dmitri. Just never real."

His hands paused on her waist. "Obsidian."

Fine. "Obsidian."

Perhaps it was better this way. Dmitri and Hollis and the lie between them could die a painful death. She'd forged herself anew when it ended, taking on the mantle of Gemma Townsend.

And Gemma, flirtatious, calculating Gemma, knew no heartbreak.

"And you're right." Obsidian's hands began to take a leisurely path up her body, sweeping beneath her arms, his fingers brushing ever so faintly against the sides of her breasts. "None of it was real."

She did not feel that faint twinge in her heart.

It didn't exist.

Gemma steeled herself as his hands began to slide lower, firm over her hips. She had the truth. He'd never loved her.

Now she needed to escape.

"Why sir," she protested in a mocking voice, "how dare you take such liberties when we've barely been reacquainted."

He paused, his hand caressing the rounded curve of her bottom. "I seem to recall you had no compunctions about allowing me such liberties in the past."

Gemma sucked in a sharp breath as his hand slid lower. Seductress or not, she hadn't been prepared for the feelings his touch awoke in her. They weren't a lie. Those leather-clad fingers stroked along the crevice of her bottom, shockingly intimate and yet strangely distant. No heat there. Not yet. Kicking her feet apart until her heeled boots were spread, he caressed his way up her body.

"If you're searching for a weapon," she whispered, "you're looking in the wrong place. Those are my breasts."

"Noted." Fingers patted her down, sliding along her arms, her sides, her waist.

He even slid a leather-gloved hand through her hair, and Gemma had to contain a gasp as his fist clenched there momentarily.

A flush of heat swept through her.

Oh, dear.

Don't you dare, she told herself sharply, but her nipples disobeyed the directive. And suddenly she was in the past again, on her hands and knees, with Dm— Obsidian buried to the hilt within her, his fist in her hair wrenching her head back.

"I know you have it upon you somewhere."

"What would you be referring to?" Her voice came out a little lower than expected.

"Don't make me strip you naked," he threatened. "You have a lock pick."

"I told you. It was magic."

"Can you never utter a single word of the truth?"

Not if I can help it.

Because the truth hurt.

He resumed his search, kneeling behind her. Hands slid up under her skirts, stroking the backs of her calves. His touch had been impersonal until now.

But it slowed as he reached her thighs, a vague hint of unease evident in his hesitation.

The combination of danger and action left her feeling a little light-headed.

He wasn't the only one frozen.

"Nothing between my thighs," she whispered, "but you're quite welcome to check. As I recall, you did wonderful things with those fingers."

"Shut up."

"Though your mouth was better," Gemma mused, and then bit her lip when his thumb dug into the back of her thigh in warning. She was getting to him. She knew it.

His hands retreated down the back of her legs, and he yanked her off-balance as he lifted her foot.

A swift tug on her laces, and he tugged her left boot off. Then the right.

"Nothing in there either," Gemma pointed out.

Obsidian straightened. "Are you enjoying this?"

"Should I not be?"

He seemed affronted by the pleasure she took in goading him.

"It's been months since I've felt another's touch," Gemma said, with a faint shrug of her shoulders. Over a year, if she were being honest. "And never doubt I can do the job myself, but there's something to be said for having someone else's hands on your skin." She lowered her voice a little coyly, as if whispering a confession. "Rough hands. That time in the museum when you stole your first kiss? We were arguing. You shoved me against the wall and pinned me there and kissed me as if you couldn't get enough of me. I loved every minute of it."

Harsh fingers tugged at the buttons down the spine of her gown. Gemma turned her head, but his hand was suddenly on her wrist, pushing it insistently back against the wall.

Had she pushed him too far?

Or could she push him further?

"And one might add, judging by the way you pinned me to the table downstairs, you are not entirely unaffected either. That wasn't a gun pressed between my thighs, Obsidian."

"I forgot how dangerous you are," he replied, the steel of his body caging her in from behind.

You, sir, have no idea.

"And yes," he whispered, sweeping her hair to the side, his lips skating over the back of her neck. "I am not unaffected." Firm hands slid down her sides, parting the back of her dress.

A tongue swept across the nubbin at the top of her spine.

Gemma froze as prickles of arousal swept through her.

"Do you want to know something?" His thumb slid along the laced stretch of her corset. Hooking his fingers in the bottom laces, he began to haul it tight. Gemma's breath caught as her corset squeezed. "I don't think I'm the only one not unaffected. Am I, *moy sladkiy yad?*"

Sweet poison, am I? She hissed out a breath as her corset drew tighter. A damning slickness between her thighs betrayed her.

Two could play this game.

She'd forgotten that.

Her lungs arrested as the corset compressed her breasts. *Submit,* said his touch, and Gemma found she couldn't breathe. A fuzzy light-headed sensation swept through her, danger arousing her to the point of intoxication. Teeth bit into the hard muscle tracing from her neck to her shoulder.

A soft cry escaped her.

And then he let her go, and her corset slackened, allowing the trapped blood in her veins to flood into blood-starved skin. The rush of sudden sensation was blinding. But the way he controlled her so deftly turned her into a puddle of mush.

Gemma gasped, fingers curling against the stone. *Dangerous, dangerous man.* For he remembered what she liked, if nothing else.

"Are you wet, Miss Townsend?" His breath ghosted along the back of her neck, his voice softly amused with her unraveled state. "If I search between your thighs again, will your wetness slick my gloves? Could I taste it, if I put those fingers to my lips?"

Anger burned within her. He sounded so mocking. "Why don't you test your theory?"

"What's wrong, Miss Townsend? You like to flirt. You like to talk," he said, slipping her sleeve down over her shoulder. "I remember that. You ran rings around half the Blood—"

"Never you," she admitted. It was the first thing that caught her attention when he'd been trying to distract her from her target all those years ago.

A handsome man intercepting her on the dance floor, insisting upon a dance.

She'd catalogued him in an instant. Tall, his shoulders straining within the well-fitted coat he wore. A full, dangerous mouth that drew her gaze for a second look. Silvery hair that cascaded to his shoulders, the color somewhat akin to moonlight on snow. Unlike the rest of the Blood Court, he'd worn no extravagant cravat, and his waistcoat was black.

One of Sergey's many "friends" but her target had been Sergey. And handsome men came and went. There would be others.

Except....

Nothing she'd ever said had been able to sway him from her side. Everywhere she looked, Dmitri was simply *there*. Sergey's guard dog, she'd groused to Malloryn one night when he'd wanted to know why she was finding this mission so difficult. She'd flirted, she'd handed him a ringing set down, she'd argued, then tried cool distance. Dmitri took it all in his stride, his gray eyes mocking her, as if he knew exactly what she was doing.

And Gemma had found herself distracted from her mission.

The seductress found herself seduced.

But she hadn't been the only one.

"Sometimes me," Obsidian admitted quietly. "But not this time. I know what you are now."

"Do you?"

"And if you think I'm going to fall into your honeyed trap, then you can think again."

He gave a little tug on her dress, nudging it to her hips and revealing every inch of her corset and chemise.

Gemma shivered as the chill of the room bit her skin. Wait. This was not quite going the way she'd planned. "What the hell are you doing? You've searched me from top to toe. It's not as though my dress contains some secret weapon."

"Not true," he pointed out, in a raw voice. "You are your greatest weapon." Fisting both hands in the edges of her gown, he wrenched them apart.

Fabric tore. Gemma gasped, as he stripped the fabric from her body as if it were mere cotton. "That's my favorite dress!"

"Was." He ripped it down her arms, stripping the sleeves over her hands. "I'm certain you have others."

"No, you don't understand." She glanced down at the forsaken remains of her gown in a puddle on the ground around her feet. "It's a Madame *Lefoux*. It cost me a fortune. The silk.... The silk is all the way from the White Court in China."

"Then buy another one."

Am I going to have the chance?

"Just what are you intending to do?" she asked suspiciously. Flirtation or not, she refused to give this bastard a single piece of her. "Because the answer is no."

"Nothing."

He stepped back, allowing her to turn and face him.

"Did you really think it was going to be so easy? That I would soften for your pretty words, for the soft gasp on your lips?"

She'd thought he'd been falling into the smoky lure of her trap, but as he wrenched the dress out from under her, she realized she'd been mistaken. One look at the hard planes of his face told her the truth; she alone had felt the flush of heat through her veins as a need long dormant rose within her.

Obsidian's cold eyes met hers.

He curved his hand around her throat, a faint, threatening caress. "Every word from your lying little mouth only confirms my suspicions. You're manipulative from the top of your head to your toes. Sex is merely a weapon to you. Every word you utter is a lie. Thank you. For reminding me exactly who you are."

She clutched his hand.

They glared at each other, his thumb stroking her throat, and God damn her but she felt it all the way within.

"I'm not the only liar," Gemma spat, feeling like he'd stripped the ground out from under her feet.

For a second her body had betrayed her, desperately wanting his hands on her naked flesh, but it was more than that. Somewhere within the scarred ashes of what remained of her heart, she'd felt something stir.

You're happy he's alive.

And he hates you.

It was more than she could bear in that moment.

His cheek tensed, then he looked away and let her go.

"You won't be going very far without your gown or boots." He hauled the hessian sack toward him, and Gemma's gaze shot to it as something within it clanked.

"What are you doing?"

He withdrew a long chain with a manacle on either end. "You've already proved a simple cell cannot hold you."

Gemma tried to dart to the side, but his arm locked around her waist and he hauled her back against his chest, her stockinged feet kicking helplessly.

He took her down, pinning her to the marble slab in the center of the room. There were a dozen ways she could have gotten away—a thumb to his eye, two sharp fingers stabbed into his throat—but some part of her softened.

To escape right now meant she'd have to seriously injure him, and she wasn't certain she had it in her, especially not after his recent revelations.

Besides. Obsidian was *dhampir*; she wasn't convinced she could actually flee without somehow killing him.

Better to wait.

He thought stripping her down to her corset made her vulnerable. Ha. More fool him.

"Damn you." She kicked out at him, making a convincing act of protest. It wouldn't do to give in too early. He might grow suspicious.

Capturing her foot, he locked the manacle around her ankle and set the other end through an iron ring at the base of the marble slab.

By the time he pushed to his feet, both of them were panting.

Gemma flinched at the cold marble beneath her and wrapped her shivering arms around herself. "It's freezing in here without my gown."

"You'll survive." He bent to snatch her dress from the floor, balling it into his gloved fists before he threw it into the hallway, far away from the bars.

"You were never cruel."

Anger flushed his face. "That was before you drugged me and set my fucking bed on fire."

"What?" Gemma drew back. "No, I didn't."

"The last night we lay together, I was drugged, and you were the one who gave me the glass of wine. Someone conveniently set my room on fire. I barely managed to escape with my life, but there was no sign of *you*."

Gemma's mind raced. "Of course, there wasn't." Her breath caught. "I couldn't stay the night. My supposed reputation would have been ruined. But I never.... I didn't drug you. And I certainly didn't set a fire."

I loved you.

Scraping her hands through her hair, she tried to think. It had been five years ago. Was that why he'd come after her the next day?

Was that why he'd shot her?

"We've already established you're not above lying. Sleep well, Miss Townsend. Perhaps this will keep you warm." Tossing the fur cloak toward her, he turned and strode toward the barred gate.

"You say I tried to burn you alive?" she yelled. "You're the one who shot *me*."

Obsidian froze in the doorway, one hand on the gate. His head half turned toward her, but she couldn't see his face.

Only sense the sudden tension within him.

"That's not the way I remember it."

"Isn't it?" Sudden fury rose up to choke her. She cast his cloak aside. "Well, unlike others, I have proof, damn you."

Tugging open the laces of her shift, she jerked her corset lower, until the flush of her nipples strained to break free. There was none of that delicious heat warming her veins this time, however. Gemma felt cold all the way through, as she cupped her breasts to the sides and showed him the scar between them.

"I was still human when you shot me right through the left lung. The only reason I survived is because I plunged into a frozen river, and it slowed the bleeding and my heart rate enough to give Malloryn a chance to get his blood into me. So call me a liar if you will. Tell me I betrayed you. But you're a hypocrite."

Somehow Obsidian staggered up the stairs toward the small turret tower where his nest of blankets lay.

He'd lost time at some stage, remembering only the clang of the door as he slammed it shut and fled from the woman in the makeshift cell below.

Her words kept hammering at the inside of his head, leaving him near blind in one eye. *"You're the one who shot me."*

"No," he whispered.

She was an enemy spy.

"She was an enemy spy," he breathed, sinking his fingers into his hair and tugging to ease the sudden sharp pain in his head.

She deliberately seduced you, seeking to use you.

"She deliberately seduced me, seeking to use me."

She tried to kill you.

"She...."

He saw the scar between her breasts.

Heard again the violent ricochet of a weapon firing. His vision sharpened along the barrel of a smoking pistol, and Hollis came into focus instead.

Red bloomed in the middle of her chest like the painted dot on a target. Hollis jerked back in surprise, her body backlit by the lights in the distance as her arms flung wide, a word on her painted red lips.

"Dmitri—"

Shock painted itself across her face, rippling through her.

She was falling backward. Vanishing right before his eyes. He lowered the smoking weapon, sound rushing back into the world as he blinked out of the semitrance he'd found himself in and realized she was gone.

Sprinting toward the edge of the canal, he gasped as time seemed to slam back into being. Ice slicked the surface of the river, covered in a faint layer of snow, except for the ragged hole right below him. Dark waters churned through the ice, but there was no sign of Hollis. His hand shook, the scent of gunpowder leaving an acrid scent in his nose.

I killed her.

His hands shook.

I shot her.

The pistol fell from nerveless hands, and then the world around him vanished as a harsh voice intruded.

Pain sheared through his knees. Obsidian blinked, and found himself on the floor in the turret room, blood dripping from his nose. What the hell was that? He'd never remembered that before.

"She was an enemy spy."

He knew that voice. Saw the light shining in his eyes as it swung from side to side, binding his gaze to it.

"She tried to kill you."

Those words, branded into his head. He punched the floor, tearing his gloves.

"She betrayed you."

No.

"She never loved you."

"Remember the fire, Dmitri?"

And he could smell it now, almost feel the heat on his skin as he woke to find the bed canopy alight and flames dripping down the walls, trapping him inside the room where he'd made love to her.

"She tried to kill you."

What the hell was the truth?

Because both images felt like actual memories, and suddenly he didn't know which one was real—and which was the lie.

CHAPTER NINE

"If you think you can just kidnap me and leave me here to rot, then you have another think coming!" Gemma snapped, rattling the bars on the cell.

Silence.

Nothing.

"Dmitri?" she yelled.

There was no answer. That bloody rutting bastard. She pushed away from the bars, shaking with a combination of fear and fury. The chain around her ankle scraped over the slate floors, hauling her up just short of the sealed windows. She was still wearing her cursed corset, undergarments, and stockings, and her skin itched as if it wanted to be free of the confining garments. The heavy drape of the fur cloak protected her from the afternoon chill.

No sign of him. She'd spent yesterday calling out to him, but he'd never come. The only hint he hadn't abandoned her entirely was the flask of blood she'd found in her cell when she woke, which was somewhat disconcerting, because she thought she slept lightly.

Be patient, she'd told herself, though the wait grated on her nerves. Gemma knew she wasn't built for patience. She was built for action.

And what would her friends think right now? Would they be looking for her?

What would Malloryn think?

What was going on out there in the world? Were they still hunting the Chameleon? What if the assassin struck now, while she was out of the picture and the queen was vulnerable?

"Damn you to heck," Gemma cursed, glaring through the thin bars.

She had her lock pick still.

The only problem was, she wasn't certain if Obsidian was merely ignoring her, or whether he was no longer in the manor.

You have one chance to escape. Don't you dare waste it on impatience.

He'd ignored her curses.

He'd ignored her yells, and the way she rattled the bars.

But Gemma wasn't about to give up.

Try and ignore me now, you cold-blooded bastard.

She started singing. Loudly. "Oh, there was a young Nighthawk from Matlock...."

Gemma threw herself into the chorus with an obnoxious gusto that would do an opera singer proud. Fourteen verses in, footsteps echoed along the hallway.

Her heart shifted gears and Gemma peered through the bars, trying to see down the narrow corridor. "Obsidian?"

She wasn't going to call him Dmitri. Not anymore. The man she'd once known was dead—he'd told her that himself. All that was left now was the icy facade that wore the same face as the man who'd stolen her heart.

Once, a long time ago.

As if the thought of him conjured him, a dark shape began to take form. Gemma's shoulders slumped in a mixture of relief and frustration. She'd almost thought herself alone. She'd nearly decided to pick the lock, which would have been a disaster, for then he'd know she still carried her pick.

"What the hell is all this racket?" Obsidian demanded.

"I was trying to get your attention."

"Well you got it," he growled. "Along with half the neighborhood. You sound like a strangled cat. Is this some new method of torture?"

Gemma's eyes narrowed on him through the bars. "I'll have you know I have an excellent singing voice."

"If you're trying to convince me you're telling the truth about what happened between us, perhaps you'd best prove you're *not* an exceptional liar. You said that with a completely straight face."

"I *am*. I took singing lessons last year. My tutor, Francois, said I had an ear for certain octaves."

"Now that," Obsidian said, "is a man who knows how to skirt the truth."

Gemma subsided with ill grace.

He watched her pace, his gaze narrowing to thin slits as he caught a glimpse of her pale stockings through the swish of the cloak.

You were the one who stripped me. So you can suffer the consequences.

Far be it from her to blush and shield flashes of her skin like a virgin. She knew men found her form pleasing. She was counting upon it.

Yet the sudden heat in his eyes cast her plan back in her face.

Her skin itched from the inside out. "You've barely fed me. I've been trying to take small sips, but there's scarcely an inch of blood left in the flask you provided, and my... my hunger is beginning to make itself known."

The color drained out of her vision as if just thinking of it roused the predator within her.

Not. Now. She sucked in a sharp breath. The craving virus stoked the fires of a person's primal self. When the hunger rose, she stopped thinking. All she wanted was blood or sex. Or maybe to kill something.

She wanted his fist in her hair as he tilted her head back, revealing her throat....

Gemma clenched her fist, letting the bite of her nails against her palm distract her. What the devil had that been all about? She wasn't prey; she was the predator.

"Unfortunately, blood's a little short in supply," Obsidian countered. "Someone blew up two of the draining factories last month and poisoned the other three. We're all on rations."

It was Gemma's turn to narrow her eyes. "Did you have anything to do with that debacle and the Sons of Gilead?"

"I watched. It made a merry bonfire."

This time it was her turn to pace. "Why? Why would you do such a thing? Why try and destroy this fragile peace in London? People will die because you took away the ability to feed most of London's blue bloods. Who are you working for?"

"People already die," Obsidian replied coldly. "And it's a nice attempt, Miss Townsend, but I'm not planning on telling you a damned thing."

"I'd prefer it if you called me Gemma. We *are* acquainted, after all."

"Are we?" Obsidian slid closer to the bars, not quite daring to step all the way into the light. "Sometimes I wonder if I know you at all."

Of course. He wasn't glaring at her for any particular reason—no doubt the morning sunlight hurt his eyes. If he chanced to step into it, his skin would redden and burn a little. It was the one advantage she owned over him—Obsidian might be stronger and faster, but he couldn't stomach the light of day.

His gaze met hers, and he smiled a little. "But you're not lying about your thirst, at least. Look at it itching all the way through you."

"Bite this," she breathed in pure frustration, biting her clenched fist at him. It was the sort of insult she'd heard among the Echelon, in reference to telling a blue blood he'd find no easy prey here, but a fist instead.

"My preference is something a little softer." Obsidian's eyelids drooped lazily, and she had the flushed sensation he was trying not to glance at her stockinged feet.

Never one to miss a chance, Gemma let the cloak fall open a hint. "If you want something a little softer, then you're going to have to come on this side of the bars."

His face shuttered immediately. "As fascinating as this little conversation is, Miss Townsend, I was trying to sleep. What do you want?"

"Freedom."

"You're wasting my time—and your breath." Obsidian shook his head, and then turned to go.

Gemma rushed the bars, grabbing hold of them. "No, wait!"

He paused.

Half turned his head toward her.

"I want... water to wash with. Hot water. And soap. Preferably something perfumed."

"I'm not certain you understand the predicament you're in." Rattling the bars, he gave her a pointed look. "You're on the wrong side of these. I don't have to take orders from you."

"It's been two days," she growled out. "I am tired, thirsty, and wretchedly cold. I stink."

"Blue bloods have no personal scent."

"I *feel* like I stink," she growled out. "One is not meant to be laced so tightly for so long."

"Miss Townsend."

"Hot water," she begged. "Even a small bowl of it. I would do anything for a bowl of hot water and soap."

Those dangerous eyes turned sleepy-lidded. "Anything?"

"Anything," she breathed.

"Fine." He slid his hands into his trouser pockets. "Drop the cloak."

Gemma tugged the strings of his cloak loose, letting it slide from her shoulders. The heavy fur-lined fabric pooled around her bare ankles, the sudden biting chill of the air pebbling her skin. "And now, Obsidian?"

"Ghost was right," he said coldly, looking his fill. "You will do anything, stoop to any level, in order to ensnare me."

A game to see how far she would let him push her.

Damn him.

Gemma hauled the cloak up around her shoulders. "Not all of us have the luxury of power. You have something I want. I have nothing to bargain with. If you're hoping to shame me, then please take your smirking face elsewhere. I am done with being shamed. All I wanted was a simple luxury. Clearly, I miscalculated your level of empathy." Somehow she laughed. "The mistake, I believe, was in thinking you had any."

Hauling the warm fur around her bare arms, she retreated to the marble slab she'd been sleeping on and turned away from him before deliberately raising her voice to earsplitting levels. "Oh, there was a young Nighthawk from Matlock—"

"Ghost." She let the word fall into the still air as Obsidian appeared at evening with a fresh flask of blood.

She hadn't been thinking earlier, but trapped in this barred room, all she had was time to think and resurrect every word spoken between them.

The Company of Rogues knew they faced an unknown alliance of *dhampir*. Created by Dr. Erasmus Cremorne at Falkirk Asylum, according to the information Malloryn had handed her, most of the *dhampir* patients had died when the asylum burned to the ground.

It wasn't a project the common people of London would have felt easy with; trying to force the evolution of blue bloods that were fated to turn into vampires. Vampires were monstrous entities, capable of tearing entire streets of people to pieces. Back in Georgian times, there'd been a spate of vampire attacks, resulting in the Year of Blood, before the Echelon had brought in strict rules.

Any blue blood who reached craving virus levels of 70 percent or higher was to be reported to the authorities as standing on the edge of the Fade, that moment in time when the color began to bleach from their bodies in preparation for the transformation into a vampire.

Yet, it was only in recent years they'd discovered there was one more way for a blue blood to evolve.

The Falkirk project had been kept quiet. Meddling with blue bloods almost on the verge of becoming vampires? The human classes would have rioted.

So Falkirk burned, all the records within it were lost, and it was only in the past year, with *dhampir* surfacing out of the dregs of myth, that Malloryn began to find traces of information about the project.

There was no way of telling how many *dhampir* were arrayed against them.

Gemma needed that information.

Suddenly, escape was not the first thought in her mind. Could she do some good here? Could she gain Obsidian's trust? Learn more about who COR faced?

"Ghost is your fellow *dhampir*, is he not?" she continued, as Obsidian shot her a sharp look. "And he knows about me." She paused. "He knows about Russia, and what lay between us."

And he had warned Obsidian away from her.

"He's the one who sent that *dhampir* to kill me, isn't he?"

The muscle in Obsidian's jaw flexed. "You're not going to gain anything else from me, Miss Townsend."

Oh, I already have.

"I never realized why your hair was so pale in Russia. I thought it your natural coloring, or perhaps you were close to the Fade. We had no inkling then, of *dhampir*. You were at Falkirk, weren't you?"

A flinch.

"Or was it the Russian court who experimented upon you?" No flinch. "No. You were born Russian, I suspect, but you were experimented upon here. When did you arrive in England? Were you a blue blood before you were sent to Falkirk? You had to be. According to the Duke of Caine's records on the facility, only blue bloods were interred there—"

"Do you want this, or not?" His hand clutched tight around the flask, knuckles splayed white.

Struck a nerve, by the look of it. "I'm only curious," Gemma protested, uncrossing her legs from where she sat on the marble slab and pushing to her feet. "There's not a great deal to do to pass the time, apart from think. You can only blame yourself for not providing adequate entertainment."

And she couldn't help thinking about the past.

Her feelings... had been real, had they not? But how could her love have existed when he'd been a virtual stranger? She knew nothing about him, nor he her. Only a bunch of carefully concocted lies the pair of them wove as they danced about each other.

It made a mockery of what they'd shared.

I loved a man who didn't exist.

"Don't be too curious." He withdrew the flask as she reached for it, and Gemma's eyes narrowed.

Slowly, he let her take it.

"Drink," he commanded abruptly. "Then turn around and place your hands behind you."

Gemma unscrewed the flask with greedy hands, tipping it to her lips. She preferred to take her blood in her cup of hot tea, or laced into her wine, but beggars couldn't be choosers. The second it hit her throat, the hunger exploded through her, flaming through her veins like a fuse racing toward a stick of dynamite. Fatigue sloughed away from her, and the constant bone-deep chill vanished.

She gulped down half the flask before she realized he was watching her.

"You've been starving me," she pointed out, patting the blood from her lips. "This is hardly the situation for etiquette."

One did not gulp one's blood as if one was an animal. It was meant to be sipped and savored, to prove you had complete control over the violence of your hunger. Especially when one was a woman and prone to "hysterics" and hence had more to prove when it came to controlling oneself.

But right then, she didn't care.

"Are you done?" he murmured, holding out a thin rope.

And Gemma remembered the other part of his request. She lowered the flask, then set if on the floor and slowly turned around, forcing her wrists together. She needed to gain his trust.

She wasn't sure if he had hers.

"Where are you taking me?"

"Somewhere you requested," Obsidian said softly, tugging the ropes around her wrists tight.

"Is that...." Gemma's jaw dropped as Obsidian pushed her through the door into a tiled room. "A bath."

Steam curled off the elegant bath in the center of the wash chamber. Bubbles popped on the surface, and though the room held the chill of autumn, the scent of lavender filled the damp air. A single candle burned on the vanity.

"I was forced to fix the boiler," he said, "but the tap still works."

He'd done more than merely fix the boiler. The room was swept clean, though dust was piled in the corner. From the state of the rest of the dying manor, she suspected he'd cleaned the bath too.

"Thank you." Gemma glanced at him from beneath her lashes. "You found soap."

"As requested." A blank, blank face. "There is also a clean gown and undergarments on the vanity, though the sizing may not be quite right."

What was going on here? She didn't think it a kindness. No, he wanted something.

Was this the plan all along? Capture her, soften her, then... learn something from her? She still didn't know why he'd taken her.

Or....

"Are you planning on watching?"

Hard hands spun her around, tugging the knot of the rope free. "Would you enjoy that?"

"I'm not entirely certain I've forgiven you for earlier." She realized she was staring at the bath. "Though I suspect I could work up to it."

A lot of things could be forgiven for hot water and soap.

"Don't try anything. I'm not going anywhere," he said, as she rubbed at her wrists. "Don't waste your time. You have twenty minutes."

Then he turned back to the door and gave her his back, as if to prove he had no damned intentions of watching at all.

Gemma cleared her throat. "There is one slight problem."

Long strands of brown hair brushed his collar as he turned his face in profile. Though he clearly dyed it, there was a faint ashen color leaching through, as if the silver blond sought to reassert itself. "Miss Townsend," he warned.

"I have a friend to assist me at the safe house." Sweeping her tangled black hair over her shoulder, she turned around, presenting the problem to him. "Consider yourself lucky you are not a woman and can dress yourself. I cannot unlace my corset without assistance."

"I swear to God, Gemma." His voice came out hard, and a little part of thrilled at the sound of her name on his lips.

"It's not a trick," she shot over her shoulder. "Have you ever tried to wear one of these infernal contraptions? And it isn't as if you had any compunction about stripping me out of my dress the other night. Unless, of course, now you suddenly do, hmm?"

"Fine." Drawing his knife, he jerked her around again.

Obsidian sliced the ribbons apart along her spine, the corset gaping with an abrupt jerk.

Gemma caught it to her breasts, her pulse suddenly pounding. "That corset was pink velvet with seed pearls hand-stitched to it! It came from Emerson's!"

"It was ruined anyway."

She stared down in dismay. "It cost me an entire week's worth of wages!"

"Then perhaps the Duke of Malloryn should be paying you more. It's just an article of clothing. You can replace it."

He didn't understand. She'd spent her entire childhood dressed in a nondescript training outfit every other Falcon trainee wore. They'd called her cadet, and shaved her head for the first twelve years—all the better to prevent another student from gaining a crucial hold during their bouts. When she'd won her way free of the Falcons, Gemma had found herself fighting to find her identity. *She* was the one who chose her gowns now, silks and velvets and frivolous undergarments that clung like a second skin.

Decadent colors she'd never been allowed to wear; gorgeous boots she'd spent a small fortune upon. As a spy, there was little she could own that held any value, and no point in collecting items of a personal nature just in case she had to flee if her cover was broken and leave them behind. Her wardrobe was the one aspect of her life she could control, that could remind her of who she was now.

It was as much a part of the construction of Gemma Townsend as her devious little mind. It made her feel real.

But how could she even explain such a thing to him?

"Warn me next time," she told him, a little breathlessly. He had not so much as marked her skin. "I almost reacted to the knife."

Flipping the blade into his fingers, Obsidian gave her a slow, heated look as he sheathed it at his hip. "You'll never get it off me, so don't give me that look."

Gemma shot him a devastating smile as she turned to face him. "I wouldn't dream of it."

She let the corset go and it fluttered to the ground, taking his gaze with it. Knowing when she didn't need to speak to make her point, she turned and slinked her way toward the steaming bath, her fingers tucking under the hem of her shift.

A pause.

A glance over her shoulder.

Obsidian's eyes met hers, flashing black with the hunger, before he turned and very pointedly gave her his back. "Be swift."

Like hell. She'd earned her bath.

Stripping the shift up her body, Gemma made good use of the movements, knowing he'd hear every last rustle of fabric. The imagination was a powerful weapon. Her drawers hit the floor. Finally she was bare, except for her stockings, and as she peeled the last one down her leg, she balled it up and threw it at his back.

Obsidian reacted as if he'd been shot, but Gemma had turned away and stepped into the bath by then, not caring whether he watched or not.

Hot. Water.

Soap.

Bubbles.

Oh, God. She sank up to her throat in the heat, moaning a little. "You have no idea how good this feels."

Was it her imagination, or were his shoulders a little stiffer?

All her frustration swept away as Gemma made good use of the soap, slicking it across her arms and down her breasts. Delving it between her thighs. Down her legs. Water splashed and dripped on the floor. A mischievous mood afflicted her, and she tossed a handful of it in his direction.

Obsidian shot her a glare as it splashed against his legs, and Gemma bit her lip, catching the flash of his glance across her bubble-coated breasts.

"It's safe to look," she taunted. "Unless you wish to keep trying to pretend you don't want to? It's all right, Obsidian. I'll keep your little secret."

"Enjoy it. It's going to be the last bath you get." A rough, heavy sentence, almost growled out.

"Do you think you could wash my back?" She cupped the soap and glanced up at him from beneath her lashes.

Then she couldn't help herself. Laughter burst from her at the expression on his face: one part murder; one part frustration; and two parts pure, unadulterated hunger.

"Were you always this frustrating?"

"Most likely." She let her gaze rove over the broad planes of his shoulders. Goodness, the man could fill out a coat nicely. "Were you always this cold and controlled? You're not the man I remember, but then... that could always have been an act."

"I wasn't the one acting."

"No? Do you know what I think?" She lifted one of her legs and rested her heel on the edge of the bath. "You say I'm the actress, but I never chased *you*, Obsidian. Sergey was my target. Not you. And every damned time I got close to him, you would appear and intercept me, and I did my best to drive you away. That wasn't an act. I never tried to pretend to be anything to you, because I never had to. You were the one who was charming and reckless. You challenged me constantly. And yet, here you are, and none of that remains." She flicked water in his direction. "It makes me wonder... just who was fooling who?"

He'd laced his arms over his chest. "Perhaps I *was* charming. Perhaps I had a reason, back then."

"Perhaps, perhaps, perhaps," Gemma growled, smashing her fist into the water. "Can you not ever grant me a straight answer?"

He stared at the wall for so long, she had to look to see if he'd heard her.

"I don't know."

"Was I that insignificant?" She lay back in the cooling water. "Could you not be bothered remembering me?"

Obsidian had crossed to the vanity, examining the old vial of perfumed oil there. "No. I *don't* remember."

It took her breath. Gemma sat up, sloshing water everywhere. *That's not the way I remember it*, he'd said yesterday. "What do you mean?"

"I have very little recollection of Russia," he said in that silken-soft voice that stirred through her. He set the vial down. "I didn't remember shooting you until you mentioned it. All I remember is the fire. Kissing you. Once.

Flashes of the first time we met. You were an enemy spy who seduced me. You tried to kill me."

She didn't know what to say.

"I didn't try to kill you," Gemma whispered. "I had nothing to do with the fire, I swear. By the time I slipped from your bed you were fast asleep, but I didn't think it unusual. And then it was hours later when the outcry went up. My chambers were right next to Malloryn's at the other end of the house. We shuffled out into the snow, and when I realized your end of the house was aflame, I tried to find you but you were gone."

"You're lying."

For the first time she gained the impression he wasn't saying it to her.

"Your cover had been blown. Malloryn discovered you were working for Balfour, and warned me to stay away from you. The next time I saw you it was night," Gemma continued. "I was walking home from a friend's. I'd been trying to find word of what happened to you, and Malloryn caught me. He was lecturing me when you appeared out of nowhere." She saw it all over again. Dmitri stalking toward her through the snowy night. The burst of relief she'd felt when she realized he was alive. Unharmed. Malloryn calling out to her from behind, *"Damn it, Hollis, get out of the way!"*

"No!" she'd cried, throwing her arms wide, so Malloryn couldn't take the shot.

"I ran toward you, but it was as if it wasn't you at all. You looked at me so coldly. It felt so wrong. And I slowed to a halt right in the middle of the bridge, alerted by some instinct. And that's when you shot me."

The slam of a weight into her chest, as if she'd been hit by a freight train. Tumbling backward over the bridge, and smashing straight through the ice. Cold. So very, very cold.

Gemma rubbed at her chest, and the faint scar there where it still sometimes ached.

"When I woke I was on an airship, being evacuated to England. Malloryn saw everything happen, and he'd hauled me out.

"I heard about the explosion while aboard. I didn't... I didn't know what to think. I thought you were dead, and a part of me was so angry at you, because I'd loved you, and you'd tried to kill me. But I didn't want you to die."

Obsidian cocked his head, as if he were trying to pick through her story. "Why would I believe you?"

"The question you should be asking yourself is why did you think I tried to kill you? If you cannot remember what happened in Saint Petersburg, then someone had to have told you. Do you trust their version of events? Or do you trust mine? What reason would I have to lie to you?"

Obsidian stared at her flatly.

Then he pulled his pocket watch out of his waistcoat and examined the time. "Your twenty minutes is over. I'll leave you to get dressed."

Then he was gone, and Gemma didn't know what to think.

CHAPTER TEN

What reason would I have to lie to you?

Damn her. The words played over and over in Obsidian's head, twisting and warping his memories until he could almost smell the smoke curling off the pistol in his hand, and see Gemma's eyes widen in shock.

I shot her. She's not lying about that. But why? Why did I do it?

Why can't I remember?

He couldn't afford to let any of his turmoil show. Not right now with both Dr. Richter and Ghost watching him like a pack of hounds circling an injured calf.

"Tell me," Dr. Richter said, picking up one of his infernal notebooks. "Have you been suffering from any strange dreams or... recollections that might seem like memories?"

Obsidian hadn't been able to avoid this assessment session. Ghost insisted, the message had said, and he'd come here directly, his fist still crumpled around the scroll of paper one of the acolyte's had given him when they tracked him down near the tower.

"Memories?" Obsidian's heart kicked hard, and the doctor glanced at the machine on the counter as the arrow on the pendulum ticked, just faintly. Obsidian eased out a breath, his chest straining against the leather straps that bound him to the chair. "No. Should I?"

He lied as easily as he breathed. He hadn't been able to, once. He remembered that. But now he knew all the little quirks they'd be looking for. The right words to say.

Richter examined his *dissimuler* device, examining the counterweights. The faintest pressure could set the pendulum moving; a sign of a swift intake of breath, a rapid shift of his heart rate, or muscular tension. The doctor claimed it could help discern a man's truth.

But he'd managed to outwit it years ago.

Obsidian stayed as still as a cobra about to strike, forcing his heart to still to a slow, steady beat. His body held the silence of a sniper taking a breath before he peered through his rifle and pulled the trigger. He let all of his inner turmoil—his thoughts—wash out of him, leaving nothing behind except for a sudden, intense clarity.

"Hollis Beechworth. Do you recognize this name?"

"She tried to kill me," he said, by rote.

"Very good." The doctor made a notation in his notebook. "And Gemma Townsend? What does this name mean to you?"

"One of Malloryn's spies. She was once Hollis Beechworth. She seduced me, then tried to kill me in Russia."

"Excellent."

The doctor put his notebook aside and picked up the leather mouthpiece. "Open, if you will."

Obsidian allowed the intrusion, breathing heavily through his nose as the doctor strapped it into place, some of his hair pulling as it was caught in the buckle. He stared directly at the far wall, the *dissimuler* pendulum making a rabid clicking noise as his heart rate accelerated and his breathing quickened.

A dull pit of fear blossomed within him.

He couldn't afford to forget again. Not now, with Gemma locked up in Mably House, and Ghost's assassins out there searching for her.

And the truth beckoning....

"It's all right," Richter assured him, patting him on the shoulder. "This is an assessment, nothing more. I promise."

The doctor picked up a long cylindrical advice. With a twist of the far end, light erupted from the pinhole at the opposite end. Richter clasped his chin and lifted the light to his eyes.

Obsidian flinched, momentarily blinded. Spit slid down his jaw as a growl tried to escape the leather mouthpiece strapped to his head. *You submitted to this.* But no matter how often he told himself such a thing, he couldn't escape the frenetic impulse urging him to burst out of his straps.

He felt like a caged animal.

The sudden flashing images of Richter drawing his cortex resectioning device into place around Obsidian's head, and strapping the helmet tightly made his gut churn. He couldn't hear the rasp of a leather belt slapping into place without feeling a chill down his spine anymore.

I'll have him schedule a reconditioning appointment for you....

No. Richter had promised. Just an assessment.

"Pupils responsive." Dr. Richter murmured, drawing the ocular spyglass away. "No sign of muscle spasm in his face, nor eyelids. No slurring of speech."

"And?" Ghost asked, from where he watched the process in the shadows.

Dr. Richter stepped back from the chair Obsidian was bound to, rubbing his hand over his mouth. "There's no sign of malfunction with the neural regulating actuator implant."

"Nothing?" Ghost sounded disappointed.

"Not as far as I can tell." The doctor unstrapped the leather buckle locking Obsidian's mouthpiece in place. "My apologies. A necessary precaution with your teeth."

Obsidian's chest heaved, the panic a little easier to rein in now he was no longer so tightly arrayed.

Vile tasting thing. He spat the mouthpiece free, breathing hard as he glared at Ghost through the strands of his hair. "So much for that theory."

"He has been increasingly insubordinate of late," Ghost said coldly.

"I do as commanded." Obsidian stared blankly at his overseer. "I wasn't aware I wasn't supposed to speak my mind as I did it. Perhaps you'd be better off investing in some of those new automatons they're selling to the docks? They don't speak back, or so I am told. Or send for one of your lickspittles if you want someone to kiss your ass. You seem to forget where we came from. *Brother.*"

"Lickspittles?" the doctor asked, cleaning the ocular spyglass.

"The new recruits," Ghost replied.

"Ah."

"Or better yet," Obsidian said softly, the muscles in his arms flexing as he tested the leather straps that bound him to the doctor's examination chair. "Why don't you just sentence me the way you did to Zero?"

Ghost paused in his pacing, one of his white eyebrows arching. "*That's* what this is about."

The doctor had been in the process of dusting off his hands, and froze. "Miss Annabelle? I thought she died by the hands of the Duke of Malloryn's agents."

"No. She died by the Wraith's hands," Ghost said, meeting Obsidian's gaze.

"Don't call me that."

A vein throbbed in his temples. Obsidian's lip curled off his teeth. The Wraith. He'd seen the bastard's cold eyes in the mirror when he returned from a mission and needed to wash the blood off his hands, off his face. Heard the ringing in his ears when the Wraith was activated, and it felt like something else took over his body and all that was left of him became a silent bystander. All he knew of the world narrowed down to that piercing sound, as though he stood right under one of the enormous bells at the top of the Ivory Tower as someone beat upon it. The very world vibrated around him until hours later, when the ringing finally stopped, he would find himself lying helplessly in the dirt somewhere, blood dripping from his nose.

And no idea how he got there.

Ghost stepped closer, sneering a little. "Did Zero call you a traitor as you did it?"

"No."

She begged instead. And then I held her while the Black Vein I gave her killed her.

Annabelle's words damned him every bloody night he closed his eyes. "*Do you think that he won't d-do the same... to you—?*"

He hadn't wanted her to die alone. It was the first time he'd ever been able to find his way out of the vibration, enough to gain some control over his body. Enough to hold her as the Black Vein tore through her veins, and obliterated her heart.

Something happened within him that night.

When he slipped out of Malloryn's safe house after her body took its last breath, he'd felt the ground spiraling beneath him.

First Omega turned on Ghost, and died.

Then Zero was "terminated".

Who was left of their fractured family when Ghost was the one who'd engineered both their deaths?

X? Raving mad and locked in his cell below, with his muzzle permanently strapped in place?

Silas? The one true brother Obsidian still called by that name?

Dido, who'd gone off to Russia with Lord Balfour, her loyalties shifting from her brethren to the spymaster?

And why the hell did his head pound so much when he caught a hint of Gemma's scent?

"You terminated Miss Annabelle?" Richter asked.

"Zero betrayed us," Ghost said coldly, as the doctor cleaned his spectacles, looking a little distressed. He'd been the one who'd warned Zero's conditioning was failing. "She would have ruined us, and eventually Malloryn would have broken her down and gotten the information he wanted from her. She needed to be eliminated before she became a larger problem."

"All she wanted was revenge," Obsidian whispered. His fingers flexed. It was all any of them had ever wanted. In the beginning.

Revenge against Caine, Casavian, and Vickers—the three dukes who'd sponsored the Falkirk project and condemned him to his fate.

"We are getting revenge," Ghost said.

"Against who?" Obsidian looked up. "Malloryn? What did the Duke of Malloryn ever do to *us*?"

Dangerous, dangerous words. Lord Balfour had taken them from the streets following the burning of Falkirk. He'd given them everything, as Ghost often preached.

But I can't seem to remember what, precisely, he gave us.

Or why we play his little games for him?

"Careful. You're speaking treason now," Ghost whispered.

Gemma. Think of Gemma.

"Forgive me." Obsidian let his head and shoulders slump. His head was aching again. "I forget so much, sometimes I merely wonder...."

"You see?" Ghost said, to the doctor. "There's clearly a problem with either the neural implant or his conditioning."

"I warned you that you can't keep doing this to them," Dr. Richter cast aside his cleaning cloth with a flurry that betrayed his feelings regarding Zero's death. "What if there's some form of scarring building up? Who knows what is happening inside his brain? You saw what repeated bouts of reconditioning did to Annabelle."

Guilt trembled in the doctor's voice.

"And you made your choice ten years ago," Ghost said, stepping closer to the man and towering over him. "Don't grow squeamish now. I think a reconditioning session necessary."

Dr. Richter's lips grew pinched. "It's only been a month since Obsidian first caught sight of Miss Townsend and you insisted upon a session. I urge caution—"

"We cannot afford to have a fraction within our cause at this moment."

"And you cannot afford to melt his brains out of his ears," the doctor countered sharply. "*Dhampir* heal from almost anything, including the cerebral cortex resectioning. Eventually. But his last reconditioning put him down for nearly three days before he could be used again. He needs time to recover between bouts. I won't do it."

"*Won't* do it?" Ghost lashed out, capturing the good doctor by the throat.

Richter kicked ineffectually as Ghost hauled him into the air, his notebook and spring pen clattering to the floor as his hand lashed out.

Obsidian's lashes fluttered half-closed as he watched it all unfold emotionlessly.

There was something wrong with his conditioning. He'd suspected it for weeks.

It had something to do with Gemma Townsend.

Whatever the doctor did to him, his failsafe's began to collapse the second he'd laid eyes upon her.

Even now his head began to ache right behind his left eye, as if the mere thought of her shattered something inside his brain.

One last constraint, perhaps.

The conditioning is necessary, the doctor had told him.

It helps to control the rage inside you, Ghost had assured him.

Don't you want to forget the pain?

Don't you want to make it all go away?

Obsidian didn't know what he wanted. He didn't know what the hell he believed in anymore. Too many patchwork memories.

Who are you? The Wraith? Obsidian? The thought slithered through his back brain like a sibilant whisper.

Or...

She'd called him Dmitri.

And he had a sudden flash of remembrance of a warm body in his arms, Hollis's laughter in his ear, as he tumbled her onto a fur rug in front of a blazing fire, careless of the world around them. Careless of anything other than the feel of her skirts crumpling beneath his hand, and the smooth kiss of her skin beneath his fingertips....

The pendulum swung again as his lungs expanded sharply, but Obsidian was the only one who noticed.

"It doesn't... matter—" the doctor choked out, "—what you do to... m-me. Without me—"

Ghost let him collapse against the bench, where the doctor sputtered and coughed, grasping at his throat.

"Without me," Richter wheezed, "you can't... control them. Lord Balfour... gave me... jurisdiction over... these matters." He pushed himself up into a sitting position. "If you push the reconditioning too far, then you will kill them. And then... *you* will deal with Balfour's rage."

Obsidian stared thoughtfully at the doctor. The mere thought of Richter's rooms made him flinch, as if some part of his subconscious knew more about what the doctor did to him, than his conscious mind. But the man seemed to be arguing on his behalf.

"So be it," Ghost spat. "But if he slips his leash, then you shall be the one who earns Balfour's wrath. Not I."

What were they truly doing to him with the reconditioning?

Obsidian felt like dozens of pieces of memory floated around him like obnoxious jigsaw puzzle pieces, refusing to slot into place. He was missing something. Some important piece of the puzzle that would make all those memories become whole.

And it had to do with Russia.

Gemma held the key to his past.

To his identity.

Could he trust her to tell the truth? He barely recalled St. Petersburg. Only fire. A pair of scorching kisses. A smoking pistol.

And the sound of someone screaming.

Someone who might have been him.

Gemma Townsend is a liar and a seductress, Ghost's whisper taunted him.

But as he watched Ghost quit the room in a fury, while the doctor trembled and cursed under his breath, Obsidian suddenly wondered whether he could trust Ghost either.

CHAPTER ELEVEN

"Tell me about Russia."

Gemma paused with her glass of blud-wein at her lips. She should have known he'd had ulterior motives when he brought the small table into her observatory.

"What precisely were you interested in knowing? It's a lovely place, if one likes snow, vodka, ornate palaces, and bloodthirsty scheming princes."

"No." Obsidian stilled, his silver-tipped lashes fluttering low over his eyes. "You claim my recollection of what occurred in Russia is wrong. Tell me about us. About the first time we met."

Us.

Gemma's smile melted off her face, and she swallowed. "What would you like to know?" she asked carefully, watching the shift of intense emotion flicker across his face.

"You say you loved me. I find it difficult to believe. I was working for the enemy—"

"I wasn't aware of that," she pointed out, "until it was too late."

"And yet, you were a trained spy, one of Malloryn's best. Love is a weapon to a woman like you. I find it difficult to believe you fell prey to it."

Gemma set her glass down. "Do you think me entirely immune to the lighter emotions? I spent my entire childhood locking away everything I dared to feel before it could betray me. It didn't mean I didn't feel those emotions, it just meant I didn't dare reveal them. When Malloryn showed me a new world those old habits stayed with me, but sometimes I succumb to certain weaknesses. Sometimes I make mistakes."

Her longing to be accepted and loved had been her downfall more than once.

"So I was a mistake?"

"Clearly," she snapped. "I thought what we shared in Russia was real. And you nearly killed me. Lesson learned. Love is a weakness that shouldn't exist for people like us."

Vibrating with anger, she turned her face abruptly away, before she could reveal too much. She should have mocked him. *Love? Of course, what I felt wasn't real. It was all a game.* But the very concept irritated something within her.

She felt strangely defensive.

"Your childhood?" Obsidian asked softly, setting one of his knives down and reaching for the other. The scent of oil on the rag in his hand was quite overwhelming. "From what Ghost has told me, you were training to be a Falcon before you defected to Malloryn's side."

"I didn't defect, so much as I was thrown away."

"Oh."

"It's a long story—"

"We have the entire night ahead of us."

Gemma sighed. She needed him to start trusting her, but this felt like scratching the scab of an old wound.

"My mother sold me to the Falcons when I was a little girl. There was a school up near the border of Scotland, ostensibly a boarding school. I cried myself to sleep every night for a month, before an older girl woke me one night with a knife to my throat and told me if she caught me sniveling again, she'd silence me forever.

"Then the classes started. Working with a knife; any sort of rifle or pistol; poisons; forgery; dancing; lock-picking; etiquette; flirtation; strangling a man with your bare hands....

"Every year from the age of ten, we faced our year-end tests, where we were given the name of another student in our class and told to either kill them—or be killed. Those that survived graduated the year level. By the time I reached my final year, there were barely twenty of us left in the class, and you didn't dare make friends." She'd learned that lesson when she was twelve and Lizzie picked her name out of the hat.

"It's one thing to be trained as a child assassin, but the Falcons take only the best. To 'graduate' you're given the name of someone to kill. Succeed and you are one of them. Fail and you are dead. I was the first to be granted a name, and it was Malloryn's."

Gemma took an unsteady breath. "I knew he was the new head of his house, recently risen to the duchy, but little beyond that. I studied him for weeks. Watched his house, watched his every move. And one night I broke into his bedroom and waited for him. He staggered in around six in the morning, and I put the pistol to his head and... hesitated. One second of uncertainty changed my life forever. It was one thing to kill for survival during our year-end tests, quite another to ruthlessly murder someone. It's the first time...." Her voice trailed off. "I always struggled with that instinct. Malloryn used the moment to disarm me, and turned my own pistol on me. I was lying on my back on the floor, certain this was the end, when he lowered the pistol. He offered me a chance to work for him, instead."

Gemma would never forget that night.

"You had me," the duke had said coldly, staring at her along the line of the pistol. *"Why didn't you pull the trigger?"*

She hadn't known how to answer. All her training prepared her for interrogation, but her mind refused to work with death staring her in the face. *"I don't know. I didn't.... I just...."*

And Malloryn lowered the pistol as Gemma started shaking violently.

He checked the pistol, examined the bullets. *"You're a Falcon. Or training to be one."*

She'd nodded.

"How old are you?"

"Nearly sixteen."

And then Malloryn knelt in front of her, with the pistol held in a slack grip between his thighs. *"You do realize you were never expected to succeed? They meant for you to die here. They wanted me to kill you."*

"How do you know that?"

He'd given her a thin smile. *"Because I know things. And I know who sent you."*

"That seems convenient for Malloryn," Obsidian said. "An ex-Falcon who served Balfour and might know some of his secrets.... Of course he granted you mercy."

"He *saved* my life," Gemma declared, suddenly infuriated. "Malloryn was the first person who ever looked at me and saw something worth fighting for—and no, I am not so foolish as to think it a sense of sudden altruism. He gained something from our bargain too, but he gave a chance, Obsidian. That's more than I can say for Lord Balfour and his Falcons."

"You bear a grudge against Balfour?"

"The night Malloryn killed him was the best night of my life," Gemma replied. "He deserves to rot for what he did to me."

And to all those poor children who were buried in unmarked graves at Falconridge.

Obsidian swished the rag over the knife in his hands, suddenly giving it his full attention. "And then Malloryn sent you to Russia. It must have irritated him greatly to see one of his most loyal agents betray him with the enemy."

Gemma pursed her lips. "He was angry, yes."

Disappointed, mostly.

And it was the disappointment that stung.

"Tell me about Russia. Tell me about us. From your perspective."

"So you can mock me?"

"So I can ascertain the truth of what happened. You were right. Something about Russia doesn't quite add up, but I'm not certain who is lying to me. You. Or Ghost."

He believed her?

Gemma looked at him sharply, but there was no sign of any inner turmoil on his face. He simply continued oiling the blade he was polishing.

Perhaps she wasn't the only one hiding behind a mask.

"Sergey was my mark," Gemma's voice softened a little as she saw it all. "We were there ostensibly to secure the alliance between the Tzarina and the prince consort, though the treaty was Lord Balfour's idea and hence, Malloryn wished to prevent it. Malloryn instructed me to get close to Sergey to discover which of the empress's granddaughters she was favoring as next in line for the throne. There was talk Catherine had begun to enter the Fade, though she'd been in seclusion for so long, nobody truly knew.

"As Master of the Imperial Ravens, and the new Prince of Tsaritsyn, Sergey had her favor, and was said to be vying for the hand of one of her granddaughters. If anyone knew Catherine's preference, it would be him. He had one weakness. He liked women and frequently flitted from mistress to mistress. I'd done my research, and planned everything, down to our very meeting. Sergey preferred curvaceous blondes who rode well, hunted, and gave him a challenge. I fit the brief. It should have been easy."

"But?"

"But." Her gaze lifted to his, and even after all this time she couldn't stop herself from taking a swift, shallow intake of breath. "The one thing I hadn't accounted for was you."

Then....

The woman who called herself Hollis Beechworth, took a deep breath as the Duke of Malloryn led her to the top of the staircase in the Winter Palace.

A servant appeared out of nowhere offering a glass of champagne, which she accepted.

"Are you ready?" Malloryn murmured, surveying the enormous ballroom as if he owned it.

"Seek. Enamor. Destroy," Hollis told him in return, with a sultry lift of her shoulder and a saucy smile. "It seems simple to me."

Malloryn gave her an astute look. This was her first official mission for him.

Oh, there'd been many other small tasks. Pretending to be other people, luring targets into admitting a particular bit of information, a little bit of break and entering, forging certain notes, taking transcriptions of others.... All done in the shadows of night, where her gift for recall helped her excel. She could read a page once and manage to remember almost everything on it hours later.

But this was the first time Malloryn had ever asked her to play a role in public.

She felt almost giddy with the thrill of it; of finally being able to repay him for sparing her life all those years ago.

"There's Sergey Grigoriev," Malloryn murmured, his glance flickering across the room. "I want you to get close to him and discover what he knows of the Empress's condition, and where her familial affections lie."

Hollis drained the glass of champagne, watching the enigmatic stranger across the room smiling like a shark. Tall. Handsome. Dressed all in black, with an ornate golden Orthodox cross hanging against his black coat. "He's mine."

The press of Malloryn's hand on the small of her back stilled her descent.

"Be careful," he said, his expression unblinking. "The Blood Court is a dangerous place, and there are rumors Grigoriev murdered his uncle, aunt and younger cousins for the title he now holds. He's a dangerous player in this game, Hollis."

"Careful is my middle name," she protested.

Malloryn gave her an arched brow.

"I won't fail you."

Then she swept down the stairs on his arm, aware of all the eyes turning to survey her.

Miss Hollis Beechworth. Malloryn's young cousin. Here to potentially cement an alliance between the British Empire and Russia, by marriage, if nothing else.

A simple role, helped by the seclusion of the real Hollis Beechworth, who despised Malloryn.

They were introduced, and Malloryn set his shark's smile in place as he swept her into the crush of silk organza.

Circling the room, she nodded at one Russian aristocrat, and laughed as another bumped into her with a smile that showed a little too much teeth. Hollis made light commentary as she was introduced to dozens of people, responding in limited Russian.

Malloryn caught her eye, and tipped his head.

Time to roll the die.

Slipping another glass of champagne from the servant's tray, Hollis headed in a meandering path toward Sergey.

He stood in a coterie of elegant gentleman, his gaze flashing across her as she swayed toward him. Then back, clearly enamored with her appearance. Time to cast the lure.

Shoulders back, she caught the eye of the strapping officer beside Sergey, then glanced beneath her lashes and moved toward him, focusing all her attention upon him. Out of the corner of her vision she caught a brief flicker of Sergey frowning, and smiled inwardly.

In her experience, men dreamed of what they couldn't have. And powerful men wanted what other men had. He was used to being fawned over, but he liked to do the chasing himself.

The bait was cast.

The officer seemed startled by her attention. His mustache quivered when she smiled at him, and he took a startled drink of his champagne, his gold medallions gleaming in the candlelight.

She was almost there when a tall, dark blot of shadow stepped in her path.

Hollis blinked as she looked up—and up—into gray eyes the color of stormy seas. For a second all she could see were his thick lashes, tipped with blond, and the faint crease between his brows. Her breath caught. The newcomer wore strict black from head-to-toe, but it only served to highlight his handsome features.

"You seem lost. May I assist you?" he asked in Russian.

"Pardon," she replied in French. "My Russian is a little rusty."

A blatant lie.

At least some of her wits were still with her.

"As is my French," he replied, in slightly accented English, and graced her with a smile that made a thrill run through her.

Good grief. Whoever he was, he mustn't smile often, for the results would be catastrophic. Women all across the ballroom would swoon, and then there'd be bloodshed, as the Blood nobles looked to see who'd caught their eye. Hollis realized she was staring, and swiftly gathered herself.

You've seen handsome men before. Focus.

"You're with the English delegation."

"Lady Hollis Beechworth," she replied, blushing at will.

"A dance, Lady Beechworth?"

Damn him. Hollis pasted a smile on her face, though she noted the sudden intensity in Sergey's eyes as he glanced at the way their hands interlocked. Instantly, she changed directions, her smile softening, becoming warmer as she stared up into those intense gray eyes. "I should be delighted.... Though I'm afraid I didn't quite catch your name."

"Captain Lieutenant Dmitri Zhukov." He lifted her gloved hand to his lips, a glint of humor warming the arctic depths of his irises. At the very last moment, he deftly turned her hand, his lips finding the inside of her wrist instead and his gaze boldly locked upon hers.

A faint fleeting gesture, but suddenly it sucked all the air out of the room.

She was well-versed in the art of court etiquette.

And the language of the blue blood world.

A kiss to the back of the hand? *How lovely to make your acquaintance.*

A kiss to the fingertips? *I desire to make more of your acquaintance.*

But a kiss to the inside of a woman's wrist?

I intend to make you mine, that gesture said, and while he wouldn't be the first man who'd ever tried to claim her thusly, the heated look in his eyes as he did it sent a lash of intrigued interested through her.

Dmitri Zhukov held a quiet sort of confidence about him she found intriguing. As Hollis swallowed, her gaze dropped to his lips. Every inch of this man moved with purpose and dominance. If he kissed her, it would not be a question.

If he kissed her, she would not be the one with the upper hand.

Don't you dare. You are here on a mission.

Sergey's the target.

Not... Not this man.

"Are you enjoying Russia?" he countered, as he swept her into the *assah,* a dance designed in England to display a thrall's assets most beautifully to her blue blood master.

Hollis had never been any man's prey, but the smoky allure of the exotic music stole over her, as Dmitri slid his left hand possessively over her waist, and captured her other hand. And she felt it strike a chord within her, as Dmitri took possession of her with purpose. Not a single ounce of hesitation filled him. He moved like captured lightning. Gripped her like a man who intended to never let her go.

"I'm enjoying it a little more now," she admitted huskily.

The faintest of smiles touched his mouth.

"You have a dangerous smile, Captain Lieutenant."

"I never smile."

"And yet you are," she accused. "Don't deny it. I saw it with my own eyes."

"Perhaps I'm enjoying Russia a little more now too."

Gemma's breath caught, but she didn't have time to reply, for he swept her into a quick shuffle that required her concentration. She'd never felt so off-balance before. Men were usually easy to wrap around her little finger, but every glint of those dangerous eyes assured her he wouldn't be easy to tame.

"How precisely, are you acquainted with Prince Sergey Grigoriev?" she asked, because she had a job to do.

"Why would you assume I am?"

"Because he's watching you quite intently."

Dmitri swept her around, capturing her wrists in both hands and leaning his mouth close to her ear. "It's not me he's watching. But you knew that."

A step forward.

A step back.

"Why are *you* so interested in him?" he asked.

"I wasn't aware I was."

"You must be," he teased, "because usually when a woman's in my arms, she's not asking questions about another man."

"He's a Prince of the Blood," Hollis breathed, slipping back into her preordained role. "What young lady of quality wouldn't be interested in him?"

He tipped his head toward her. "True."

"Are you a friend of Sergey's?"

"No."

Interesting. "A relative?"

They looked a little alike, but the Russian court were fastidious about keeping their bloodlines pure, and—

"No."

"Do you know how to answer a question with more than one word?"

There. The faintest hint of warmth in his eyes. "Occasionally."

Gemma couldn't stop herself from smiling. Her real smile this time, not the seductive one she often fabricated. "You, sir, are an enigma."

And there was nothing she enjoyed more than a mystery.

"I'm nothing of the sort," Dmitri replied, sweeping her beneath his hand. The soft caress of his fingertips brushed her waist as she spun, his thumb stroking the silk there just long enough to make her realize

"I promise you won't remain a mystery for long," she retorted a little breathlessly, as she spun back into his arms.

The dying strains of the *assah* whispered through the air, as they drew to a halt.

"It seems our time together is over."

Dmitri met her eyes, and his own twinkled. "I like to think it is just beginning. Until next time, Lady Beechworth."

"One presumes there is a next time."

"Oh, there will be."

He kissed her hand again—the back of it this time—but his eyes smoldered as he took his leave.

What an interesting man. She was still smiling when she turned to look for Sergey.

Only to realize he'd vanished during the course of the dance.

And she hadn't noticed at all.

CHAPTER TWELVE

Obsidian rested one arm against the open arch of an abandoned clock tower, staring at his target. The Ivory Tower speared into the heavens, but despite its height and glory, he barely saw it.

If you cannot remember what happened in Saint Petersburg, then someone had to have told you. Do you trust their version of events?

Curse her to hell.

The first time you kissed me, I forgot the role I was supposed to be playing, the game I'd set into place. I forgot everything, but the taste of your mouth.

Gemma was playing with his mind, manipulating him. He knew it. It was what she did.

And yet, there was a faint whisper of doubt deep in his heart.

Could he believe what she'd told him?

Had she truly loved him?

Opening his clenched fist, he stared down at the button he'd taken from her dress. There was no scent on it, no reason to consider it a memento, but he couldn't stop his thumb from rasping over the soft silk and thinking of her skin.

Footsteps echoed through the gloom of the clock tower's attic, disturbing a pair of nesting pigeons who cooed in sudden nervousness. Obsidian cocked his head, but he'd heard the door open below, and seen the familiar figure enter.

"Are you just goin' to stare at it all night?" Silas asked, stalking out of the shadows behind him. "Ghost's growin' impatient."

Obsidian snapped his fist closed and slid the button into his pocket, mastering his expression before he turned to his brother.

"Lord Balfour is expecting an update as soon as possible. You know how Ghost gets," Silas said with a shrug.

"Ghost is going to get us dead if he's not patient."

"You're the assassin," Silas said. "I trust your instincts. But I don't trust his temper."

Trust. Silas just *had* to repeat that word.

Obsidian had trusted Ghost once.

"This is not a task to rush," Obsidian said. "The Tower's guarded by over five hundred guards. There are cannons mounted on the walls, and a metaljacket legion held in reserve. The stables are full of the Trojan cavalry. And we have only thirty-eight *dhampir.*"

"The tower's full of secret passages," Silas countered. "The humanists got in during the revolution, so surely we can do it."

"And the Duke of Malloryn was working with the humanists," Obsidian pointed out. "What do you think the first thing he would have done when they took the tower is? Do you think he'd just leave all those passages open?

Undefended? Every tunnel I've found so far has been filled with rubble. He blew them all."

Silas rubbed at his mouth as he squatted in the open window. "Good point."

"Bloody Malloryn." Obsidian turned his gaze back to the tower. "The only way inside it is to use someone they'd never expect."

"Project: Chameleon?"

They both knew how he felt about that.

"Ghost might have already played that card," he said roughly. "Killing Jonathan Carlyle was a foolish move. Now they know they're vulnerable. The Coldrush Guards have been like a kicked ant nest ever since."

"His neural implant was malfunctioning. It was only a matter of time before it killed him, and they found it. He needed to die." Silas swung his legs over the edge of the tower. "How would you do it?"

Obsidian shot him a sharp look.

"How would you kill the queen?"

He stared at the tower, considering his skill set. "The tower's impenetrable."

Not for you. You can get inside any building."

"Even for me. I've spent weeks testing its weaknesses. The guard's rounds are too irregular, the walls too steep. And the queen's personal chambers are at the very pinnacle. Getting to her means going through an entire tower's worth of defenses. You could fly over it in a dirigible and come in from the top, but they've mounted cannons on the wall to counter airships.

"If I wanted to kill the queen, I wouldn't enter the tower at all," he mused. "I'd wait until she left it."

Silas made a frustrated sound. "She's holed up tighter than a nun's britches, what with them riots in the streets."

"Malloryn's wedding gives us a chance. She won't miss that."

"Imagine Malloryn's face if the queen died under his watch. Hell of a weddin' gift." Silas gave an evil smile. "Compliments of Balfour."

Obsidian nodded, pacing in front of the open tower as he cracked his knuckles. "It could work. She'll have to take a steam-carriage through the streets, which makes her vulnerable. Then there's the wedding venue itself. The Hamilton's house is nowhere near as well-protected as Malloryn's manor."

He felt eyes watching him.

"What's troublin' you, mate?" Silas finally asked.

I have one of Malloryn's spies locked up in the Duke of Vickers's abandoned manor, and I can't kill her.

And then... there was her story.

She was an enemy spy.

She tried to kill you.

The faint echo of pain whispered through his head.

I thought what we shared in Russia was real....

"Do you ever wonder if Ghost has ever lied to you?"

Silas stiffened. "You're asking dangerous questions."

"We swore an oath," he said quietly, dragging out an old milk crate and sinking onto it. "Brothers by blood. Forged in Falkirk. And then he sent the Wraith to kill Zero when she betrayed him. I... I didn't realize until it was too late."

He could still see her face sometimes. Begging him for mercy as he injected her with Black Vein and held her while she died.

"Zero would have killed *us*."

"Do you think so?" He clasped his hands between his knees. "All she ever wanted was revenge upon the people who hurt her and threw her in Falkirk. He gave the order to kill her, Silas. He didn't give a damn about her. He used me to do it."

Indeed, Ghost's last words had been, *"She's served her purpose. Put her out of her misery."*

As if Zero's abilities were the only value she had for him.

"She was mad as hatters, damn it." Silas pushed to his feet. "Bloody hell. We can't talk about this."

"Why not?"

Silas raked a hand through his hair. "Because Ghost'll *kill us* if he ever catches wind of it."

"There's no one here but you and me."

"Aye. And when Dr. Richter puts you under? You ever wonder what exactly he pulls out of your head? Or what he puts in there?"

Obsidian froze.

"Because I do." Silas stabbed his temple. "Sometimes I wonder if I can even trust meself. I ain't havin' this conversation, not even with you, brother. I'm due for reconditionin' in a week, and I don't want to inadvertently betray either of us to Ghost." He clapped Obsidian on the shoulder, squeezed hard. "I'll mention the Malloryn element to Ghost. But it wouldn't hurt to keep taking a tilt at the tower. I'll see you tomorrow night."

"Aye." Obsidian stared out across the expanse of rooftops as Silas patted him on the back and vanished. He needed to return to Mably House before Gemma woke. She'd fallen into a stupor minutes after she drank the drugged cup of blud-wein he'd given her tonight, but he couldn't trust she'd still be under.

You ever wonder what exactly he pulls out of your head? Or what he puts in there?

A shiver ran down his spine as he pushed to his feet.

Because if Silas was right, then could he trust himself?

"Did you discover what he's up to?" Ghost asked as Silas hauled himself up into the steam hack.

He slumped on the seat and stared at the leader of the *dhampir*.

"Obsidian thinks tryin' to break into the Tower is a barmy idea," Silas replied, scratching at his jaw. Curse Obsidian. He had to give Ghost something. "Mentioned Malloryn's weddin' instead, maybe takin' a crack at the queen then."

"That's not what I was asking about," Ghost chided, tugging on his leather gloves.

Silas flushed with cold. Betray Obsidian to this bastard? Or protect the one last brother he truly had?

Are you sure Richter's not going to pull it out of your head later anyway? You're screwed, mate, either way.

Silas stared out the window. It was one thing to have his head on the chopping block, but to deliberately take this step felt like choosing sides. And he knew what Ghost had ordered done to Zero and Omega. There weren't no blood between them. There never truly had been.

But Obsidian. They were the only two originals left with any sense of bond.

Could he betray his brother to save his own skin?

"Why is he spending so much time at Mably House?" Ghost mused, stretching one arm across the back of his seat as the hack's boilers started hissing and it pulled away from the curb. "My trainee didn't dare get any closer to the house, but he said Obsidian's tracking beacon has been there for days. He's up to something."

And Ghost was clearly having Obsidian watched for his own reasons.

Him or you. Make your choice. Silas bowed his head and reached into his pocket for the small object.

"He was toyin' with this when I walked in." He flicked it toward Ghost, who snatched it out of the air. "I slipped it out his pocket when I left."

Ghost looked up sharply when he saw what it was. "A button. A lady's button."

"I think there's a reason no one can get near Gemma Townsend. And it's got little to do with *her* skills."

Gemma lay still for almost an hour after Obsidian vanished.

Then she cracked one eye open, the taste of laudanum in her mouth.

It was almost insulting that he thought she wouldn't have tasted the laudanum-hemlock mix. The second she'd felt the familiar heaviness sweep through her veins, she'd made the quick decision to allow her body to relax into a light slumber, wondering what he was up to.

The last thing she'd been aware of was Obsidian laying her down upon the marble slab and chaining her to it. She was almost certain he'd brushed a piece of hair off his face, then he'd sighed under his breath. "Time to get to work."

Swinging her legs off the marble slab, Gemma eyed the chain around her ankle with a glare. Time to remove this cursed thing. She didn't know what he was up to, but there could be only one good reason to try and drug her.

He'd left the house.

Though she'd been making progress with him, she couldn't stop thinking about COR and the Chameleon.

They needed her.

And Obsidian was nowhere near close to telling her a damned thing.

He'd made that clear earlier.

Gemma reached for the dead plant in the pot nearby, and dug around in the dirt for her lock pick. It was the matter of seconds to unlatch the manacle. Another to grab his cloak and swing it over her shoulders as she hurried to the door.

Boots, gown, and lock pick. Now she had all three.

"Thank you, my love, for providing me with a dress." She smiled to herself as she tumbled the lock on the barred gates.

The iron gate seemed to squeal on its hinges as she eased it open, and Gemma winced.

Slipping through the bars, she held her breath and listened.

Nothing.

This time she made her way through the back halls, taking the servants hallways when she could. Moonlight flickered through the windows as she passed, quiet as a mouse. Every step she took seemed to shake off the heaviness that still lingered within her.

A door creaked somewhere in the house.

Gemma froze, ducking behind a curtain into a glassed alcove. Damn. He must have returned. Her heartbeat ticked out the seconds, and she popped her ears, trying to hear more.

The second he saw the empty observatory, she'd be in trouble. She had to move. Quickly.

Gemma eased into the hallway, creeping along the hall runner and keeping to the shadows as much as she could as she made her way down to the servant's section of the house.

She was just slipping beneath the arched doorway that led into the kitchens when something moved behind her.

A hand slammed over her mouth, another hand dragging her back against a hard, male chest. Gemma was about to drive a heel to his instep when she sensed the stillness within him and the familiar strength of his arms. One of his damned biceps was almost the size of her head.

"Don't move," Obsidian whispered.

His attention was elsewhere. His gaze locked on the ceiling above them, as though he was listening to something else.

A chill ran through her.

Maybe it was COR, come to rescue her. But instinct told her there wouldn't have been that quiver of concern in his voice if her friends had arrived. He was faster, stronger, and far harder to kill than a regular blue blood, *and* he was a trained assassin.

Pressing her back to the wall, he kept his hand over her mouth, and then eased away from her, peering back into the hallway.

Gemma gently bit his fingers, more to capture his attention than anything else.

Pale eyes met hers, his brows drawn down in a serious frown. Gemma crooked her eyebrow, more of an, *"I won't yell if you take your hand away,"* than anything else.

Maybe it was her imagination, but for a second *her* Dmitri was there as he gently slid his gloved hand away from her lips.

The knife whispered free from its sheath, his fingers locking around the hilt in a threatening grip. Gemma's fingers itched for a knife of her own.

A timber board creaked overhead.

They both looked up.

Someone whispered something in the silence of the house. Obsidian held up two fingers, his brows drawing together as he looked at her. She understood his frustration. Two unknown assailants, and a reluctant prisoner.

Gemma jerked her head toward the back door. *Let's get out of here.*

She knew bad odds when she saw them.

He grabbed her wrist as she slipped toward the door and shook his head. Tugging her toward the pantry, he knelt and eased a trapdoor in the floor open, gesturing her into the darkness within.

Taking his hand, she let him drop her down into a narrow passage. Then he followed, landing right beside her, and reached up to tug the trapdoor closed.

Any hint of light vanished.

"This way." He breathed the words in her ear, then captured her hand and tugged her forward. "They'll be watching the house. This leads into the storm water drains."

Of course. During the Echelon's peak, it had been common for blue bloods to attempt to elevate their position within their house via a stealthy assassination—or ten. Every manor had a handful of exits, just in case.

"I can't see a damned thing," she whispered, staggering after him.

She'd often trained with a blindfold. Being blind wasn't a problem; being forced to rely upon *him* was. Because she didn't trust him. How could she?

"Follow me."

Then they were feeling their way down a flight of damp stone steps, the air growing colder and moss slicking the tunnel walls beneath her outstretched fingers.

Water splashed ahead of them. The tunnel led down into the sewers, and Gemma wrinkled her nose. Wet. Damn it. She'd just gotten jolly well clean. No help for it. She was forced to wade into the frigid waters, the invading chill seeping into her boots.

"Where are we going? Who was it? What's—"

"Be quiet, and keep moving," he hissed, planting a hand firmly in the middle of her back. "Unless you want your throat slit."

On and on, through dark tunnels. Wading through ever deepening water. A glance over her shoulder revealed a faint phosphorescent light bobbing along behind them. "They're following us."

Obsidian froze. Light streamed into the sewer ahead of them through some grate, highlighting his stark, expressionless face. "Damn it. They're not following us. They're following me."

Reaching up with the knife, he felt under the back of his hairline, and then made a sharp jerking motion with the blade. Blood flavored the air, and when he withdrew his hand, his fingers were slick with it.

"What are you doing?" She caught a glimpse of a tiny silver disc in his hand, faint silvery legs spreading away from its body like a spider's legs.

Obsidian turned and threw the tiny device down the other tunnel. "Move, Gemma."

A tracking device. She slammed a hand to his chest when he moved to push past her, spat on her fingers, and then reached up to smear her saliva across the small wound. "They'll be able to scent the blood. My saliva will help the cut heal."

He nodded.

She splashed through the tunnels ahead of him, chasing the rippling blue light. They came to an intersection, the sluggish water starting to move faster past her boots. "Which way?"

He glanced toward the rushing sound down the tunnel to their right. "This way."

Behind them, a shout echoed.

Had their assailants discovered the tracking beacon?

There was a sharp drop ahead of them, water rushing toward it. Gemma skidded to a halt on the edge of it. "What are we going to do now?"

"Do you trust me?"

The jury was still undecided. "Perhaps."

He grabbed her arm and looked over the lip of the spillway.

"No. Absolutely not." The darkened waters gleamed far below them, water draining rapidly toward some hidden grate. London was full of underground rivers, and this section of London was frequently flooded when the ELU Underground Railway Project collapsed. The government had installed a steam-driven drainage plant to maintain the water levels.

"No choice."

"I am *wearing* a dress," she hissed. "Do you have any idea how heavy—"

"Don't scream." Obsidian slammed a hand between her breasts, and Gemma lurched off the edge of the circular hole. Arms windmilling, she caught a scream behind her teeth and plunged into the darkened well.

She slammed into a sheet of water, plummeting like a stone. Bubbles streamed from her mouth, and she clawed toward the surface.

An enormous shadow smashed into the water beside her, sending her rocking from the impact.

Gemma surfaced with a gasp, her skirts threatening to drag her under again. Kicking hard, she struggled to keep her head above water. Panic bloomed within her. Drowning was the one fear she owned.

Water closed over her head as her body plunged beneath the frigid waters of the Griboedov River. She'd smashed through the thin layer of ice on the surface, the shock of cold water stealing her breath in a gasp of bubbles until her lungs were flooding with it, drowning her....

She caught a mouthful of water now, her throat closing as she spat desperately. Gemma panicked.

"I've got you." Strong hands captured her shoulders, and then Obsidian hauled her against him. "Shhh, Gemma. We cannot afford to make a sound."

Shh?

Shh?

Gemma clung to him, her lungs heaving. "I am going to kill you when we're out of this mess."

But her fingers tangled in his wet shirt, and her heart beat a sharp staccato in her chest, belying the firmness of her voice.

His arm snagged around her waist as he hauled her out of the circle of light that was painted on the inky waters. With her skirts dragging at her body, she felt shockingly vulnerable. If he released her, she'd eventually vanish beneath this unknown depth.

"Don't let me go," she gasped.

Obsidian's pale gaze locked on hers as if he'd finally sensed some of the turmoil hidden beneath her cool expression.

A spillway hovered under a stone arch, water pouring through it. This was how the levels had split. It sucked the pair of them toward it.

Obsidian kicked them beneath the faint overhang of the tunnel, pressing them both against the bars there. His hand rubbed circles on her back, as the other clung to one of the bars. "I won't ever let you go," he breathed in her ear. "Now, be quiet."

Gemma sucked in a sharp sob and simply pressed her head to his chest.

Difficult to stop her legs from thrashing in the wet cage of her skirts. She couldn't remember the last time she'd been forced to rely upon someone else. Or trusted them enough to do so.

Malloryn, perhaps, but then he'd earned her undying loyalty when he pulled her from the Griboedov and resuscitated her.

Now?

She had no choice.

It had nothing to do with the sound of Obsidian's voice, so like the Dmitri she remembered. Nothing to do with the familiar touch of his hands. Love had betrayed her all those years ago. She couldn't afford to trust in it again, ensnared in a dream that had never existed.

Footsteps splashed through the tunnel above them. Obsidian's grip on her tightened, and Gemma returned the embrace, trying to slow her racing heart.

The pair of them barely dared breathe, locked together under the overhang of the grate.

"Any sign of them?" someone called in a low voice.

"No. He cut the bleedin' tracker out of his head."

"Hell. What are we going to tell Ghost?" The splashing sounded like it was growing distant. "This is three times she's escaped death."

"Aye, well, she had help the first couple."

Then they were gone.

Gemma's heart pounded as she lifted her gaze to Obsidian's face. *Three* times? How many attempts had these *dhampir* made to kill her?

146

"We need to get out of here," he breathed, still looking up, completely oblivious to the shock rampaging through her.

But Gemma's heart pounded madly.

Because she finally had some inkling of his intentions toward her.

He hadn't kidnapped her in order to kill her.

He'd done it to keep her safe.

CHAPTER THIRTEEN

"I swear to God this is the last straw," Gemma spat. "You locked me in an abandoned manor, threw me into a bloody well, and now this? *Again?*"

Obsidian peered into the streets, trying to ignore her, which was particularly difficult when she hit that strident note at the end. "It's for your own good."

"Have I not proved I can be trusted?" Her voice turned pleading, as she toweled her hair dry. They'd washed under a water pump outside, and most of her clothes were still dripping. "There have been a hundred ways I could have escaped you today, but no, I played along."

"Which doesn't negate the fact you were trying to run when I returned to Mably House."

He'd barely managed to return to the manor when he saw the lanterns flickering through the boarded-up windows. Every inch of him had gone cold, and he'd rushed to the observatory.

Only to find it empty.

Somehow his fellow *dhampir* had found him, and now they knew he was keeping her safe.

Hell and damnation. What was he going to do?

"Who were we running from?" Gemma demanded, straining against the cuffs that bound her hands together.

That was the problem. She'd always been too smart for her own good. And she'd been furious when he'd hauled the cuffs from his waistcoat, insisting on putting them on her.

"It's none of your business." Obsidian let the curtains fall back into place, flinching as the glare of the afternoon sunlight left bands of white across his vision. He could barely remember the days when he'd been able to stomach the light of day. It was the only thing he missed from his life before his transformation.

Or one of the few things he truly recalled of it.

Sunlight would force his brethren out of action for the day. He'd managed to get the pair of them all the way across the city to a safe house of his own, using the drains to protect himself from the light.

Perhaps he'd known it would always come to this. Some unconscious part of him must have suspected he'd need somewhere safe, somewhere even Silas wasn't aware of.

"None of my b-business? They were *dhampir*," she said, through chattering teeth. "They were hunting us. Or should I say, me?"

Obsidian turned and surveyed his unwilling captive.

With her black hair tangled and knotted from the water, she should have looked like a drowned rat, but despite her trembling lip and pale skin, Gemma drew his eyes like a lodestone.

"I'm not stupid," she warned, her lips almost blue with cold.

No. Never that.

"And I *will* d-discover the truth."

"Turn around," he told her, unlocking one of the cuffs from her wrists and then snapping it to the exposed pipe on the wall before she could take advantage of his empathy.

"You don't need the cuffs. I couldn't run even if I w-wished to," Gemma told him through chattering teeth. "Besides, it seems a forgone conclusion you'd catch me before I took two steps. You're faster than I am, unhampered by wet skirts, and you blindfolded me for the last part of the journey, so I have no clue where we even are right now."

"I wasn't worried about you running." No, he'd seen the way her gaze dipped to his belt and the array of knives there.

"I thought we'd grown past that?"

"That doesn't mean I trust you.'"

"Likewise. What I am curious about is precisely what you intend to do with me." Gemma slanted a look at him from beneath the dangerous fan of her black lashes. They were spiked together with water. "Kidnapping usually serves a purpose. You haven't made any demands of Malloryn, as far as I can work out. You haven't tortured me for information. You've barely spoken to me. Apart from your penchant for handcuffs, I'd think you quite content to lock me away for an undetermined period of time." Her expression shifted, her shoulder lifting coquettishly. "One could be mistaken for thinking this an obsession. And yet, you also seem to have no intentions of touching me unless necessary."

Curse her quick mind. He turned away from her, fractured memories of her bleeding through his mind like the broken pieces of a stained glass window.

He knew they should fit together somehow, and yet all he managed was fragments.

The quick flash of her laughter.

Hollis tucking a scrap of paper down her bodice with a knowing little smile, as if aware of how it drew his eyes.

The feel of her hand sliding down his naked abdomen.

Waking from a drugged stupor to flames creeping up his bed hangings, and her lithe body conveniently vanished from the bed.

Obsidian pressed a hand to his temples as they throbbed.

She's a weakness you cannot afford.

Months of aversion therapy flashed through his mind, sending a searing wave of pain across his nerves. He could almost feel the leather mouthpiece between his teeth, preventing him from biting his own tongue off as Ghost fisted a handful of his hair and wrenched his head back, "Tell me about the girl. The one you betrayed your brothers for."

"She's a lying, treacherous bitch," he'd finally spat, and then Dr. Richter shocked him with electric current one more time, just to reinforce the message.

The conditioning worked well.

It had been years since he'd thought of Gemma without feeling a flinch along his nerves. He'd even stood there in Ghost's parlor four months ago when they first arrived in London and stared dully at her photograph when Ghost pinned Malloryn's allies to the board—the targets he and his team of *dhampir* were preparing to destroy. Nothing in him had stirred at the sight of her pretty heart-shaped face, except for pain, and he'd locked eyes on his Master and said flatly, *"She's mine."*

He'd meant as a target. The knot of pain and past that tied him and Gemma together was something he'd vowed to finally erase.

Until the second he watched one of Ghost's minions try to end her life... and realized whatever she'd once meant to him, those ties still bound him.

"Dmitri?" she whispered, pulling him out of the fragmented mire of the past.

"Dmitri's dead," he said tonelessly. "There is only Obsidian."

"I'm not entirely certain that's the truth."

He looked at her sharply.

"Obsidian would have let me drown today. Obsidian would have killed me himself. Do you know what I think? I think someone wants me dead, and Dmitri kidnapped me so this mysterious person who was hunting us couldn't get their hands on me."

"Do you? It sounds almost as plausible as your tale of our past."

"It's an outlandish theory," Gemma admitted, her lip still shivering. "But they're the best ones. So what now?" She examined their accommodations. "It's a little less roomy than my observatory." Her gaze fell on the bed. "And I have an atrocious habit of sprawling across the entire bed when I sleep, so it looks like it shall be close quarters. E-elbows at two paces. That kind of thing."

Their eyes met again.

He knew what she was doing. Pushing him. A flirtatious challenge to see just what he intended to do with her.

"Who said you're getting the bed?" Obsidian arched a defiant brow.

"Y-you blackguard. You w-would take the bed yourself?"

I'd rather have you in it.

Under me.

The burst of odd familiarity swept over him, as if they'd done this a hundred times before, but it was the sudden surge of the hunger that made him look away.

Disconcerting. His memories of her were still thin, but it was the look in her eye he recognized.

He couldn't afford to touch her.

Because a part of him knew she would destroy him.

"Is there a-any chance they have a bath h-here?" Gemma slumped against the wall. "I don't think I've ever been so wretchedly cold in my entire life as I have b-been this week."

"Then you haven't lived through a Russian winter," he murmured. "And it's unlikely there's a bath. I can fetch you a basin of warm water and soap."

"Do you think.... Do you think you could help me out of m-my dress then?" Gemma tried to undo the buttons down her spine, but clearly couldn't quite reach. "U-unless you want to untie my other hand?"

"We're not playing this game again."

"I'm wet, Obsidian. And cold. Don't worry, I have more intention of giving all my affections to those lovely thick blankets on the bed. You have nothing to fear."

"I don't fear you."

"No?"

"Turn around," he said, grabbing her by the shoulders and forcing her to turn.

The row of buttons down her spine gleamed. Obsidian scraped the tangled snarl of her hair forward over her shoulder, and then set to work on the top button. Her skin felt clammy to the touch. It seemed she'd been telling the truth. For him to have even noticed, she had to be cold indeed.

"You were born in Russia," she murmured, glancing over her shoulder as she launched her opening gambit.

"*Da.*" He concentrated on her buttons and nothing else. "My mother was Russian. She gave me a name from her country, and taught me her language. Sergey always told me I had a terrible accent, like a serf."

"I don't know." Gemma gave a minute shrug. "I quite liked it, and you sounded like the rest of the court to me."

Curse her.

"What happened to her?"

A knot of pain twisted deep inside him. "I don't remember."

This time, Gemma almost turned all the way around.

He stepped back. "Your buttons are undone. I'm certain you can manage the rest yourself."

Gemma held up her manacled wrist.

Obsidian unlatched it, just enough to strip the sleeve of her gown over her hand. Her fingers felt like ice. He paused, but she'd find no warmth from him. *Dhampir* were as cold-blooded as blue bloods.

And yet....

He rubbed his hand up her arm, feeling the burr of her goose bumps. Gemma tensed, but then she began to soften, her lashes closing in quiet approval. He used friction to warm her, and the gown began to slip down her body, revealing the upthrust mounds of her breasts. Soft and creamy globes that threatened to spill from her damp bodice.

"What do you mean, you cannot remember your mother?" She lifted her eyes to his.

He stepped back as she tugged her other sleeve down, revealing the straps of her chemise.

"I have little recollection of my life before Falkirk."

"And seemingly little recollection since it," she pointed out.

What would she say if she knew the truth?

His "conditioning" with Dr. Richter saw to his scattered memories, he suspected. It used to always make him "feel better" after a session with the doctor, but now....

Just what were they doing to him?

And how long had they been doing it to him?

"I lost track of her once I was sent to Falkirk. I remember her name. Marina. She became a cook at an inn, I believe. I remember the way she would swear in Russian. And I remember her nightmares. But little else."

He frowned. What little he could recall of his childhood didn't seem to fit the story. He remembered other children laughing and playing in the snow with him; a man bent over an enormous desk in a gilded study, pointing to some sort of ledger or book; a smiling woman in elegant court attire bending down to kiss his forehead before she was handed up into a carriage....

Fire. Always fire.

He could not recall anything more of Marina than the scent of vodka, her plain wool gowns, and a certain grim-faced intensity as she dragged him down the gangway of a steamship.

She'd fled from something in her homeland.

His father, perhaps.

And she'd never stopped looking over her shoulder for someone.

"A man came to examine me one day when I was fifteen," he murmured. "I had the craving, though I don't know how I got it. His name was Dr. Erasmus Cremorne. He worked with rogue blue bloods like me, he said, to help control the craving. They had a treatment program at Falkirk. Marina had signed me up for it. It was the last time I saw her."

"I'm so sorry." Gemma's hand stilled on his arm.

And Obsidian hauled himself out of the past. The savage beast within him—the hunger—felt like it finally eased its grip upon him at the stroke of her hand. Not soothed. Never that. The proprietary urges he felt toward her only sank their claws in tighter. But he was almost certain the darkness within him would kneel at her feet and surrender itself to her, if she only kept touching him like this.

"I never knew my mother," Gemma whispered. "I always wanted to track her down and ask why she'd sold me to the Falcons. Who could do that to a little girl?"

Who indeed? He wanted to tear someone apart at the flare of rage her words wrought in him, to protect her, but the very intensity of his sudden emotions alerted him. Obsidian surfaced from the depths of the hunger through sheer will, blinking at the sudden lightness of the world around him.

What was happening to him? What was she doing to him?

Ensorceling me.

Wrapping him around her little finger, inch by inch.

Mine, whispered his darker half. Obsidian's teeth ached, his lip curling back off his right fang as his gaze dropped to her throat.

He had the sudden, insistent urge to bury his teeth in her throat and claim her. Bloodletting was an intimate thing, never to be taken by force. But he wanted it now. He wanted to crush her in his arms and bury himself in her body. The hunger rushed through him like oil thrown upon a fire, engulfing his vision until he could barely see. Only hear the throb of her pulse.

The world went black.

His cock hardened, thrusting insistently against the placket on his breeches.

"Obsidian?" Those wide eyes locked on his mouth, but he could no longer see the pretty blue depths of her irises. Only gray. The entire world around him was gray. "Do you have... fangs?"

Fangs. The thought hauled him out of the darkness. Shit. How close had he come to losing control?

Obsidian shoved away from her abruptly, turning toward the wall. It was better when she wasn't touching him, but not... not gone.

"But... how?" she whispered.

"They grew in several years after my transformation." All the better to pierce her skin with, and suckle the sweet blood from her veins. His cock flexed, and he fought the urge to turn back toward her.

"I didn't notice them before."

"They descend when I'm hungry."

"Like... an erection?"

Only Gemma could say such a thing.

Damn her for saying such a thing.

And then he could feel a soft touch on his back, fingers trailing down the muscle on the side of his spine. The hunger's vise on his lungs choked tighter, hauling him back into dark depths—

"Don't touch me," he snapped, jerking away from her.

Her hand fell from his back.

Obsidian whirled around, pressure tightening around his chest. "I don't ever want you to touch me."

"Then what *do* you want from me?"

Everything. "I want to erase you from my life." He closed his eyes. "I have no memories of you, Gemma, because I asked them to remove them. I asked them to send me for conditioning after Russia. I wanted to forget you."

Her full lips parted in a gasp, the pain in her gaze imprinting itself upon him.

Then she visibly swallowed. "You tried to forget me."

"Yes."

And yet, no matter how he tried, he couldn't seem to manage it. Some tie still tethered him to her. The second he'd laid eyes upon her, the block in his head began to dissolve. Wisps of memory were coming back with every second he spent in her company. It hurt. Even now he could feel the stabbing pain of Richter's machine sliding like a needle through his eye socket.

"Do you know what I think?" Her voice roughened, her eyes flashing fire.

"What?"

"I think you couldn't forget me if you tried."

Dangerous, dangerous words. Obsidian tensed, aware of the heat suddenly filling her eyes. Challenge gleamed there as Gemma took a step toward him, the gown slipping to her waist.

She gave a little wiggle, and the skirts tumbled to a pink mess on the floor around her stockinged feet. She wasn't wearing a corset, and her damp chemise was crushed to her body, highlighting each inch of her skin. Her puckered nipples gleamed rosy through the thin white cotton,

"Oh, yes," she whispered, sliding her hands down the curve of her hips. "Do you think you can forget this?"

Their eyes met.

"Gemma," he warned.

"What's wrong?" Her fingers toyed with the hem of the shift.

"Don't you dare," he managed to rasp, taking a step back as she stepped forward.

"I'm testing a theory." She dragged it up several inches, revealing her smooth thighs. Pretty pink garters tied her stockings there, and he wanted to tug them loose with his teeth.

Instantly his fangs descended again, his mouth flushed with heat.

"What sort of theory? Because this one's going to end with you flat on your back."

"I loved you," she whispered. "And while I'm not entirely certain what lies between us now, I know you're lying. Does it make it easier to say you want to forget me? Do you know what I think? I don't think you wanted to forget me at all. I think... you wanted to forget what happened on that bridge when you shot me."

"I guess we'll never know."

A hand slid up his chest as Gemma stepped forward, the very swish of her hips predatory. "There's one way to find out."

His fingers locked around her wrist. "You're playing a dangerous game. I'm not the same man I was."

If I ever was that man.

The index finger on her other hand hooked in the top of his pants as Gemma nibbled on her soft lower lip. "You still feel the same."

He held his breath as the back of her knuckles brushed against the tented suggestion in his trousers. His hips gave an involuntary thrust.

Gemma grew bolder, stroking her knuckles up his hard length. Every aspect of her face sharpened as the hunger rose. Her own eyes darkened, until the blackness spilled across her irises like the velvety sweep of midnight. She turned her hand and cupped him, squeezing hard.

"Gemma."

She was impossible.

And he wanted her so damned much.

Obsidian grabbed hold of the back of her neck and dragged her mouth toward his. Every inch of her pressed against him as she kissed him. Finally. There was no more pain, no more voices arguing in his head. Just her. The taste of her tongue as she slicked it against his, and the sensation of her cold body as he wrapped his arms around her and hauled her up.

No more time for doubt.

No time to think.

Gemma's thighs wrapped around his waist, gripping him tightly. He staggered sideways until he felt her back hit the wall. Rocking into the vise of her thighs, he captured her mouth in a punishing kiss. *Do you still love me now?* It hurt, pain screaming through him as his conditioning kicked in, but he couldn't stop himself, no matter how much he tried. Soft hands raked through his hair, but he didn't want soft. Her gentleness would break him.

Capturing her fingers between his, he yanked her hands over her head, pressing the backs of her wrists to the wall. The position gave him all the power between them, and yet he knew, deep in his heart, she held the upper hand somehow.

Gemma bit his lip, drawing back to let him see the triumph in her eyes.

"Fine," he whispered, in a voice taut with suppressed hunger. Another searing streak of white left him swaying. "You want to fuck? You think that means anything to me? You think there's anything left? Then let's fuck...."

Gemma blew a strand of dark hair from her face, glaring up at him, her chest rising and falling with the force of her breath. "I know it means more to you than you'll admit. I know you too well, all your tells... and I'm willing to put it all on black—"

Put it all on black.... *Her laughter sliced through him, her arm draped around his neck as she urged his hand forward across the green baize. "Do it," she'd whispered in his ear, nipping the fleshy lobe there. "Put it all on black, darling. I know we'll win. Together we're invincible."*

He'd... forgotten about that.

Obsidian blinked his way back from the past, staring into her eyes now. The fierce challenge that gleamed in those stormy depths was irresistible. She thought she had him. She was prepared to risk everything on this one move.

The electric lash of conditioning seared him again. He slid his fingers from hers, capturing her wrists. His touch wasn't kind. And he thrust into the vee of her hips, pinning her to the wall with his hard body, almost moaning as his erection dug into her belly. A subtle shift of his hips, and then he was riding over the small nubbin between her thighs.

"Yes," Gemma gasped, tilting her throat back and revealing the slim column there. The pulse thumping beside it.

Heat filled his mouth, his lip curling as the sound of her heartbeat began to overwhelm him.

Then he could no longer deny himself. He bit her. There. Teeth sinking into soft skin as she gasped and jerked and ground herself against him. He wanted her hot blood in his mouth, but if he took that step he didn't think he could come back from it. He kept his bite light enough to sting, not deep enough to penetrate.

Gemma cried out, as if the sensation lashed through her.

The scent of her arousal drove him wild. He wasn't thinking anymore. Pain came in surges, whiteness blinding him again and again. But the sensation of her body began to sink through, to penetrate the oblivion. Obsidian yanked her shift up in a crumpled mess about her hips, cupping her between the legs and earning a sharp inhale from her. "This doesn't change a damned thing. And maybe you're willing to *put it all on black*, but you're not the only one who can take risks here."

"I remember the first time you took me." She gasped as he rubbed the heel of his palm against her pussy, and then began to stroke her through her drawers. Gemma bit her lip as he worked her. "I remember making love—"

"You were my enemy," he snarled, working his fingers through her drawers and shoving two of them inside her. Hot, wet heat enveloped him, making him shudder for a second. He forced the weakness away as he curled his fingers, stroking her inside. "You seduced me because you wanted to destroy me. And all we ever did was fuck."

Shocked eyes met his, her body clenching around him as he brutally crushed his thumb against her clit and began to work her there.

"Prove it," she said.

Gemma writhed, and he took immense pleasure in the unmasked emotions that ruined her pretty face. She couldn't hide how much she wanted him now. Nor could she pretend he wasn't working her body like a well-oiled machine.

"Prove that"—a gasp—"all I ever meant to you was this."

Fine. His mind went hot with incandescent rage. Thrusting his fingers inside her, again and again, he wrung every last little gasp from her lying lips. "I hate you."

Her poisonous body tightened around his fingers as he brought her to the edge. "I hate every lying word that leaves those pretty lips. Every memory I have of you is poison."

Wide eyes locked on his, her fleshy lip locked between her teeth as she stifled a moan. *No, you don't*, said those eyes, and then he was pushing her over the edge, burying his face against her throat to hide from the truth as she screamed with pleasure.

She couldn't fake this.

And nor could he.

His heart pounded in his chest as her body milked his fingers, a spasm running all the way through her. She was gasping in air, all her weight pulling against the hand that pinned her wrists to the wall and her chest heaving against his, those soft curves melting against his hard frame. Slowly her head fell forward, her breath stirring the hair beside his ear. The pain in his head was endless—*he bit down on the leather strap, screaming through a hoarse throat as waves of electric current ran through him*—but he was also tearing her drawers away from her, drowning in the scent of her hot arousal. Forcing the here and now to sweep the past from his memories. He wanted oblivion, but as he cast her drawers aside, he hesitated.

Oblivion came at a price.

"Do it," Gemma breathed as he looked down and met her devilish eyes.

A price he needed to pay....

Turning and thrusting her forward over the table, Obsidian shoved the shift up over her hips and freed his aching cock from the button flap on his trousers. He could have taken her then, but something in him demanded more. He slid a hand up the curve of her spine, pinning her flat to the table even as he drove a knee between her thighs.

"Is this what you want, curse you?"

And she laughed, damn her, the sound vibrating through her back. Her voice came out husky in reply. "I always did like it a little bit rough...."

Curse her.

He found her slick wetness, rubbing the crown of his cock through it. Blood and mercy, he was dying with want of a fuck. Needed to be within her. Now.

Obsidian thrust.

Hard and deep, filling her to the hilt. Gemma gasped, tight inner muscles clamping around him as he slid his hand up her back and dug his fingers into the soft muscle just under her scalp. Her face was turned, her cheek pressed to the table. He drew back and slammed within her again, tearing a soft cry from her lips and a shudder from the table. Its legs squealed over the floor, his hips slamming into the soft flesh of her bottom. The ripple of impact drove across her thigh, and he dug his fingers into the curve of her ass. He took her with animalistic passion, driving in and out of her until she was crying out, her fingers curling helplessly across the table varnish. Pleasure choked her as she screamed.

The table hit the wall, and suddenly it couldn't go any further. Obsidian drove himself inside her, the hunger flooding through him, roaring his claim upon her as he marked it on her flesh.

"It *means nothing*," he said hoarsely. "You mean nothing." Another hard thrust.

Gemma clenched her inner muscles.

He drove into her once more. Twice. A hot hand gripped him by the balls as orgasm exploded through him. Biting his lip, he threw his head back and pumped his pleasure inside her until he collapsed over her wilted body, drained of everything.

No more pain.

Just her. Just pleasure, twitching through his cock.

"Oh, my God," Gemma panted, her body flinching with aftershock.

Utterly spent, he wilted over her, the weight of his body crushing her to the table. Gemma gasped for breath beneath him, and he realized his weight was too heavy. Somehow he pushed away an inch, his biceps flexing. He withdrew from her body, his cock bobbing in the cold. It was almost like being plunged under icy water; the shock of it left him bereft.

Her stockinged feet hit the floor and her knees almost buckled. He captured her in his arms, half turning her. She shook like a newborn foal.

"I didn't hurt you?"

Gemma grabbed a fistful of his hair and kissed him again, softly this time. Not so much to mark his flesh, but to steal his soul.

He had to get away from her before it was too late.

Gemma staggered against the table as he let her go, her thighs slick with his seed and her shift caressing the full white globes of her breasts. Her knees quivered as she met his gaze with wide-eyed shock.

He wanted to take her again. Rut his way into her, throw her down on the bed and sink his fangs within her flesh until she screamed his name.

"Who's lying now?" Gemma whispered, as if she saw it all in his eyes.

"I assume that would be you," he grated out between his teeth as he stepped way from her, hastily buttoning himself back up. "It's always been you."

Her knowing eyes locked on him, as if she could see right through him.

And suddenly he couldn't stay here in the room with her. Obsidian strode toward the door, slamming it shut behind him.

Then he collapsed against the wood, his hands shaking and his stomach twisting with nausea, a sign he'd pushed the conditioning too far.

Who's lying now?

Indeed.

Obsidian lowered his hands away from his face, knowing he was about to collapse. Somehow he pushed away from the door—heading anywhere, as long as it was away from her—his heart thundering in his chest.

There would be no coming back from this.

CHAPTER FOURTEEN

After several long, fruitless days, the tracking beacon finally ignited just as Ingrid and Byrnes crossed into Clerkenwell territory one evening.

Ingrid gasped as she felt the device pulse inside the pocket of her coat. "Byrnes!"

Her husband peered over her shoulder as she tugged the device free, watching the arrow spinning madly, round and round.

Malloryn had insisted all of them be implanted with a tracking beacon when they first started working for COR. The second Gemma went missing, he'd sent the pair of them out into the streets searching for her.

The tracking device had a limit of half a mile upon it, which meant they had to be close. Gemma was nearby.

Hopefully alive.

"Got her," he said.

Ingrid met her husband's eyes. "We need to fetch Malloryn. Now."

Because she'd seen the signs of a struggle in the museum and knew someone had taken Gemma by force.

Instinct propelled her forward, driving her to wade into battle immediately, but Ingrid fought it down. They had no idea what—or who—they were facing.

"I'll run and fetch the others," Byrnes said, pointing to the tracking device. "Wait here for me."

The wild roused within her, prepared to go to war.

But Ingrid stifled the sensation. "Aye, aye, captain. But if you don't hurry, I'm going in."

Gemma was nothing if not practical.

After a restless afternoon spent tossing on the bed— the one she lay alone within—she used the basin of warm water Obsidian brought her to remove the scent of sex from her skin. It had been delivered to the door with a swift knock, but there'd been no sign of the actual man himself when she opened it. He'd remembered her earlier request for scented soap—God knew where he'd found it—and by the time she dragged the itchy woolen blankets around her nude body, she smelled like a lavender farm.

"I want to erase you from my life." The words had cut her deep, though she should not have felt them at all.

"I have no memories of you, Gemma, because I asked them to remove them...." A knife to the chest.

"I wanted to forget you."

Only fragments remained of her heart. Utter fragments.

He saved your life yesterday, she countered. *And presumably twice more.*

That didn't sound like someone who hated her.

And do you think he'd have found your favorite soap if there wasn't a part of him that cared?

And then, of course, there'd been that cataclysmic clash on the table. Heat flushed through her as she caught a glimpse of the marked wall. She'd intended to push him past the brink, but the intensity of the encounter made her breath catch.

No matter what had happened between them, this man was the only one who'd ever shattered the firm guards around her heart.

He'd decimated her, leaving her quivering in the aftermath. A brutal, hard fuck, their emotions clashing like a storm of fury that erupted over them. Everything she couldn't say to him spilling between them as he kissed her. Pleasure, so intense it stole her breath, and then the shuddering climax of his claiming. It was the barest of tastes, her aching heart needing something more from him. An empty pleasure, for though she'd intended to seduce him all along, all she'd gained was physical pleasure.

It vexed her.

For days she'd been thinking if she could only get him to kiss her, everything would change. Seduction had never failed her before.

But he doesn't trust you, and he knows how you operate.

Gemma rubbed her chest. How else was she meant to reach him? Flirting was easy. Kissing and sex were but a brief foray into her arsenal, but they'd failed to even move him. What was she meant to do? Bare her heart to him?

Trust *him?*

She'd done that once, and look where it got her. Drowning on her own blood in an icy river.

A shudder swam through her. She didn't even know what she wanted from him.

The truth was, she could have escaped a half dozen times if she'd wanted to.

She was lingering here for some reason unknown even to herself, and it had nothing to do with Malloryn, the Rogues, or even the *dhampir.*

It had to do with him.

What the hell are you doing, Gemma? Where does this end? Because you know it's going to end.

They couldn't stay locked away from the world forever.

There was a whole world out there trying to tear them apart. Malloryn and the Rogues. Obsidian's *dhampir.* All the secrets that swirled between them.

And two opposing missions.

The *dhampir* wished to destroy her London. But they would do so over her dead body.

You have to give him up. The last time you gave in to your heart, you nearly died. The Winter Palace was bombed.

And now London faced worse than that.

Gemma tugged the blanket around her naked body and paced to the window, feeling restless. It wasn't the first pain she'd felt in her life. She'd lost almost everything at various stages—her mother, her childhood friends, her heart, Dmitri.... This, too, could be overcome.

But none of this made any sense.

How did they even strip his memories from him?

What the hell was "conditioning?"

A sharp rap sounded at the door, heralding the very devil currently plaguing her thoughts. Gemma eased out a breath, her stomach suddenly filled with butterflies. "Come in."

Obsidian slipped inside, his hair still damp—presumably he'd washed elsewhere—and clothes in his arms. Every inch of him looked hard and merciless, as if he'd spent the day putting himself back together somewhere, but his fingers curled into the wool of the dress he was holding, just a faint sign he wasn't quite as composed as he seemed.

They stared at each other.

He with his back to the door, barely daring to enter, and she by the window, watching as evening encroached. The faint spill of sunset lit his pale skin and pinkened his white shirt. It strained over the bulk of his chest, drawing her attention to the corded muscle in his forearms. Once again his shirtsleeves were rolled up, revealing a sprinkling of fine silvery hairs, like spider silk. A dark knot of tattoos swirled down the inside of his forearm.

"Well." A flush of heat worked its way down her throat. One would think her the veriest maid. "Hullo again."

It was as if her words broke the stalemate. "This will help to warm you," he said, crossing to the bed and dumping the pile of clothes he'd fetched upon it. "You slept well?"

"Tolerably." How polite they were this evening. Oh, no, neither of them was affected by what had happened earlier that morning at all. Gemma's eyes narrowed. "You've brought me warm clothes."

Because he'd known how cold she was.

Keeping any hint of her turmoil off her face, she crossed to the bed, rubbing the thick wool of the skirt. Her eyebrows rose. "I suppose 'warm' is definitely one word we could use to describe this dress."

Along with hideous.

And what was he doing? Raiding lady's wardrobes throughout the city? Or stealing them from washing lines? She had a brief image of him stalking the London night, in pursuit of female undergarments. Despite her circumstances, Gemma couldn't retain her laugh.

"What's so amusing?" Obsidian asked suspiciously.

Gemma couldn't help herself. She gave into the urge, a choked giggle escaping her. "Nothing."

"You don't like the dress."

"No, I appreciate it, I do." She captured his wrist, squeezing softly, trying to thank him for the considerate thought. "I just... I'm not certain if you intend to dress me like a nun." Gemma turned and held up the heavy brown wool gown, shaking it out. "After what happened this morning, one would think you wanted to cover every inch of me."

Obsidian turned away from her, scraping a hand over his face. "It's not as though I can escape you. There was little else that looked to fit you."

"Kind of difficult to forget, is it not?"

He crossed his arms over his chest. "Incredibly difficult. But then I keep telling myself this will end. I might as well enjoy the pleasures to be found in the meantime."

I see.

"And how does it end?" She asked the question that had been plaguing her all morning. "Your fellow *dhampir* wish to kill me. Are you going to keep me locked away forever? I suspect they'll eventually notice you're missing."

"They already know I'm involved." He paced a little. "They must have followed me to Mably House."

Gemma froze. She hadn't considered the implications when he cut the tracking device from his skin, but he'd been giving up one of the ties of his allegiance as he did it. "What does that mean for you?"

He turned those stark gray eyes upon her, hands clasped behind his back. "Ghost needs me. He cannot afford to punish me too severely, and if... if it comes down to the pair of us, I'm probably the only one who could strike him down. He knows that. He'll be wary."

"How does he need you?"

His expression shuttered. "I cannot tell you the answer to that."

"Cannot? Or will not?" She held the blanket together as she reached for her shift. Damn him.

Turning around, he gave her his back. "Will not. We're not allies, Gemma. I don't even know if I can trust you. We share an immediate, short-term goal."

"Keeping me alive."

"Indeed."

She stared at the broad planes of his back. "This is ridiculous. It's not as though you've not seen every inch of me," she said dryly, tossing the blanket aside and hauling the shift over her head, and then the scratchy wool gown. It was precisely as wretched as she'd expected.

"I knew this morning was a mistake," he growled. "You're not going to let me forget it, are you?"

Gemma laughed. "What do you think? Button me up?"

"I swear you're trying to torture me."

"Every. Day," she promised with a faint smile, gathering her hair into a knot and presenting her back to him. Obsidian tugged her gown together and swiftly did the buttons up. "But I think you're not as innocent as you claim to be."

"No?"

His hands came to rest on her waist. Gemma stilled, her heart beating a ragged little tattoo in her chest.

"Are you trying to tell me you suffer too?" His breath whispered across the back of her neck. Then soft, dangerous lips trailed along the line of her shoulder.

Gemma closed her eyes and shivered.

"I think you know the answer to that," she breathed.

The softest of kisses painted itself across her neck. The gentle press of his tongue lashed against her pulse.

Gemma bit her lip. She could handle what happened this morning. That had been pure frustration. A storm of lust. But this? This sought to ruin her.

His hands stilled on her waist, his lips lifting from her neck.

"Don't you dare stop," she protested, but the second the words spilled from her lips, she knew something was wrong.

Obsidian looked up, a chill expression sliding over his face and his eyes tracking some invisible movement. "There's someone on the roof."

Instantly Gemma stepped out of his reach, danger dampening the sudden flush of heat through her body. "*Dhampir*? How did they find us?"

"They couldn't have tracked us," he replied, drawing the knife from the sheath at his hip.

No. Not *us*. But there was someone who could have tracked *her*. Gemma froze. Oh, shit. She couldn't feel the tracking beacon in the back of her scalp, but every hair along her spine lifted.

COR had come for her.

Her gaze focused, locking on the lethal figure in front of her, her heart turning into a ball of lead.

She stood within a nightmare. All she'd wanted was her freedom, but now she stood on the verge of it. The people she loved would be closing in, and the man she held feelings for would face them.

This didn't end well, no matter which way she looked.

As he'd pointed out, they weren't allies.

And if Malloryn caught a glimpse of him, he wouldn't hesitate to cut Obsidian down.

Gemma's heart started pounding. "We should go out the back."

"I can hear a couple of voices. We don't know how many of them there are." Obsidian strode toward the window on cat-silent feet, bracing his knife along his forearm. "There was no one following us last night, I swear," he murmured, glancing out into the dying sunset.

She had to get him out of here before this confrontation turned deadly. Gemma hauled her boots on, lacing them swiftly as her mind raced. "Either way, I think it best to flee. You don't know how many people you face, and you cannot handle them all at once."

"Here," he said, tossing her one of his knives, and she froze as she caught it, her hand locking with familiarity around the grip. "Now there are two of us. I've seen you in action."

Oh, no. He thought they were working together. She opened her hand around the leather grip, the scent of oiled steel kicking her impulses into overdrive.

He had trusted her enough to give her one of his knives. She felt ill.

A whistle pierced the air. Charlie, from the low fluting sound of it.

"Obsidian," she breathed, trying to catch his attention.

He pressed a gloved finger to his lips, setting his back against the wall beside the window.

"Don't come in!" she screamed, just as a figure swung through the window, spraying glass across the room.

Everything burst into motion.

Obsidian shot her a sharp look, and then he lunged toward the intruder. Charlie rolled across the floor in a tight ball, finding his feet and lashing back with a cutthroat razor.

It nicked Obsidian's forearm, but she could see his own knife lifting—

Gemma threw herself into him, slamming him back against the wall before he could bring it down into Charlie's unprotected back. A shadow rippled at the edge of her vision. Byrnes flipping into the room right on Charlie's heels.

"Gemma." Obsidian sounded shocked as she slammed his knife hand against the wall.

"They're my friends!"

She saw the realization creep over his face, as if he knew what she was saying. *You're choosing them.* His gray eyes shuttered, locking down tight on the swift gleam of betrayal.

But that was not what she was saying at all.

Obsidian shoved her away from him, and Gemma went down, sprawling across the mattress in a spill of skirts.

Charlie yelled, and Gemma arched her spine, then flipped to her feet, catching her heel under the bloody hem of her skirt. Damn her skirts. She needed her leather working breeches right now.

Working in unison, Charlie and Byrnes circled Obsidian, darting in at the same time to force him to split his attention. Byrnes's blade lashed out, and dark blood spattered across the white walls. She saw the frustration on Obsidian's face as he jumped back, Charlie's razor whistling through the air where his abdomen had been. He slammed a hand down on Charlie's wrist, and then spun shockingly fast, his boot driving Charlie into the wall with a crack of plaster.

"Oof." Charlie fell to his knees.

Gemma's ears were ringing. He hadn't used the knife. She didn't know what that meant.

But her side had no such compunctions.

"You all right, Charlie?" With his back to her, Byrnes feinted in, spinning in a whirl to avoid Obsidian's counterstrike, light gleaming off his blade—

Leaping off the bed, Gemma caught the heavy beam of the rafter, and swung her legs up, hammering her heels into Byrnes's back. He slammed against the wall, pushing off it in surprise when he saw her drop to the floor with the knife clutched in her hand.

"Don't kill him!" she yelled, but footsteps were pounding up the stairs. Reinforcements.

Obsidian shot her one last unreadable look, and then he bolted toward the window and leaped through it.

"Gem?" Charlie panted, pushing to his feet. "You okay?"

She was fine. But she knew how Malloryn worked.

He of all people knew what he faced. Charlie and Byrnes were the distraction.

Sprinting toward the window, Gemma slammed her boot on the sill, and jumped through the open hole, her fist clenching around Obsidian's knife.

Gravity caught her in its hold, and her skirts whistled up around her breasts as she plunged toward the sharply sloping rooftop below her. Gemma landed with a jolt that nearly flipped her forward, but she adjusted swiftly, skating down the slick tiles. A pair of gargoyles leered at the bottom of the gutter, and Obsidian paused there, his head whipping toward her, and then turning to lock on one of the gargoyles.

Time slowed down, almost as if she moved through thick treacle.

Malloryn ducked out from behind the statue, lifting an electrode-stimulating gun. She barely had a chance to cry warning. The arrowhead hissed from it as he pulled the trigger, the sharp prong sinking into Obsidian's chest.

Current arced along the thin metal chain attached to the end of the arrowhead, and Obsidian's body jerked as Malloryn ruthlessly shocked him. Obsidian's feet went out from under him, his back slamming to the tiles and a spark flashing as his knife flew from his hand. Moving lethally, Malloryn reached into his coat to draw his second pistol, and Gemma could see it all unfold in a flash.

He'd be packing the armor-piercing bullets the Falcons had used, or one of the chemical Firebolt bullets that exploded on impact.

"No!" Gemma screamed, flipping the perfectly balanced blade of Obsidian's knife into her fingers, and then flinging it with all her might as she rode the tiles toward them.

Silver flashed, winking in the gaslight from the streets.

As Malloryn drew the pistol in one smooth motion, her knife slammed into it, flinging it from his grip.

And then she was there, crouched over Obsidian protectively as Malloryn whipped his second pistol out.

It locked upon her, the duke's mouth falling open in shock. "Gemma?"

She flung her arms up around her head. "Don't shoot!"

Malloryn froze, breathing hard. The whine of the current down the thin chain evaporated as he took his finger off the pulse. "What the hell are you doing?"

She bent and tore the inert prong from Obsidian's chest, flinging it away from him. His chest heaved erratically, the leather glove on his right hand seared where he'd been holding the knife. Glazed gray eyes met hers, widening in shock. Gemma squeezed his left hand.

"Thank you," she whispered, "for not killing Charlie and Byrnes."

Because she knew he could have.

Obsidian's gaze slid past her, and Gemma turned, shielding him with her body. Malloryn's pistol never wavered.

"Gemma, get out of the way." Malloryn's entire expression hardened.

"No." Her heart beat wildly as she stared the duke in the eye. Lightning lashed over the city in the distance, highlighting the sharp slope of his cheekbones.

She'd failed him once.

She'd vowed never to do it again.

Behind her she could hear Obsidian groaning as he rolled to his side. Still far too vulnerable.

Wind whipped through her hair as she slowly straightened, tearing tendrils of it from her messy chignon. Her skirts rose to cover him. "He didn't hurt me. He never intended to hurt me."

Malloryn's jaw locked tight and he took a step toward her, his finger twitching on the trigger. "Get out of the way. I won't ask you again. This man is responsible for a threat against the queen."

"No." She stared defiantly back, and the look on Malloryn's face nearly broke her. "I *cannot* allow you to hurt him."

"Because he showed so much mercy when it was you in his sights," Malloryn snarled.

She could hear movement behind her, Obsidian clambering to his feet. His hand gripped her skirt, as if he needed help to steady himself. Electrical current was one of the few weapons any man—be he human, blue blood, or *dhampir*—was vulnerable to.

There was no way they could ever be together. She knew that.

"Go," she whispered, tearing her gaze from Malloryn's just long enough to push at Obsidian's chest.

Obsidian's gaze slid over her shoulder, locking on Malloryn with a faint air of menace.

"Don't you dare." Malloryn wasn't the only one whose bullet she needed to stop right now. If it came down to the duke versus the *dhampir* assassin, she wasn't entirely certain how the cards would fall.

Malloryn was only a blue blood, but he knew what he was facing. He'd have made precautions to allow for the nature of his opponent, and he wouldn't hesitate to use them. The Duke of Malloryn didn't lose.

And she couldn't lose either of them.

"Please go," she whispered.

Obsidian's hand captured hers, his gloved fingers stroking the back of her hand for just a second.

"You want me to be safe from your companions?" Gemma grabbed two fistfuls of Obsidian's waistcoat, keeping her body between him and the duke. "COR will keep me safe. And we couldn't... we couldn't continue the way we were. Walk away and erase me from your life. Forget me, just as you promised. You know the truth now. We both know the truth. This can end without either of us getting hurt."

It wasn't as if there was any way they could ever be together.

Her loyalty was to the duke and the queen. To London. She would *not* compromise the core of her beliefs, not even for him.

If only she was a mere Capulet.

His hand clasped hers, darkness sweeping through his eyes. "You were right. I don't think I can erase you. If I could, it would have happened when they sent me for reconditioning."

"Try harder," she snapped.

A thoughtful look came into his eyes, and then he grabbed her by the back of the head and kissed her. Hard. Brutal. Goodbye.

Letting her go, he took a step away from her, shooting Malloryn one last look, and then he was gone, stepping off the rooftop into the streets below and vanishing into the shadows of the night.

Gemma sank to her knees.

For the second time in her life, she'd betrayed Malloryn for the sake of her wretched heart.

CHAPTER FIFTEEN

At least Malloryn waited until they were home.

"Nearly there, Gem," Ingrid murmured, helping her up the stairs toward the main entrance of the safe house.

Malloryn strode toward the front door as if he could barely look at her. He'd ridden in front with Herbert on the way home and spoken not a word to her. Tension vibrated through his lean form. A storm brewed within him, despite the cold look on his face, and Gemma couldn't stop herself from glancing at him to gauge the full effect of his fury.

A tropical cyclone, she decided. Ready to burst from his skin the second she opened her mouth.

"*We're* incredibly pleased you're back." Ingrid squeezed her hand, and Gemma was suddenly grateful for her tall verwulfen friend.

"Speak for yourself," Byrnes called. "At least my blud-wein collection's been safe from a certain blud-wein thief. I haven't missed you at all."

Ingrid swung a lazy punch in his direction, but he avoided it with a laugh. Gemma mock scowled at him, but his joking eased the knot of tension within her.

She couldn't quite manage a smile in return, though she tried. "Thank you."

Byrnes squeezed her shoulder.

Ava burst through the front door in a flurry of lace. The young scientist had been forced to stay behind, but she scurried down the steps and threw her arms around Gemma. "Oh, my goodness! You're alive."

And there was the welcome she needed. Gemma lost herself in Ava's embrace, squeezing hard to try and choke down the urge to cry.

So much had happened in the space of a few days. Obsidian, alive. The Chameleon, also alive. A threat to the queen. Her heart, ripped clean out of her chest, as she came face-to-face with the ghosts of the past and realized there was so much more to it than what she'd thought.

It was easy to lock her heart away when she'd told herself the man she loved had shot her without remorse. Easy to tell herself none of it had been real. *He played you. He was an enemy spy who pulled the wool over your eyes.*

Except now there was a whisper of doubt in her mind.

Obsidian could barely remember the past.

He certainly couldn't explain what had happened.

Or why.

He had barely any recollection of shooting her, only the aftermath. It was as though he'd pulled the trigger, and came back to himself just in time to watch her fall.

This is not the first time this has happened, said the assassin-trained part of her mind that never stopped thinking.

Gemma no longer knew what was real, and what was not.

Whatever she'd felt for Obsidian, those feelings clearly lingered. She'd thrown herself between him and Malloryn without a hesitation.

But could she trust those feelings?

Could she trust *him*?

Her heart was a mess, and her thoughts didn't help.

"Come on," Ava said, drawing back from her embrace. "You look like you could use a hot bath and a glass of blud-wein."

"A bath sounds heavenly."

Ingrid nudged her husband in the ribs as they turned for the door.

"Really?" Byrnes protested. "Why am I the only one who suddenly has blud-wein?"

"Well, you could ask Malloryn," Gemma pointed out.

"She's not back a minute and she's throwing me to the wolves?" Byrnes shot her a look. "Fine. I'll fetch the blud-wein."

The second Gemma was through the front door, the tension within her eased a fraction. Home. She was finally home.

At the top of the stairs, Malloryn glanced down at her, then turned and stalked toward his study.

And suddenly the tension was back. "How mad is he?"

"Want me to thrash him?" Ingrid growled.

"No. Thank you, Ingrid, but I think.... I think I'd best talk to him," she whispered.

Three pairs of eyes watched her walk stiffly up the stairs, as if she walked to her doom.

Perhaps she did.

She'd felt this way after her failure in Russia. It was the only other time she'd seen such disappointment in Malloryn's eyes.

But there was no point in putting it off. She needed to face him and deal with the consequences before she could enjoy her glass of blud-wein and her bath.

When she knocked on the open door to his study, she found Malloryn staring into the fireplace, resting his arm on the mantle. His fingers curled laxly around a glass of brandy, and he didn't so much as flinch when she closed the door behind her.

"What the hell were you thinking?" he asked roughly.

That I couldn't let you kill him. Gemma remained silent, though indignation burned through her.

"I thought you were dead," he growled out.

"Well, apparently he didn't wish to kill me."

"And then you bloody well leaped between us. I nearly *shot* you."

"You didn't—"

"Only because my reflexes are excellent. I keep asking myself, *why*? And the only thing I can come up with is that you weren't thinking at all. Damn it, Gemma. This is the second time you've let your emotions cloud your judgment when it comes to this man. Do you not realize he's the enemy?"

"I don't know if he—"

"Because I do." Malloryn slammed a hand to his chest. "I know he's the enemy, and all I can see is Russia happening all over again, and—"

"I'm sorry if my emotions are so cursed inconvenient to you!" Heat seared the backs of her eyes, but at least the craving virus protected her from shedding any bloody tears. "Do you think I want to feel this way? Do you think I have any damned choice?" Her voice rose. "I *loved* him. Do you even know what that means? Have you ever, in your entire life, known what it feels like to care for someone more than yourself?"

Malloryn flinched.

"Love?" His tone turned the word into an insult. "If that is love, then no, I don't know what it means. And I don't want to."

A hot fist of fury burned within her, and she poured herself a brandy because he wasn't damned well going to. "Say what you want to me, but don't you dare try and pretend how I felt—how I *feel*"—there. She'd said it—"is inconsequential."

"He shot you in the fucking chest."

"I know!" Gemma paced in front of the fire with her brandy. She could still see Obsidian's face as she showed him the scar between her breasts. "I'll never forget that night. But there was something I was missing until now.... When he shot me that night I thought my cover was blown, and he was furious with me for betraying him. But I can remember the expression on his face, Malloryn. Or the lack of one rather. That wasn't fury. That wasn't betrayal. There was nothing of my Dmitri in his face. Nothing at all. When he pulled that trigger, he might as well have been shooting at a target."

"Well, he wasn't. If you think for one second he didn't intend to kill you that night, then you've lost all your wits. Because I was there too, Gemma. I remember everything too. How can you forgive that?"

"Because the only other time I've ever seen a man look that blank when he pulled a trigger is when Jonathan Carlyle murdered Lord Randall," she whispered.

Malloryn drew up shortly.

All this time, she'd summoned the look on Dmitri's face when he shot her, forcing herself to accept the fact she'd been played. The Dmitri she'd known, who laughed at her jokes and deliberately sabotaged her efforts to seduce her mark, had been nowhere in that moment. She'd always told herself it was because the Dmitri she'd known had never existed.

A role. An act. An enemy spy toying with her emotions.

But what if there was another explanation?

"I know you think my mind choked with emotion, but Obsidian kept me locked away in the Duke of Vickers's abandoned manor for days. I've done nothing but bloody well think, and there is something about what happened that night in Saint Petersburg I am missing. And I couldn't help but start thinking about Carlyle." She dragged her hand through her ruined coiffure. "You've always told me to trust my instincts. And they are screaming at me right now that there is something wrong with the facts in front of me. Carlyle broke down in tears when he realized he'd murdered Lord Randall. His story never *changed*, Malloryn, because there was nothing *to* change. It was exactly as he believed it. He couldn't *remember* what happened. He didn't want to kill Randall. And when Obsidian shot me on that bridge in Saint Petersburg, he might as well have been an automaton. There was nothing inside him. Just a blank canvas. A weapon. And he barely remembers it. When he took me this time, Obsidian didn't want to kill me. He refused to hurt me." She took a deep breath. "And when a pair of his fellow *dhampir* found us, he fled with me. Malloryn, after all he's done to me, I know it's hard to believe, but Obsidian was trying to protect me."

The duke's face remained expressionless.

"Remember that time I was attacked in the museum?" she pleaded, desperately needing someone else to understand, as if it would give credence to her theory. "Someone rescued me. Someone killed the *dhampir* who tried to hurt me. My CV levels went through the roof, and Ava said there was something wrong with my blood. I shouldn't have healed as swiftly as I did, and yet, it was a miracle. Or... more to the point, some *dhampir* used his evolved blood to heal me. It's the only rational explanation. It was him. I know it was him. He's been following me for weeks now, like some cursed guardian angel, protecting me from his brethren's attempts to assassinate me."

The duke turned away from her, scraping a hand over his mouth. "Did you learn anything?" he growled out. "Please tell me you at least discovered who's pulling the strings behind the scenes."

She swallowed hard, nursing the brandy. "I.... He didn't trust me enough."

A sound of pure frustration vibrated through his throat as he turned away from her.

"If you let me try and reach him again, perhaps I can—"

"For fuck's sake. *Fuck*." Turning suddenly, Malloryn threw his empty glass at the wall. It shattered with a loud crash. "Stop thinking he's not a threat to you."

He might as well have slapped her.

To see Malloryn undone by emotion was shocking.

Gemma dragged Ingrid's coat tightly around her shoulders, feeling small and cold. *You failed. Again.*

She'd promised herself she'd never feel this way after those dark days following Russia.

Promised herself no man would ever bring her this low.

"But I—"

"*No*." Malloryn released a sharp breath, forcibly putting himself back together right in front of her eyes. "No. You're off duty."

"*What?* Why?"

"I don't know, Gemma." Malloryn's lips pressed tightly together. "Can I trust you?"

She gaped.

"Oh, not your loyalty. Never that." He turned his piercing gaze upon her. "But can I trust you not to let emotion rule you? We both know you cannot confront him and keep your wits about you. If it comes down to a choice between the right thing to do and protecting him, I know which option you will choose."

There was a hollow feeling deep within her.

Malloryn had taken her from the darkness as a child. He'd taught her there was more to life than survival and death. She'd never known a family, but he'd been the one person she'd always looked up to—indeed, she'd spent the last ten years of her life trying to please him. To disappoint him like this felt like carving her own heart out of her chest with a spoon.

He didn't believe her.

No. Worse. He didn't believe *in* her.

"You're off the Chameleon case," he repeated quietly.

Gemma hung her head. "Yes, Your Grace."

And then, unable to bear his disapproval any longer, she turned and strode blindly for the door.

The door opened quietly.

The second he smelled her perfume, Malloryn knew who it was. Nobody else would dare enter the room while he was in this mood. And she couldn't resist.

"Get out," he said flatly, nursing his brandy.

He knew he wasn't himself.

It was happening all over again, and he couldn't help seeing Gemma's body jerk as Obsidian shot her that night in Russia, again and again.

Not her. Please not her.

He needed her off this case before she could be injured. He'd thought he could manage his feelings toward her when he brought her back into this operation, but the last few days had been a recurring nightmare he couldn't seem to wake from. It brought the past rushing back to him; Catherine's smile haunting him every time he saw the same smile on Gemma's face.

"You can't protect her from the world," Isabella murmured, wrapping her arms around him from behind.

"It's not the world I want to protect her from."

He pushed away from her, unable to bear a comforting touch, even from her. There was a spiraling sensation in his chest. A feeling events were spinning out of control.

"She said you'd taken her off the case."

"It's for her own good." He'd never imagined Gemma would be facing Dmitri again.

"She thinks she's failed you again."

"Failed me?" He jerked his head to stare at the woman who'd once been his mistress. "How...? But...?"

"Russia, Malloryn." Isabella rolled her eyes. "You have no idea, do you? For all your frightful intelligence, you are severely blinded to those closest to you. Have you ever told Gemma what she means to you?"

"She means nothing more than—"

"Stop *lying* to yourself." Isabella glared at him. "I know you see Catherine every time you look at Gemma."

"It's not what you think."

"Oh, I'm aware of that. Do you think I would ever have seduced you if I thought your heart lay elsewhere? Gemma's the one weakness you own though."

"It's...." He tried to explain it.

"You couldn't protect Catherine," Isabella continued in a firm voice, "and you watched Gemma nearly die in your arms. I know Russia frightened you more than you'll ever admit. I watched you change when you realized what she meant to you. You've always tried to keep Gemma at arm's length. You're astonishingly protective of her, for a man who doesn't care." She stepped closer. "You disapprove of her love life like a curmudgeonly older uncle; you sent her away for all those years as if you wanted to keep her out of harm's way; she exasperates you; you lecture her all the damned time.... Malloryn, I know what she means to you. She's like a sister, isn't she?"

"Catherine's little sister," he breathed.

Isabella reared back. "What?"

"Not by blood," he murmured, his shoulders sinking. "I've checked. I cannot find any record of it, though they look so damned alike it's uncanny. But... it feels as though she keeps Catherine's memory alive for me."

"Oh, Malloryn." Isabella reached for him, leaning up on her toes to kiss him, sympathy in her eyes.

He turned away, and her lips fell upon his cheek, pausing there as she felt his denial.

"Isabella, I can't. I'm getting married tomorrow." His voice tightened. "This does no good to either of us."

To you.

Isabella lowered her heels to the ground, her jaw clenching. "Of course. This was an arrangement from the start."

Guilt stirred through him, for he was coming to realize something that had escaped his notice until recently.

It had stopped being an arrangement in her eyes at some point, and he'd missed the warning signs.

They'd worked together for years.

Indeed, almost as long as he'd known Gemma.

Isabella had been widowed young, and at first they'd shared that. Two souls who'd lost the loves of their lives and came together to share something purely physical. He'd told her things he'd never admitted to anyone else, but the way he felt about her...

It was friendship, and nothing more.

"You're a beautiful, intelligent woman who has the entire world at her feet," he said softly. Gently. "You deserve more than I can give you."

She gave a false laugh, reeling away from him. "Oh, God. Please, stop. You are so blind, Malloryn, so blind...."

And as he watched her slam the door behind him, he felt the familiar burn of guilt.

He'd driven both of them away. No Gemma. No Isabella.

It was better this way.

Malloryn turned, surveying the map on his wall, all the recent catastrophic events picked out upon it in red string. A spider web if one knew what one was looking for. A trap, slowly closing around London, around him.

He knew patterns. He could sense the storm coming.

And there was a churning sensation in his gut as he stared at the puzzle pieces in front of him, his mind coldly putting them together.

You know what this is.

This was personal.

Someone out there was pulling strings, as if just watching and waiting for him to realize what he faced. He'd known peace for three years, but this had all the makings of an old game, finally resurrected.

It bore a certain signature he'd been trying to overlook.

It couldn't be who he suspected.

It wasn't possible.

"I buried him myself," he whispered.

But someone had reopened the game between them, and this time, Malloryn was the one with everything to lose.

A sharp rap sounded on her door.

Fresh from her bath, Gemma gave it a dull look. "Yes?"

"Are you up to company?" Ingrid called. "Ava wanted to make certain you were all right."

Gemma strode toward the door and opened it, surprised to see the two of them there.

"We bring gifts," Ingrid said, lifting a green glass bottle. Another was hidden behind her back. "I've raided Byrnes's cabinet."

"Is he going to demand repayment?"

"Already accounted for, Gem. I'll pay the price."

"With a pound of flesh?"

Ingrid gave her a wolfish smile. "It's a great hardship, I know, but I am prepared to make this sacrifice for the sake of our friendship."

"That *is* incredibly selfless of you," Ava said, with a choked laugh. She was new enough to the world of physical pleasure she still blushed whenever Ingrid and Gemma teased her.

Gemma stepped aside, gesturing them inside her room. After the heartbreaking moment in Malloryn's study, she desperately needed the pair of them.

"Tell us everything," Ingrid demanded, then snagged the cork between her teeth and popped the bottle open. "Blud-wein for the pair of you." She filled the glasses Ava held up, the liquid thick and viscous. "And brandy for me, as drinking blood-laced wine is vile."

Gemma tipped the glass to her lips and drained the entire damned thing.

"Oh, dear," Ava said when she lowered the empty glass. "That bad, huh?"

Ingrid lounged on the bed, handing the bottle over.

"I hope you brought more for Ava," Gemma said, taking the bottle for herself and knowing neither of them would protest. Bugger the glass. Screw etiquette. "Here's to Malloryn choking on his own tongue."

She drank to that.

Ava produced a flask from inside her apron pocket. "You definitely deserve the entire bottle. Don't worry about me. Kincaid's been corrupting me, and I had a feeling we'd all have sore heads in the morning so I came prepared. Blud-wein's not my poison of choice, either."

"A blue blood who doesn't like blood. What are we going to do with you, Ava?" Gemma shook her head. "Oh, well. More for me."

"So... apparently we share a common interest in *dhampir* men," Ingrid prodded. "I never knew you had such wicked secrets."

Gemma took a seat next to her, and Ava knelt on the end of her bed.

"I have some bad news for you," she told Ingrid. "Apparently Byrnes is due to eventually grow a set of razor-sharp canine teeth."

Ingrid had her glass to her lips and almost sprayed brandy across the room. "*What?*"

Ava thumped Ingrid's back as she choked.

Gemma explained, hooking her index fingers into little curls and tucking them under her lip to mimic fangs. "Like Dracula."

"I always wondered if Bram Stoker took the blue blood myth and embellished it. We've never had fangs, after all." Ava frowned, and then suddenly grew excited. "But what if he had somehow encountered some sort of story about *dhampir* somewhere? What if—"

Ingrid tossed a pillow at her. "No, Ava! No talk of craving viruses and the origin of the *dhampir* tonight. I want to know more about Byrnes's teeth. The man's a menace as it is."

"Well, we all know there's been an increase in Byrnes's, ahem, stamina. Apparently, his bloodlust's going to go through the roof as well, from what I understand," Gemma said.

"Too late for that warning," Ingrid muttered into her glass.

Her eyes shot to the other woman's neck. Then Gemma snatched her wrist. Not a mark upon her. "Ingrid Miller. Just where is your husband biting you?"

"Don't worry. I bite him back."

"What sort of menace?"

"Can't corrupt innocent ears," Ingrid said, with a wink.

"Oh, it's not as if we cannot hear the pair of you every damned night," Ava protested. "And I shall have you know—"

"Not Kincaid!" Both Gemma and Ingrid plugged their fingers into their ears.

"Please," Gemma protested, "the man is an extremely fine specimen, but ever since I found out he has a cock on him like a battering ram, I can barely look him in the eye."

"And all the things he says to you!" Ingrid clapped a hand over her eyes. "You made *me* blush, and I don't have a chaste bone in my body."

"You're just jealous because Byrnes wouldn't know poetry if it bit him on the ass. Between you and Byrnes, you're the one with a gift for rhyming slang," Gemma pointed out.

Ingrid clinked glasses with her. Last month, she'd finally confessed to a certain risqué bet between her and Byrnes that had apparently ended with him tied to his bed, naked, with a poem scrawled across his chest.

Considering he'd been found by several of his former Nighthawk brethren, he'd spent a year vowing revenge upon Ingrid.

According to Byrnes, he could no longer show his face around the Guild of Nighthawks, because every time he did, they started singing the poem.

"What Kincaid was whispering in Ava's ear has little to do with poetry," Ingrid continued.

Ava blushed. "I blame the pair of you. I'd never imbibed so much before. I cannot believe I even admitted he says such things."

The three of them collapsed in laughter.

Gemma felt the weight of the last few days slough off her as she laughed. This was exactly what she'd needed. "So what else have I missed?"

"Well, while you were off seducing the enemy, Malloryn's had the whip in hand," Ingrid admitted. "No rest for the wicked. Ava's been busy with the autopsies of the three victims from Thorne Tower; Malloryn and Kincaid have been trying to organize the guard protection for the queen; and Charlie, Byrnes, and I have been scouring the streets trying to find you."

Malloryn's best trackers. It surprised her, for he should have had them on the Carlyle case.

"Did you find anything unusual in Jonathan Carlyle's autopsy?"

Ava shook her head. "No. Most of his brain was mush, unfortunately. He'd been tortured and starved, and he was emaciated. You were right though. The bullet in his head was etched with a diamond."

That itch was back. The one that said something about the Carlyle murder struck her as wrong.

Obsidian's lack of memories. Carlyle's lack of memories. How were the pair of them connected?

"Uh-oh," Ingrid murmured. "I recognize that expression. What thought is bothering you?"

Malloryn hadn't understood. He was such a cold bastard; he could barely look an emotion in the eye and respect what it was telling him.

But these two....

Gemma let the entire story of her past spill from her lips.

By the time she'd finished, both of them were frowning.

"I can have another look," Ava said. "Cause of death was fairly easy to ascertain, so I wasn't searching for anything else." She hesitated. "What *should* I be looking for?"

"I don't know," Gemma admitted. "Something just doesn't feel right about this entire case."

"Trust your instincts," Ingrid said, "and have another drink."

"At least someone believes in my instincts."

"Everyone knows you pick up on things we don't," Ingrid protested.

"Unless, of course, you're the Duke of Malloryn, in which case I'm merely conjuring theories to try and rationalize my overly emotional decision-making processes."

It came out a little harder than she'd expected.

"He's been on edge ever since you were taken, Gem," Ava said hesitantly. "I wouldn't take his words seriously."

"Malloryn sent us searching all over London for you. He even joined us in the end, when there was no sign of you. I won't say I thought you were dead, but the tracking device was silent for two days. Even I was starting to...." Ingrid gave a shrug, unable to complete the sentence. Her irises flared bronze as the wolf roused within her.

Verwulfen were incredibly protective of those they considered their own.

"What happened?" Ava whispered.

Gemma had explained the past she and Obsidian shared, but she'd glossed over the recent events.

"The usual." The hollow burn of resentment ached within her. She lifted the bottle of blud-wein directly to her lips. "I failed Malloryn."

She sensed Ingrid and Ava exchanging a look as she swallowed

"I fail to see how any of what happened was a failure," Ingrid growled. "You did your best to survive a dangerous situation. And to be honest, when we broke in, I didn't gain the impression your feelings were one-sided. Obsidian's first instinct was to protect you."

A gentle hand rested on her knee as Gemma lowered the bottle.

"Malloryn's had his britches in a knot all week," Ava said firmly. "Don't take his words personally. He's barely slept since you went missing. And then there's the queen. Someone tried to break into the Ivory Tower two nights ago, as if to test its resources, and they couldn't catch him—"

"And of course, let us not forget Malloryn's forthcoming wedding, though I daresay he's trying to."

Gemma's grip tightened around the neck of the bottle. Oh, heck. The wedding. Her mind raced, counting days. When was— "Tomorrow," she whispered.

Ingrid rolled her eyes. "Byrnes can hardly wait. Wants to see Malloryn get his comeuppance."

"Half the Echelon wants to see Malloryn get his comeuppance," Ava added.

Gemma tried to find a smile, but couldn't.

"You couldn't have timed your escape better if you'd tried." Ava accepted the glass Ingrid gave her. "Malloryn's been in such a lather we weren't certain if he was going to call off the wedding to find you, and Byrnes has been beside himself that it would skew the results of the betting pool."

"Byrnes doesn't deal with stress well," Ingrid added, as if realizing how that sounded. "He focuses outwardly on other things in order to hide his true feelings. He was genuinely worried, Gemma. He could barely sleep."

"I know." Her voice roughened as she stared down into her own glass. These people were becoming more like her family than the unknown woman who'd birthed her and then sold her to Balfour's Falcons. "Thank you."

No tears warmed her eyes—as a blue blood she was physically incapable of crying—but she was fairly certain she was going to lose her composure.

Ava gave her a gentle hug, and Ingrid chinked her glass against Gemma's.

"To getting you back."

They all threw their glasses back, and the blud-wein burned down Gemma's raw throat.

Ingrid topped up all three glasses. "To Malloryn's wedding."

Again.

A warm, fuzzy sensation began to burn through her veins as the blud-wein splashed into their glasses again. Ingrid poured like a woman hell-bent on getting top-hammered.

"And to the Company of Rogues, who are my newfound family," Ingrid said in a softer voice, and Gemma realized she wasn't the only one who'd known little to no familial love.

Ava had been raised by a banker who didn't know what to do with her once she'd been kidnapped and turned into a blue blood; Ingrid had been captured by English raiders from somewhere in Scandinavia as a child and forced into a cage for the amusement of blue blood lords....

And Gemma?

She'd had friends once, in the training camps of the Falcons, before she realized they'd be pitted against each other during their final years and forced to do anything to survive. She'd never dared let anyone get close to her after that horrifying revelation, using her armor of flirtation and charm to prevent anyone from slipping under her skin.

But these people had hunted for her when she'd been taken. They were here now because they knew she was sick at heart.

No matter what sort of twisted mess she felt for Dmitri, she needed this too.

"To the pair of you. You are my family," she whispered, her fingers shaking around the glass. "And I will do my very best to keep you all safe, no matter what comes. I love you both."

The blud-wein burned.

They'd need another bottle if this continued.

"Oh, my goodness." Ava fanned her face. "Stop it. You're both going to have me sobbing, and then Kincaid will want to know what's wrong, and I won't be able to explain it, because he has the sensitivity of a rock sometimes...."

"You should try living with Byrnes." Ingrid lifted the bottle and snorted. "He'd be trying to sort out the problem and coming up with analytical explanations for why I'm crying. If he asks, I'm merely going to remove my gown. That distracts him in no time."

And Gemma suffered another little moment of aching pain as the pair of them bantered back and forth, because if she was being honest with herself, the need for family wasn't the only ache that pulsed within her....

She wanted this too.

CHAPTER SIXTEEN

Obsidian stared across the crowded tavern, watching as humanity laughed raucously and swilled beer. The noise enveloped him, but he was very aware he didn't belong here. The smell was quite overwhelming: the press of human body odor, the likes of which had rarely met water if he wasn't mistaken; rotten teeth; and a certain yeasty scent which underlaid everything.

He honestly couldn't fathom why Silas liked this place so much.

Tapping the blunt end of his cheroot in the tray, Obsidian lifted it to his lips and inhaled, considering his next steps. Every inch of his body ached. Whatever Malloryn had shocked him with, it had sent his heart stammering for a good hour afterwards. His fingers were burned, though the craving virus rapidly healed him.

And Gemma was gone.

It was that, perhaps, that hurt the most.

Perhaps? Even his inner voice mocked him.

What the hell had she been thinking, throwing herself between him and the duke? She could have been shot.

And hell, if there was anything that could convince him she spoke the truth about the past it was what had happened tonight. Gemma had risked her life and everything she stood for in order to protect him. Obsidian's hands shook a little as he exhaled a cloud of smoke. His heart skipped a beat, and instantly he sought to master himself again; to still his breath, taking a long slow inhale of air, much the same way he prepared to pull a trigger, but different now, for the turmoil was inside him.

There was no future with Gemma.

There never had been, but despite all that was lost to him, the sudden sharp ache of yearning took him by surprise.

He barely remembered her, and yet, some part of him felt like he'd known her for years. To be in her company was like stepping into warm, golden sunlight, a welcoming embrace of heat he hadn't felt in years. Like being a marble statue brought to life; a man whose heart finally beat in his chest after years of stillness.

He missed the sunlight.

He missed warmth.

He missed *her*.

And he couldn't go back to his brothers.

If there'd been *dhampir* agents in Mably House, then they knew what he'd been up to with Gemma.

And if they knew, then Ghost was aware of everything.

The door crashed open, letting the blustery wind of night inside. Barely anyone glanced that way, but Obsidian ground out his cheroot as Silas finally slipped in through the front door.

Silas paused when their eyes met. He nodded, dragging his long scarf from his throat, and then crossed the packed tavern to slink into the other side of the red leather booth as if he'd been expecting to see Obsidian here all along. This was his favorite drinking hole, a vice both Obsidian and Ghost abhorred.

"What the hell was you thinkin'?" Silas growled, shoving the damp wool scarf on the table. "Are you mad? Ghost is furious."

Fury never quite described Ghost's rages.

"Hence why I haven't returned," he said, with a faint, unamused smile though his fingers still shook with the shock of it all.

"I swear to God, you're goin' to put me in an early grave." Silas shook his head. "I knew it seemed unusual. Two *dhampir* agents sent after Gemma Townsend and none of them survived? I kept askin' myself: Is she that good? Trained ex-Falcon or not, she's still only a blue blood. But then I began to wonder... what if there was someone watchin' over her? A guardian angel, if you will? Someone who could handle two *dhampir* with ease. Someone with an interest in keepin' her alive."

"*You* betrayed me to Ghost."

Silas looked away, capturing the barmaid's eye and holding up a single finger. "He already knew. He's had two of the acolytes trailin' you from a distance."

Obsidian looked at him sharply.

"You wouldn't have seen them. They were instructed to track the beacon and stay a distance of five clicks from it. Ghost became curious about why you was spendin' so much time at Mably House."

Just how long had Ghost been having him watched?

And why?

"You don't find that bothersome?" he asked.

Silas sighed and slumped back against the seat. "Course I do. Cut mine out months back. I leave it where I want them to think I am. Usually a place like this. I don't actually like this pig swill."

His gaze dropped to Obsidian's ruined gloves.

"Looks like you've had a hell of a day. Miss Townsend stick you a few times?"

"No." He didn't want to talk about it.

"Someone made you bleed. I'd like to meet the man who got the drop on you."

"It was Malloryn and his friends."

He watched Silas choke on his smile, swearing under his breath. "Jesus. You had a run-in with ol' ice britches himself? He still walkin'?"

Obsidian released a tense breath, glancing across the tavern. "There was some interference."

"Miss Townsend," Silas said knowingly.

"She didn't want me to kill her friends."

"And since when do you take orders from a piece of skirt?" Silas held his hands up sharply when Obsidian's glare turned icy. "'Pologies. She's got you twisted up in knots again, ain't she?"

"Again?"

Silas looked grim. "This ain't the first time, mate. You were smitten with her in Russia."

"Before I shot her," he stated very carefully.

Silence.

"I've got to be honest with you, mate." Silas's lips thinned. "I ain't here of my own reckonin'. Ghost told me to track you down."

Instantly, he stilled.

"Why?" Obsidian let the hilt of his favorite blade slip from his sleeve into his hand.

"Guess he thought I might be the only one to survive an encounter with the Wraith. Wanted me to pass on a little message."

"Don't call me that."

"No?" Silas drummed his fingers on the table. "Are you going to use the knife?"

Of course he'd noticed.

"Do I have reason to? *Brother*?" he returned, just as softly.

Silas glanced down, as if in thought, but Obsidian could see his hand shifting. He wasn't the only one who carried a knife up his sleeve.

"Anything else I can get you, sirs?"

The barmaid was suddenly there, and neither of them had noticed her coming. Obsidian sat back in his chair as she leaned forward to mop up the ring of beer on the table that some previous resident had left. She thunked a foaming tankard of ale in front of Silas. "The special of the day's the mutton stew, though I recommend the shepherd's pie."

"No, thank you," Obsidian said, not taking his gaze off his closest friend. "I don't think we're interested in eating."

"As you wish." The barmaid dried her hands on her apron with a saucy look in Silas's direction, before moving to the next table.

"What sort of message does Ghost want you to deliver?"

"Not the bloody kind," Silas said. "If I ever got that instruction, you wouldn't see hide nor hair of me ever again. I know who wins an encounter between the likes of us. I'd be on the nearest airship to the Americas before you could so much as sneeze."

"The message?"

Silas sighed. "He wants you to come in for reconditionin'. Said she's clearly been twistin' your head again. He could forgive that."

"Ghost forgives nothing."

"Aye, but he knows he needs you. Balfour's twistin' the thumbscrews, and nobody else has got your skills."

True. Obsidian rubbed at his mouth as Silas took a mouthful of his ale.

While a blue blood could still enjoy food and drink in moderate proportions, the *dhampir* struggled to consume food they'd once found pleasurable. Silas forced it down.

"And what else is he going to insist upon?"

"You know the price."

Gemma's life.

"No," he said, so softly Silas shivered. "If he touches one hair on her head, I will kill him. Brother or not. Balfour or not." He leaned toward Silas, staring his brother in the eye. "Tell him if he thinks I cannot get to him, then he is mistaken. If he hurts her, then the last thing he will ever see is my knife. Or better yet... he will never see me coming at all."

Silas eased out a breath. "You're one intense bastard when you want to be. I think my balls just shriveled up a wee bit. But I'll tell him you said that. I think I might enjoy watchin' him go a little paler round the gills. Now he's got his crew of sycophants, he's been gettin' a little too big for his boots."

Obsidian traced the wet ring Silas's mug had left behind. In the space of a few days, Gemma had torn his life apart. There was no place for him at her side, and yet... what else did he have? "If he wishes me to come in, then I will consider it. And *my* price is Gemma's life."

He couldn't keep watching over her like this.

Sooner or later one of his brethren would slip past him, and then he would lose her for good.

"I will come in. I will accept his orders. I will play my part. But Gemma is not to be touched. He needs to rescind the assassination order."

"You want to tell Ghost what he is or ain't to do?"

Something stirred within Obsidian. He'd spent too many years bowing to Ghost's will because he simply didn't care enough to fight him.

Now he cared.

"Yes."

"Well, now. I guess this means we know where you stand on the Gemma Townsend issue." Silas peered into his glass as if it contained the mysteries of the universe. "I watched him torture the memory of her out of your mind after Russia. Ghost was furious your loyalty had been swayed. You would scream, again and again, as he put you under and reprogrammed you. You forgot her. Became naught more that Ghost's pet assassin.

"And now here she is, walkin' back into your life, and it's like I'm watchin' something come alive within you. And I can't help but wonder... what would it be like to know that sense of loyalty to someone? Stronger than what we forged in the Cremorne Institute. Unbreakable."

Taking a deep breath, Silas carefully placed both hands on the top of the table. "Just tell me one thing... Is she worth it?"

Obsidian had no answer to that. His and Gemma's relationship had always been a thing fraught with danger. There'd been moments of lust between them, fragments of... quiet times where he could remember her kissing him, and feeling as if the entire world lay in his grasp.

So much had been lost. No, stolen from him.

He didn't know if there was an *us* or a *them*. All he knew was he had to save her.

But he tried to put the concept into words for his oldest friend.

"We've had no peace. We've never had a chance to be. She is pain, and suffering, and torment to me, but she is also hope, and light, and laughter. Perhaps we'll never have that peace. Or a chance to discover if there could ever be more. But is the cost of my life worth the price of hers? Yes. I think I would die for her, and there would be no bitterness earned in pursuing such oblivion. As long as she lived. As long as I knew she was still out there, safe. I would pay any price for her."

"Let us hope it don't come to that," Silas murmured. "You're the only bastard I actually give a damn about."

"You're only saying that because you want to stay in my good graces."

Silas tipped the tankard of ale toward him. "There's that too, you mad bugger."

CHAPTER SEVENTEEN

Gemma rapped on the door to Malloryn's private chambers at the Hamilton residence in Kensington. "You sent for me?"

There'd been a message waiting with Herbert that morning when she hauled herself out of bed and downstairs for some very much needed tea. Her one consolation was that Ava and Ingrid were in a similar condition.

Inside the room, she saw the duke examining his choice of cufflinks as his valet watched on. Malloryn's icy gaze flickered to her, and then he turned to his valet. "A moment, Edwards. Perhaps you can see if the bride needs anything."

The valet vanished and Gemma shut the door behind her.

The ceremony was to take place in the formal chambers of the Hamilton house. In light of the threat against the queen, it wasn't ideal, but it had been too late to make other arrangements.

Malloryn shot her a cool look. "The guests should be arriving shortly. I'm sure Ingrid and Ava filled you in on events last night?"

The queen would be in attendance today, and while the Company of Rogues had been busy while she'd been gone, they'd made no headway on the Chameleon issue.

"She has, though I was under the impression I was no longer working the Chameleon case."

He ignored the bite to her voice. "Are you recovered?"

The request took her aback. She hadn't even been entirely certain she was still on the guest list. "Yes."

"Good." He peered at himself in the mirror, his expression blank as he fiddled with his right cufflink. "I need you to be focused today, Gemma. While I'm not certain whether to return you to the field to face your ex-lover again, I would like you to assist with the queen's safety. You would see any threat coming long before the rest of her guards."

A truce then.

Despite her aching head, there was a clarity within her this morning she hadn't owned the night before.

And as much as Malloryn drove her crazy, she did care for him. Perhaps more than he allowed anyone else to do.

"Here," she murmured, crossing over to him. "You're butchering this."

Malloryn gave himself and his cufflinks over to her.

Gemma swiftly did them up, and then straightened the shoulders of the black velvet coat he wore. Every inch of him looked dangerous and dashing. His close-cropped dark auburn hair gleamed in the gaslight, and his usual assortment of rings splayed across his fingers. All eyes would see a man who held an incredible amount of power, and wielded it with a dispassionate hand, but they'd never realize how loyal and true he was to those he considered his.

"Perfect. You look perfect," she said with some satisfaction, for he'd tasked her months ago with choosing his wardrobe for the occasion.

"How is Isabella this morning?" he murmured.

"Do you really want to know?"

For the first time, Malloryn looked uncomfortable. "She's barely speaking to me. We quarreled."

"I know."

"About the wedding."

"I know."

Malloryn met her gaze, looking utterly perplexed. "She knew going into this there would never be anything between us. It's the only reason I let her seduce me. I shouldn't have. I knew better than to mix business with pleasure, but I thought she understood that."

"Oh, Malloryn." Gemma sighed and tugged his coat closed, starting on the buttons on his chest. "Despite your omnipotence, you have absolutely no idea about women's hearts, do you?"

"I don't want to hurt her, but...there's not....I don't—"

"I know." Gemma stepped back, brushing lint off his sleeve. "Your heart died with Catherine. Isabella knew better. She's told me as much a hundred times, but it doesn't negate the fact that deep in her heart she felt something for you. She knows you have to marry Miss Hamilton, and perhaps... perhaps it's best this ends now, before she gets her heart well and truly broken."

Logically it made sense, but her heart ached for her friend. She'd barely seen Isabella since she returned, so caught up in her own heartbreak she had scarcely given the other woman a thought. She'd try and find her tonight, once this was all over, and see if Isabella needed a shoulder to cry on.

"Go and get married," Gemma said, turning toward the door. "And be kind to your future wife, because despite the fact Miss Hamilton manipulated you into this wedding, she has a heart too."

"One would beg to differ." His voice roughened. "Which is the only reason I'm going through with this. I would never say this to her face, but in a way Adele suits my purposes. She's callous and cold, and she will never desire more from me than I am prepared to give."

Gemma shook her head. He'd never learn.

"Gemma?"

She paused with one hand on the door.

"I may have spoken hastily last night." Malloryn shifted his cravat, as if it were suddenly choking him. "It's not that I don't understand. You never knew who your parents were—Balfour took you off the streets and trained you to be a weapon, but the second I saw you, I knew there was more to you than that. There was too much compassion within you to survive as one of Balfour's Falcons. He thought it a weakness, but I saw more. Your sense of empathy was the one thing that allowed me to lure you away from him. It's what makes you so valuable to me, for I know you believe in the cause we're undertaking. I know you want to see a better London, and that gives you incentive to fight harder than any of the others I could have chosen for this role.

"It's your greatest strength—but it's also your downfall." He cleared his throat. "I won't pretend I understand it, but I know Obsidian means more to you than I can imagine. I just hope you mean enough to him."

She looked away. "I know there's no future between us."

There couldn't be.

Not with Dmitri on one side of the line, and her on the other.

"I hope there is," Malloryn murmured. "Because you're not like me, and... as much as I complain about it at times, there is a certain optimistic part of me that would like to see you happy. You deserve happiness."

"Are you *actually* saying there's a secret little romantic part of you?"

"Heaven forbid. Maybe I'm nervous. I'm babbling. Now go." He gestured to the door, his entire demeanor changing as if he'd let down his defenses and found it too overbearing to continue. Strictly business once more. "I want you to keep a close eye on the queen today. You're the last line of defense, Gemma. I've got enough guards on hand to fight off the entire army of New Catalan, but as we well know, that hasn't stopped him in the past, and you know him best."

Him.

The Chameleon.

"You think he'll strike today?"

"It's the first time she's been out of the Tower in a week," Malloryn replied grimly. "I tried to talk her out of it, but she insisted."

Gemma had seen the guest list. Half the Echelon was to be in attendance. Numerous opportunities for anyone to get close to the queen.

"This is aimed at you," she said. "He wanted you to know he's going to try. If it's going to happen, then today is the perfect day for it."

Malloryn grimaced. "The thought crossed my mind."

"Have you warned your fiancée?"

Malloryn blinked.

"You do realize she has a right to know a dangerous assassin may just ruin the wedding."

"I honestly hadn't given her a thought."

Poor Miss Hamilton. This marriage was probably going to be worse than she'd expected.

"Go and warn her," Gemma said, grabbing his arm and lacing her arm through it. "It's the right thing to do."

"I think I'd rather chew nails."

"You have to beard the dragon in her bedchamber at some stage."

He gave her a chilling look. "Miss Hamilton's bedchamber and my presence shall never meet. I know you're hoping for something more to this, Gemma, but I think your recent captivity has rotted your brain. Now go and find the queen."

That sounded more like the Malloryn she knew.

"Only if you warn Miss Hamilton. The queen shall be safe as houses. I won't fail you," she promised.

Malloryn gave her an odd look as he escorted her to the door. "You never have."

But Gemma couldn't help thinking of Russia.

Malloryn paused before the half-open door with his hand raised to knock. Movement shifted inside, but none of it the sounds associated with what he'd have expected of a happy bride preparing for her moment of victory. Indeed, there was a definite hush over the room.

Curse Gemma for making him do this.

"You look beautiful, miss," said a soft, gentle voice.

"Do I?" This was even quieter, almost toneless. "Perhaps I'll steal my husband's heart when he sees me in this dress." A soft laugh. "If he had one, that is."

"Yes, miss."

A sigh. Malloryn shifted slightly so he could see. Adele stared in her cheval mirror, wearing a gown of blushing pink that set off the creamy perfection of her skin. She didn't look like a happy bride. Indeed, her face was expressionless and her eyes looked tired. Someone had gathered all that blonde hair back into a neat chignon, with her veil clasped just beneath it. The effect was stirring. Innocent. Despite his feelings on the marriage, he couldn't deny Adele was stunningly beautiful.

For a viper.

"Has my mother come down yet?" Adele asked.

The maid paused. "Not yet, miss. I'm sure she will."

"That makes one of us," Adele murmured under her breath. "Thank you, Emily. I daresay I won't be returning to this miserable place after the wedding, but you've been my one spot of brightness in this household. I've left a small favor for you in the envelope on my nightstand, along with a reference just in case. Make sure you gather it before my mother sees it."

"Miss, you're too kind." Emily bobbed a curtsy, and for a moment looked like she was going to cry. "It will be all right. You'll see. You'll be a duchess soon."

Adele's head bowed. "We shall see."

She almost looked sad. A moment of unease shivered down the back of Malloryn's neck, but the maid had turned and was halfway to the door when she spotted him.

"Your Grace!" she blurted.

Malloryn slipped inside, noting his fiancée's startled glance as the maid made her escape. She even shut the door behind them, a gross mistake of decency—if not for the fact he was already well and truly trapped. At least this conversation could be had in private.

"Malloryn." Adele turned, her vast array of skirts slowly changing direction with her. "Isn't it bad luck to see the bride before the wedding?"

"I didn't think it would make a difference." It wasn't as though this was a real marriage, after all. But he didn't call it a sham to her face. Malloryn looked her up and down, and to his surprise Adele actually held her breath. That stopped him in his tracks as he remembered what she'd said about stealing his heart. A jest, of course, for both of them knew the truth behind this mockery, but for the first time he simply examined her, rather than dismissing her.

Sunlight streamed through the window, turning her hair radiant with gilt. The neckline was demure, with full-length sleeves complete with little pearl buttons. For a moment, a part of him almost stirred, tempted to unwrap this little present someone had given him. Perhaps that was what made him the angriest about this entire situation: despite his feelings on the matter, he wanted her. Wanted to discover each and every inch, even as he knew he could not. After all, he himself had set the terms for this marriage. He would do his duty, but he owed her nothing else.

He refused to owe her anything else.

Adele tipped her chin up, a brow arching. "Do I meet your approval, Your Grace?"

"It needs a little something," he said.

Adele turned back around, eyeing herself critically in the mirror. "If my mother had her way, it would be a tiara."

"Too much," he told her, eyeing the spread of jewelry on the dresser.

"That's what I told her." Adele toyed with a clutch of pearls, and then traced her fingers over a set of diamonds beside it. "But I do need something to cover the scars."

Faint slash marks marred her neck, some old, some new. Malloryn said nothing as he stepped behind her. Others whispered the Duke of Malloryn was getting used goods—never within *his* hearing, of course—but Adele had never been an innocent, and he'd known that.

"The pearls are too plain for a future duchess," he said, snagging the glittery twist of diamonds and reaching around her to hold them in front of her throat.

Adele froze. Her pulse leapt in her neck and her hand hovered there. "They were my grandmother's."

The diamonds looked too harsh. Malloryn rested them lightly against her skin. Standing behind her like this, he could see the heady thump of her pulse in the side of her neck. Silence stretched between them. When he met Adele's eyes in the mirror, her pupils were dilated, and she looked almost hungry herself.

She knew what had caught his interest.

She wanted it.

Malloryn discarded the diamonds. "Wear the pearls then. I don't think it matters."

With that, he turned his back to her, examining the well-made bed and the pretty upholstered chair in the corner, behind a small packed trunk. All her things, packed in a single trunk? He'd expected dozens.

"So, what brings you to my boudoir?" Adele asked, fiddling with the pearls. "I thought it would be the last place you'd ever set foot in, Your Grace... considering your claims this marriage will yield a cold marriage bed."

"It will." He turned around. "I came to warn you actually. I've received word this wedding may not go entirely without hitch."

"Oh? The bride's going to get cold feet, is she?"

"One can hope."

Their eyes met again, and this time Adele almost smiled. She'd settled on the pearls after all. They didn't suit the dress, but he could see she was satisfied with her choice. *My grandmother's....* For a moment he was almost curious. It was clear her mother had washed her hands of her daughter, and from what he'd heard earlier, there was no love lost between them, but there'd been something almost wistful in her words when she'd said her grandmother's name.

Don't. Don't think of her as anything other than what she is. Easier that way for both of them.

"So what does that mean?" Adele asked politely. "Not without a hitch?"

"I have heard nothing specific, but if anyone were going to take the chance to get at me, today would be a good opportunity."

"You expect it," she said, watching him very closely.

"I do." After all, if this truly were his oldest enemy, this would be too good an opportunity. "Be prepared for anything. I'll have men on hand, so if someone attacks or attempts to blow the manor up, they'll get you out immediately. You remember Byrnes?"

"That grim-faced Nighthawk who doesn't know how to smile?"

"That's the one. He'll come for you if something happens."

Adele shivered. "Who do you suspect?"

"Someone who doesn't like me very much."

"So it could be anyone then?"

Touché. The girl was swift of tongue. "I see the anticipation of your scheming finally blossoming into its reward has taken none of the edge off you."

"You're the one you said I was a viper, through and through." Adele paused, looking thoughtful. "If something does happen, do you think anyone will be hurt? I have friends, Malloryn.... My sister.... They'll all be here today."

"The matter will be dealt with. I don't intend to have anyone killed at my wedding. It's a bad omen."

"Malloryn." This was said in a warning tone. "I do wish you'd tell me what was going on and who has threatened you."

"Well, you'd have the most motive." He watched concern flicker in her eyes, and slowly changed his mind. "But then, that would disrupt this wedding. And you want to be married."

Adele gave him her sweet smile, the one that made the hackles on the back of his neck rise. "Of course I do, Your Grace. Who wouldn't want to marry a duke?"

Pretty words, but so lacking in inflection he couldn't help but doubt them.

"Why did you wish to marry me?" he finally asked. The question had been tickling at the back of his mind.

Adele fussed with her gown, tilting her shoulder this way and that, as if her image was the only thing on her mind. Green eyes met his in the mirror. "It was your charm, Malloryn. It quite swept me off my feet."

He didn't know what had prompted the question, and regretted having asked. He and Adele had settled into a well-practiced duel at this stage; thrust, parry, disengage. Clearly she had no interest in meeting him in the middle. "So be it. If that is the case then I shall see you at the ceremony."

And he turned toward the door.

He was almost there when she broke the stalemate.

"You never asked."

Malloryn paused in the doorway. "Asked about what?"

"That night in Lord Abernathy's garden. You never asked who had cut me."

His gaze narrowed on her. "All right. You have my attention."

"You presumed it was me." There she stood in her princess gown, defiant and arrogant.

"I presumed it was you. Or some... acquaintance."

"Conspirator, you mean?"

This time he couldn't stop a faint smile. "Let us be blunt then. I assumed you had organized for some blue blood to do the deed."

There. The words were said, but they didn't seem to have the effect he'd been after.

Adele stood in the too-tidy remnants of what had once been her room, as proud as any queen. "What if it wasn't a conspirator? Did you ever think of that?"

He had not. Malloryn's eyelids grew sleepy as he examined her. It wouldn't have been the first time some debutante had been attacked. But... could he trust her? Adele was sometimes shockingly ruthless. "It was a rather enormous coincidence. You, rushing out of the shadows all bloodied and breathless, straight into my arms, just as half the Echelon happened to stroll around the hedge. You breathed not a word of protest when my honor was besmirched, except to claim we were anticipating our engagement."

"I won't lie. I saw you there and the moment I realized who you were, I thought you might help me. You've made your stance quite clear about the thrall-hunters. Believe it or not, I considered you the lesser of two evils." She smiled, but there was no humor in it. "Which says something, I believe."

Anger stirred, deep in his veins. This was precisely what he'd meant to counter when he came up with the law regarding those blue bloods who sought to take a woman's blood by force. His voice hardened. "Who, Adele?"

"Does it matter?" She was smoothing her skirts again, a nervous habit, he assumed.

Malloryn took a step toward her. "Yes. It does. If you were afraid of someone... I could forgive that."

This time he wasn't imagining the fear that flickered through those green eyes. Adele looked away. "I cannot give you a name."

"Then I cannot believe you."

She was one of the best liars he'd ever encountered, after all.

"Adele, if you are telling the truth, then know this... I am very, very good at discovering secrets. If someone did threaten you, then I will find him. And I will make him pay for what he did to you. But beyond that... nothing changes. Do you understand?"

She stared at herself in the mirror, swallowing faintly as she smoothed her gown over her hips. "I understand."

"I'll see you at the altar then."

You can do this. You'll be safe now, and no blue blood will ever be able to touch you again....

Adele stared at her pinched expression in the mirror.

The pearls looked wrong.

But they're Grandmother's, and if there's anyone you want standing at your side today, it's her. Or the memory of her.

She would have wanted to be here on your wedding day.

"My mockery of a wedding day," she whispered, clutching the pearls as if they were strangling her.

Heat flooded Adele's eyes. She couldn't breathe. And her corset was too tight. All she'd wanted was for her sister to be at her side this morning, but her mother wouldn't even allow her that.

I wash my hands of you, Adele. I am done. Once this is over, I expect never to see you darken my door again, do you understand?

Do you understand? the Duke of Malloryn had asked.

Oh, yes, she understood all too well. Adele caught hold of the edge of her old bed, clenching her eyes shut as she put herself back together, piece by piece. After all, it was clear the only person she would ever be able to rely upon was herself.

Slowly, she released the shuddering breath she was holding. *You have a heart of ice.*

Nerves of steel.

A will of iron.

Nothing could touch her anymore. Not if she didn't *let* it touch her. Malloryn might hate her for trapping him like this, but at least she would be safe, and then she could use her pin money to rescue her younger sister, Harriet, from the path her parents had forced her down years ago.

Harriet would never have to go through what Adele had.

No matter what she had to do.

Adele swallowed the burning lump in her throat and opened her eyes, meeting her emotionless gaze in the mirror.

All she needed to do was suffer through this ceremony and she'd finally be free. Malloryn had sworn never to touch her. They would live separate lives.

Harriet would be safe.

And that was when something moved behind her in the reflection.

A wet hand clamped over her mouth, jerking her back against a hard body before she could even scream. Not a hand. A handkerchief. It smelled like— She wanted to gag, but her eyes were fluttering, her lungs caught in a chemical haze. A hint of a pale figure loomed behind her in the reflection, his hair the color of bleached bone.

Adele's knees weakened, her fist flailing helplessly.

Malloryn would probably be relieved.

Because she was fairly certain she wasn't going to make it to her own wedding....

The world vanished around her as Adele's body slumped.

CHAPTER EIGHTEEN

The Duke of Malloryn stood at the altar, his hands crossed in front of him as he stared directly at the garland of flowers.

"Nervous?" Leo Barrons asked, at his side.

There was no one else he could have asked to stand with him. Malloryn's gaze flickered to his friend, and he arched a brow. "Do I have cause to be nervous?"

"It's your wedding day," Barrons mused with a faint smile. "Aren't all grooms nervous?"

"Were you?"

"No." Barrons's glance slid toward his wife in the crowd, his dark eyes softening. "Mina was all I ever wanted, so I was bloody thrilled to finally claim her for my own."

Thrilled.

Malloryn's lips pressed firmly together as a sudden lashing of anger sliced through him. As calm as he might claim to be, he hated feeling manipulated like this. Resentment burned within him like a smoldering coal nothing could extinguish. Most of the time he thought he had it under control, but the entire day rubbed him the wrong way.

He just wanted this over and done with so he could set his mind to other matters.

Then Adele could go her way, and he could go his, and never the twain should meet.

It's not Adele's fault you're feeling this way, he told himself. *You can't blame her for choosing the wrong flowers.*

His gaze slid to the flower wreaths; gorgeous red roses and sprays of carnations. And his heart gave an unfamiliar squeeze in his chest as Catherine's image came to mind.

It might have been seventeen years since he'd pledged his heart to her, but he rarely thought of her these days. He refused to, the memories tainted by what had happened to her.

Yet now, the sight of her favorite flower—a red rose—had his skin itching from the inside out with all the ways this felt wrong.

This should have been *her* day, but Lord Balfour had robbed him of that chance all those years ago when he put a bullet through her heart. Malloryn had been too late to save her, and all he could do was hold her limp body in his arms and scream his bitter rage at Balfour.

"Easy," Barrons warned, and Malloryn realized the color had faded from the world as the hunger within him rose to the surface.

"I'm fine."

This entire day conspired to make him sweat. He glanced at the queen, and saw Gemma in place behind her. Their eyes met, and he gave her a faint nod.

Time ticked by.

Where the bloody hell was Adele? He had the sudden brief suspicion the bride had actually run away, but then laughed under his breath. Some punters would hope so as he knew there was a betting book in the Company of Rogues about whether he'd actually go through with this, but he knew Adele far too well. One didn't plan a military campaign like this just to cry free at the last moment.

She wanted to marry him. He just wasn't entirely certain why.

"You never asked...." Her whisper stirred through his memory. Damn her, why did she have to say that? Was this another game she played? Malloryn had ice water in his veins, and one of the reasons he'd agreed to go through with this was because Adele did too.

Don't you dare think of her as though she's the victim in all this.

"Malloryn," Barrons murmured, pulling out his pocket watch and checking it.

"She'll be here," he said, ignoring the whispers and rustling fabric behind him in the ballroom of Adele's parents' home.

Someone cleared their throat.

If she didn't make an appearance soon, he was going to punch something.

Ten minutes passed. The whispers grew and finally Malloryn's temper snapped. The bloody little bitch. She'd actually decided to cry free. He couldn't believe it.

Mrs. Hamilton gave him a thin, nervous smile. "I'll go see what the holdup is."

That was when Ingrid slid into the room, looking breathless. Their eyes met across the expanse of the ballroom, and hers were wide and startled.

A sense of tension leached through his body as she gestured quickly with her fingers to let him know she needed to speak with him.

Malloryn made his excuses, pasting a smile on his face as he nodded to the guests and strode toward her. "Where is she?" he demanded through gritted teeth.

"I don't know," she whispered. "I waited outside her door for twenty minutes, but it finally got the better of me. Malloryn, the room's empty. There's no sign of Adele, only the breeze whispering through the window."

Gone.

She'd actually done it.

Fled from this wedding, made him a laughingstock....

Malloryn headed for the stairs, taking them briskly. "Fetch Byrnes and Gemma. I swear I'm going to *thrash* Adele when I get my hands on her."

Malloryn prowled Adele's bedchambers, tossing aside pillows and books as if that would provide some clue as to his missing bride.

Time to tread carefully, judging by the expression on his face. Gemma examined the room. Curtains blowing in the faint breeze, the sill all the way up. No signs of a struggle.

Malloryn finally gave up, scraping a hand over his mouth. "I don't understand. Surely she would have left a letter behind to explain her actions. And she *wanted* to get married."

Gemma crossed to the open window, kneeling to examine the latch. A tiny chip of paint was missing, but if someone had broken in, then they were an expert.

"You swear you heard nothing?" he asked Ingrid.

"I arrived a minute or two after you left, according to the guard I replaced," Ingrid admitted. "I didn't hear a thing."

"How the hell did she escape? She was wearing her damned wedding dress. The thing must have weighed half a ton." Malloryn spun toward the door. "Where's the guard you replaced? Where's her sister? If Adele was going to run, then she may have confided in the girl. What was her name? Harriet?"

A tiny thread of pale pink was caught on the sill. Gemma tugged the piece of silk free and straightened. "Malloryn."

He turned abruptly, moments away from striding through the door.

"She went through the window." Gemma held the silk strand up.

Byrnes arrived, entering the room like a bleak, black-clad incongruity among all the pink wallpaper. The thick overcast clouds and fog outside meant he could move about during the day, but he was limited to the inside of the house. Sunlight burned his skin these days.

Ava scurried in behind him, whispering in Malloryn's ear. "I questioned her sister and mother, but neither of them knows anything. The sister's upset. She swore Adele would never run. She wouldn't tell me why she was so certain, but she stressed the fact Adele needed to be married."

"What's that smell?" Byrnes asked, exchanging glances with Ingrid and rubbing his nose.

"I can't smell a damned thing," Ingrid admitted. "Gemma?"

She shook her head, but focused on Byrnes. "Your senses are stronger than either of ours. What do you think it is? All I'm getting is perfume."

"It's... something chemical." His nose screwed up as he stalked the room, trying to track the scent. "I recognize it from somewhere, though I'm not certain where."

Malloryn watched him like a hawk. "Concentrate, Byrnes."

"It's ether," said Ava, taking a slow sniff. "I use it myself sometimes when I assist Dr. Gibson at the Nighthawks Guild. It's quite familiar to me."

Everyone in the room grew still.

"Ether?" Malloryn repeated, his face tight and feral. "Why would Adele's room smell like ether?"

Gemma's heart dropped through her abdomen as everything became ruthlessly clear. "Oh, no."

"Oh, no?" Malloryn's gaze cut to hers.

"It was never the queen he was after today." Perhaps the Chameleon knew he couldn't get to the real target today with all the security, but there'd been hardly anyone watching the bride. "He's taken Adele in her place."

Just to prove he could.

Malloryn's face paled as he strode for the door. "Alert the guards. Search the house. I want everyone out in the gardens looking for him. I'll alert Barrons and leave him to sort the queen's contingent out. He can keep her safe."

They had to get Miss Hamilton back before the Chameleon killed her.

Coldrush Guards swarmed through the Hamiltons' gardens.

There was no sign of the bride, and Malloryn's voice had turned lethal as he barked orders, though his expression held no outside trace of his turmoil.

Gemma caught a hint of some of the wedding guests' whispers: *What a shock ending to this fiasco of a wedding; Malloryn couldn't even get his bride to the altar; has someone taken her?*

Half a dozen of the blasted peacocks were on the balcony, watching proceedings with an amused eye. Some of them even had champagne. Bets were being placed, which made her feel a little uncomfortable, for while COR had opened a betting book on the event, none of them had done it with malicious intentions.

Gemma glared at them. She wasn't going to let Malloryn become a laughingstock. And the poor girl might still be alive.

Think, damn you. You know him best.

The Chameleon liked to take credit for his kills.

He'd begun to send Malloryn a bullet-ridden playing card before them with a clue as to his target.

He wants to taunt Malloryn.

Taking Miss Hamilton was nothing more than an insult. A means to strike at Malloryn, as if to say, *I can take anyone you care to protect.*

He knew Malloryn.

He knew the day's program, and the house.

It's always an inside job....

And it was clear Miss Hamilton was no longer on the premises. Gemma's head turned, and she slipped to the gate at the edge of the garden. There'd been guards here earlier, but perhaps they'd joined the search?

The scent of blood caught her attention.

A minute amount, but any sign of it might be a clue.

Gemma strode into the streets. A single dark crimson droplet of blood marred the cobbles. It seemed surreal to find an area of Kensington so devoid of traffic, but Malloryn had insisted the streets be cleared for half a mile around, what with the queen in residence.

Guards loomed at the roadblock to the north of the street.

But Gemma's head turned south, her nostrils flaring as she followed the trail of blood.

A single drop splashed here and there; dark enough to be a blue blood with a low CV level. She tracked it to a narrow lane, where she found a man stashed behind a pile of refuse, stripped of his clothes. The pale linen of his undergarments was stark white. Someone bleached them, which argued for certain uniform standards. His hair was close-cropped, almost military style. Clean-shaven. Polished Hessian boots. Blood dripped from his ear where someone had most likely stabbed a stiletto directly into his brain. Some of the blood was thickened, congealing, which gave her a timeline.

A Coldrush guard.

This was how the Chameleon got in.

She started putting events together in her mind. The Chameleon took the guard out first, as cleanly as he could, and dressed in his uniform before returning to the guard's post. There should have been a second guard, but she had no idea where he'd gone. Dead, perhaps, the body hidden.

The guests started arriving.

Everyone retired to the ballroom for the ceremony.

And that was when he made his move.

Discarding the decorative overlay of her bustle, Gemma hurried back to the foggy street. All her gowns had been modified to her specifications to make it easier to move within them. A froth of gold lace spilled through the two slits on either sides of her skirt, a subtle display of gorgeous fabric that disguised the fact the slits gave her room to move. One second she could be ready for the wedding of the year, the next, able to kick a man in the face.

Gemma drew her pistol out of her reticule, as well as a curious brass gauntlet she'd stolen from Jack's laboratory.

He didn't want her testing it yet, as he hadn't quite gotten the power pack sorted, but she'd been preparing to protect the queen and needed every edge she could get. Slipping the ultraviolet illuminator gauntlet on her hand, she locked it into place.

Time was running out. Miss Hamilton might be killed at any moment. Curse it. She wasn't wearing one of the aural communicators they used on jobs, having removed it for the ceremony. She had her two favorite sai strapped to her thighs, a knife up her sleeve, the pistol, a garrote in her necklace, and a decorative stiletto pinned in her hair, but she was woefully unprepared for this.

Where? Where would he have taken Miss Hamilton?

Gemma's heart raced as she surveyed the area. A cricket ground resided in the distance, the ornate gates of a cemetery, and a dozen small residences....

Malloryn. It all had to do with Malloryn.

It was as if something drew her toward the cemetery.

Instinct, perhaps.

Brompton Cemetery. One of the Magnificent Seven, and home to a grave she knew far too well. Catherine Tate. The young woman Malloryn had allegedly given his heart to when he was younger, though he'd only ever spoken of it once.

He still visited occasionally.

What were the chances the duke's fiancée was stolen from her home on her wedding day, and the blood trail led toward the cemetery Malloryn's first love was interred within?

"You son of a bitch," she whispered.

There was too much poetic justice for it to have been mere happenstance. Gemma started running.

How were the *dhampir* and the Chameleon connected?

Everything they've done has been with Malloryn in mind. Why not the Chameleon?

She was more convinced than ever of a link between Obsidian, his fellow *dhampir*, and the Chameleon.

Obsidian was an assassin; he'd shot her once without a flicker of remorse on his face.

He'd been in Malloryn's original safe house and killed his fellow *dhampir*, Zero, before she could succumb to Malloryn's questioning.

He'd worked for Lord Balfour, Malloryn's greatest enemy, before Malloryn cut the spymaster's throat and killed him.

What if the real Chameleon had been closer to her than she'd ever expected?

No. No. He'd been back and forth to Russia several times upon Balfour's whims. Surely Obsidian couldn't be responsible for the fifteen deaths the Chameleon claimed. She would have to check the timeline and see if she could place Obsidian out of the country when one of the assassinations occurred.

And Carlyle? How did he fit?

Too many puzzle pieces, not enough of the pattern to see.

But she couldn't deny there were links between her ex-lover and the assassin she was hunting.

And he hadn't trusted her enough to reveal a damned thing.

Gemma passed beneath the arched gateway, drawing the second pistol she always carried. It made a loud sound in the stillness of the fog as she drew back the hammer on both of them. Heart pounding, she moved between the colonnades that led toward the domed chapel ahead, scanning the graves and memorials that surrounded her.

Too many places for the Chameleon to hide. It made her skin crawl being out in the open like this. During a sunny day it was almost peaceful here, but with a malicious layer of fog serving as ground cover there was an eerie sensation that chilled her spine.

The scent of blood drew her like a lodestone toward the chapel, gravel crunching under her feet. Each memorial seemed to float in the fog like a disembodied figure, stark angels staring at her with empty eyes.

Sound whispered to her right. Gemma spun, staring through the pistol's sights, her pulse suddenly hammering.

Nothing moved.

But as her vision finally resolved, she could make out a yawning black crevice leading down into the bowels of the earth.

The perfect place to hide a not-quite-duchess.

The perfect place for an ambush.

Catacombs existed below the colonnade. A pair of marble angels watched her pass by, stained by the repeated attentions of the local pigeons. Gemma crept down the sloping path leading directly to the mouth of the catacombs, fog swirling away from her skirts. Two pillars stood on either side of the door, and she could smell blood again, as if someone lured her into the shadows like some gothic version of *Hansel and Gretel*.

This doesn't make me nervous at all.

Movement stirred behind her.

Gemma spun, tracking the darkness. Only the swirling fog indicated someone else was out there. All her senses went on alert, the color leaching out of her vision as it sharpened. She stepped between two headstones, using them as cover, crossing one foot carefully over the other as she searched the shadows for an assailant.

The tiny hairs down the back of her neck prickled.

Behind her.

Gemma spun around, both pistols locked on the shadowy figure emerging from the fog.

Pale brown hair tumbling to his collar, the familiar harsh slant of his cheekbones.... The breath burst out of her as Obsidian appeared, gloved hands held in the air. Dressed entirely in black as if he melted from out of the shadows themselves, he strode toward her with an intense stare. Gemma's heart skipped a beat; a combination of the danger of the situation, and a sudden jolt of *something* she couldn't name.

"Are you insane?" she whispered hoarsely. "What are you *doing* here?"

I nearly shot you.

His pale gaze raked the shadows of the graveyard, and he pressed a finger to his lips. "*You shouldn't be here,*" he mouthed.

A horrible suspicion dawned in her breast. "Please tell me you're not here for the reason I think you are."

He moved like a sudden blur, capturing her from behind and slamming a hand over her mouth. Gemma found herself hauled back against that hard body, her skirts crumpling between them.

Instinct almost made her pull the trigger, but she froze instead. He wouldn't hurt her. He'd gone to great lengths not to hurt her.

Instead, she softened against his chest, her heart pounding madly in her ears as Obsidian drew her back into the shadows of the catacombs. Somewhere out there in the foggy evening, something else moved.

They weren't alone.

CHAPTER NINETEEN

Curse her to hell.

Obsidian rested his back against the brick wall of the catacombs, the rapid thump of Gemma's heart echoing in the darkness.

This was the worst scenario he'd ever imagined, with Silas moving out there in the cemetery, almost invisible in the fog. If Silas saw Gemma he wouldn't hesitate to shoot her. And Silas was the only *dhampir* Obsidian wasn't certain he could actually kill.

Gemma wriggled, her skirts pressed against his groin.

"Don't. Move," he breathed in her ear.

She seemed to understand.

Seconds stretched out. Minutes. The heat of her body began to warm him, and the faint scent of her perfume imprinted itself on his skin. All he could hear was the steady *thump-thump* of her racing heart, and the sound of it began to call the darkness within him. Shadows deepened as his eyesight became clearer. He rarely saw the world in color anymore, for the hunger was always just beneath the surface, but something about Gemma called to another part of him. Color drained back *into* the world, until he could make out her vibrant, berry-stained skirts.

The pink of her lips.

The creamy perfection of her skin.

His gaze locked on the pulse in her throat, and there was a rush of blood through his cock as his teeth began to ache. The diamond-shaped canines had grown in several years after his initial transformation, as if to give him a predatory edge. Some blue bloods of the Echelon used to file their teeth into points, but for a *dhampir* they were a natural enhancement.

Gemma's head tilted to the side as she glanced back over her shoulder at him. One eyebrow arched in pointed exasperation as if to say, *really?*

His fists clenched in her skirts as he whispered, "I haven't drank today."

"And this is definitely the right situation," she breathed back, wriggling her bottom a little, as if to confirm he was indeed erect.

That was the problem with being *dhampir*. Or perhaps it was merely Gemma. "It's always the right situation."

The hunger never truly went away anymore, but he'd thought he'd had a leash on it until *she* walked back into his life.

"There is a young woman missing. And one of your brethren took her." Her eyes flashed murder as she turned around, her hand laid flatly against his chest. "Please tell me your companion *isn't* the goddamn Chameleon."

"He isn't the Chameleon."

The pistol wavered against his chest, and he saw indecision flood through her. "You know who it is."

"Gemma...."

"Don't you lie to me."

"Fine." His expression tightened. "I won't lie. But this is one fight you are better off staying out of."

"I have to stop him," she said.

"*Nyet*. If you walk out there, you'll die."

"If I don't, then Miss Hamilton will die."

"Better her than you," he said.

Shouts echoed.

Tension slid through him as he turned toward the mouth of the catacombs.

"No," Gemma blurted, slamming her hand to his chest and forcing him back against the wall. "They're my friends."

Yesterday swam between them.

It was the exact same thing she'd said then, and he'd thought she'd chosen them.

Until she stepped between Malloryn's gun and his fallen body.

He looked down at her. Black curls danced around her defiant face, and something long dormant warmed within his frozen chest. Gemma would defy the world for those she loved, no matter what it cost her. And somehow, she'd decided he was important enough to be protected.

If her friends were out there, then so was Silas....

How the hell was he going to get Gemma away from here? She wore that mulish expression he knew so well. If he tried to throw her over his shoulder again, he had a feeling she'd try and castrate him.

"You're not prepared to face Silas," he told her. "He's not like me, Gemma. He won't spare your life. Your friends are here. Let them rescue—"

"I'm sorry," Gemma whispered.

"For what?"

A sudden sharp, lancing pain went through his side. Obsidian grabbed her arm, but a wave of weakness went through him. She'd stabbed him just under the ribs with a tiny dart she'd pulled from her bracelet.

"Just a little hemlock," she murmured, bracing his weight against her body. "You'll be able to move again in a couple of minutes."

"Gemma!" His legs weren't working, a chill spreading out from the area she'd injured. As the poison worked through his system, it took his strength with it. "Damn it."

Obsidian went down on one knee, barely able to twitch his toes. His fingers curved around her arm, locking tight, but she pried them off.

"Well, what do you know?" Gemma whispered, catching him under the arms and hauling him into the darkness of the catacombs. "It seems all a blue bloods strengths—and weaknesses—are exacerbated when one is made into a *dhampir*. I'm sorry. But I can't let him kill an innocent girl."

Obsidian slumped to the ground, barely able to twitch his little finger. *Gemma.* He tried to speak, but even his throat muscles were paralyzed. *Don't. Damn you, don't go out there.*

The last he saw of her was her vibrant dark pink skirts as she vanished up the ramp into the cemetery.

Lights flashed in the foggy cemetery as Gemma scanned the darkness. She heard voices; Coldrush Guards. Byrnes. Perhaps even Malloryn.

Her heart started beating faster. The *dhampir* she'd seen was out there somewhere, she knew it. And every beacon of light and loud shout betrayed the presence of those trying to rescue Miss Hamilton. It would keep her target's attention while she moved like a shadow in the night.

A foggy, poorly lit night.

Perfect grounds for an ambush.

Yes. But which one of you is going to walk into the trap? He's a dhampir.

Taking Obsidian down with hemlock when he was distracted was one thing; managing to kill a creature that was faster, stronger, and invulnerable to all but a thrust straight to the heart quite another.

And this one wouldn't hesitate to harm her.

Gemma powered the illuminating gauntlet on her hand, feeling the slight hum of its vibration. An untried prototype, it might be the only edge she had in this fight, though the enormous covered eye in the center of the gauntlet had only enough power to give her one blast.

"All I need," she whispered, setting out into the night.

Where would he have taken Miss Hamilton?

The faintest scent of blood had her turning deeper into the cemetery, away from the searchers and toward the end of the colonnade.

The sensation of being watched raised every hair on her body. No sign of anything moving out there, though the fog was thicker on the ground and sound was muted. Could be just her mind playing tricks on her. Gemma jumped as an owl suddenly hooted nearby. Her pulse rocketed through her veins, and she forced herself to swallow. The surge of energy through her veins was both a boon and a curse. She felt ready to leap right out of her skin.

The scent of blood grew stronger, and she suffered a horrible moment of doubt as her footsteps quickened. *Please let me be in time.*

The fog ahead of her stirred, sweeping away from a tall memorial as if someone drew the theatre curtains on a stage. Movement. Gemma raised her pistol, creeping forward with slow careful steps. A shape was beginning to form, slumped against the memorial, the scent of blood growing stronger—

A pale flash of movement leaped toward her from the side, and Gemma spun and hammered three shots directly into the blur with her armor-piercing bullets.

The *dhampir* vanished behind a headstone, but she heard him wheeze and swear under his breath. "Damn you. That was me favorite coat."

It threw her off.

"What?"

Shouts echoed nearby as the searchers heard her gunfire. Gemma circled the headstone, only to find nothing there.

A faint laugh echoed behind her. "I begin to see why Obsidian has a soft spot for you, Miss Townsend. Brave, beautiful, and intelligent. What man could resist? It's a pity you've also caught the eye of Ghost. But he doesn't want your heart. Just your head. Thinks you've caused enough problems, turnin' our best assassin against him."

"I didn't do a damned thing. *He* kidnapped me."

She pressed the charge button on the illuminator. It began to whine. The *dhampir* stalked her through the fog, and Gemma forced herself to tilt her head to listen. If she mistimed this she was dead.

"This isn't personal, Miss Townsend."

There. To her right.

"Though I might be inclined to make it such." His voice roughened, but it was now to her left. Toying with her. "You're going to get him killed."

"I can sway the Duke of Malloryn. He won't harm Obsidian."

"I weren't talkin' about Malloryn."

Silence.

A cold feeling rippled down her spine.

Gemma closed her eyes, her hearing focusing intently. There. The faintest sound of gravel shifting, as if beneath someone's foot.

Right behind her.

Gemma spun, stabbing the button of the illuminator, and not daring to open her eyes. A bright light flashed, searing her closed eyelids, and someone screamed.

One second of intense light, and then the whine died down.

Gemma shot into the night, spraying bullet fire in a half-circle in front of her, before she dared open her eyes. She'd lost her night vision. Blackened shapes reared around her, and she almost tripped on a headstone, blinking furiously.

A shape moaned on the ground to her left.

"Bloody hell. What did you just do to me?"

Gemma turned her pistol upon him. One bullet left, if she was counting accurately.

"Pull the trigger and the girl dies," he gasped.

Gemma froze.

"Where is she?" she demanded.

The bastard panted, hand clapped over his chest and one side of his face burned as he pushed to his hands and knees. Behind him, she could hear the shouting growing louder. "Out of the way, luv. I know a certain someone who wouldn't 'preciate it if I ripped your head off your shoulders. It's the only thing savin' your life right now. I just have to keep tellin' myself that."

"Strange. I was fairly certain I had a target on my back. Several of your brethren have tried to murder me in the last month."

"And where are they now?" He staggered to his feet. "Bottom of the Thames? I suppose we *could* ask our mutual friend."

"Don't move." She focused her pistol right on his heart.

"You're runnin' out of time, Miss Townsend. You have barely a minute to save the girl's life, so you'll have to make a decision. The girl. Or me."

Gemma's teeth clenched. "What do you mean?"

"I had my orders. Malloryn's not supposed to find her 'til it's too late, but if someone else were to get to her first, well... I did as instructed. Tick, tock, Miss Townsend."

The *dhampir* vanished into the fog, and Gemma turned helplessly toward the pale figure she'd seen in front of the memorial.

Blood.

Sprinting toward the mound, she could just make out the beginnings of pale skirts. Miss Hamilton lay sprawled on her back, her eyes closed and her arms curled around a small ticking package.

Oh, no. Gemma slid to the young woman's side, feeling for a pulse in her throat. There. Thready and weak, but there. There was a lump on the side of her head.

She examined the bomb. Less than twenty seconds remained on the clock face attached to it, and a thin wire was attached to the bracelet on the young woman's wrist. A single move and it would detonate, she was sure. "It's all right, Miss Hamilton. I've got you. You're going to live, I promise."

Curse him.

Curse them all.

Gemma eased out a slow breath as she slid her fingers around the very edge of the package. *One. Two. Three.*

She tore the bomb free and flung it, throwing herself over the girl. The fiery detonation washed over her, raining a hail of marble pebbles down over her. They stung her skin and pelted into her legs, but she'd heal.

Malloryn suddenly slid to a halt at her side, spraying gravel. "Miss Hamilton? Is she all right?"

Gemma's ears were ringing as she lifted herself up. "I think so."

Malloryn pressed a hand to Miss Hamilton's forehead. "She feels like ice. Where's the Chameleon?" he barked, stripping out of his coat.

"I don't know. I shot him, but I had to save Miss Hamilton."

And was that really the Chameleon?

Obsidian had told her it wasn't, and the *dhampir's* mocking voice and sarcastic tone sounded nothing like those of a cold-blooded killer.

She needed to return to the catacombs and question a certain enemy agent before any of the others stumbled upon him.

Malloryn's lips thinned, but he nodded. "You made the right choice."

Easing his coat around his fiancée's shoulders, Malloryn hauled her dead weight up into his arms. Golden ringlets tumbled over his sleeve, and Miss Hamilton moaned.

Malloryn looked down at her with a strange look on his face. "Well. The odds certainly weren't in my favor today. Tell me... was anyone betting an assassin would kidnap the bride before she could say *I do*, or does no one win the kitty?"

"*Malloryn.*"

The smile he gave her had a knife-edge to it. "Thank you, Gemma. You saved her life. Take the night off. You look like you need a good sleep. Tomorrow, we renew the hunt." His smile vanished as he glanced up at the memorial in front of him, and the elegant scrolled writing embossed across it. *Catherine Tate*. For a second, his expression froze, and then he looked down again, balancing his fiancée in his arms.

"I want the Chameleon's head," he said in a lethal voice, "and I will have it."

CHAPTER TWENTY

The bride was home safely, disaster averted, and the Company of Rogues dispersed for the night, grateful for having survived the day in one piece. There'd been no sign of Obsidian in the catacombs, and Gemma wasn't certain whether she was relieved or not.

He wasn't going to appreciate being hemlocked.

And she had quite the bone to pick with him in regards to Miss Hamilton.

Gemma retreated to her bedchambers, peeling off her long leather gloves as she entered the room.

Tossing the gloves aside, she felt the cool breeze on her skin, and—

The window was open, the curtains blowing in a way reminiscent of Miss Hamilton's bedchambers. Fatigue sloughed off her in an instant and Gemma slipped her hand through her slit skirts and drew one of the sai sheathed against her thigh as she pressed her back to the wall, dropping her handful of pins on the carpet. The room was empty; nothing moved.

But her heart raced in the stillness of the night.

Someone had been in here.

And then her eye locked on the single sheet of folded paper on the bed. Only one person could have gotten into her rooms undetected, despite the risks.

All the tension eased out of her, replaced by something that burned a little hotter, a little tighter, and she gritted her teeth as she stalked toward the letter. *Damn him.*

Saint Petersburg haunted her. Stolen moments in the midst of chaos; secret rendezvous where they could pretend they were alone in the world without an entire spy war between them. They'd traded notes then, using a plethora of servants and tactics such as breaking into each other's rooms, just like this.

Stealing away at a ball to kiss him in a shadowed alcove. A day at the Hermitage Museum, where Gemma marveled at the art and pretended she was merely a young woman strolling with her beau. An afternoon tucked away in a carriage, exploring the canals and streets. Sipping svekolnik, a cold borscht soup. Laughing as they lay naked under a blanket, before a blazing fire. All they'd ever truly had were moments.

Gemma flicked the note open. If he thought to sway her with nostalgic memories, then he was sorely mistaken, especially after the day's events.

We need to talk. Come and find me. If you can....

"Son of a bitch," she growled, screwing the piece of paper into a crumpled mess and heading for the window.

Talk? Ha. They certainly did have much to discuss.

Two minutes later she was slipping over the rooftops, a foggy London spread beneath her. Lamplight glowed in the fog, like little fuzzy will-o'-the-wisps. Gemma surveyed the roofline.

Where would he be?

A single candle lingered in the open window of a neglected tower to her right. Gemma's gaze locked on it.

Of course he would have to make her climb a bloody tower in her heeled boots and the gown she'd worn to the wedding.

Fine. Gemma withdrew the other sai from her left thigh and gripped it between her teeth. It left her free to tuck a loop of her skirts into the leather holster wrapped intimately around her thigh, revealing a healthy slice of her gossamer stockings. She hauled herself up the interlacing brickwork, her toes finding crevices between the coarse bricks and her fingers clinging in minute cracks.

Gemma gained the window ledge, and a figure loomed out of the shadows, dressed in stark, imposing black. A violent grace filled every step he made; a lethal intensity. He'd stripped to his leather waistcoat, and the broad planes of his chest and shoulders filled out his shirt, but that was the last thing she wanted to notice right now.

"Here," Obsidian murmured, offering her his hand.

Like hell.

Gemma scrambled over the ledge and plucked the sai from her teeth. "What the hell did you think you were doing, leaving a note on my bed like that? Are you trying to get yourself killed? The house is *watched*, damn you. Herbert's been instructed to shoot all pale-haired intruders with a dart laced with Black Vein. Not even you could survive that."

Obsidian refused to back away, and her fury roused at the fact she had to look up to see his face. The bloody bastard had almost a foot of height on her.

"He would have to notice me."

"Herbert is a trained assassin." Somehow she managed to grind the words out between her teeth. "One of Malloryn's best."

"He's not that good. It's not the first time I've been in your room, Gemma."

Her fist curled around the sai, and she gave in to the instinctive rush of her fury and sliced the top button of his waistcoat with a flick of her wrist. It felt good. Even as he captured her wrist and forcibly took the sai from her.

It didn't matter. She had another.

The edge of violence thickened between them, and instinctively she settled into a defensive stance, prepared to take him down if he made a single move. Tension shivered through the air, as their eyes met. Then Obsidian whirled the sai in his fingers and captured the needle-sharp prong in the center, examining the balance.

He offered it to her. "This is my favorite waistcoat."

"You made me climb the damned tower in a dress."

"You didn't have to. You could have removed it." Heat curled through his dark eyes; a faint taunting smile curved his mouth. *I dare you*, his eyes said, and her breath caught, because there was *her* Dmitri. "As this week has proven, you seem to enjoy flaunting yourself."

It was as though pieces of him were swimming to the surface, inch by inch.

The hardest part of the last week in captivity had been watching the man she'd once loved and not recognizing a damned thing about him.

But he was still there.

"And you seemed to enjoy pretending you weren't looking."

His lashes fluttered lower. "I was looking."

"I know."

"I couldn't help myself," he admitted, his thumb stroking her fingers as she took possession of her sai. "You have a way of twisting me into knots."

Her breath caught, leaving her feeling somewhat disconcerted. "Don't think your words can turn me up sweet. Shall we cut to the chase?"

"You hemlocked me," Obsidian stated flatly.

"You lied to me," she snapped back.

"I fail to see how."

"You know who the Chameleon is."

He turned away, unable to look her in the face, and a horrible suspicion filled her. "Leave it alone, Gemma."

"Is it you?" she whispered.

He stared at the floor, his head bent. "Not this time."

Not this time? "What the hell does that mean?"

"Haven't you figured it out yet?" His head turned, his gaze tracking hers.

Gemma took a rushed step toward him, and then paused. "Today, your friend was the Chameleon," she whispered. "But you have played this part in the past."

Of course. That was why the Chameleon had always been so bloody difficult to capture; it had never been one person. All those misleading witness statements—young, old, bearded, gray-haired....

She'd never truly been hunting for one assassin.

And Jonathan Carlyle paid the price for all the others.

"Oh, my goodness," she whispered. "Who's the current Chameleon? Who's going after the queen?"

Obsidian shook his head. "I can't tell you that."

He'd said too much.

"You mean you won't. You could stop this," she whispered. "There would be no more deaths, no more chaos in the city. There could be peace—"

"This doesn't stop until the Duke of Malloryn is dead," he growled out, clenching his fist. "It ends when everything he's ever loved is ash, his entire life's work smashed into rubble around him."

The expression on her face—

"I *am* part of his work," she said, taking a step back from him. "I have been there every step of the way as Malloryn fought to build something I believe in. I love him, Obsidian. He's my family. Would you see *me* smashed aside, beneath this... this cursed vendetta?"

She didn't understand.

"I was trying to remove you from the equation."

Gemma started shaking her head, her fingers curled into helpless fists. "*No.* No, no, no. This isn't happening. Don't you dare say you kidnapped me so I would be safe when everyone I loved was slaughtered. Don't you dare say you tried to protect *me* at the expense of everyone else."

His heart was an empty, gaping hole in his chest.

"I couldn't let you die. But I can't stop the others from being caught in the crossfire."

"You son of a bitch." She shoved him, pushed again when he staggered back a step.

"My hands are tied."

"Bullshit," she shot back. "You don't have to work for Ghost. Every time you take his orders, you make a choice."

"This is bigger than Ghost. Bigger than me. The second I make a countermove, I'm dead, Gemma. Or worse, you are. Do you have *any* idea what you're facing?"

"No, I damned well don't know what we're facing. Why don't you tell me?"

The second he did, she was dead.

Ghost would never let him go, and Gemma would never forfeit her ideals. Especially not with her hatred for Balfour driving her to take him down. Obsidian couldn't stop the cataclysmic clash they were headed toward.

Or could he?

"Run away with me," he whispered.

Gemma's head jerked up. "What?"

Obsidian cupped her face in his hands. The words were as much a surprise to him as they were to her, but the second he breathed them into the world, he gave them life. They swelled, filling the gaping hole in his chest. An answer. A damned answer where neither of them needed to yield. "You and me. We could leave all this behind us. Run away together and never look back."

The more he thought of it, the more alluring the idea became.

"No more *dhampir*. No more killing. No more ruin. We could flee to the Americas. Create a new life for ourselves." He desperately needed her to say *yes*. "All I need is you."

But he knew her answer even before she opened her mouth to reply.

Agony gleamed in her blue eyes. "Obsidian—"

The desperate need to still her words slammed through him, and he took her mouth, trapping the answer inside her. If she couldn't give it life, then he could linger here, in a dream world where they could be together.

Gemma kissed him back, her fingers twining through his hair, and her mouth just as hungry as his. Obsidian's hand slid down over the curve of her ass, and he hauled her against him, grabbing a fistful of what remained of her bustle. The crush of her breasts against his chest ignited the blood rushing through his veins, and her belly pressed against the flushed rousing of his cock. All he needed was

Gemma. He devoured her with quick, helpless kisses until he could barely breathe.

Until he was dizzy with it—

She pushed against his chest, drawing back with a gasp. "*No*. No, I can't. You're asking me to throw away the lives of everyone I love. And I will not do that. Not even for you."

Stalemate.

He'd always known it would come to this.

"Gemma...."

"Please," she whispered, taking his hands. "Please help me stop them. With you on our side, we cannot fail."

"Gemma." He pressed his forehead to hers. "The second I betray them, I'm dead."

Or worse.

They would turn him against her again.

"Malloryn will protect you. I know he will."

"Stop." He clasped his fingers over her lips, stilling the words. "You can't hide me from what's inside me. It doesn't matter where I go in this cursed city. My only hope is to leave the country—to get as far out of Ghost's range as I possibly can."

Stillness leached through her, and she looked up.

"I am not the man I once was, Gemma." He tried to make her see. "Malloryn had you all implanted with a tracking beacon when you began to work for him, didn't he?"

Suspicion darkened her eyes. "You removed yours."

"I have what is called a neural regulating actuator implant in my brain. It took me years to even realize it was there. I have these... moments... where I black out. I lose time sometimes. And my memories are full of holes. Sometimes I can wake to find myself in a place with no idea how I got there."

"What are you trying to say?"

"There is a Dr. Richter working for Ghost. He's spent years perfecting the implant, and it killed most of the initial trial patients. It forces you to obey. You don't even know what you're doing."

Her mind was racing behind her eyes, but they suddenly lifted to his, and he could see the truth dawning in them like a sunrise.

"You shot me," she whispered.

He brushed his knuckles down the sides of her cheeks, unable to meet her gaze. "I can't remember pulling the trigger," he confessed. "All I can see is the moment you started falling. The last thing I knew before that moment was drinking a glass of blood with Silas as he checked my burns. And then I was on the bridge, and you were gone." His voice roughened. "It's all starting to come back to me. I thought I'd killed you. I couldn't stop thinking of the look on your face when you fell. I tried to find your body, but there was no sign of you, and then the explosion happened.... I barely escaped with my life. But I would never—"

"Shhh," Gemma whispered, pressing her fingertips to his lips. "It all makes a perfect sort of sense. Your face was so blank I thought everything had been a lie. I thought you'd played me for a fool."

"Everything... in my head. It's a mess. Nothing makes sense. I don't know what is real."

Gemma captured his wrist, her expression gentle as she lifted his hand to the center of her chest. "This is real," she whispered.

His palm splayed across her smooth skin, feeling the kick of her heartbeat beneath the skin.

She lifted on her toes, brushing her mouth against his, her breath stirring his sensitive lips. "*This* is real."

Taking his hand, she slid it sideways to cup the curve of her breast. "And this is real."

His mouth softened under hers, thumb stroking the smooth slope of her breast as his tongue brushed against hers.

He needed her so much right now. The world was spinning off its axis, her words echoing in his head, *please help me stop them*.

But she didn't understand.

He couldn't help her, when he might be the very tool used against her.

A single spoken phrase, and perhaps he'd be staring down the line of a pistol again, without even seeing her on the other end of it. He knew what Richter and Ghost did to him. There was no point hoping he could fight it, when he damned well hadn't been able to in the past.

What the hell was he going to do?

If Ghost accepted his terms and spared Gemma's life in exchange for him returning to the fold, then she'd never forgive him for what happened to her friends. He couldn't flee without her, leaving her to face certain death at the hands of his brethren.

And he couldn't force her to run with him, for she'd never forgive him.

No matter where he looked there was no answer.

Only the feel of Gemma's mouth beneath his, anchoring him to the world; the heat of her body stealing through him until it began to melt even the frozen vestiges of his own heart.

This. This was all they had.

Obsidian slammed her against the wall, pinning her hands to the brick above her head. Harsh gasps tore through her, leaving her breasts straining. His gaze dipped lower, drawn unbidden to the heaving globes.

She's always been your weakness, Ghost's voice whispered, and he wasn't certain if it was the neural implant or not, messing with his head.

Obsidian's mouth found hers in the darkness, trying to gain some clarity. Gemma bit him sharply.

His fist curled in her skirts. He wanted to tear them up, to search beneath them for the wet, slick heat he was sure to find. Instead he coaxed them, inch by inch, letting the anticipation build as he met her eyes. His knuckles brushed against her inner thigh, sweet torture that stirred the raging heat within him. So soft. An unconscious caress he began to direct, turning his thumb into her flesh and letting it rasp dangerously close to her hip, toying with the thin lace that hemmed the edge of her drawers.

Gemma's dangerous mouth parted, her lips shaping around a soft moan—

"You ruin me," she whispered.

The words cut through him like a knife. He closed his eyes, concentrated on the sensation of her skin beneath his.

A kiss to her throat as she arched her neck to allow him access. His gums ached, the points of his vampiric canines feeling like they lengthened as he saw her pulse kick.

But blood was not the only thing he wanted from her tonight.

He wanted all of her.

Obsidian went to one knee, lifting her heel to his thigh. The slit of split skirts draped across her knee, and he shoved them up so he could see the fine silk of her stockings.

When his knuckles grazed the inside of her thigh, goose bumps pebbled across her skin.

He kissed her knee. Her leather garter, where her thigh holsters hung. Slipped the remaining sai from its sheath.

"Are you trying to disarm me?" Gemma whispered, a sultry look in her eyes as she sank one hand through his hair.

His cupped palm slid up the back of her other thigh, finding the second weapon. It hit the floor with a steely clang. "Perhaps I don't want to take out an eye."

"Mmm." Her fingers clenched in his hair. "Whatever would you be doing between my thighs that would endanger your beautiful face?"

"This." He breathed across her skin as his lips skated up her thigh. One tug of the soft leather strap circling her thigh, and the holster hung loose. The second one fell to his conquering touch.

Gemma's breath caught as he hooked his fingers under her drawers and tugged them lower. She lifted her heel from his knee just enough to let them slide to the floor before he replaced it. Supple leather caressed her calf, giving way to the gossamer silk of her stockings. But beneath the fall of her skirts she was bare, and they both knew it.

Obsidian turned his face into the musky depths of her inner thighs, suckling the skin there, laving it with his tongue. One hand clenched in the sleek muscle of her ass, and he glanced up from beneath his lashes as he let her feel the rasp of his teeth—and his intentions.

A breathless moment stretched out as he waited for her to decide.

He'd been dreaming of marking her beautiful skin for days. His cock clenched at the thought.

Gemma stroked her hand through his hair, her chest rising and falling, her eyes glazed with black as her own hunger woke. "Do it." A smoky whisper.

Obsidian sank his teeth into her.

Gemma cried out, her fist locking in his hair, but it wasn't pain he heard in her voice. Shock, perhaps. Then her blood flooded his mouth, and he lost himself to the sensation of claiming her.

All these years he'd wanted to brand himself on her skin, but he'd never dared. He could remember that, at least.

A blue blood's saliva held chemicals within it that could bring a woman—or man—to release. His was no different.

Suckling hard, he heard the shocked sounds as her body began to tighten. Gemma's hands captured the sides of his head. "Dmitri," she breathed, throwing her head back with abandon. "Please. Oh, *God*."

Gemma's fingers curled into fists in his hair. Finding the wet slit of her, he brushed his knuckles against her clitoris. Again. And again. Echoing the pull of his mouth, until her wetness slicked over his fingers. Obsidian worked two of his fingers inside her, setting his thumb into place as he fucked her with his hand. His thumb found her hot and swollen. Right *there*. Her body tightened around him, as she gasped and tried to grab onto the wall above her head with one hand.

A soft cry stole from her full mouth.

Gemma embraced pleasure as if she'd been made for it, completely unabashed in her glory. It stole his entire attention. This was no longer about his pleasure, despite the raging need of his erection. Wiping his mouth, he licked the faint marks to heal them, his pulse throbbing in his ears as he withdrew his fingers from her slick body.

"Dmitri," she begged. "Don't you dare stop."

"Wasn't planning to."

And then he claimed her ass in both hands, and captured her sweet pussy with his mouth, spearing his tongue inside her. Her skirts fell around his head, and Gemma screamed as he worked her clitoris with hot lashing strokes of his tongue. Her hips bucked violently, and he could hear her begging. Not for release this time, but mercy.

Breathing hard, he withdrew, though he had no plans for mercy. Not this time.

It was all he could do to restrain himself, to hold her up as she shuddered.

"Gemma," he whispered.

"Still alive," she breathed, her passion-flushed eyes meeting his. A sudden smile radiated across her face. "Barely."

That smile sank into his heart like an arrow.

Gemma was a light in the darkness, the sun itself, breathing warmth through him until he could almost remember what it felt like to be a man.

Letting her skirts fall as she collapsed against the wall, he stood, his hands caressing the dangerous curves of her body.

"You are mine," he whispered.

No matter what he had to do, he could not walk away from her.

Not this time.

Grasping her hips, he turned her around, forcing her to put her hands on the wall. Gemma's chest heaved on a sob, and her head hung as she sought to collect herself from utter devastation.

His devastation.

A faint smile curved his lips as he felt her thighs trembling, and then caught there as he remembered her earlier words. This was the only sort of claim he could accept from her. Only this.

Because the only thing that could eclipse the radiance of her light, was the darkness of his soul.

You ruin me.

He clenched his eyes shut, seeing that smoking pistol again. Feeling the utter devastation slice through him as he saw her fall.

To have her, was to be her death.

But just this once, he wanted to let himself love her.

Slipping the bejeweled stiletto from her hair, he let it hit the floor. Thick raven locks tumbled down over her shoulders from the twist she'd wrapped it in. Obsidian draped it to the side, kissing the back of her neck. A shiver went through her, and her head lifted as if she finally became aware of what he was doing to her.

He tugged the knife from her sleeve and discarded it with all the rest.

"That's not going to take out your eye," she whispered, as he turned to the row of buttons down her spine.

"Maybe. I'm not entirely certain how much you've forgiven me yet."

"I wouldn't aim for your eye."

Button by button, her gown fell to his determined siege. He'd caught glimpses of her skin in the observatory, but it wasn't enough. "Straight through the heart."

"I always aim for the heart," she purred.

Far too true. "I think you've had my heart since the moment I first saw you. What is left of it has always been yours."

Gemma stilled.

He rested his forehead against the perfumed sweep of her hair as he slipped the gown from her shoulders. Obsidian slid his hands inside its gaping fabric and pushed it down to her hips. The silk of her corset flowed beneath his fingers, and he placed scattered kisses across her bare shoulders as her dress tumbled to the floor. Her corset was the palest of pinks, like the color of her nipples. He bit her again, sinking his teeth into the base of her neck, not quite hard enough to break the skin.

His hand slid down her shift, tugging it up and revealing her bare bottom. Sliding it between her thighs, he found her wet, slick heat and thrust two of his fingers within her.

Gemma's spine arched, her body milking him as she gasped.

He worked her with kisses, trailing his fangs across her shoulders. He worked her with his fingers, circling the lush button of her clitoris until she bit his arm and screamed again.

Turning her around, he pushed her back against the wall. The pale pink of her corset tugged lower, almost revealing the top of her nipples. Cupping her breasts through the straightened silk, he teased one free of its strict encasing, his mouth finding her nipple. Not so gentle anymore. He tugged on the tight little bud, sucking it into his mouth. The room began to vanish around him. *Mine*, the darkness within him whispered as he wrought pleasure upon her skin.

Just this once, he told it.

Gemma moaned and clasped his other hand, drawing it to the lush curve of her other breast. "Harder," she breathed in his ear.

He bit her nipple, pressing his hips between her thighs.

Then a hand worked between them determinedly, and Gemma's eyes held a challenge as she found him through his trousers. The feel of her touch rocked him. Any hint of patience vanished as Gemma tore at his buttons, spilling his erection into her hands.

"I want you inside me," she demanded.

Hauling her up, he set her back to the wall, pressing her hips wide with his thighs. The rounded head of his cock slicked through her wetness, back and forth, back and forth, as Gemma moaned.

"Now," she commanded.

Capturing her mouth, he thrust inside her. Gemma's body clutched at him like a glove, her silken inner muscles clamping down around him.

The last time he'd taken her had been pure, unrelenting fucking. He took her hard now, thrusting within her as she bit his throat, but the entire air of the situation changed.

The war waged between them was brutal upon his heart.

Come with me, he told her with his body.

Stay with me, she replied, reaching up to capture his mouth and lay waste to all his best intentions.

She was torn between two causes, the ache of indecision twisting within her. He felt it in every inch of her body, every tortured caress, as if she too knew their time was fleeting.

And there was no answer.

He came with a hard cry, burying his face in her throat as Gemma stroked his hair.

This. This was heaven.

Could he truly forsake this?

Gemma cupped his face between her hands and kissed him again. The soft stroke of her tongue toyed with his, as she kissed him lazily, breathlessly. "Stay with me."

Obsidian bowed his head against hers, his heart cracking open as if she'd torn it apart with both hands.

He wanted to destroy anything that could ever threaten her.

He'd burn the world to ashes for her.

And yet, she asked him for the one thing he couldn't give her.

Could he?

By the time he'd collapsed over her, cradled in the brace of her thighs, he knew there was no way to avoid the oncoming collision. A decision would have to be made, but why the hell did he have to be the one to make it?

"Please," she whispered, as he listed his head. "Come with me."

"Gemma...."

"I know Malloryn would have you. Work with me to save the London I love."

"It's not..." He drew out of her body, a shudder running through him. "It's not that easy."

"It is."

"Gemma, I told you about the neural implant. Mine is a special kind, with a particular feature. It can send an electrical pulse through my brain if they detonate the neural implant. It would kill me, unless... unless I was out of range. I don't know how far that range lies."

Gemma paled. "You have a bomb in your head?"

"Of a kind. The only one it kills is me. I cannot betray my brothers. Not even if I wished to."

CHAPTER
TWENTY-ONE

Gemma knew she was in trouble when she managed to get through most of breakfast without breathing a word of what happened to her friends.

There was no sign of Ava and Kincaid this morning—Byrnes had told her they'd spent the night at the Guild of Nighthawks, with Ava working on a second autopsy of the three men killed in Thorne Tower.

Malloryn was clearly off managing affairs within the Echelon and trying to save face after yesterday's dilemma.

Which left Byrnes, Ingrid, Charlie, and Isabella at the breakfast table.

The words kept crawling up her throat.

Obsidian was here.

I was with him last night.

There is a bomb in his head.

What the hell was she going to do? She'd barely slept a wink after their encounter, hearing his words every time she closed her eyes. She'd seen him wavering, his loyalty shifting to her, but what could she do to stop Ghost from killing him if he did?

Run away with me....

He'd known it was their only option, if he had any chance of surviving. And for the first time, she genuinely thought about it. It wasn't a matter of breaking her oaths, or casting aside her loyalty to Malloryn.

She just needed to save his life.

What the hell are you thinking?

You know they'll think you a fool.

You barely know him.

Dmitri no longer existed, not in the sense she'd known him, and could she trust what had burned between them?

Obsidian was but pieces of his whole, but sometimes when he looked at her, she saw *her* Dmitri. This man had nearly killed her in Russia, and yet there were so many unanswered questions between them. The way he'd kissed her, as if she meant the world to him. The way he'd saved her life several times, watching over her like some fallen guardian angel.

She needed to know if what she'd felt all those years ago was real.

Run away with me.... It would solve the immediate problem of the implant in his head being activated.

But what if they find you?

Ghost would never let them go. Perhaps they'd have months, years, but they'd always be on the run, looking over their shoulders for a pale-haired assassin. Would Obsidian simply drop dead in the streets in front of her one day when she couldn't even see the threat?

It wasn't an option.

And Malloryn.... He'd be so incredibly disappointed in her.

So she didn't say a thing. None of the Rogues would understand anyway. As far as they were aware, Obsidian was the enemy. He'd shot her. It was only now she understood why.

It forces you to obey....

You don't even know what you're doing....

The loss of memories. Actions one would never expect a certain person to take. Jonathan Carlyle had always pled his innocence, and she felt ill to think the poor bastard might have actually *been* innocent. Of intent, at least. She finally had a link between Carlyle and Obsidian.

There was a lump in her throat, as thick as a fist.

An inside job.

An ever-changing description from the witnesses.

It finally, *finally* made sense.

What if the Chameleon wasn't one person, but dozens? Mindless assassins sent to execute their targets without a bloody clue what was inside their heads?

But if so, then that meant this conspiracy stretched back further than she'd ever have imagined.

Because the Chameleon had been in action for years.

Dr. Richter had created the device. Obsidian refused to tell her more, as if he could somehow keep her away from a confrontation with this "Ghost". But the Chameleon was tied to the *dhampir.*

And whoever was pulling their strings had been working for the prince consort all those years ago.

But how the hell could she give the Rogues that information without revealing her treachery?

Malloryn would forbid her to ever see Obsidian again. He'd make sure she was watched.

How the hell could she protect Obsidian from what was inside his head if Malloryn learned the truth and locked her away? How could she protect the Queen or London if she *didn't* speak up?

Where the hell are you, Ava? Please find the implant in Jonathan Carlyle's head, so I can somehow lead this investigation in the right direction without betraying my interest in Obsidian.

Gemma squirmed as she chased the spoonful of coddled eggs across her plate. She didn't require food, but sometimes she liked the taste of it, and yet this morning her mouth tasted like ash.

"If you stare at it any longer, Gem, it's going to grow legs and crawl away," Charlie muttered beside her.

She looked up sharply.

"Sure you know what you're doing?" he murmured under his breath as Byrnes and Ingrid argued across the table over whether yesterday's events could be construed as the bride crying off or Malloryn reneging.

That stupid bet.

Nobody was paying them any attention.

"What do you mean?" she breathed.

"I know where you were last night," Charlie mouthed silently.

The heat drained out of her face.

His hand found hers under the table and squeezed.

"I'm not going to tell anyone," he whispered, leaning close to her ear so only she could hear the words.

Of all the Rogues, Charlie was probably the one she felt the most relaxed around. He was like the younger brother she'd never had, albeit the kind of brother who'd glue her shoes to the floor because he thought it was funny.

She hadn't realized how much a part of her needed to hear someone endorse her feelings. He wasn't trying to protect her like Malloryn; nor was he staring at her like she had two heads like Byrnes. Charlie knew what it felt like to be at the mercy of one's heart: While he hadn't given Gemma the girl's name, he'd told her about a long lost love on a dirigible flight to Brighton two months ago.

"It's never going to happen," he'd told her, with a bittersweet smile, when she'd pressed him to make a move. *"She hates me."*

"Love and hate are but two sides of the same coin, Charlie."

God, what a simplistic platitude.

"And it's none of my business," he pointed out now. "But I just hope you know what you're doing. I shouldn't like to see you hurt."

"I'm not going to get hurt."

Charlie winked. "Good. Because if you did then I would have to have a word with him, and after the other day, I'm fairly certain that's not going to end well for me."

"Oh, Charlie." She shoved his shoulder, but he barely moved.

Twenty-two and built like a tree.

"Nice try, Gem," he said, spearing a piece of egg off her plate. "But I'm going to be too big for you to thrash sometime soon."

She rolled her eyes. "The bigger they are, Charlie...."

He grinned.

And yet, her smile slid off her face.

"What's wrong?" he asked, turning deadly serious. "You look as grim as an undertaker this morning."

Gemma shook her head swiftly. Then paused. She and Charlie had a special connection. They'd both kept each other's secrets in the past. Gemma met the dangerous blue of his eyes and whispered, "I think I know why Jonathan Carlyle killed Lord Randall. I think I know how the Chameleon is never caught."

"How?"

"I can't say."

"You need to tell Malloryn."

She stole a glance toward Byrnes and Ingrid. The pair of them were looking at each other in that heated way they sometimes did, as if nobody else existed. It seemed the argument had drawn to a stalemate. "I *can't*."

She swiftly explained the situation with the Chameleon and Obsidian.

Charlie's face paled. "An implant in his head?"

"I think that's how the Chameleon is deployed."

"Then who would they be sending after the Queen?"

"I don't know. I don't even know how to look for signs of it."

Charlie's brows drew together thoughtfully. "You need to get the truth out of him."

Easier said than done. Obsidian had made it quite clear he didn't want her involved.

"I need Ava to find that implant," she breathed in his ear. "Then I can push the investigation without revealing Obsidian's role in it. You know Malloryn won't let me near him if he realizes the truth, and I can't watch him die. Please, Charlie. I need help."

He nodded brusquely. "Keep an eye on Obsidian. I'll head to the Guild and see what Ava has found."

"What are the two of you up to?" said a sharp voice. "He's a little young to corrupt, isn't he, Gemma?"

Caught. Gemma stared over the top of her cup of bloodied tea, her vision finally focused on Isabella. The baroness looked terrible as she pushed her own coddled eggs across the plate.

"We were merely discussing how long Malloryn intends to keep me out of the field," Gemma murmured. "You should be getting some rest. Have you been sleeping?"

The baroness looked up, her eyes bloodshot. She stared at Gemma for such a long time, Gemma began to feel a little uncomfortable.

"Is everything all right?"

A faint, mocking twist of the baroness's mouth. Of course. She must have heard about the debacle at the wedding.

"Would you care to take a stroll?" Isabella finally murmured. "I feel the need for some fresh air."

"That sounds perfect."

She wasn't the only one suffering from heartbreak—though hers had an entirely different cause.

Gemma shot Charlie a significant look and he nodded.

"I'll go prompt Ava," he mouthed, and Gemma eased out a sigh of relief that at least she had one ally.

This afternoon, she intended to track down a certain elusive *dhampir*, but first she needed to discover if her suspicions were correct—and Jonathan Carlyle had a neural implant in his head.

They strolled arm in arm through the park nearby, though Isabella remained strangely quiet.

"The ceremony was canceled," Gemma murmured, squeezing Isabella's hand. "I'm so sorry I haven't been there for you in the past few days. Everything has been so hectic."

"I hear you rescued Miss Hamilton," Isabella said tonelessly.

Gemma hesitated. "Isabella, she's a young woman. She didn't deserve what happened to her."

"I know." Isabella's eye was twitching, as if she'd lost control of the muscle there. "I don't blame Miss Hamilton. She took her chance, and she captured her duke. But that duke had a choice. No. I don't particularly wish her well, but I don't blame Miss Hamilton."

An awkward silence descended.

A squirrel scampered across the grass in front of them, turning to watch them pass.

"Has he called off the wedding?"

It was the barest whisper.

Gemma hesitated. "I don't know. He's intent upon capturing this Chameleon at the moment. And Miss Hamilton will take several days to recover. There's still hope."

"No." Tendrils of Isabella's black hair ripped past her in the wind. "I am done with Malloryn." She pressed her lips firmly together, as if she wanted to say something more.

Gemma wrapped her arms around the baroness, squeezing her tight. "More fool Malloryn. He doesn't know what he's missing out on."

"Gemma, please don't." The baroness pushed away from her. "You're making this harder for me."

"Ingrid and Ava were there for me when I needed them. I can do no less for you." And Isabella was so cool and detached, she found it difficult to make friends.

Gemma was probably the only one who considered herself such.

"You've always been my true friend," Isabella whispered, drawing back from the embrace. "And yet, do you know how many times I've hated you?"

Gemma looked at her sharply. "What?"

Isabella turned and stared across the gardens. "I wanted what you had so effortlessly. I wanted Malloryn's affections, even as I knew I would never own them. I knew, and still I forged ahead, trying to fool myself. And I hated you for the place you held in his heart."

"There's nothing between Malloryn and—"

"You look like Catherine," Isabella said sharply, turning those glittering green eyes upon her. "Eerily so.

When you were sent to assassinate Malloryn, he couldn't kill you, and I didn't dare tell you why. It hurts him to look at your face. That's why he sent you away to be trained as a spy upon the Continent. He couldn't bear to look at you for such a long time. You could be her sister. He *thinks* of you as her sister, Gemma. He loves you, as much as Malloryn probably can, and he's gone out of his way to protect you over the years. He swore he'd never let you suffer the same fate."

Isabella's words took the ground out from under her. "But... I...."

She looked like Catherine?

Isabella would know. She'd been working with Malloryn before Gemma was sent to kill him.

He thought of her as a sister?

It hurts him to look at your face.

For the first time in her life, she didn't know what to say. There was a horrible mix of emotions within her. She'd always wondered why he'd saved her life the night she tried to take his.

I hated you....

"I thought you should know," Isabella murmured, drawing her cape jacket tightly around her shoulders. "You shouldn't hug me. I don't deserve it."

"Everybody deserves a hug," she whispered, but she couldn't find it in herself to resume the embrace. Shock rampaged through her.

"I'm sorry. I shouldn't have said such a thing."

"No, I'm... I'm fine."

She wasn't fine at all. So many things suddenly fell into place. She felt like crying.

"And he's not angry at you for the way you feel about Dmitri," Isabella said quietly. "You never failed him. He never, ever thought you failed him in Russia. Indeed, perhaps it was quite the opposite."

If she could shed tears, she was fairly certain she would be right now. Gemma scrubbed at her face. "Oh, heck." She felt all flushed and hot, and knew her cheeks would be a blotchy mess. "Here I am trying to comfort you, and you're destroying me. I'm supposed to be able to hold myself together better than this."

"I'd say I'm sorry, but I'm not," Isabella murmured, turning toward the gate. "I just wanted you to know. I hope you'll forgive me one day."

Gemma trailed after her, feeling all puffy and horrid. "There is *nothing* to forgive."

"I've done terrible things, Gemma, and I don't know how to take them back." Isabella's voice grew very small as they slipped through the park gate and started making their way back to the safe house. "I don't know if there's any hope for me. There's so much anger inside me. I wanted to hurt him back. And now it's too late."

"What are you talking about?"

Isabella's eyes gleamed as they slipped down the back lane toward the walled garden behind the safe house. "I don't deserve your friendship. Promise me you won't hate me when all is said and done."

"Oh, tosh. You're not in charge of my feelings for you. If I say you're a friend, then you're a friend." She squeezed Isabella's arm. "And I couldn't hate you. I honestly couldn't. We'll sort this... this Malloryn thing out."

He thought of her as a sister?

It was still so incredulous she had no clue what to think about it all.

"Gemma!" Isabella's eyes widened, the first sign Gemma had of something wrong.

"Hello, Miss Townsend."

A voice right behind her.

She spun around, lashing out with the knife that slid so easily to hand, but it was too late. Something smashed across her temples, and Gemma barely had a chance to stagger before her body went out from under her....

The candle flickered in the breeze as Obsidian waited in the tower overlooking Malloryn's safe house.

He'd left a note on Gemma's bed again, but that had been hours ago. Long enough for the candle to eat its way halfway down its length.

He couldn't afford to linger much longer.

Ghost wished to meet with him, according to a message from Silas. He wasn't certain if he returned the sentiment. The more he thought about it, the more he longed for the nights he spent with Gemma.

But Ghost would never let him go.

Not willingly.

The brotherhood of *dhampir* had been forged in loyalty, all those years ago, but loyalty cut both ways.

Would Ghost accept his offer? Gemma's life in exchange for Obsidian's?

The thought of surrendering his will to that of the other *dhampir* made his stomach crawl, but what choice did he have?

He couldn't run—she wouldn't go. And one press of the control device that Ghost kept in his breast pocket would obliterate the device in his head, ending his life. If Ghost didn't need his "Wraith" so badly, he had the feeling it would have ended already.

This is not loyalty.

This is not brotherhood.

It was only now, when he had no choice, he saw the truth.

You could kill him, whispered a dark part of himself that always lingered beneath the surface.

Kill Ghost and the threat to Gemma dissipated.

Except he'd always wondered what Richter had programmed into him during his conditioning sessions. A single word might resurrect the Wraith, stopping him in his tracks and turning him into a weapon—for their own use.

How he hated the fucking implant in his head.

Pacing in front of the window in the tower, Obsidian peered into the still night as the sudden hiss of a steam carriage barreling down the street caught his attention. The Duke of Malloryn leapt down from it before it had even finished moving, and launched himself up the steps to the door of the safe house and through it.

Something was wrong.

A chill ran down his spine. No one emerged. Lights flickered in the windows, and he could hear raised voices.

A whisper of dread curled through his veins.

He had no reason to believe Gemma lay at the heart of this sudden disturbance, but she hadn't come.

Stepping up onto the window ledge, Obsidian launched himself into the night, the tails of his coat whistling up around his arms. He landed, knees braced, on the roof below him, and then sprinted across the edge of it and leaped onto the roof beside it.

Three seconds later, he was hovering on Malloryn's roof, squatting down by the man's study window to listen.

Sharp words echoed within. Three, four voices perhaps. Despite his exceptional hearing, there was a faint undercurrent of static vibration that squealed through his ears. One of those high-pitched devices that made it difficult to listen to conversations, no doubt.

Nothing to be learned here.

He strode along the gutter, grabbing the edge of it just over Gemma's room, and then swinging down onto her open windowsill. The room within was dark, but he froze there for a second, listening.

Nothing moved within. The argument in Malloryn's study obliterated all other noise, but when his gaze shot to her bed, he saw the faint indentation where his letter had lain.

It was gone.

Slipping through the window, he paused again, the hairs prickling along the back of his neck at the risk he took. *Are you trying to get yourself killed?* Gemma's voice echoed in his ears. Drawing the pistol from its holster, he laid it flat along his thigh as he scanned the room.

Everything lay exactly as he'd last seen it when he'd been delivering his note. The note that was now missing.

"Looking for this?" said a voice behind him.

Obsidian spun, pistol raised upon the man who stepped out of the shadows behind the immense wardrobe.

Malloryn.

Dressed strictly in an unadorned black leather outfit he'd never seen the duke wear before, Malloryn glared at him menacingly over the top of what appeared to be a dartgun. Obsidian stilled. His pistol was trained right between the duke's eyes, but it didn't matter where Malloryn hit him if those darts contained the Black Vein serum.

The duke held something up between two fingers. A note written in Russian. He was possibly the only one in the house who could read it, besides Gemma.

"Same time," the duke murmured, disapproval stark in his voice. "'Same place.' She's been meeting with you again."

And keeping it secret.

The pair of them stared at each other over the length of their weapons in silence, and he knew some part of this man itched to pull the trigger.

"Where is she?" Obsidian asked softly.

A muscle ticked in the duke's jaw. "Give me one damned good reason to tell you anything."

He'd spent months studying this man.

Watching his every movement, helping to plan his downfall.

He had no love of Malloryn—no true emotion, either way—but he'd heard Gemma's voice soften when she spoke of the duke. *Family*, she'd called him. He couldn't imagine the icy duke returning the sentiment, but that wasn't merely rage blanking the duke's expression. Obsidian saw the reflection of his own concern in the man's eyes.

And Malloryn was the one who'd saved her life in Russia when he nearly ended it.

It was a simple equation. Gemma was clearly missing. Both he and Malloryn wanted her back. Ghost wanted her dead.

The question he'd been asking himself for days finally had an answer.

Just whose side will you choose?

Gemma's.

Not Ghost's. Not Malloryn's. Only Gemma had the ability to sway him.

And he needed Malloryn alive if he was going to be able to find her.

Obsidian raised his pistol in the air, uncocking it. Staring into the duke's eyes, he holstered it within his coat and held his hands up in surrender. "Where is she? What's happened?"

Malloryn eased the dartgun lower, but he didn't take his finger off the trigger. "If you so much as breathe in my direction, I will shoot you. You know what this does?"

"I know what it does."

"Good." Malloryn tossed the note aside, and it fluttered to the floor like a dying moth. "There was an attack upon the baroness and Gemma. When Isabella came to in an alley, Gemma was missing. She's still missing. We don't where she is, though I've sent Byrnes and Ingrid out with the tracking device. You were my prime suspect until I found your note."

Obsidian's head turned toward the noise in the study. "You knew I'd come."

And he'd staged an argument so Obsidian would think the way was clear.

A dangerous man.

He'd never been so careless before, but the thought of Gemma in danger obliterated his natural caution.

"I was hoping you would have her," Malloryn said, then lowered the dartgun completely.

"How much blood was there?"

"Minimal. They struck Gemma over the head, according to the baroness, then turned the bludgeon upon her."

"When?"

"Four hours ago. I just received the message."

"What did the assailant look like?"

Malloryn arched a brow. "Look in the mirror. He was one of yours. Where would he take her? What would he intend to do with her?"

Obsidian froze.

It could be dozens of places. Balfour had operations all over London; little terrorist cells quietly at work, unaware of each other.

But if it had been Ghost or one of the acolytes who'd taken her, she'd have been dead in the street.

Silas.

His head turned unerringly toward his brother's preferred stalking grounds. He had to move quickly. Balfour had insisted upon putting a bullet through her heart, and then staging her for Malloryn to find, but Silas might not do the job himself.

Ghost wanted that pleasure, which meant he had a window of several hours if Ghost was to be the one who pulled the trigger.

She might already be dead.

No.

Obsidian took a step back, toward the window, unwilling to waste anymore time.

The dartgun tracked him instantly.

"If you shoot me," he mocked, "then your chances of getting her back slim dramatically."

"Damn it." Malloryn jerked his finger off the trigger. "Where are you going? Where is she? Tell me where they'd take her—"

"I don't follow your orders."

"If we don't work together—"

"I'll get her back," he promised, as he slipped over the sill. "Just stay out of my way. You're not my ally, Malloryn."

"No?" Malloryn shot him one last dangerous smile. "Just how do you think this ends? There's no hope you'll turn her—your side wants her dead. And Gemma believes in what we're doing here. This is not merely a game for her. Perhaps she loves you, but I know her heart. She will never betray her cause, not even for you. Not even for love."

His eyes narrowed, the truth ringing in the duke's voice.

Malloryn offered him a faint nod, man to man. "And she won't run. Gemma's sense of loyalty is one of her greatest assets. So it seems you are left with a dilemma. There's a part of me that will never forgive you for what you did to her in Saint Petersburg. I don't even know if I trust you. But the only chance you ever have of being with her is to form an alliance with me. And I might be prepared to overlook certain past indiscretions in exchange for everything you know about the enemy's operation."

Their eyes met.

The duke still didn't know who he was facing.

And it was somewhat telling that he was planning on letting Obsidian go to save Gemma's life, rather than keeping him here to ferret out every little secret he might know.

"Think about it," Malloryn said softly as he lowered the dartgun. "Now go and get her back before it's too late."

Obsidian said nothing as he leaped down into the street.

He would deal with Malloryn's offer later.

CHAPTER TWENTY-TWO

Gemma blinked awake, her head pounding as though she'd been into Byrnes's blud-wein. The entire cabinet of it. The world seemed to split into two, her vision pitching sideways before she righted herself.

Forcing herself to straighten, she closed her eyes and breathed through her nose until she'd regained her balance. This time, the world didn't sway when she opened her eyes. Hoorah for the craving virus.

She forced herself to take stock of her situation.

Bound to a rickety chair in the middle of what appeared to be an abandoned warehouse. Pigeons cooing in the rafters. Dust motes swirling in the patches of light that streamed through the barely boarded-up windows. Across the room, a guard slumped in a chair.

Somehow she was still alive.

The last thing she remembered was—

Isabella's eyes widening. The *dhampir*. He'd hit her from behind, and now...

Now she was here.

She'd been expecting a ditch, if she were honest. Or to not wake at all. Were they seeking to prolong her death? Or was her attacker fetching this Ghost that Obsidian spoke about?

Or was it a trap? She could vaguely recall Isabella babbling about Malloryn thinking of her as a little sister.

They'd failed to kill his fiancée.

Perhaps she was next?

I have a suggestion, Gemma, old girl, how about we consider these questions when we're as far away from here as possible?

She was fairly certain she had a concussion.

Gemma squirmed. Knife in her boot, mysteriously missing. Thigh holsters gone. Nothing up her sleeves. No jewelry.

Good grief. Her favorite stiletto was still in her hair. How the devil had they taken everything else and missed that?

And they must have cut her thigh holsters off her, which was quite vexing. They'd been custom made, curse it. Did they have any idea how much she'd paid for those damned holsters?

The chair first.

Her ropes next.

And then the guard.

Gemma's gaze focused on the solitary guard slumping in a chair against the wall, his chin nodding onto his chest. For a second there were two of him, then she blinked and her vision cleared again. This might be a bit of a problem. His hair was the color of bleached bone, and his skin maggot-pale. *Dhampir?* Or a blue blood well into the Fade?

And just what sort of condition was she in?

"Hullo," she called, snagging his attention. "May I trouble you for something to drink?"

Her mouth *did* taste like several of the pigeons overhead had made good use of it, but honestly, she just needed to lure him closer.

The *dhampir* jerked his head up as if embarrassed to be caught napping on the job. He looked young. And suspicious. "I'm not supposed to talk to you."

"What are they afraid of?" she asked. "I appear to be tied to a chair."

Completely helpless. She batted big, innocent eyes at him.

"You *killed* two of my brothers. I know what you're capable of."

Hmm. The two *dhampir* Obsidian had dispatched. "I'm afraid I don't know what you're talking about. *Please.* You can point a gun at me. I'm just so thirsty."

He considered her request, then reached into his coat and produced a battered leather flask. *Dhampir* thirst was much stronger than a blue blood's, so she'd been counting on him having one.

He avoided the patches of sunlight that gilded the floor, wincing at their brightness as he moved closer. The middle of the day by the look of it. Somewhere up there, some god was smiling upon her. Unscrewing the flask, he drew his pistol and then stared at her.

"I promise I won't bite," she said, with what she knew was her most becoming smile. "You're the one with the teeth."

The *dhampir* held the flask to her lips and the pistol to her temple. His nostrils flared nervously. "I'm not supposed to kill you yet. But if you move a single muscle...."

"I understand."

The taste of blood filled her mouth, and Gemma's nerves relaxed as the hunger whispered through her veins. No point in wasting it, and it would assist with her healing.

Even now, her vision was becoming a little clearer, though the back of her head still throbbed.

"Enough," he murmured after she'd drunk her fill. He tipped the flask away from her mouth.

She let some of the blood dribble down her chin, as if he'd surprised her. It splashed across her breasts, and his gaze jerked unconsciously lower.

Gemma kicked the pistol out of his hand, and then slammed her heel into his knee. Shoving herself into the air, she threw herself backward, smashing the chair to pieces and flipping to her feet. The suddenly loose rope sloughed from her wrist, and Gemma wasted no time. She had a sharpened stake from the chair in her hand, and she slammed it through his chest as he threw himself at her.

It all happened in an instant.

The young *dhampir* gasped, his arms wrapping around her and his weight sending her staggering backward. Gemma angled the thrust right up beneath his sternum, knowing she hit the heart. She worked it a little deeper as he coughed, black blood spraying across her cheek.

"Never presume a pistol gives you the upper hand," she whispered, but the lesson came too late as the light faded from his eyes.

Gemma eased his body to the floor. She almost felt a little guilty. He barely had fangs. Just these little baby canines with the faintest sharp edge. Obsidian had said there were *dhampir* in training. Had they left one of them to guard her? It made no sense, which meant her suspicions were confirmed.

She wasn't the target.

She was the bait.

There'd be other *dhampir* out there, far more dangerous than this one.

She had to get out of here before Malloryn and the others walked into a trap.

Rifling through his coat, she found a pair of knives stashed about his person. Not as well-crafted as her own, but they'd do in a pinch. Stalking toward the pistol, she checked how many bullets she had, and then snapped the barrel shut.

Instinct told her to get the hell out of here and spring the trap before it was too late, but there were... a lot of crates. And they had a very familiar scent about them.

Snatching a crowbar from a nearby bench, she jacked the lid off one of the crates, her heart dropping through her chest when she saw what was inside it.

Oh, heck.

Explosives.

He couldn't find her.

Obsidian's worst fears were coming true. Hours passed as he searched all of Silas's usual haunts. Then the entire night. Panic began to bloom in his chest as he expanded his search to include every known safe house and cell that belonged to Lord Balfour.

And then the sun rose.

Desperation became his driving force. He stole a cloak and hat to shield his skin from the searing sunlight, and staggered into the city, slipping from shadow to shadow.

What the hell had he done?

He'd told Ghost the cost of his compliance depended upon Gemma's safety, and then Ghost had gone out and kidnapped her.

What if this was Ghost's answer?

I will kill him. Slowly.

But first, he needed to find her. No matter what.

He was just nearing the East End docks, and one of the munitions factories Ghost had abandoned last year, when he caught a glimpse of a pair of familiar figures.

Obsidian ducked behind a pile of crates.

"Device is clicking," the tall verwulfen friend of Gemma's muttered. "I've got two clicks, so she's got to be less than three hundred yards away."

Gemma was here. His gaze slid unerringly toward the warehouse on the end of the docks, and his knife slid into his hand.

Then he paused.

Why put her here? The warehouse was near empty, was it not? Everything about the situation had the makings of a trap.

Obsidian crept through the fog, slipping after the pair of Rogues. They moved well, using shadows to hide in as they checked the device.

"Getting closer," Ingrid murmured. "Which one is it?"

And Obsidian made a decision.

He cleared his throat. Loudly.

Instantly, the tall ex-Nighthawk spun around, his pistol locking upon Obsidian. He stepped out from the crate he'd been using for cover, hands in the air.

Caleb Byrnes stared at him, and then slowly lowered the pistol.

"If you wanted us dead, we wouldn't have heard you coming," Byrnes said, drawing a swift conclusion. "Hence, you don't want us dead."

"Correct."

Byrnes's eyes narrowed, but he slowly put up his weapon. "Do you know where she is?"

"Factory to your right. We were using it last year to smuggle weapons into London, but dock authority was becoming a nuisance, so Ghost shifted to another location. It hasn't been used of late."

"What are we facing?"

"No idea." *We?* He still wasn't certain how he felt about this entire situation. "I haven't checked in since I captured Gemma."

"Smells like a trap," Ingrid said.

"I agree."

"Then perhaps we can form some sort of alliance?"

A sudden rumble shook the docks.

Obsidian looked down at his feet, then up.

An enormous ball of fire suddenly swept into the sky, the warehouse simply exploding. All three of them dove for cover.

"I think we found her," Byrnes said, ducking behind a crate as debris rained down upon them.

Ingrid coughed. "Gemma? Oh, my God, is she still alive?"

Obsidian's head snapped up, his pupils aching as they dilated in the intense glare from the fire.

Gemma.

And what the hell?

That factory should have been empty.

Gemma sprinted along the street, the wall of flames behind her crackling with heat. A piece of burning debris shot past her, sparks and ash tumbling from the sky like a hail of flaming rain.

"Gemma?"

She skidded to a halt as Obsidian appeared out of nowhere, covered head-to-toe in an enormous cloak.

"Dmitri?" Then she was in his arms, and he dragged her tight against his chest, spinning her around. Gemma wheezed as his embrace began to crush her a little. "Dmitri."

"Hell." He let her go enough to catch her breath. "I thought you were dead."

"There seems to be a lot of that going around."

Capturing her face in both hands, he kissed her hard and fast. Gemma's fingers twined in the back of his hair, exhilaration burning through her and igniting the sudden need to get her hands on his skin.

"Ahem." A cough behind them.

Gemma broke the kiss with a gasp.

"Jesus, Gemma." A familiar voice drew her attention. "You know Malloryn disapproves of us drawing attention to our work. You could have chosen a smaller target to ignite."

Byrnes.

And Ingrid.

"I was low on options at the time," she replied.

"And I should like to point out," Byrnes said, "you have terrible taste in men."

"So do I, apparently," Ingrid growled, giving him a nudge.

Gemma slid down the front of Obsidian, glancing between the three of them. Nobody seemed to be on the defensive. "What's going on? What are you all doing here?"

"Together?" Byrnes teased.

"We had a common desire between us," Obsidian murmured, resting his hand on the small of her back.

"Probably going to return to trying to kill each other tomorrow," Byrnes said with a shrug. "Though I suspect Malloryn's got plans. He had that gleam in his eye."

"Plans?"

Obsidian's lips thinned. "It seems the Duke of Malloryn and I are overdue a chat."

Silas strode through the door to Ghost's personal quarters, and paused as the scent of blood hit him like a punch in the throat.

Puddles of blood soaked into the rugs. Two pale bodies lay slumped in various disarray. Ghost stood amongst the carnage, wiping the blood from his pale hands with a linen handkerchief. He fussed at the creases between his fingers, and cursed at the mess under his rings.

"Busy afternoon?" Silas surveyed the room.

"Apparently there was a failure at our warehouse in the East End. You know how I abhor failure among those who have been given our gift."

Silas picked his way among the damp patches. "I assume that was the explosion that took out our East End stockpile?"

Despite the blood, Ghost appeared far too mellow, considering how well he took setbacks. It made Silas tread a little carefully as he eased the file labeled Coldrush Project onto the *dhampir's* desk.

Ghost picked a pawn off his chessboard and began to clean the blood off it. "It seems Obsidian's obsession with Miss Townsend is warranted. She's a dangerously talented and beautiful young woman." Ghost tossed the bloodied handkerchief aside and carefully replaced the pawn on the board. "I was using her as bait for a trap for Malloryn, but she managed to escape and in the process blew up the entire building."

"You took Gemma Townsend captive?" Was Ghost out of his mind? "Did you not hear what Obsidian's terms were?"

"I heard them."

Silas stared at him. This was going to ignite a war between two of the most dangerous people he knew. And worse, the one person he still gave a damn about was now on the opposite side of the divide. "He'll kill you."

"He'll try."

"What are you going to do about him?"

A faint flicker of a smile, there and then gone again. "Why... nothing."

"He knows everything," Silas stressed. "We'll have to abandon this place and most of our operations."

"He won't get a chance to use the knowledge."

"What do you mean?" What was Ghost planning? And why the hell did he not know about it?

"I have had enough of this Company of Rogues. It's time to initiate Phase Two."

"You mean to activate the Chameleon."

It wasn't a question.

It also explained precisely why Ghost wasn't worried about Obsidian. Silas's heart stopped dead in the center of his chest. He swore it did.

"Rumor tells me Malloryn's called a Council meeting in the Tower tomorrow. Which means he's taken the bait. He's about to introduce our unwitting Chameleon to the queen. What was it Obsidian said? Something about how we couldn't get inside the Tower.... Well, it inspired a certain train of thought. *We* can't. But nobody said anything about the Company of Rogues."

"You're going to activate the Wraith."

Silas watched as Ghost toppled the ivory queen in the middle of the chessboard.

"It seems like poetic justice: Malloryn is going to do the one thing we never could. He's going to hand deliver our assassin to the queen."

"You cannot expect they'll take him to the Queen," he blurted. "Why the hell would Malloryn trust Obsidian? This is the barmiest idea you've ever had."

Ghost merely smiled. "Trust me, Silas. I've been putting this into motion for days now. I cannot fail."

Tomorrow, the queen would be dead, and they could initiate Phase Three.

But what would the cost be?

Damn it, he'd warned Obsidian not to lose his bloody head.

A sleek panel in the walls opened up, and a slim figure dressed strictly in black stepped into the room.

"Where have you been?" Ghost murmured as he sipped his blood and stared at the closed door through which Silas had vanished.

Couldn't trust a damned soul these days. He'd seen the secrets in his *brother's* eyes. He didn't know what Silas hid from him, but he didn't like it. First Obsidian. Now this.

"Here and there. Making sure the final pieces slot into place. You didn't tell him the truth?" the figure whispered, trailing her fingertips across the back of his shoulders.

"He is fond of Obsidian. And matters have a bad habit of getting out of late. With Obsidian joining Malloryn's forces, I cannot afford any further leaks." Ghost turned to capture her wrist. He kissed her hand, "Ah, Dido. I've missed you."

She shot him a dangerous smile as she swung her leg across his hips to straddle him. "I couldn't have stayed away for the world. Balfour wants a direct report on how matters advance. Are you ready for mayhem, my love?"

His cock hardened as he wrapped his arms around her. "Let's watch London burn together."

CHAPTER TWENTY-THREE

Obsidian carried her all the way up the stairs to Malloryn's safe house.

Gemma rested her head against his shoulder, listening to the beat of his heart. "I can walk," she pointed out. "I did just escape a *dhampir* agent and blow up a munitions factory."

"I know."

He didn't release her.

Byrnes held the door open as Obsidian strode through, shooting her a particularly arch look that said, *I hope you know what you're doing.*

Not a bloody clue. But she clung to Obsidian's neck, feeling strangely whole in his arms.

She hadn't asked him whether he'd made a decision yet, but his presence here seemed to argue for it.

It was both a relief and a sudden fear. Because if anyone had seen them today... it might already be too late.

Malloryn stood at the top of the stairs, watching as they entered. Gemma felt a little self-conscious. As nice as it was to be in Obsidian's arms, she couldn't help noticing the way Malloryn's gaze slid over them, as if cataloguing every inch of their body language.

And Obsidian had told her of the duke's offer.

It wasn't that she didn't trust Malloryn. But she knew the way his mind worked.

A *dhampir* turncoat?

The idea of all that information would be irresistible to the duke, but could she trust him with Obsidian's life?

"Put me down," she whispered.

Obsidian complied.

"My study. Now." The duke stalked down the hallway.

"Good to see you," Byrnes called after him, stripping off his gloves. "And it's our pleasure. We're glad Gemma's safe and whole too."

Malloryn stood behind his desk when they entered, pouring her a brandy. "You're well?" he asked her.

"Tolerably."

"Would love one," Byrnes said, but the duke ignored him and pushed the glass toward her.

"Found her in a warehouse in the East End docks," Ingrid said. "Or should I say, the second the warehouse blew up, we were fairly certain we had her location."

Malloryn's gaze sharpened.

"I set the charge," Gemma said, and then hurried to explain.

About the abduction, the warehouse, the *dhampir* she'd taken down. "The way I escaped... I thought they'd be tougher," she admitted.

"Or maybe you're just that good," Byrnes said.

"It *was* too easy," Obsidian said.

The entire company looked at him.

"In what respect?" Malloryn asked. "Gemma's exceptionally capable."

Obsidian shrugged. "I don't think they intended to kill her. This was a message. If they'd wanted her dead—or intended to set a trap—then it would have happened."

"How is Isabella?" Gemma asked.

She'd been struck to the back of the head, according to Byrnes, and in bed last he saw her.

"One hell of a headache," Malloryn murmured. "She was quite disorientated, and there's some sort of problem with her vision, but otherwise well. She was most distressed. Could barely get a word out and kept crying."

Worried about me. Gemma nodded. This was not the baroness's week. "I'll check on her later."

"Why would they take Gemma?" Malloryn directed this question to the man at her side. "And what message are they trying to send? That they can take any one of mine at any time?"

"It was potentially done because of me," Obsidian replied. Every inch of him remained tense, and Gemma had the feeling she was staring at two strange cats hissing at each other across the yard. "I gave Ghost an ultimatum. This was his answer."

"An ultimatum?"

Byrnes took a surreptitious step closer to Obsidian, and Gemma shot him a glare. If this all went horribly wrong, then the room was going to explode into chaos, because she wasn't going to allow her friends to hurt the man she loved.

Or vice versa.

"He wants me to return for reconditioning." The words were torn from Obsidian. "I said I would consider it on the condition Gemma was not to be harmed. He doesn't care for ultimatums, but I didn't expect him to take her hostage."

"It seems he's given you an answer." The duke faced off against Obsidian. "What now? I told you that you would have a choice. This is the moment. Them? Or us?"

"Please," she whispered, catching Obsidian's sleeve. "We have to tell them about the neural implant. If there's any chance of saving you, then perhaps we can all come up with an option?"

"The neural implant?" Malloryn said, his voice sharpening as if he sensed a dangerous tidbit of information.

Obsidian stared at her. "Gemma."

"Running away isn't an option," she told him sharply. "Jack's the best inventor I've ever met. Kincaid works with bio-mech, and Ava's brilliant when it comes to investigating a person's body. We could find a solution to the bomb in your head."

Silence.

Malloryn's head turned sharply toward her.

She couldn't stand it any longer. "You're already at risk. Helping to find me today might have finally convinced your brothers your loyalty has shifted. What if they detonate it today? You would never see it coming. This is your only hope. Please. *Please.* Tell them about the Chameleon Project and the neural implant."

"What neural implant?" Malloryn asked.

Obsidian released a slow breath. "The one in my head. The one in Jonathan Carlyle's head. The one in the head of the new Chameleon, who will be sent to assassinate the queen."

Color drained out of Malloryn's face. The others gasped.

He explained everything he'd told her the other night. A neural implant implanted in a person's head while under anesthetic. Hypnosis. Then either a remote-controlled activator, or a certain code phrase used to activate the device.

"You will not know who it is," Obsidian said softly. "But they will be within the Ivory Tower already, someone close to the queen. They will not even know themselves. It's most likely a blue blood, as the surgery heals so swiftly any sign of it is gone before they awaken. I do not know their identity. Ghost's been... difficult of late."

Malloryn looked pale. "We have to alert the queen."

The Ivory Tower had long ceased to awe her, but as Gemma strode toward the elevation chamber within it, she realized Obsidian had fallen behind.

Sunset's dying rays speared down though the hollow core of the tower, highlighting the hard planes of his face as he looked up.

"See something you like?" she teased.

"No, I just...." His mouth twisted ruefully. "I've spent weeks trying to get inside this bloody place. It seems ironic that now I'm here, only not as I expected."

Warmth spread through her. "Thank you."

Thank you for helping us.

"Don't thank me just yet," he murmured. "I've been working for Malloryn for nearly three hours, and I already want to chain his feet to an anchor and drop him in the Thames."

"The impression doesn't fade," Byrnes said, clapping him on the shoulder as he walked past.

Obsidian tensed, and she saw the way he'd almost taken the former Nighthawk's arm off.

Then he gave her a rueful shrug. *Old habits.*

She smiled, understanding the urge perfectly. When she'd broken free of the Falcons, it had taken her a long time to accept another's touch as anything other than a threat. Now she took every opportunity she had to hug her friends and kiss them on the cheek.

"You're remaining here." Malloryn gave Charlie a brief nod.

The young man hauled a set of cuffs out of his coat. "Sorry, Obsidian. But the duke insists."

Gemma's heart kicked, and she narrowed a glare upon Malloryn. "What is going on?"

"The Council meeting begins in ten minutes," Malloryn replied coolly. "I'm taking you and the baroness with me as witnesses, and Ingrid and Byrnes as guards. Obsidian can remain here with Charlie until we've spoken to the queen. If she requires his testimony, then he will be brought to the throne room."

"And the cuffs?"

"The cuffs remain." Malloryn tilted his head toward Obsidian, clearly recognizing a lethal adversary when he saw one. "If I wanted to assassinate the queen, then this seems the perfect opportunity, you understand? Who's to say *you're* not the Chameleon? You do have a neural implant in your head, after all."

"It's all right, Gemma," Obsidian said, holding his wrists out and staring flatly at Charlie. "My allegiance has only recently shifted. Malloryn's taking sensible precautions. I'll stay down here until required."

Charlie snapped the cuffs on him.

"Byrnes and Ingrid, could you wait for the next elevation booth?" Malloryn murmured as they strode toward the brass box.

Byrnes's eyebrow arched, but he pulled his wife aside. "As you wish, Your Grace."

Gemma waited until the doors to the elevation chamber closed before taking a slow, deep breath. Isabella settled at her side, staring directly at the door. She'd barely spoken since they embarked in the carriage.

Malloryn turned upon Gemma. "Just because you trust him doesn't mean I do. We are speaking of the queen's safety, damn it." He paused. "Gemma, you heard what he said about the implant. Were you not the one who told me you didn't think he recognized you when he shot you?"

"It's fine. I understand." She squeezed her hands tightly together. "I just worry they'll kill him before we have a chance to examine the device in his head. It's different to the one used on the Chameleon."

"One has to ask why they put a bomb in the head of their best assassin," Malloryn said, staring at the wall.

Gemma's mind raced. "They didn't trust him."

"And it happened right after Russia, you said."

Sweet lord. Further proof Obsidian's feelings for her had been real all along.

"Perhaps I was wrong, Gemma. I think you compromised him more than we realized. He loves you," the duke said quietly. "I never thought I should step aside when it came to Obsidian and you, but I'm certain of it. He loves you."

"I thought that word didn't exist," she said lightly, her heart pounding like a rabid badger in her chest. *Just breathe.*

"It doesn't." The baroness trembled.

"Are you all right?" Gemma asked.

"I'll be better once I'm out of this damned box," Isabella snapped, placing a hand to her temples.

"Your head aches?"

The baroness was not a blue blood, after all, able to recover from the blow to her head so easily. She'd insisted upon coming, however, snapping at Malloryn that she had a job to do and he could take his false concern elsewhere and shove it up his backside.

"I'm fine."

The doors opened with a *ping*. Due to the way the tower was designed, this was the highest one could go via the elevation chamber. They had to take the glorious double staircase that swept along the interior of the hollow core, leading up three stories to the throne room.

Isabella burst out of the elevation chamber as if she needed fresh air.

Gemma gave Malloryn a sharp look. "Have you said something to her?" she hissed under her breath.

"I haven't said a damned thing." He stared after Isabella, and then glanced down at his hand, splaying his fingers.

Gemma's breath caught when she saw the wedding ring on his finger. *Oh.* It all made a great deal of sense. "You married Miss Hamilton?"

"I am *not* going to be a laughingstock," he said tightly.

"When?"

"Quite frankly, Gemma, it was a private ceremony, and I don't feel like sharing the precise moment." He stormed out of the box. "That way no one wins your bloody bet."

She followed a little more slowly.

The bet had clearly rubbed him a little rawer than he'd have liked, especially in the wake of his disastrous "wedding" day.

Poor Isabella.

The baroness strode ahead of them, her skirts swishing over the carpet. They were practically running after her to keep up.

Then the baroness slammed to an abrupt halt.

"Isabella?" Gemma frowned at Malloryn.

The other woman didn't move.

Malloryn's lips thinned. "I should never have let her come." He stalked forward. "Fetch a doctor, Gemma."

"No."

A single, emotionless word.

The baroness slowly turned, her hand sweeping up, the pistol in it locking right on the middle of Malloryn's chest.

Gemma froze.

"Do you know, I always thought you had a heart, Malloryn," the baroness said coldly. "But if I pull the trigger, do you think you'll even feel it?"

"Isabella." Gemma's breath came out in a rush as a horrible, horrible certainty filled her.

You will not know who it is....

Not someone close to the queen. But someone who would be brought into close proximity.

And Malloryn had always suspected a leak.

"You," Malloryn said as all the pieces started to click into place. "You're the Chameleon."

Isabella held the gun on him, but the second Gemma stepped forward, it wavered toward her—then back again. "Don't move. Don't speak. You think I don't know how the pair of you work?" A bitter smile transformed her red-painted mouth. "You think I don't know that no matter how much the pair of you meant to me, your allegiance to each other was stronger? I've spent years on the outside looking in. Years giving everything of myself, only to fade into oblivion the second either of you walked through the door."

She didn't understand. He could not give her his heart, and if his suspicions were true and Balfour *was* still alive... he would strike at those closest to Malloryn first. "Isabella—"

"I said *shut up.*"

The pistol locked on him again, but this time it shook. "I could have *loved you,*" Isabella spat. "I *did* love you. And then you married that stupid brat. You discarded me like a piece of soiled linen, as if your damned wife would care where you were spending your nights—"

"It's got nothing to do with Adele," he replied, holding his hands up and trying to stall for time. Every second he spent here talking to her was a second in which she couldn't get close to the queen to carry out her deadly mission. "I never meant to hurt you. I didn't realize you owned feelings for me...." He stopped abruptly, for was that not what Gemma had been trying to tell him for months? "I merely thought to end things amicably, before you could get hurt."

"I begged you not to marry her," she snarled.

"I had no *choice.*"

"You're a duke, Malloryn! Adele Hamilton is dirt beneath your shoe. If you'd wanted to deny her, you could have."

And seen all his recent work with the Thrall Bill undone?

He clenched his jaw as her eyes filled with tears. "I'm sorry. I didn't.... I didn't pay you enough attention. But you don't have to do this."

"It's too late for apologies."

Gemma sidled closer, remaining silent and fading into the background.

Malloryn stepped forward so Isabella's attention remained upon him. "If you put the pistol down, it's not too late—"

Isabella laughed. "I know you too well, Malloryn. Besides, it *is* too late. Never say I'm not the type to lie in my bed once I've made it. This only ends one way."

"How could you work with the enemy?" he whispered, but the answer was clear. *A woman scorned....*

It was his own damned fault because he'd toyed with her heart without ever looking closely enough to see the damage he was doing. Their mésalliance had been borne of lust and practicalities; he'd allowed her to seduce him because he'd never, ever thought Isabella Rouchard had a heart. It had always been a mutually beneficial affair in his eyes.

What was the first rule he'd ever learned in this game of houses?

Love and dalliances were both far too dangerous for a man who couldn't afford to let a woman in. He'd had a rule once: One night only. So nobody should be harmed.

You blundered. Badly.

And then he'd accused the others of emotionally compromising themselves, when he'd been the one to walk blindly into such a swamp.

"I wanted to see you suffer," Isabella whispered, the kohl around her eyes leaking down her pale cheeks. "I wanted to make you hurt, the way I was hurting—"

"I never wanted to hurt you."

"Well, I do!" she snarled. "I want you to damn well know what it feels like to have your heart ripped out of your chest."

"Isabella," Gemma whispered, stepping closer. "You're not sounding at all like yourself. Put the gun down."

Isabella curled her fist, and pressed it to her temples. "Stop it! Stop talking to me. You're making it hurt."

Making it hurt.... Malloryn's blood ran cold. Gemma was right. None of this sounded like his old friend.

"The neural implant doesn't always work." Obsidian's voice in his mind. *"Sometimes, if it's implanted in the wrong part of the brain, you can see changes to its bearer's personality. It puts a pressure point there that wasn't there before...."*

He had a sudden blinding realization: All these years she'd been content to keep their arrangement practical, and yet she'd been so overwrought in the past few months in a way he couldn't understand.

He'd never, ever have thought to question her loyalty. She'd been with him from the start.

But what if her *loyalty* wasn't in doubt?

"Gemma." He caught her eye and tried to communicate his thoughts with her, tapping a finger to his temples.

Gemma's eyes widened, and then she turned back to the baroness.

"Put the pistol down, Isabella," he soothed, hearing the elevation chamber return, no doubt with Byrnes and Ingrid. His heart started pounding. *Thank all the gods.* They were nearly here. "You don't want to hurt yourself. I don't want you to be hurt. You can still walk away from all this." He took a step toward her. "I'll make sure you're treated well."

"And I'll make sure he keeps his word," Gemma whispered, just behind him. "Please, Isabella. Don't do this."

Isabella started laughing. "Oh, God. Listen to you. You're saying exactly what he told me you'd say."

"He?" Malloryn's hearing intensified, a prickle of tension running over the hairs on his arms.

Isabella stepped back out of reach, hate twisting her smile into something ugly. "The Master."

"You know who it is."

Everything stopped.

The world around him abruptly stood still.

Time.

Movement.

The only sound was the pulse of his heart. Balfour. It had to be Balfour.

But Isabella had hated the other lord. They'd spent years working together to bring him down. How could she betray him to *Balfour?*

"Malloryn, don't," Gemma warned. "Isabella, please. We don't care about the Master. Only you. Please put the pistol down. It's over."

Byrnes and Ingrid skidded around the corner of the stairs, sliding to a halt when they saw the scene.

"I know who it is," Isabella said, glancing toward Byrnes and Ingrid. "I know what he wants. He wants to see you suffer, Malloryn. He made you a promise once. But you'll be last, Malloryn. You'll be there to watch them all fall. Do you know who it is yet?"

Of all his former enemies there was only one who'd hated him this much.

"He wants you to see your beloved city burn."

It struck him like a bullet to the chest.

"He wants you to see your queen die."

The heat drained from his face.

"He wants to take all your playing pieces off the board. One. By. One."

No. His heart became a frozen pulp in his chest, his ears ringing. Her words confirmed every little doubt he'd been having lately.

"I killed him," he whispered, as she confirmed every suspicion he'd had.

"Did you?" Isabella's laughter rang like the tolling of bells. "You never know how much the craving virus can heal."

The body went into the ground. I saw him buried. I put him in the fucking coffin myself, where he could rot, just as the queen ordered. He stared at her through a world that felt like it was turning in slow circles around him, as if he were caught in the middle of a waltz. Shook his head slowly as all his nightmares came true.

I cut his throat.

Stabbed him in the heart.

Shoveled the fucking dirt over him myself.

How could a man survive that, blue blood or not?

"Now you know," Isabella whispered. "Now you know who you're dealing with. He wants you to know he's out there. He wants you to be looking over your damned shoulder every second of every day. Wondering who he's going to take next."

"You won't get near the queen," he said softly. "It's over."

"I was never meant to get near the queen. This bullet isn't for her." She clicked the safety off, her hands shaking and tears streaming down her face. Those green eyes begged him to save her, even as her mouth spat those hateful words. "You challenged him once. You said there was nothing of your heart left to take, but he wanted to test this theory.

"Goodbye, Malloryn. Just remember, this time the joke shall be on you. I was never the Chameleon. Just the one meant to set her in play." Isabella put the pistol to her chin, her face going blank through her veil of kohl-lined tears. "London Bridge is falling down...."

Malloryn jerked forward, one hand outstretched. "Don't! Don't do it, Isabella."

"Falling down, falling down."

Tears streamed down her face as she stared at nothing.

"Wait!" he yelled as she pulled the trigger.

And then it was too late.

CHAPTER TWENTY-FOUR

"Malloryn!" Byrnes yelled, sounding so far away.

Malloryn caught Isabella in his arms as her body slumped toward the floor, shock searing through his chest. The weight of her slumped against him as he went to his knees, trying to lay her down.

There was blood all over his hands.

Blood all over her skirts.

Her hair—

He had the distant feeling he'd never be able to wash it off.

"Isabella?" A foolish question, for he'd seen the glorious light from her eyes vanish.

"Is she—?" Ingrid paused, a step away from him, visibly swallowing down her words.

Clearly realized how futile they would be.

"He got to her," Malloryn choked out, a hollow ringing sound echoing in his ears. "He put a fucking neural implant in her head and turned her against me."

"Who got to her?" Ingrid asked.

"*Balfour.*"

"Balfour? As in Lord Balfour? The prince consort's spymaster?"

"Isn't he dead?" Byrnes added.

Malloryn rocked Isabella in his arms, clenching his eyes shut against the pain. He'd never loved her, but she'd been a friend, a lover.... If he'd paid her more attention, would he have seen the faint signs of her personality change? Would he have noticed the way the enemy was twisting her to his will?

Could he have saved her?

"London Bridge is falling down," came a soft voice behind him.

A familiar voice, but with each word, there was less and less inflection in her tone, as if what remained of *her* washed out of the words. He didn't know what set him off, but all the hairs on the back of his neck lifted.

Malloryn turned his head slowly.

Gemma stood there, staring blankly at nothing.

Gemma, who hadn't come rushing to Isabella's side despite their friendship.

A second epiphany burst through him like a starburst, sending a chill down his spine.

Just remember, this time the joke shall be on you. I was never the Chameleon. Just the one meant to set her in play....

It felt too easy... The way I escaped.

I thought they'd be tougher....

Taking Gemma had never been a trap meant for him, but a means for Gemma to recover from her surgery. She'd have been suspicious if she'd woken in the streets, dumped in some alley.

So they'd set the scene for her to escape.

"Gemma?" he asked as the full implication of Isabella's words hit him.

A blank doll stared back.

"Chameleon," she whispered again, as if she could hear some other voice and was merely repeating the instructions.

And then those blue eyes locked on him with a sudden, eerie intensity.

"Malloryn," she said.

Not her. No.

"Byrnes. Ingrid. Get the hell out of here." Setting Isabella down, he started to stand. "Get to the queen."

Gemma reached for the pair of pistols sheathed at her hips—

Malloryn threw himself down, rolling across the carpet, his hands reaching for his own pistols and finding them.

Bullets spat past him, and he heard Byrnes swearing. "What the hell? *Gemma?*"

"Get down!" Malloryn yelled.

He came up into the perfect firing position, and—

She didn't even bother to protect herself.

Simply strode toward him like some lethal weapon, her eyes blank and dull, and her pistols tracking Ingrid and Byrnes as the pair of them darted for cover.

The perfect assassin.

And he'd brought her here.

"Malloryn?" Byrnes yelled, his pistol in hand as he shielded Ingrid with his body.

He heard the question in his agent's voice.

And for the first time in years, he didn't know what to do.

He had a clean shot. Both his pistols locked right on the center of her chest as she swung back to face him.

And he couldn't do it.

"Disarm her," he yelled, rolling across the carpet as Gemma shot at him.

An explosion of sound echoed, heat roaring across his skin as her bullet sank into the wall. She was packing those bloody exploding bullets.

Bodies slammed against each other, Byrnes a pale blur as he tried to take her down.

Gemma lost one of her pistols. She spun, ripping something from the holster at her hip.

"Stop!" Malloryn screamed as he saw what she'd reached for.

Black Vein darts.

The only thing that could kill Byrnes.

Byrnes's eyes widened as if he realized, and he blocked her blow as she stabbed at him.

Gemma ducked under Byrnes's arm, spinning beneath his grip as she drove her knee into the side of his. It was like watching a blur. *Chop. Chop. Block. Punch.*

Byrnes met every blow, his forearms slapping against hers, but Malloryn could see he hadn't expected her to match him for speed.

Dhampir were faster than blue bloods.

But Gemma had been training as an assassin since she was a child. They'd stripped her reaction time from her, so everything was pure reflex. They'd taught her how to read the movement, so she was always several steps ahead.

Every time Byrnes countered one of her blows, she was ready for him, already disengaging and striking elsewhere.

Byrnes grunted as another knee took him high in the thigh.

"Step back!" Malloryn demanded, pistol trained on the pair of them.

He couldn't get a clean shot.

The dart flashed silver in the light as Gemma lifted it high, and Malloryn could see the beginning choreography of Gemma's final move as she lured Byrnes into a combination that would prove fatal.

"Ingrid!" Malloryn yelled as Byrnes took a terminal half step too far to the side, leaving himself open.

Ingrid slammed into Byrnes as Gemma drove the dart in. She screamed in verwulfen rage as the dart drove into her back. The pair of them crashed to the floor, but Malloryn had no time to see if Ingrid would be okay.

They'd never tested Black Vein on verwulfen before.

He took the shot.

Aimed for Gemma's knee.

A blur of movement, and Gemma cried out as his bullet clipped her in the side of the thigh.

Snarling in fury, she turned and threw one of her daggers at him.

It missed.

Her arm drew back again. He of all people knew exactly how many knives she had on her.

He'd given her the entire fucking set.

Malloryn threw himself behind a nearby statue, catching another glint of silver coming at him. It ricocheted off the marble, nearly taking his ear off. Malloryn didn't dare flinch—using the statue as cover, he aimed over the top of it.

"Get out of here!" he yelled at Byrnes and Ingrid. "Protect the queen!"

Byrnes dragged Ingrid to her feet, shoving his limping wife toward safety as he tried to pull the embedded dart from her back.

And Gemma hesitated for that fraction of a moment, torn between following them and moving in to finish him off.

His vision narrowed along the line of the pistol, Gemma's red coat becoming little more than a blurred target behind it.

A split second as she turned....

Malloryn cocked the weapon.

His lungs arrested.

The world vanished.

It would all be over....

Take the shot.

Not her, screamed something in his brain. Not the girl who'd saved his life all those years ago when he'd had nothing but ashes in his life. When she'd been the only thing that gave him hope in the endless black.

Breathing hard, Gemma spun around as if she sensed it, giving him the perfect shot.

Right between her breasts.

It was a mistake.

He knew it was a mistake.

But he lowered the pistol and shot her in the knee.

Her right leg went out from under her, and she nearly fell. Gemma screamed, her eyes bleeding to pure black as the craving arose in her.

"It's done," he said hoarsely as he stepped out from behind the statue.

She drew another pistol.

You'll be there to watch them all fall....

Balfour didn't want him dead. It was the only chance they had.

You're the only one who can stop her.

He stepped directly into the hallway, away from the statue he'd been using to shield himself, calling Gemma—and Balfour's bluff.

"Malloryn," she repeated, lifting her pistols toward the ceiling, as if she knew he wasn't to be touched.

A shaky breath left him.

"Put the pistols down, Gemma," he said, pointing both of his directly at her chest as he stepped forward. "I don't want to hurt you—"

Gemma shot him in the shoulder.

He staggered back, realizing the abrupt error in his thinking. Blue bloods could survive a great deal.

If the pair of us went to war, you win. When it comes to pulling the trigger on you, I hesitate. You don't....

How the tables were turned.

Gemma drilled a second bullet into his upper chest, and he hit the floor, the breath slamming out of him.

He couldn't stop her.

Not without killing her.

And even then he didn't know if he was good enough. Not when she was like this.

But he was the only one who *might* be able to take Gemma down face-to-face like this. He just had to get the pistol off her.

Then he gritted his teeth, and hauled himself to his feet, standing between Gemma and the doors to the throne room.

"All right, Gem." Malloryn spat blood. "Let's dance. I know you can't kill me."

She lifted the pistol and smiled an eerie smile. "True. But Balfour wants you alive. Ghost didn't say anything about being unharmed."

Ingrid lurched along the hallway beside her husband, her heart racing and the rush of blood stirring all her instincts. Something wet and sticky dripped down her back, and in some distant part of her brain she knew she'd been injured, but the wild within her had her in its grip, and all she could feel was the fury roaring through her veins.

"Lock the throne room doors!" Byrnes called to the pair of Coldrush Guards who'd snapped into a defensive stance as they heard them coming.

The pair of them looked puzzled, and Ingrid snarled at them. "Where's the queen? Is the queen inside?"

"Court's in session," said one of the guards.

"Where's your lieutenant?" Byrnes skidded to a halt. "Clear the court! There's an assassin in the Tower."

That inspired a flurry of activity.

"Yes, sir!" One man shoved the double doors that led to the throne room open.

Behind them, a sudden hail of gunfire barked.

Ingrid jerked. *Malloryn?*

She stared along the hallway, but there was no sign of him. Only the distant muzzle flash of light flickering in the darkened shadows.

If anyone could stop Gemma, it would be him.

Her verwulfen heart gave a solid squeeze. If only he could do it without hurting her friend....

They could get Gemma back. They had to.

They just needed to work out how to snap her out of this spell she was in.

"We need to get the queen out of here," Ingrid said, meeting Byrnes's eyes. "Just in case."

He nodded. "Are you all right?"

"Fine." Her heartbeat throbbed in her ears. The Black Vein made her feel strange, but it didn't seem to be working upon her the way it would have done to him. "Well, it didn't kill me, so it seems verwulfen are immune to Black Vein."

Something locked around her upper arm. A hand. Byrnes frowned. "You're limping."

"Gemma kicked me in the knee. I'm fine."

"Doesn't mean that poison's not circulating through your system."

"Concentrate, Byrnes. We've got a job to do."

He let her go, but she knew he wouldn't like it.

"What the hell's going on out here?" Jasper Lynch, the Duke of Bleight—and the husband of her best friend, Rosa, came striding through the double doors.

Behind him, she could make out dozens of craned necks, and an entire throne room full of ruffles and silk. Court was in session.

"There's an assassin loose in the Tower and we think she's after the queen," Byrnes said.

Lynch's gray gaze sharpened. "An assassin? How the hell did they get past the guards at the gates and the bottom of the Tower?"

"Long story," Byrnes replied.

"Can you get the queen out?" Ingrid asked. She suddenly realized the gunfire had died down.

Only silence remained.

A prickling of hairs rose along her arms.

"The throne room's secure," Lynch said. Which meant there was no way out, barring through these doors. Hidden passages riddled the tower, but not here, in the heart of the court.

Ingrid head turned toward the scene of the carnage.

There was a shadow rippling over the walls, growing larger as it stalked toward them.

Ingrid shoved Lynch back inside. "Barricade the doors. Whatever you do, don't open them."

He nodded.

The doors slammed shut, and she heard the rasp of something being slid through the handles.

A shadow made of curves and malice, smoke smoldering from the pair of pistols she held, Gemma finally strode into view. Her hips swayed like an exotic snake being charmed, her eyes blank and empty holes as she stared through them to the throne room doors.

"Malloryn's down," Ingrid breathed.

And Malloryn was the most dangerous one of them all. She couldn't believe it.

Was he...? Was he dead?

"What do we do?" she asked Byrnes.

A certain sort of coldness came over his expression, as he turned to meet Gemma. "We stop her."

"No!" Ingrid grabbed his arm, a growl erupting from her throat. "*No.*"

"We don't have a choice," he snapped. "You saw her. She won't hesitate. Malloryn was right; she's lethal. And if we try to take her down without harming her, then she'll kill us." His voice tightened. "She'll kill you, Ingrid. I saw it in her eyes. And I can't allow that."

Ingrid's heart raced, as her thoughts started shifting. Becoming one with the wild inside her. *Friend,* beat the pulse of her verwulfen heart. *Gemma was a friend.*

"No," she said, feeling the wild bleed into her eyes, as everything sped up just a little. "I've got an idea of how to bring her out of this. Stall her."

The hallway circled the interior of the Tower. The only way down was past Gemma—or via the elevation chamber.

"Ingrid!"

"Stall her," she shot over her shoulder. Without her in the line of fire, he'd be able to focus his full attention on taking Gemma down. "And don't get hurt."

Then she was racing down the other branch of the double staircase, away from Gemma, heading for the elevation chamber.

And the one chance any of them had of getting out of this alive without having to kill Gemma.

Gunfire echoed through the hollow core of the Tower.

Obsidian stared up through the interior, his heart beating a little faster. Something was going on. People yelled, and the odd scream punctuated the air, followed by another burst of gunfire.

He pushed his palm against his forehead, his other wrist forced to rise thanks to the cuffs, as he heard that static buzzing in his ears.

Gemma was up there.

And someone was firing his frequencies.

"What the hell is going on?" Charlie whispered, stepping forward into the circle of light that fell through a nearby window and looking up. He unholstered his pistol as lights began ticking through the elevation chamber box. *Level six. Level five. Level four....* Someone was coming down.

"We need to get up there," Obsidian rasped.

The other man shot him a smoky look. "The last place I'm taking you is anywhere near the queen."

"You don't understand," he snarled, pushing his finger against his forehead hard enough to make his skull ache. "Someone's firing the frequencies. I'll bet my life the Chameleon is up there. And so is Gemma."

Charlie stared at him.

"If she dies," he promised softly, "there's not a damned thing in this world that can stop me from killing you."

Charlie glanced at the descending elevation chamber, and then swore under his breath. "I'll go. You're staying here." He gestured toward a nearby door, fumbling with the keys to the handcuffs. "I'm going to chain you to that door. I strongly suggest you don't—"

Obsidian moved like lightning, slamming his elbow up under Charlie's chin.

Charlie's head snapped back, and he hit the floor hard.

Obsidian knelt on his chest in a single fluid motion and grabbed him by the throat. "Don't get up."

He helped himself to the keys, unlocking his right cuff.

Charlie blinked beneath him, and then grabbed Obsidian's wrist. A swivel of his hips, and his legs locked around Obsidian's waist. They crashed to the floor.

Flung apart with a grunt and a pair of punches.

The keys went sliding across the marble, and he still wore the cuff on his left wrist.

Stubborn bloody bastard.

He rolled to his feet as Charlie drove a boot at his face. Obsidian slapped it aside, feinting forward and slamming a punch to Charlie's ribs. A clenched fist smashed into the side of his face, making his ears ring. Charlie ducked under his retaliating blow, and the pair of them broke apart, facing each other with feet spread.

The young man could move.

"You've been training with Gemma," he noted.

Charlie glared at him and spat blood as he brought his fists up. He stepped between Obsidian and the elevation chamber. "Like I said, you're not going anywhere."

It was a shame. He almost liked the young man.

Obsidian feinted to the left, then ducked under the next wide-flung punch, his fingers locking around Charlie's wrist. He twisted, hooking Charlie's arm over his back, and then with a thrust of his thighs, he rolled Charlie over his shoulder and slammed his back to the floor.

Two quick movements, and suddenly Charlie was lying flat on his stomach, one of the cuffs slapped around his wrist. Obsidian twisted the loop of chain around Charlie's other wrist, pinning them behind the young man, and kicked the keys toward himself with his boot.

A flick of the wrist, and he was free.

He snapped the second cuff around Charlie's wrist.

"Shit," the young man swore. He squirmed, his arms tied behind him. "*Bloody hell.*"

"You did better than expected," Obsidian said. "Gemma likes you. She wouldn't want me to hurt you."

"Where the hell do you think you're going?"

"To find Gemma. If someone's shooting at people, she'll be in the midst of it."

The elevation chamber pinged just as he reached the doors and began to slide open.

Ingrid staggered out, blood splashed across her shirt and her eyes wild.

A dash of quick footsteps alerted him.

An arm wrapped around his throat, yanking him back against a bigger body. Charlie got him in a chokehold, no sign of the cuffs.

"Sorry," Charlie gasped. "But I can't let you near the queen."

Obsidian hammered his head back and felt a sharp crack as the back of his head smashed into Charlie's nose. The young man fell back, but one of the cuffs was snapped around Obsidian's right wrist, binding the pair of them together.

"Guess you ain't going anywhere without me," Charlie said.

"How did you—?"

Charlie rubbed at his bleeding nose. "I'm the best thief in the business. You didn't think a set of cuffs was going to hold me?"

Fine. Obsidian stepped forward as Charlie danced lightly on his feet—

"We don't have time for this."

A boot swept his legs out from under him. Obsidian twisted like a cat as he went down, but there was no stopping the fall. He hit the marble and rolled, flinging his hands up to protect his throat as Ingrid pressed her boot there.

He gripped the boot, his breath rushing through him, and thought about it.

"I don't know what's going on, but I need you up there." Her eyes were pure bronze, given over entirely to the wolf within. "It's Gemma. Gemma's the Chameleon. And you're my only chance of stopping her without having to put a bullet in her head."

Gemma.

A chill ran through him.

A stillness.

"How?"

He sat up abruptly as Ingrid stepped back, all the heat in his body seeming to retreat.

"*What?*" Charlie groaned as he rolled to his side. She'd taken him down too.

"I'll explain in the elevation chamber," she snapped, hauling Obsidian to his feet. "Something's come over her— her eyes are so blank it looks like there's nobody inside, and Isabella said she wasn't the Chameleon, Gemma was, and Malloryn's down—"

"The neural implant," he whispered.

But when had—?

Of course. When the baroness and Gemma were assaulted. Gemma had escaped, but it had been almost twenty-four hours she'd been missing for. Long enough for the doctor to implant the neural implant if they were prepared, and her CV levels were high enough to heal any sign of the swift surgery.

They'd all thought she'd escaped, but had she?

Or had Ghost deliberately let her go?

Rage burned through him like a combustion engine stoked high.

"What neural implant?" Charlie demanded. He hadn't been in the original briefing.

"Keys?" Ingrid snapped, and Charlie unlocked the pair of them from their cuffs.

"There's a device implanted in her brain," Obsidian said as Ingrid stabbed the buttons to the throne room floor. "Gemma's still in there, but it's overriding her control of her body. She'll do things she'd never want to do, hurt people she'd never want to hurt."

She wouldn't be able to stop herself.

He *knew* the feeling far too well.

"How do we stop her?" Ingrid smelled like panic. "She's going after the queen. Byrnes is trying to slow her down, but if he can't lock her out of the throne room.... If she gets inside.... We have to stop her from killing the queen. He'll have to *stop* her."

The fucking elevation chamber wasn't moving fast enough. He paced the small cage, knowing what she was saying. The only way to stop Gemma was to kill her. "Leave Gemma to me."

"She'll try and kill you."

A hollow sensation echoed around his heart. "I *know*."

Because he'd been there once himself, on the inside looking out as his body pulled the trigger, no matter how much he screamed inside....

It was all starting to come back to him. All the things he'd never wanted to remember.

A sudden concussive force slammed the elevation chamber from side to side. Obsidian staggered into Charlie, then pushed away from the walls as the chamber stabilized. They weren't moving.

"What was that?" Ingrid demanded.

"Explosion." He looked up through the roof.

"She's taken out the power grid to the elevation chamber," Charlie said, stabbing buttons and trying to work the lever. "She knows we're coming. We're not moving."

"We're trapped in here," Ingrid snarled.

A second explosion rocked them.

He could hear a winch squealing as if the weight of the chamber strained the pulley system above them. They had to be close to the top. The explosion sounded like it had come from barely fifty feet away.

Screams.

Someone yelling.

"Damn it!" Ingrid tried to push her fingers through the double doors. A thin gap of light splayed through. Muscle flexed beneath her sleeves, but the doors held firm.

"Locking mechanism's in place," Charlie said, prying open the electrical panel that operated the door and surveying the wires inside. "Give me a minute or two."

No time for this.

Obsidian looked up.

Punching a hole through one of the brass panels on the ceiling, he hooked his hands on either sides of the hole, then curled his body and slammed his heels up through the roof. Brass rivets popped and strained. He kicked again. Light shone through.

"Or we could do that," Charlie muttered below him.

"Follow me," Obsidian called, and hooked his legs up through the opening he'd created before curling his body up after him.

The throne room doors were blown off their hinges, smoke pouring through them.

"Caleb!" Ingrid slid to the side of her fallen husband, trying to discover where he was bleeding. Byrnes gritted his teeth and clapped a hand against his side, dark blood staining his fingers.

"Couldn't take her down," Byrnes gasped. "She was trying to kill me."

And Byrnes had been trying to merely incapacitate her.

"I need you to get one of those electric stunners the guards use," Obsidian told Charlie and Ingrid, because the last thing he needed was someone else getting in the way. "I'll stop her from reaching the queen, but I need the stunner to destroy the neural implant's hold on her."

A dozen guards in blue and gold were hovered around the queen on the dais. Blue blood lords and their ladies screamed and scrambled to get out of the way as Gemma advanced, scattering like a flock of rampaging peacocks.

But Gemma herself moved like a lethal vision, bending to roll a handful of her smoke bombs across the floor toward the line of Coldrush Guards that remained the last line of defense for the precarious human queen.

"Ready," shouted a Coldrush lieutenant as the line of his guards knelt and locked their rifles upon Gemma. "Aim—"

She'd never survive.

Obsidian was sprinting before he knew it, fists pumping at his sides.

She stared to turn toward him, pistols coming up, but he smashed into her.

"Fire!" someone bellowed.

They slammed into the marble floors, sliding into the brass circle where blue blood duels were fought. Bullets spat past them, whining through the air.

Then the bombs exploded, and suddenly the air was thick and roiling with black smoke as the chemical elements inside them mixed. Several of the guards started coughing and spluttering.

"I can't see her!" someone yelled.

"Get the queen out!"

"Did you miss me?" Obsidian asked her, as Gemma stared up at him for one breathless second.

He urged her to see him.

To know him.

But there was nothing but blankness in her expression, and suddenly he realized how she must have felt all those years ago, to see the man she loved betray her.

Crouching low, he gestured for her to come at him. If she was focused on him, the she couldn't hurt anyone else.

A vicious leg swept toward him, smashing into his jaw.

Then Gemma was upon him in a single leap, her thighs locking around his face and throat. Slamming her fists down upon his head, she threw her body weight to the side, but he leaned back into it, spinning her through the air instead.

An elbow rammed into his ear.

Obsidian squatted and slammed her back onto the floor, trying to pin her with his body weight. He thrust his arm across her throat to try and choke her out. If he could make her black out, he'd have a chance to secure her without injuring her. Gemma gasped, momentarily winded. Those thick, dark lashes blinked once. Twice. Blood flooded her face, mottling her skin.

"Go to sleep, sweetheart," he whispered. "You've got to go to sleep so we can get this thing out of you."

She smashed the flat of her palm into his elbow, and his arm slipped.

Then it was like holding a writhing, spitting cat that knew he'd almost taken her down. Gemma fought to kill now, holding nothing back, and it was all he could do not to hurt her.

"Don't shoot!" Ingrid yelled nearby. "Get me one of your stunners!"

Every move he made was countered. A thumb gouged toward his eye, and the second he flinched back, her legs were swiveling and locking around his waist. They rolled, and he threw his weight across her, so they rolled again.

A shadow blurred over her shoulder as they flipped.

Then something smashed down over her shoulder. He felt the arm give as it popped from its socket. Gemma screamed.

Obsidian flipped her onto her stomach, forcing her other arm up behind her beck. Ingrid knelt on her, holding the long pole of a stunner with its loop of wire around the end.

They got the loop of the shocker around Gemma's throat as she kicked and thrashed. He didn't dare let go of her as Ingrid stepped back and gripped the end of the stunner.

"Shock her!"

Ingrid's eyes narrowed, and he saw her realize he understood he'd be hit with the current too.

"*Do it.*"

The first lance of electricity sparked through him, slamming into his elbow as if a lead pipe had hit him there, and then arcing through his gut and throat. Obsidian's heels drummed on the ground, a scream vibrating in his throat as current poured through him.

He lost control of his entire body.

Lost his grip on Gemma.

Pain vanished instantly, as if it was finally, blessedly over.

Obsidian collapsed on the ground. He'd somehow landed face-first, and slumped there, gasping and dribbling on the floor. Every nerve in his body shook, and the world around him swam.

"Gem—"

He could sense people crowding in. Sense skirts swishing past him, and shoes.

"Where the hell is Malloryn?" one of the dukes on the council demanded.

There'd been files on all of them.

Photographs of their faces printed and pinned to the wall so all the *dhampir* would know their faces.

Lynch. The Duke of Bleight.

"I don't know. He tried to stop her." Ingrid.

"Arrest her!" The Coldrush Guards swarmed past him to the still figure lying on the floor of the throne room, motionless.

No.

Obsidian managed to find strength from somewhere, and pushed to his hands and knees.

They slapped cuffs on her. Hauled her upright, where she screamed as her shoulder popped again, and then slumped in their arms unconscious.

"Lynch." Byrnes snagged the duke's arm. "It wasn't her. There's some kind of neural implant in her head that made her do this. You can't let them hurt her."

The duke's implacable gray gaze swept across Obsidian, then raked over Gemma as if he saw everything in a single moment. "I'll take charge."

He strode after her, and Byrnes breathed a sigh of relief.

Someone knelt at Obsidian's side, helping to steady him. Charlie. "Well. Guess you weren't the one we needed to watch."

"I need to be there," Obsidian gasped, struggling to stand, "when she wakes."

Charlie sighed and slipped under his shoulder. "You shouldn't be going anywhere."

"Lynch has got it in hand," Byrnes said, still looking somewhat shocked. He crossed to his wife's side and examined the blood on the back of her shirt.

"No. You don't understand." He grabbed Charlie's wrist. "Gemma loves you all, especially Malloryn. If he's dead...."

If she'd killed him....

"This will destroy her."

CHAPTER TWENTY-FIVE

Adele Hamilton— No. Adele *Cavill*, she had to remember, fled along the hallway, her fists full of skirts, and her sister at her side.

"This way," she snapped to Hattie.

Round and round they went, clambering down the enormous double staircase that circled the hollow interior of the Ivory Tower.

She didn't know what was going on. Hattie had been having a minor attack of hysteria in the powder room when an explosion rippled through the tower. But Adele hadn't been part of this court for so many years without learning when to run, and the one thing in this world she loved was her younger sister.

She had to get Hattie safely out of here.

"Adele!" Hattie gasped, staggering into a wall. "I don't think... I can run... anymore."

Each breath Adele took strained her own corset until it felt like her ribs were trapped in a vise. She'd barely recovered from her assault on the day of her first wedding attempt. Adele collapsed against her younger sister's side, grabbing her by the wrist. Hattie's cheeks were flushed with exertion.

"I don't know if it's safe to stop," she said, glancing up. Shouts echoed down through the tower. "I don't know what's going on—and I don't intend to find out."

Blue bloods were dangerous, and it was the humans around them—like her and her sister—who often suffered when they were caught up in blue blood schemes.

There was no knowing where her husband was, but he could take care of himself.

Indeed, she'd be surprised if Malloryn even gave her a thought.

It would probably be convenient if I died here today.

Not if she could help it.

"Oh, my goodness!" Hattie suddenly burst out. "Is that blood? There's a... a dead woman."

Adele's head snapped sharply around.

A trail of darkened blood smeared the red carpets just around the corner. A handprint of bluish red marred the perfect ivory walls, and a door leading into the room beyond swung eerily open.

In the middle of the carpet lay a woman in bloodred skirts, her dark hair tumbled across the floor and a coat covering her face.

"Is she—?"

"Stay here." Adele's ears started ringing, as she swept toward the fallen stranger.

There was no pulse in the woman's throat, and someone had clasped her hands across her breasts in a position of repose. Adele swallowed hard and lifted the coat to see who had—

She let it fall the second she saw what remained. Gorge rising, Adele turned away swiftly. *Oh, my goodness.* Hattie stared at her in shock, her lovely blonde curls swept into an elegant chignon and her face paling when she saw the horror on Adele's.

"Who is it?" Hattie whispered.

Adele could barely speak. She pressed the back of her hand to her lips. Baroness Schröder. Her husband's mistress.

That poor woman.

And I hated her.

"What's going on?" Hattie's voice grew small. "They're fighting upstairs, and there's a dead woman in the halls, and..." Her green gaze flickered to the bloody handprint on the wall and the door that lay ajar. "And someone's hurt."

Adele recognized the darker color of the blood. Whoever was bleeding, they weren't human.

And someone had killed the baroness.

A blue blood?

Adele swallowed hard. There was no time to give in to hysteria. "Stay here. I'll see if he's still breathing." There were so few female blue bloods it had to be a man who'd left that much blood on the floors.

"Are you certain that's wise?"

An excellent point. If they were injured, then they might be potentially dangerous. Who knew what the craving might do to a blue blood who was weakened—and hungry? "You hurry past. I'll try and latch the door so he can't come after us."

"I don't want to be out here with her!"

"She's not going to hurt you. She's dead. I'll shut the door so we can safely pass."

Adele prepared the hemlock ring on her finger, flicking one of the fine silver thorns out. Hemlock beaded at the tip like a raindrop.

One that could drop a blue blood where he stood.

Creeping toward the door, she reached for the handle, a nervous flutter turning her insides to mush. If someone leapt out at her she was probably going to scream.

Then hemlock him.

Except there was nothing moving in the room inside.

Adele's breath broke from her lips in relief, and she swiftly yanked the door toward her to close it and—

That was when she saw the man's boots.

Adele froze.

A man lay on the floor inside, a bloody trail leading from the door to his body, as if he'd dragged himself as far as he could before he passed out. Buckskin trousers caressed a firm backside and the white silk of his waistcoat—court attire—was ruined.

She took a cautious step inside, prepared to flee at any moment if he leapt up from the floor, but he didn't move.

One hand was outflung, his fingers slackened as if he'd been trying to reach for something.

There was a gun on the floor, barely three feet from his outstretched arm.

And worse.

Adele would recognize the gold signet ring on his finger anywhere.

"Malloryn," she gasped, shoving the door open wide enough to allow her skirts.

Her husband lay unmoving, a spreading pool of darkened blood puddling beneath his chest. For a second she thought him dead, but the faint wheeze of air through his chest revealed life—even if the sound of it seemed like a steam engine on its last gasps.

Adele rushed to her fallen husband's side, rolling him onto his side.

He wasn't moving.

Was barely breathing at all. Blood ruined his trousers, both knees a sticky and wet mess. Bruises mottled the side of his face, and his chest—

He'd been shot at least four or five times.

Adele took stock. This hadn't been an altercation between a blue blood and his mistress. There was no way the baroness had managed to inflict this much damage upon him. Someone else had done this.

"Is he dead?" Hattie whispered from her vantage point in the doorway.

Adele found the flickering pulse in his throat. Blue bloods were insanely difficult to kill, but the blood.... Everywhere.

"You've barely been married a handful of days, and you might already be a widow."

Adele leaned over him. With his eyelashes closed over those dangerously piercing eyes, and his lips faintly parted, Malloryn looked almost peaceful. Nothing like the broodingly intense duke who'd told her the night of their wedding she'd be keeping a cold married bed for the rest of her life.

"Do as you will, Adele. I don't give a damn. As long as you don't do it near me."

"You'll inherit enough to live your own life, Adele," Hattie said in a wondering voice. "Mother and Father shall never be able to touch you again, and you won't have to deal with *him* ever again."

"*Hattie,*" she admonished.

She didn't want her husband dead. She never had.

He wasn't... cruel.

Merely indifferent.

He hates you, a little voice whispered.

But he'd saved her from a life of penniless dependence upon her mother and father, who'd been pushing her to make an alliance with lords she hated—and couldn't trust. Malloryn didn't *have* to marry her, after all.

She owed him.

And he needed blood.

Badly.

"Shut the door," she said firmly as she flipped open Malloryn's waistcoat, searching in his pocket for the small bloodletting kit every blue blood lord carried about his person.

Hattie gasped. "You're not going to bleed yourself! Adele, he's unconscious and injured! You know the rules."

Every thrall worth her brass knew the rules.

Blue bloods were dangerous in an unconscious or injured state. During their lessons in etiquette, pianoforte, flesh rights, blood rights, and dancing, their instructor had told both girls what to do in the event they gained a happy thrall contract.

Don't ever approach an injured blue blood.

Don't ever cut yourself in front of a hungry blue blood.

Don't ever fight him if he grabs you, or cuts you. It only excites them more.

Surrender. Surrender and you might just live.

Well, she was done surrendering. She'd finally found a way to protect herself, and Malloryn wasn't going to bloody well thwart her now.

"I cannot just leave him here! He needs blood." And like it or not, she was the only one who was available to offer it.

It would barely hurt at all.

She knew from experience, even as her heart gave a threatening lurch. Adele gritted her teeth as a flash of memory overtook her, leaving her momentarily struggling on a garden bench under the weight of Lord Abagnale as he shoved her down and slashed her throat and took what he wanted from her, regardless of how much she begged.

She locked it all away, refusing to allow those *vile creatures* to drag her back into the shadows that haunted her. She was Adele Cavill. She wasn't about to let a bunch of pasty-faced vultures scare her.

And Malloryn could tear at her all he liked. The hemlock ring on her finger wet her knuckles, ready to hand him a hefty dose of paralysis if he lost control of himself.

It might almost be worth it to see the look of shock on his face if she had him on the ground at her feet, and at her mercy.

We'll see who doesn't give a damn then.

"Get out of here," Adele said firmly as she found his kit and removed the thin lancet he used.

Setting it to her wrist, she paused. The wrist was less intimate, but she needed her hands free so she could paralyze him if she needed.

It had to be the throat.

Adele undid her ornate choker from where it hid her scars and dropped the pearls on the floor.

Hattie's eyes widened in fright. "Adele!"

"Go. He won't hurt me."

And this was something she didn't want another to witness.

She didn't want to scare her sister, for Hattie was still young enough to believe she'd make a happy arrangement and be loved and cherished by her future master.

Adele couldn't bring herself to shatter Hattie's foolish dreams.

Hattie slammed the door shut, leaving her in the dark with her husband.

Adele cut herself swiftly, dragging her fingers across the small mark. Another scar to add to her collection, for she doubted Malloryn would have the wherewithal to use his saliva to heal her wounds at the end.

"Malloryn?" she whispered, reaching out with bloodied fingers to waft them beneath his nose.

His head turned as he drew in a sudden, sharp breath.

Adele let her fingertips trace his mouth. It was the closest she'd ever been to him, and her heart was suddenly pounding.

If one was being strictly honest with oneself, then one could concede one's husband was a physically fine specimen.

And that was almost the outmost limit of "ones" she could allow in a single sentence.

Perfect chiseled lips. The slant of a hawkish grace to his cheekbones. The allure of his broad shoulders, and those lean hips that cast an excellent cut to his coat and trousers.

Malloryn was the epitome of dangerous, moving with all the fine instincts of a predator in broadcloth. She often watched him when he thought her eye elsewhere, for it wasn't as though she'd ever know him. Physically.

But for one brief second, she was allowed to touch him....

His tongue darted out, touching the sensitive pads of her fingertips and tasting the blood there. A drop of blood slid down over her collarbone and pooled between the hollow of her breasts.

His lashes fluttered.

Black pupils absorbed all the merciless color from his eyes, and her breath caught when she saw how deep in the darkness he was. He wouldn't even know her in this moment, and it was said that a blue blood in the grip of the craving was at the mercy of his basest, most primal instincts.

Malloryn hated her for what she'd done to him.

What if he tore her apart?

The thin veneer of civility was gone. Obliterated. All that remained was hunger and need and sheer, furious desire. There was no sign of her ice-cold husband in his black eyes when he looked up at her. The craving had him in its thrall.

He lifted his head, the air wheezing through his punctured lung. Adele swallowed hard and helped ease him to her throat.

"You need a little blood, Your Grace," she whispered, for brash, calculating Adele was nowhere to be seen.

Traitor.

All that was left was her stammering pulse and the sudden tension in her lower abdomen, and a small blossoming seed of hope she'd thought she'd extinguished.

Malloryn's breath exhaled across the upper slope of her breasts, his gaze locking on that trail of blood as she drew him higher. Something cool and wet met her skin, and she gasped in surprise as she realized it was His Grace's tongue. He licked the blood from between her breasts, his hand sliding up the slope of her ribs just beneath the curve of her breasts.

Instantly, heat flushed through her. "Your Grace!"

Well within his rights, of course, but she'd never been touched there. The experience was worlds away from the diagrams she'd been shown and the exotic painted pictures of how precisely a man would take a woman.

And a part of her wanted him to move that hand higher, until it lay on her skin, cupping the soft weight of her breast....

Not to be, of course.

For that was when the predator awoke.

Fingers curled around her throat, wrenching her head to the side, and Adele gasped as her husband rose above her with swift demonic hunger, his tongue tracing from her breasts to her throat.

Hunting the source of it.

The shock of his heavy weight slamming her down to the floor drove the breath from her lungs. Then his cool mouth was upon her throat, and he sucked. Hard. Adele cried out as a pulse of aching need lit through her body, ending right between her legs. It was the first time he'd willingly touched her, apart from the moment he slid the ring on her finger during their consort ceremony.

"Malloryn!"

Her legs were spread obscenely, Malloryn's narrow hips pressing insistently between them. This wasn't what she'd expected.

Don't fight him.

It was hard to disobey her instincts, her skirts crushed between them and her hand fisted in his hair.

Adele lay back and surrendered, her heart pounding rashly through her veins and the ring resting innocuously against the back of his neck. A single twist of her hand and he'd be poisoned.

But she needed to get some blood into him first.

It took long moments to realize this was not the same as all the other times she'd been forcibly bled.

Malloryn's cologne was so familiar, she couldn't mistake whom she was with. And she'd chosen to allow this, which made all the difference. His thumb began to stroke her throat as he drank, sliding down to her collarbone, then lower, as if tracing the pattern of her veins. Fingertips brushed the lace covering her breasts, and Adele died a small death as she squirmed beneath him.

Oh, God.

It felt... incredibly good.

There was also, she suddenly realized, a rather insistent part of him pressing intimately against her thigh.

"Malloryn?" she gasped as his hips thrust against her.

She was no innocent. There'd been rather detailed lessons on a young lady's flesh rights and what to expect if she chose to give them to her new protector.

The act of taking blood was a sensual one, with the chemicals in a blue blood's saliva inducing release. Indeed, though she'd never felt the merest hint of pleasure in all the times she'd been cut and bled, she could feel it curling through her now with insidious, stroking fingers.

The situation changed.

Adele's swollen breasts pressed into her stays, the flesh between her thighs growing damp as Malloryn rocked against her. His hand cupped her breast, squeezing faintly, and Adele's eyes went wide with shock, for she was fairly certain he was going to deflower her on the floor of the Ivory Tower in a pool of blood if she wasn't careful.

"Malloryn! Stop!" She slammed an open palm to his shoulder.

He drew back with a gasp.

Rested his forehead on her shoulder for a long, drawn-out moment, his hand stilling on the curve of her breast.

Adele lay equally still, her heart rabbiting in her chest as though a dozen hounds hunted it.

Well. This was awkward.

She cleared her throat. "Your Grace. Are you feeling better?"

"Adele?" he rasped, as if her identity until that moment had been uncertain.

For a brief second, Adele regretted not hemlocking him. "Of course it's me. Who did you damned well think you were... rolling about on the floor with?"

Malloryn raised his head, his mouth dark with her blood, the move driving his hips between her thighs as he strained to lift himself.

Adele squeaked.

He looked utterly horrified and jerked his hand away from her breast. "What the devil are you doing?"

"What does it look like?" she snapped.

He stared at her, those black eyes still hungry, but a vague hint of uncertainty resting within them, as if he actually *didn't* know what she'd been doing.

"Relax, Your Grace," she said in an acid voice, though her cheeks flamed. "I was hardly trying to force a consummation. I found you on the floor. You were barely breathing, and you needed blood. Ergo, I gave you blood. Our current predicament is due purely to your intentions."

He pushed to a sitting position, tearing a handkerchief from his waistcoat pocket and blotting the blood from his lips as if he'd been poisoned. "*You* gave me blood?"

Somehow Adele pushed to her feet, swaying a little as her head swam. Her skirts were all in disarray. Her body rampaged. She nearly tipped over, but Malloryn was suddenly tucked under her arm.

"You've given too much," he accused, as if she'd had a choice in the matter.

"Again, not by choice."

He'd overwhelmed her. Not by force, but by sensation.

Adele suffered the horrible feeling she'd been about to reach her pleasure beneath her husband.

Malloryn caught her chin firmly, examining the gash on her throat. She thought he muttered "Rutting hell" under his breath before he leaned down swiftly and licked the wound to try and seal it.

The small gesture almost made her eyes dampen.

She had a dozen scars there. Small, white little slashes that marred the perfection of the throat. *Used goods*, in a blue blood world.

There was no need to, but she appreciated the effort, for no one else had ever given a damn.

"You need to sit," he snarled, towing her toward a nearby chair. "What the hell's going on? How did you get down here?" He looked around sharply as if a thought occurred. "The *queen.*"

"Haven't you heard all the ruckus?" she asked in a bemused voice, still feeling. "I'm fairly certain someone set off an explosion near the throne room. And there's a body in the hallway. Your mistress, I think."

There went the last traces of his discomposure. Malloryn went shockingly still, reverting to his icy persona.

"Are you all right?" he demanded.

She nodded. "Hattie's out in the hall. I didn't want her to see."

"Good. Stay here."

Then he limped toward the door, his right leg dragging, as if he'd already forgotten her.

Light began to penetrate her closed eyelids. A gentle hand stirred through her hair. Gemma blinked awake, the familiar shape of a man's lips bare inches from her own. Ashen brown hair fanned around his face like a halo.

"Dima?" she whispered.

Fingertips traced her cheek. "I'm here. I wanted to be here when you woke up."

Woke up?

God. She felt like every inch of her had been pummeled, and her throat burned. Gemma tried to lift her hand, but it was trapped against her body. What on earth—?

"Here. Take it easy." Obsidian helped her to sit.

Gemma swayed, looking at the heavy stone walls and the barred door. Her left arm was strapped across her chest in a leather sling somewhat akin to a straitjacket, and every inch of her body ached. Pain pounded behind her temples, like an ice pick straight through her right eye.

"Where am I?" she slurred.

What had happened? Was that blood on her split skirts?

"We're in Thorne Tower."

Thorne Tower?

Home to traitors, violent murderers, and dangerous political dissidents. And this time she was on the other side of the bars. Gemma's head jerked up, and suddenly it all came rushing back to her in a jumbled mess. There was blood splashed through her memories. Byrnes screaming at her. A flash of Ingrid's face. The *bang-bang-bang* of the gun in her hand, and an odd image of Malloryn crawling away from her, leaving a smear of blood behind him as she stalked toward him, bringing the pistol up—

"Where is Malloryn?" she whispered hoarsely, because her memories ended there, watching him crawl for the forlorn pistol on the ground as she lifted her pistol and pointed it at the back of his head.

"I don't know. They weren't going to lock me up, but I insisted. I didn't want you to be alone. The last I heard he was missing."

The hot flush of not-tears swept through the back of her sinuses. A sound broke from her chest; a squeaky wheeze that sounded like something dying.

Damn it. She knew herself.

She didn't miss when she meant to kill.

Obsidian held his arms out.

"You shouldn't touch me." Not when there was blood on her hands. Not when there was so much darkness staining her soul—

"I'm not afraid of your darkness, Gemma," he told her, and she realized she must have breathed the words out loud. "There's nothing inside you that could ever make me turn away. Your darkness is but a mirror to mine."

He knew.

She looked up helplessly, but he merely held his arms open as if she belonged there.

And then she was in them, and they wrapped around her, bringing with them all the absolution she'd been hoping to find.

"It's not your fault," he murmured, stroking her hair.

"They put that cursed neural implant in my head, didn't they?" All her memories were scrambled. She could barely piece together the last few days, let alone... today? Had it happened today?

"Yes. I had to shock you with one of the guards' stunners to bring you down." Obsidian began to explain, telling her everything he knew.

Oh, my goodness. Isabella was dead. Malloryn... missing. It was all too much for her.

"I'm here." He picked her up in his arms, dragging her onto his lap as he slid onto the trundle bed.

It was all starting to come back, little fragments starting to piece themselves into the pattern.

Isabella looking at her. Saying those words.

London Bridge is falling down....

Light draining out of the world until it felt like she was staring down a narrow tunnel. At the end of the tunnel she could hear Malloryn's voice. Byrnes. Ingrid. Obsidian. But it was like looking through the wrong end of a telescope.

All that remained was a high-pitched whine in her ears and a voice.

"Your mission is to kill the queen."

What happens if someone gets in my way?

"You must kill the queen."

But what if—?

"Kill. The. Queen."

A hollow silence.

"Or die trying."

Suddenly she could see it all running swiftly through her head, as if someone had sped up the action. Byrnes stepping between her and the throne room, a determined look on his face and his hands held defensively.

Men in the Coldrush uniforms sprinting toward her and then falling, one by one by one. A bullet hole slammed through a man's forehead, and Gemma squeezed her eyes shut, trying to forget the look of shock on his face as he fell.

Blood on her hands....

Splashed across her memories....

"And the... others?" she whispered, half afraid of the answer.

"Alive." A warm hand rubbed her back. "Ingrid wanted you to know she was sorry for dislocating your shoulder. And Byrnes said to tell you he's still picking bullet fragments out of his ass, but he appreciates the fact you shot him there and not in the head. He also said something about how you were wrong; you're top of the list. I don't know what he meant by that."

Gemma broke into a laugh-sob, because that sounded so like Byrnes, and yet at the same time she knew exactly what the bastard was trying to tell her. What Ingrid was trying to tell her.

This time the real sobs began, racking through her chest.

Obsidian's arms squeezed her tighter, and Gemma wrapped herself around him desperately. Her fingers curled in the slick leather of his coat, and her face nuzzled into the crook of his throat as she let it all out.

She needed this so badly.

Strong arms to protect her from the rest of the world. From herself. Kisses that scattered over her cheek and forehead, cool against the heated flush of her skin.

Someone who could understand her, who would never flinch from the darkness within her, because he had his own share of ghosts.

"The memories fade," he said softly, rubbing her back.

And she had the sudden horrible realization he spoke from experience.

Who had been there for Obsidian when he woke with blood on his hands?

What had it felt like to know it had been *her* blood?

Had he searched for her?

It was one thing to hear him speak of it, quite another to know deep in her gut exactly how it *felt* to have the blood of someone you loved on your hands.

"How do you deal with it?" she choked out. "How do you ever let yourself forget?"

"I'm not the one you should ask for advice. I wanted to forget. I wanted to carve the pain from my heart, and so I asked Ghost to put me through a year's worth of conditioning under Dr. Richter's special treatment—the kind he used for X. I got what I asked for. I lost all my memories of you. They tortured them out of me until the mere thought of you brought pain.

"It wasn't until we arrived here last year to enact Balfour's revenge scheme that I began to remember. The first time I saw you it was like a knife to the chest. I hadn't realized Ghost asked Richter to reprogram me at the same time. Every time I saw you I hated you, but I couldn't hurt you. It drove me crazy to crave your presence so much and not understand why. Touching your skin reawakened some part of me they'd locked deep within. Kissing you reignited all I'd ever felt for you. When I kidnapped you, the conditioning started to fail, and you began to bloom in my heart, until those memories started to resurface."

He looked at her intently. "Don't do what I did, *lyubov moya*. It hurts to know you were used to make others suffer. It should hurt. Gaining back everything I lost is worth all the pain in the world, just to know you again."

She swallowed.

Hard.

"And I will be there for you," he whispered, lacing their fingers together as he lowered his mouth to hers for a glancing kiss. "Every step of the way. For you are mine. You've always been mine. I will take your pain for you if you cannot bear it. I will guard your back when your heart is heavy. But you are stronger than me, and neither of us knows what is going on out there. It might not be... too bad. Don't think the worst. Not until we know the facts."

We. It made all the difference. "What now?"

He hesitated, and she felt it.

"The Council is considering what to do with you. Without Malloryn around to speak on your behalf, there was talk of execution. I believe Charlie had a word with his mentor, Blade, and both he and the Duke of Bleight pushed for the Council to hold their vote until they had all the facts, but it concerns me. The queen is frightened. She doesn't understand what happened. All she sees is how close you came to taking her life. I didn't wish to wait to discover what her verdict is, so I came with you just in case I needed to get you out."

Execution.

Her blood ran cold. All she could see were the faces of those Coldrush Guards. "Perhaps I deserve it."

"If you're going to say such foolish things, then I swear I shall leave you here to face your fate. *Da*, your body pulled the trigger," Obsidian snapped, "but you were controlled with the neural implant. The question is, my love, are you going to let those who controlled you get away with it?"

He might as well have slapped her.

"Are you going to let them win, Gemma? Because that doesn't sound very much like the woman I know."

Fury flared. She'd been so focused on what she'd done that she hadn't considered the alternatives.

Someone planted that damned thing in her head.

Someone sent her to kill the queen.

Of all the torments she'd suffered in her life, the sheer indignity of having her own will stolen from her was the worst. "You have a point."

"Good. There's one more thing you need to know.... It's Balfour, Gemma."

For a second she didn't think she'd heard him correctly. What did Lord Balfour have to do—

And then every inch of her went cold, as she realized he was watching her carefully, the muscle in his shoulders tensing as if prepared for her reaction.

"Lord Balfour is still alive," he said softly. "He's the true enemy. The one setting all the pieces into play...."

"*What?*"

She saw again the school. Her training masters. A fellow student, lying on the ground before her, the only thing standing between her and survival.

"Pull the trigger, cadet."

And she'd hesitated, until that student scrambled for his forsaken knife.

It was the first time she'd ever killed.

She'd never forget that bloodied mist.

The sound her fellow student's body made when it hit the ground.

"Good." A hand coming to rest upon her shoulder. *"Lord Balfour will be pleased with your progress, cadet. You have passed your year end exams."*

The sickening lurch in Gemma's chest almost brought up her gorge. She could never scrub that image from her mind. She could never forget the name of the man who'd shaped her.

The one who'd sent her to kill Malloryn, because she *looked* like the woman he'd once loved.

"How?" *He died.*

Obsidian brushed a strand of hair from her cheek, watching her expression as if to gauge her response. "Balfour was taking the *elixir vitae* before Malloryn cut his throat the night of the revolution. In the advanced stages of the Fade, death creates a vampire, but it only exacerbates the elixir's effects upon the craving virus. When Balfour resurrected he woke in a coffin. You have to physically remove a *dhampir's* heart or decapitate him in order to truly kill him.

"He's the one who gathered us together after Falkirk burned. He's the one we pledged our fealty to. I've been working for him for over a decade, though never in the open." A flicker of consternation crossed his face, and he pressed his hand to his head. "I can't remember why I agreed to it. All he's ever done is destroy our brotherhood, and turn Ghost into the man he is now. But Balfour's behind everything. I should have told you earlier. I-I never realized how much you hated him—how much he'd hurt you—until that night when you told me of your past. Gemma, I would never.... I would never have worked for him if I'd known what he did to you."

She couldn't seem to breathe.

Balfour.

Alive.

It all made so much sense.

She pressed her unsteady fingers to her mouth. The day's events were pure Balfour. He and Malloryn had hated each other with a passion that could burn London to the ground. Of course, he'd have wanted Malloryn to suffer.

And how better to do it than to wield her as the weapon that would cut the duke down?

This was twice now that Lord Balfour sent her to kill Malloryn.

And rage bloomed within her like a flame given oxygen.

"He's currently in Russia," Obsidian murmured. "Please say something, Gemma. I'm sorry. I should have told you."

"Yes, you should have damned well told me!" Unable to control her fury, she smashed her fist against his chest. "I hate him. I hate him so much. He stole over half my life from me. He made me what I never wanted to be."

Obsidian took the blow, and the second.

Gemma's rage snarled in her chest as she saw the look upon his face. The quiet acceptance as if he'd expected to be punished for this secret. Her third blow paused, her fist hovering in the air between them.

He too, had been forged by Balfour.

His memories stripped from him. His choices stolen. What did he know of trust? Even now, she could sense him holding a part of himself back, as if to protect himself.

He was trying.

And surely he would fail at times, for every instinct trained into him taught him to guard himself first. He'd never learned how to reveal the secret depths of his heart.

But he'd thrown his lot in with Malloryn's for *her*.

He'd betrayed everything he'd ever known for *her*.

Gemma's sudden fury drained out of her, and she opened her closed fist, splaying it wide across his chest, gasping a little at the sudden fierce ache of pain. Of understanding.

For all she'd lost, this man had lost more.

He'd lost himself.

"I didn't want you to hate me. I didn't know what to do—how to tell you. It was a shock to discover he'd had a hand in forging both of us, and then there was no time," Obsidian admitted. "I have been so lost, Gemma. Everything I ever believed.... It means nothing. Everywhere I look, I see an enemy trying to manipulate me, even Malloryn. You have been my one constant. The only guiding star I could see in any of this, but even then I wasn't sure how much I could trust you."

She swallowed the hard lump in her throat. "Balfour *used* me to hurt Malloryn. He knew it would be the one thing that could twist the knife in Malloryn's chest."

"I know." Gentle fingers brushed a strand of hair behind her ear. "He was the one who demanded we have you assassinated and delivered to Malloryn's doorstep to find. It was the first moment of my awakening. I have never felt such rage before, and I couldn't understand why. But it led me back to you. As much as I hate him for what he's done to you, I will never regret finding you again."

His head dipped, lips brushing against her ear. "I trust you, as much as I can. I trust your judgment. But to give so much of myself goes against my very nature. I will try to do better, I promise. If you could ever forgive me?"

Gemma turned her mouth to his, her hand clasped over his cheek. The roughened trace of his stubble— something she'd never felt upon his jaw before—reminded her this man was real. Flawed. And hers.

"There is nothing to forgive," she breathed, pressing her forehead to his. "And perhaps, once all is said and done, we will have a chance to learn together. For you are not the only one who knows nothing of trust."

Gemma could barely breathe as she waited for his response.

He grabbed her by the back of the neck, his mouth crashing down upon hers. Claiming her in a kiss both furious and demanding. She could sense the need in him, the question he asked. *Be mine. Please.* Gemma grabbed a fistful of his hair, her tongue thrusting into his mouth, answering as best she could.

Always.

She'd never understood what lay between them. Why him? Why, of all the men who'd sought her heart, had he been the one who stole it?

The second they'd met, she'd been drawn to him. She'd always had the sense he could see right through her carefully constructed words and flirtations. A single glance from those dangerous gray eyes stripped her to the bone, as if only he saw the real Gemma. The little girl who'd learned to lock her true self away, even as she so desperately wanted someone else to see it.

Perhaps it had been her innate conscience realizing she had met the other half of her soul. Like finding like. On the surface, they couldn't be more different if they tried.

Obsidian held himself apart, watching the world with cold, wary eyes. But she'd walked the same path as he. Buried her pain and rage beneath a smile and a laugh. Thrown herself into living her life as completely as she could, determined to beat the odds others had given her, even as nothing ever felt completely real. Different lives, yes, but still the same, at heart. She *understood* this man, in a way she'd never understood another living person.

They broke apart with a pant, though Gemma was loathe to destroy the moment. She wanted more. She wanted to allow passion to steal away all her hurt, all her pain, but that would only be using him in this moment.

When they came together again, she wanted their moment to be about them. Nothing else. No hurt. No pain. No rage. Only a consummation of love, where she could show him the secrets that lurked deep in her heart.

"We need to go," she breathed.

Obsidian nodded, drawing back from her, and looking right through her as if he saw the words imprinted on her soul. He shifted out from underneath her, slinking toward the bars. "Just in case the queen makes a hasty decision she can't take back."

"What are you doing?" Gemma whispered, as he set his hands around the bars of the cell. "Obsidian? I thought you had a lock pick."

"I like your 'magic'," he told her, granting her the faintest of smiles. "But this works for me."

Gemma staggered to her feet, her face puffy and her lips swollen. "You won't break the bars! They're reinforced and were designed specifically with blue bloods in mind.... Oh."

The bars were warping as he flexed his arms. Muscle rippled beneath the tight-fitting black coat he wore. "Why do you think I insisted upon staying with you?" His teeth were clenched together. He wrenched the bars almost half a foot apart. Another inch. Just wide enough to ease through.

Obsidian slipped through the gap, his chest scraping the bars. "Coming? Your enemy's not going to come to you."

Gemma took a shaky step. "Coming. The only problem is we're in Thorne Tower. This place is locked up tighter than a nun's drawers. How are we going to get out of here—without killing any more of the guards?"

Obsidian smiled as he stepped back into the hallway, the shadows of the bars rippling over his face. "Trust me. I have exceptional skills at getting in and out of places undetected. Now I get to use them for good."

"I want her head," the queen snarled as Malloryn staggered into the council chambers, his arm slung over Charlie's shoulders.

Queen Alexandra stood at the head of the massive circular table in the center of the room. The original one had been deliberately burned when the queen regained her throne and overthrew her husband, and this replacement was made of polished mahogany and jokingly referred to by several of the councilors as the Round Table.

"Hear me out first," he managed to gasp as Charlie directed him toward the table. "It wasn't her fault."

The queen whirled on him. "Perhaps you can explain to me how I was almost assassinated in my own damned throne room by one of *your* agents!"

He tugged the neural implant Ava had found during Jonathan Carlyle's autopsy out of his pocket and slammed it flat on the table.

"This is how they did it," he replied. "This neural implant was discovered in the brain of Jonathan Carlyle, the man we thought was the Chameleon. One of my top agents has spent the past day trying to discover what it does, but all she could say was that the device was inert. Probably made so the second Carlyle was murdered.

"However, I've managed to discover someone who does know what the neural implant is intended for. It uses complex bio-mechanics to fuse with a person's brain and override their impulses and wishes. Our enemy has discovered the means to circumvent a man's—or woman's—true loyalty and turn them into a mindless killing automaton. The Chameleon was never one person. It's a code name passed from person to person. Project: Chameleon. The next Chameleon could be anyone." He tipped his head toward the queen. "It could be your dearest friend, the Lady Aramina. It could be a trusted housemaid, her intentions overridden by this bloody thing. It could be a guard who's spent thirty years in the service of your family. You'll never know. And you'll never see them coming, because they don't even seem to realize what's happened.

"From what I can gather from events, Baroness Schröder"—even saying her name hurt—"was turned against my cause. There was an incident a few days ago where the baroness and my agent, Gemma, were the subject of a kidnapping. The baroness managed to escape with a mild concussion, though knowing what I know now, I suspect she led Gemma into a trap. Gemma vanished for the period of twenty-four hours and managed to escape the warehouse where she was being held. She and I thought it strange how lightly guarded the facility was, but...." He paused, swallowing the lump in his throat. *Always question the small things that don't add up.* How had he forgotten? "There was no sign of any injury upon her. There wouldn't be, as she's a blue blood. Gemma could barely remember what happened. She was bludgeoned, hemlocked, and then kept drugged throughout the ordeal. Her head hurt her at first, but we thought it merely a side effect from being hit from behind. Now...."

He could barely say it.

His fists clenched.

"They must have operated on her while she was drugged, and implanted the neural implant. The craving virus healed all signs of it, and she 'escaped.' This was set up from the start. A threat against you meant I'd get involved. I'd bring in my top agents and surround you with them. Gemma's the first one I'd look to in order to save your life. Her skillset is the perfect match to guard you, no matter who they sent against you."

And she's the perfect one to try and take it too.

Someone knew him so well, he'd managed to predict every damned move Malloryn made.

You are what I made you, Auvry....

Silence lingered in the chamber, like the air surrounding a funeral procession.

"How do you know what this neural implant does?" Jasper Lynch, the Duke of Bleight mused, reaching for the device.

"Because I've spent the past several weeks trying to lure one of the enemy's agents to our side. Or should I say, Gemma has." He tilted his head toward the queen. "The agent who went after you goes by the name of Gemma Townsend. She has a history with one of the *dhampir* arrayed against us. He has cast his allegiance with me. If you sentence her to death, we lose Obsidian too, and the one real chance we have of striking our enemy a blow. He knows everything about our enemy's cause, but he's only just starting to open up. I've barely had a chance to question him."

The queen paced, her gold skirts sweeping behind her like the sails of a warship leaning into an abrupt turn. "You're skating on thin ice, Malloryn."

"Gemma Townsend? Why do I know that name?" said Rosalind Lynch, the Duchess of Bleight, who'd managed to earn a place on this council of her own means and not merely as adjutant to her husband.

"She's my right hand. A former Falcon I managed to seduce from Lord Balfour's side many, many years ago. She was just a girl when they sent her to assassinate me."

"And you trust a former Falcon?" The queen sounded shocked.

"One could say all of us sitting here at this table have trusted less reputable people," he replied.

Malloryn's right knee shook and suddenly gave, leaving him staggering against the back of his empty chair. Blade caught him, kicking the chair out as he managed to seat Malloryn within it.

"'Ere, princess. Take a seat." Blade started stripping out of his coat and tore his waistcoat off.

"Thank you." Malloryn pressed it to his chest. The room was swaying, but he simply couldn't afford to let himself faint.

Not without assuring Gemma's safety.

"You should be in a bloody bed." The queen's lips pressed tightly together as her gaze raked him from head to toe. "Where's the tower physician?"

"I will be," he ground out, locking eyes with her, "once I see to the safety of my queen. And my agents."

Gauntlet thrown.

Her eyes narrowed.

"How can we trust her?" the queen demanded. "How do you know that... thing in her head isn't going to transform her again."

"Obsidian assures me Gemma's neural implant is defunct. Electricity destroys the circuit." He suddenly felt so fucking weary, he barely had the strength to lift his head. "The problem is, I think you have to trust Gemma. And Obsidian. Because I've barely even begun to delve into the issues we're currently facing. Project: Chameleon is the tip of the iceberg. There's more. And it's worse."

"What could be worse than a device being used to take over people's free will?" Rosalind Lynch demanded.

"It seems an old enemy isn't quite as dead as I'd hoped. And he's behind everything that's happened with the *dhampir* and the vampires and the SOG, and now this assassination attempt...."

"Who?" The queen's voice tightened.

Malloryn pressed Blade's waistcoat against the worst wound in his side. "Before she died, Baroness Schröder was taunting me with the fact this is all a game designed to wound *me*. She used... specific statements only one man has ever used. She said our enemy wanted me to see London burn. My queen killed. My friends murdered. And each and every thing I love destroyed."

"And I thought *I* pissed people off, beggin' your pardon, Madam Queen," Blade said. "Ain't anybody ever wanted to burn the entire bloody city to the ground because of *me*."

"It's a gift Malloryn has," Leo drawled. "Along with the ability to keep everyone in suspense. And technically, the Duke of Morioch *was* trying to burn you out of Whitechapel."

"It's not deliberate," Malloryn shot back. "I have no proof my old enemy is even still alive."

He didn't need proof. The truth burned within him, leaving him in absolutely no doubt.

"*Who?*" the queen whispered.

"Lord Balfour," he said, and watched the queen reel back as if slapped. "And while I understand your trepidation, I need Gemma, Your Highness. For if we're truly facing Balfour, then this changes *everything*."

CHAPTER
TWENTY-SIX

Obsidian took her to the tower ruins overlooking Malloryn's secret townhouse. It was their little world, safe from prying eyes and whispers. Safe from the impact of Lord Balfour, and Malloryn, and every bloody thing striving to keep them apart. They could pretend here and lose themselves in each other without giving a damn about the outside world.

Nobody would be looking for them here, and with the Ivory Tower still in turmoil she'd be safe until they could discover what had happened.

Moving around the room with a small taper, Obsidian lit each candle and then latched the windows against the night and prying eyes before turning back to Gemma.

She stood in the middle of the room, her arms wrapped around her middle and her hair hanging in tangled snarls around her heart-shaped face. Strips of skirt clung to her legs, and for once she didn't seem to give a damn about her bloody Madame Lefoux's, or whoever designed it.

No, her eyes flamed hot with intent when she looked at him. Clearly determined to forget her troubles, no matter what she had to do.

Obsidian slowly blew out the flame on the end of the taper, and smoke curled from its tip. He couldn't take his eyes off her.

She needed him.

It was that simple.

He'd never had anything to fight for before. Weapons simply did as they were told, and with his fractured memories he'd never had a reason to rebel. He couldn't even bloody recall if he'd ever tried.

But the second she'd walked back into his life, he'd seen a chance for him to break free—to be seen as something more than a tool. Nobody had ever risked their life for his, until she threw herself between him and Malloryn.

Nobody had ever cared.

But now it was his turn to look after her.

"There's a storm brewing in your eyes," Obsidian murmured, as he stalked around her in narrowing circles.

He could see the edge in her eyes. Neither of them were made for soft words or gentle touches.

Or heartfelt confessions.

He was willing to give her whatever she needed.

"There's a storm brewing in my heart." Gemma turned her head to follow his movements. "But I'm afraid if I let it out, I'll destroy the world. Ever since we left the tower, all I can think about is how to kill Balfour. I've managed to map out at least four ways to get to him, but they all involve casualties. And there's a part of me that doesn't care. I feel like I should care. I *want* to care. But all I feel is empty. No. All I feel is fury. Have you ever been frightened of what exists inside you?"

Circling her slowly, he reached out to let his fingertips trail across the muscular flex of her spine. Gemma shivered.

"Yes," he whispered.

He turned her to face him, resting his fingertips on her lips.

"Make me forget today," she begged, sliding the charred edges of his coat off his broad shoulders.

Make me forget. He saw again the pistol smoking. The empty bridge coming into focus. And the world rushing back in upon him. Obsidian shook his head as he captured her face in both hands. "You cannot forget your pain without forgetting all the goodness that comes with it," he whispered. *Trust me. I know.* "Pain is what makes the pleasures of life seem so vibrant. If you didn't know pain or loss, then you would take for granted what had been gifted to you."

He breathed her in, pressing his face to her hair, one hand curled around the back of her neck.

Mine. All mine.

"Then make it *hurt*," Gemma said, before she stretched up on her toes and captured his lips in a demanding kiss.

He tore his mouth from hers with a shudder. "*Nyet.*"

Capturing her hands, he held her there, fingers linked. Pain flashed through his synapses, but it was a dull ache now. A distant warning of the aversion therapy. The line between pleasure and pain was thin enough it could go either way; kissing her was torture in the most excruciatingly delicious sense.

But he didn't want *her* to know such a sensation. Not tonight.

"*Please.*"

"Gemma." Obsidian shook his head, swallowing hard. "Let me love you. Just this once."

Stillness spread through her as she tilted her head. "Love you?"

And there they were. The two words that had the ability to cut his heart right out of his chest.

"What would you call it?" He tried to make sense of the sudden riot in his mind. His heart was pounding, a physical response he couldn't seem to quell, despite his control.

But then, he'd never been able to control that recalcitrant organ when it came to her.

"Do you speak of taking me to bed? Or... something else?"

Obsidian laced his fingers through hers. When he felt like he had control over his facial features, he slowly looked up. "Something else. Perhaps. I have never felt rationally when it comes to you. I don't.... I don't know what I feel. But it is overwhelming. You are the beginning and the end of everything. You are all I see. You are *mine*.

"They tried to lock it all away inside me. To bind it with chains of hate, but even when I wanted to kill you, a part of me could not raise a hand. I've killed to protect you. I would die for you. And you alone have the power to bring me to my knees with a single kiss. Is this love?"

Gemma curled her fingers through his. She tried to laugh, and failed. "You're asking me? According to Malloryn my perception of the word is skewed."

"And you think the Duke of Malloryn knows what love is? He's a fool."

A laugh burst out of her.

Then the shadows came back as the day's events clearly returned.

"You make me believe," he added swiftly, "there is a place where I belong. And that place is in your arms. It doesn't matter where we are, or what we're fighting for. You are the only thing that matters to me."

Those luminous eyes were shuttered by the flicker of her lashes, but then she met his gaze, and all the pain and fear and anger washed out of her. "That's what I felt in Russia. I had a job to do, but for the first time in my life I wanted to run away with you. I wanted to leave behind all my burdens, all my duties. I wanted something I'd never wanted before. Love," she said, in a wondering tone.

If Malloryn lived, Obsidian was going to kill him for putting that doubt into her mind.

"Do you trust me, *lyubov moya*?"

"With my life."

Obsidian bent and caught her up beneath her thighs, lifting her easily. Gemma's arms slid around his broad shoulders and her thick black hair cascaded around his face.

They'd never had a moment in which to surrender to each other. There'd always been tension between them. Lies. Hot, hard kisses. Teeth in skin, as both of them sought to overwhelm the other. In Russia they'd both been playing a game, from what he could recall. Passion was easy to ignite. Sex, a means to communicate without saying a damned thing.

But this....

He lowered her onto the rough bed he'd created in the corner, and Gemma lay back like a bride surrendering to her husband on their wedding night as he knelt between her thighs.

He kissed her palm, lips skating up the inside of her wrist. Pain stabbed through his head, but he ignored it in favor of the sensation of her smooth skin beneath his lips.

Gemma arched her head back with a soft moan as he caressed the hollow of her collarbone. The thick heady rush of her pulse captured his attention, and he paused as his vision plunged into shadows, the hunger awakening within him with hungry teeth.

Obsidian hadn't been naive enough to think this could remain a gentle, teasing seduction—not when both of them had their demons—but he'd hoped he could control himself long enough to make this perfect for her.

"Kiss me," she said, pushing at his chest and rising to her elbows.

"You're so demanding."

Sliding his hand behind her neck, he captured the roughened exhale of her breath on her lips. Gemma's mouth opened under his, hot and eager. Every kiss they'd previously shared seemed to twist him into tighter knots, but this was no seduction she planned. She simply let him take, their tongues writhing against each other in abandon, her fingers curling into the lengths of his hair until a flare of pain ran through his scalp. Hungry. Rough. A little demanding....

His heart pounded in his chest as he grabbed her by the hips and dragged her against his erection. Alive. He felt alive and whole, as if a single kiss from Gemma could put all the pieces of his fractured psyche back together.

The hand against his chest grew insistent.

He spilled onto his back, and Gemma clambered astride in a cascade of skirts. Then they were kissing again, his fingers sinking into the rich, luxurious length of her hair, until she broke from his mouth and ventured lower. Soft lips grazed his jaw, his pulse. The sting of her teeth against his throat made him hiss as she bit him hard enough to bruise the skin. But it was the caress of her tongue against that mark that sent tingles shooting down his spine.

Obsidian captured her mouth again, hands cupping her face as he poured everything he had of him into the kiss. How had he ever thought he could deny what he felt for her? He might as well try and pull the moon from the sky as withstand the power Gemma had over him.

Gemma moaned, her thighs squeezing his hips as she rocked against him. "Sweet mercy, I want you naked. I want to lick every inch of your skin." Fingernails suddenly dug into his shoulders, leaving eight hard little half-moons imprinted there as she sucked in a stolen breath. "I want to bite you."

So do I. He drew her lower lip between his teeth and sucked. His shirt fell prey to her clever fingers, and Obsidian broke the kiss just long enough for her to push it from his shoulders.

Then it was her turn.

Hauling her hips against him, he ground her against his erection as he dragged her hair forward over one shoulder, just enough to catch a glimpse of the top button of her gown.

Gemma gasped, throwing her head back. Obsidian captured the curve of her breast in his mouth, the rasp of the lace scraping his mouth. He tugged at the buttons down her spine, one by one, cursing them under his breath. Small, fabric-coated buttons, each one catching in the eyelet as if they'd been devised specifically to frustrate a man's larger fingers.

To frustrate him.

"What's wrong?" she teased. "Thwarted by fashion?"

"Curse your goddamned Madame Lefoux." He finally had her gown undone, and spread both halves of it. "I'd rip it, but you have nothing else to wear."

And a penchant for her fancy gowns.

"That didn't stop you before."

"I was a little... frustrated."

"Do tell," she purred, biting the fleshy lobe of his ear.

"You know what you did to me in Vickers's manor." He pushed the sleeves from her shoulders. "You drove me half insane. All this skin I couldn't touch. Lips I didn't dare taste. You. Mocking me. Tempting me. You're the cause of my madness."

Gemma laughed, the sound spilling from her in a throaty echo as she peeled the sleeves over her hands. "You're impatient."

"I've not had you naked before."

"I was naked. You wouldn't look."

"Then consider me a fool. I didn't want to see what was right before my eyes." Yanking her gown down around her waist, he slid his palms up her ribs, capturing the generous curves of her breasts. They threatened to spill from her corset. The press of lace and silk was a riot of sensation against his fingertips, but nothing compared to the warmth of her skin.

Gemma wilted into the touch as if it was all she needed.

Pushing her right breast free of the clasp of her corset, he sucked her nipple into his mouth, using his teeth just the way she liked it. The strings on her corset were an impossible mess, but somehow he drew them loose, tugging each crisscrossed lace free until the corset settled around her hips.

He drew it over her head, and then her chemise, until she was wearing nothing but her stockings, with those red silk garters.

Of course. A laugh vibrated in his chest. Only Gemma would wear such a frivolous thing where no one could see it. A little touch of naughtiness only she would ever be aware of.

Or perhaps she'd meant for him to see it.

To always wonder what she wore beneath her gown from now on.

"You're beautiful."

The sight of her naked body was enough to ruin what was left of his control. She'd been made for a man's gaze, all creamy skin and rounded curves. An hourglass in shape and form. Unbound, the lush sway of her breasts were large enough to overflow his hands. Her body was an odd mix of hard muscle and soft, soft flesh. Without her daily training, she'd have been voluptuous.

Gemma bit her lip, as he trailed his fingers down over her throat and breasts. "You are not so hard on the eyes yourself. There's just one little problem...." Her finger snagged in the waistband of his trousers. "You're dressed and I'm not."

"Then remove them."

"It will be my pleasure," she purred, as she bent to unsnap his buttons. Gemma worked her way down his body with sinuous appeal, her feline eyes glinting with a dare as she pressed kisses down the center of his abdomen.

Intention sparked in her eyes as inched her hand into his pants and curled her fingers around his cock.

There was something about watching her head lower, that small tongue darting out to tease the smooth skin at the base of his erection, that made his ass clench and a shiver work its way up his spine.

He didn't dare breathe.

He couldn't move.

All he could do was watch as Gemma's lashes flickered up and she met his gaze, her hand twisting, stroking, driving him bloody crazy.

"Are you trying to torture me?" he gasped.

"Is it working?"

He had the brief, startled thought this was supposed to be about her. About pleasing her, making love to her, making her scream....

Somehow she'd turned the tables on him.

She always does.

"I'm fairly certain... I was meant to be... making love to *you*."

"Oh, pish. You've been in control the entire time. Now it's my turn." She pressed a kiss to the soft skin of his groin, dangerously close to where he wanted her mouth. "Oh, and Dmitri, I fully intend to make you suffer the way you made me suffer."

"You have no idea how much it hurt to keep my hands off you."

"It wasn't your hands I was worried about."

Obsidian swallowed as her hair dragged over the sensitive tip of his erection, followed by the heated clasp of her mouth. Gemma never had been shy. She swallowed him whole, the wet lash of her tongue stroking the sensitive arrow beneath the head of his cock, teasing him mercilessly—

Somehow his hands were in her hair, and he thrust up into her throat as he eased her down. The hot, wet clasp of her mouth drove all rational thought from his mind. He was losing himself, inch by inch, the base of his spine tingling as her mouth did wicked things to his cock.

"Up," he commanded, wrapping her hair around his fist and drawing her up.

Her wet lips met his, but he had no intention of stopping there. Cupping her ass, he hauled her astride him, her thighs clamping around his narrow hips.

"Dima," she gasped, as he thrust up into her wet heat, burying himself to the hilt in one smooth glide.

Tighter and hotter than her mouth. Dangerously addictive.

Obsidian held her against his chest, the fingers of one hand stroking the base of her skull as he fought to regain his equilibrium, the other toying with the lace of her garter.

But she was having none of that.

Rolling her hips, she lifted until all but the very tip of him broached her. Gemma eased back down with an inner squeeze, her nails digging into his chest.

Every inch of her body sheathed him with a silken flex that had him groaning. *Fuck.* He'd never last. Just as she no doubt intended. *Mother of God,* she moved like her very bones were flexible, as if she knew just the rhythm to drive him out of his bloody mind.

"What's wrong, my love?" Gemma gave a husky laugh.

Oh, she was a devil.

Grabbing her by the nape, Obsidian mashed his mouth against her and rolled them, driving her into the furs with a hard thrust.

Gemma moaned, and somehow he got his elbow under the back of her thigh and hooked her knee over his shoulder, pinning her open beneath his ruthless assault. He could feel her tensing as he rubbed the base of his cock against her clitoris, pushing her toward pleasure like a fast-running freight train. Fucking her so hard she could do nothing but thrash and moan, her nails biting into his shoulders.

The brief flare of pain anchored him.

He looked down into her face as she came, her pillow-shaped mouth parted and her eyes shuttered as she threw her head back with unabashed pleasure.

She was the only thing that made sense in his world.

And she was so fucking beautiful it made his chest ache.

He traced her lips, her cheeks, his fingertips learning her with an artist's touch as she moaned, his thrusts slowing. "Ever since I met you, you're all I ever wanted."

Gemma sucked his fingers into her mouth. It was all happening. Heat flashing through his balls. Her body clenching around his like a silk-gloved fist, his eyes rolling back in his head—

He couldn't stop the strangled sound leaving his throat as he gave a few more savage thrusts before he spent himself inside her with one last moan.

Obsidian slumped atop her, burying his face in the hollow of her neck as Gemma stroked a hand down his spine. Her chest rose and fell against his in harsh rhythm as they both panted.

And then she was laughing and so was he, the clench of her body echoing in time to the silvery gales of laughter she made.

"I don't know who won," she admitted.

"You came first."

Those wicked blue eyes narrowed, and she squeezed him again. "You came harder."

"That's debatable. I think I'll be feeling your nails in my back for years to come."

He could feel himself hardening inside her at the sight of that wicked smile. Obsidian gave her a gentle nudge.

"Again?" One of her black eyebrows arched.

Obsidian smiled a dangerous smile, and kissed her fingertips as he rocked inside her. "Didn't I tell you? The teeth weren't the only enhancement the elixir gave me. Are you sure you can handle me?"

Gemma wrapped her arms around him, her eyes narrowing as she locked her legs around his hips. "Oh, please. Don't you know who you're dealing with by now?"

He kissed her slowly. "Then let us put it to the test."

"I think you might have won," Gemma finally conceded, spilling onto her back beside her lover in a wobbly mess. "I concede. I don't think I have a single orgasm left in me."

"I'm sorry. You might have to repeat that," Obsidian murmured, trailing his fingers over the ripple of her upper arm. "I won?"

She punched him in the ribs, but he merely grunted and dragged her into his embrace. Every last inch of him wrapped around her, and he kissed the back of her neck lightly, as if to say, *I'm here.*

And suddenly the rest of the world was intruding, no matter how much she wanted it to go away.

Gemma rested her head on his biceps, staring at the dying flicker of the last remaining candle.

She was ruined. Emotionally. Physically. Sexually. There wasn't even enough energy within her to feel more than a mild ache when she thought of Malloryn, which was exactly what she'd wanted.

But she couldn't avoid it forever.

With the light of day would come the reality of the situation. She wished she could close her eyes and when she woke, this would all seem like some horrible dream.

But wishes were for little girls who hadn't been sold to a school of assassins.

Because that little girl learned long ago there was no point in believing in things that would never come true.

The only thing different about this time was she wasn't alone. And maybe that would be enough to get her through tomorrow and the harsh reality of all that had occurred.

"Stay with me like this?" she whispered, curling her fingers through Obsidian's.

"Always."

And Gemma surrendered to the warm darkness and the safe cocoon of Obsidian's arms.

"I have to go back," Gemma whispered, sitting in the arched window of their secret tower with a glass of blood, watching the world go by.

Watching people come in and out of the safe house.

Ava. Kincaid. Byrnes. Ingrid. Jack. And Charlie.

But never Malloryn.

The wait was killing her. She needed to know what had happened to him. And though she could stay here forever in Obsidian's arms if she pretended there wasn't an entire world out there, how long could she play pretend?

COR needed her. She needed them. Obsidian filled one half of her heart, and while she could survive with him alone, there was a part of her that needed more to be truly content.

Memories flashed through her head: Byrnes complaining about her penchant for blud-wein; teasing Charlie about how to seduce a certain girl on their long flight to Brighton last month; "borrowing" Jack's new prototype of a blast-shield for a mission; begging Kincaid to resurrect it so she could replace it before Jack noticed it was destroyed; and getting hilariously foxed on Malloryn's secret stash of sherry with Ingrid and Ava, and not realizing Ava had barely ever imbibed before.

And now she knew what they faced, she couldn't leave them to face it alone.

"Ingrid and Ava will be worried," she said, knotting her hands. "And poor Charlie…. He's such a sugarplum. I wouldn't want him to feel guilty—"

"A sugarplum?"

"He's my perfect, sweet Charlie," she replied, "and if anything ever happened to him I'd never forgive myself."

"And the queen?"

"Regardless of what the queen desires," she whispered, "I have a duty to those I love to return."

Obsidian slid onto the ledge of the open window and kissed the back of her shoulder. "As you wish."

CHAPTER TWENTY-SEVEN

Malloryn rapped at the door to his wife's bedchambers.

Wife. It still felt strange, though the ceremony had been a simple one, a swift half hour stolen the day following their attempted wedding, and he'd barely seen her since. Vows had been exchanged, papers signed, and Adele handed into the carriage that would take her to Malloryn House while he checked his pocket watch and made his way to the safe house.

Indeed, the last time he'd laid eyes upon Adele, he'd been between her thighs with her blood on his lips and—

He was not going to think of that now.

The queen had finally sent him home, insisting he see to himself as she didn't want to see him "limping around chambers" for at least a week.

There was no rest for the wicked, but he'd succumbed to her "suggestion" with ill grace. Logic dictated at least one decent day of sleep if he was to heal completely.

He'd need all his strength to face the forthcoming days, and the shocking revelation that Balfour had survived.

But there was one last person he needed to check upon before he could take himself off to bed.

"Come in," Adele called, and he pushed the door open to find her seated primly in bed, reading a book.

Her sister, Harriet, sewed quietly in the corner, her feet tucked up beneath her skirts.

Adele turned her page, engrossed in the story. "You can set the tea on the—"

"It's me."

Harriet's head jerked up. "Your Grace."

"Your Grace," Adele blurted, as if she'd thought he was the last person who'd ever enter her bedchambers.

If he was being honest, he couldn't truly blame her for the assumption.

It was the last place he wanted to be.

"Miss Hamilton." He tipped his head to Harriet before he turned his narrowing gaze upon his wife. "Duchess."

They held a long stalemate, until Adele put her book down, and cleared her throat. "Your Grace."

"You said that."

Color flooded her cheeks, and she touched one of the loose curls draped over her shoulder, as if aware she was *en dishabille*. "Yes, well. I *am* dealing with the Duke of Malloryn. His magnitude is so great he deserves at least two 'your graces'. I should not wish to offend."

Harriet's eyes widened to the size of saucers.

Ha. Clearly his wife was feeling better after their encounter in the tower. "Are you well?"

"Tolerably."

"You've regained your strength?" He began to tug his gloves off.

"Hattie's informed the staff I am strictly confined to bed until the end of the week," she replied, shooting her sister a disapproving glare.

Was that frustration he heard? He glanced at her as he slapped the gloves into the palm of his left hand. It was somewhat discomfiting to share an emotion with her.

Adele is ice and haughtiness. She's a viper who doesn't deserve an ounce of compassion.

Of course. Which is why she bled herself for your sake in the Tower....

Curse her.

"I hope you've informed your sister how dangerous your actions were." He couldn't restrain the slight edge to his voice. "And how, if she is clever, she will never, *ever* put herself in a position where she is in such danger."

"You're welcome, Your Grace." Adele visibly seethed. "Hattie recommended I wait until you ceased breathing, whereupon I'd be completely alone in this lovely big manor with all your money, but I admit I suffered an inconvenient moment of conscience."

"Adele!" her sister squeaked.

"Most of the property would revert to my heir, a distant cousin who'd likely cast you into the streets. And it wasn't as though I was dying. I'm a *blue blood.*"

"Oh, of course," Adele mocked. The blankets tumbled into her lap, revealing the fine lawn of her nightgown and the shadow of her breasts beneath it. "How could the Duke of Malloryn ever be brought so low his wife *saved* his life?"

Malloryn stared at the outline of her figure, then furiously looked away when he realized she hadn't even noticed how revealing her nightgown was. His cock gave a faint clench. *Don't you bloody well dare*, he told it silently.

He'd been two seconds away from delving his fingers into the wetness of her body in the tower when he'd finally regained his senses.

Moments away from tearing the buttons on his breeches open and fucking his way inside her, the bloodlust shifting to something *else*.

How utterly mortifying.

Adele.

Adele Hamilton.

Unwillingly consummating his marriage on the floor of the Ivory Tower with his dead mistress in the hallway outside and five bullets still inside him would have been at the top of his list of the most humiliating moments in his life.

But it could have been worse.

He'd had no sense of the world. No rational thoughts. All he'd been was a mess of need and hunger, and a sudden furious desire that still ticked through his veins, curse her inconvenient nightgown. Did she not realize how the light fell upon her?

She was clearly wearing nothing beneath the fine lawn.

The primal side of a blue blood's nature was dangerous to rouse, particularly in the presence of one's enemies. He was loath to call what he felt for Adele hate, for he wouldn't dare give her the satisfaction of such a thing, but he'd been faintly furious toward her ever since she trapped him into this farce of a marriage.

He could have killed her.

"Aren't you going to say something? A moment of conscience?" she mocked, clipping her vowels in the precise way he did. "Why, I'd have never thought you afflicted by such a grievous burden."

He cast a seething glance upon her sister. "Can you fetch your sister a robe? I should hate for her to catch a chill, though I suspect her heart is frigid enough to stave off that burden." He arched a brow toward Adele. "Is that better?"

Clearly he wasn't the only one who remembered that moment on the floor. Adele subsided with a waspish nod, as if relieved to return to the parry and thrust of their previous relationship, but her cheeks bore a rosy stain and she couldn't quite meet his eyes.

"You should speak of frigid hearts. It's been three days and this is the first you've visited," she said, instead.

Not entirely.

He'd called in on her the first night, when he'd finally staggered in on crutches, his right kneecap still shattered from where Gemma had shot him. Hattie had been sitting by her bed, fretting over Adele like a concerned mother hen, when he checked to make sure she'd recovered.

"Oh, His Grace did—"

He cut Hattie a sharp, incredulous look, and she shut her mouth abruptly as she secured the robe around Adele's shoulders.

"My apologies," he said to Adele. "I wasn't aware you were waiting for me."

"I wasn't. And stop glaring at my sister."

He forced his tone to be callously distant. "I've also been busy seeing to matters of the realm."

Adele subsided. "Important matters, I suppose."

"Indeed."

Keeping Gemma's head on her bloody shoulders. Trying to track down the source of that bloody chip, and finding nothing. Ghost was aptly named.

Making sure the queen was well guarded, all her servants forced to electrocute themselves mildly before they were allowed to see her.

Burying Isabella.

His breath caught, that dagger-sharp flare of guilt burying itself within his heart up to the hilt.

"You can burn my city. You can tear down all I've built. But you can never touch me," he'd spat at Balfour all those years ago. *"I have no heart anymore. You took it from me when you murdered Catherine. So do your damned best. You can't destroy me."*

Balfour had revealed his hand in the most devastating way of all, as if to remind him of those words.

You know this was a taunt. You know he killed Isabella to test your resolve.

And the horrible truth kept circulating through him. He'd never loved her.

But she'd loved him.

He'd heard it in her voice right before she shot herself.

Malloryn flinched. Adele was saying something, but he hadn't heard a damned word of it—

"Would you give us a moment?" he asked Harriet, his voice sounding a million miles away.

Harriet bobbed into a curtsy and then practically fled the room.

Blankets rustled. "Are you quite done terrorizing my sister?"

"Terrorizing her?"

"You frighten her," Adele shot back. "Which you would notice if you ever noticed anyone beneath you."

His eyes thinned to narrow slits. "I notice everything."

"Then what did I just say?"

Touché.

He merely stared at her, and she flushed again, though this time it was in anger.

"You notice everything *important*," she said, a hint of bitterness creeping through her voice as she tossed her covers back and slipped to the edge of the bed.

That wasn't what he'd meant at all.

She tried to stand and he limped to her side in an instant, prepared to catch her if she fell. Instinct. Etiquette.

And more than a little guilt, though he couldn't admit such a thing to *her*.

Adele froze, the rose-colored drape of her silk robe mercifully hiding her form from his gaze. "It would take more than a little bloodletting to take the wind from my sails, Your Grace."

Malloryn backed away, hands clasped behind his back. "It would probably take the entire bloody airship armada to do so."

"That almost sounded like flattery."

"It wasn't."

Her smile died. "Of course not."

They stared at each other again.

For the first time in years, he didn't know what to say. "Adele?"

"Yes."

She'd been busy tying her robe, but at his silence, she looked up.

"Thank you." He forced the words out.

There. He'd said it.

"It's not as though you were dying." She flung his own words back at him, seemingly just as discomfited as he was.

"And yet, it would have taken me days to recover if not for your assistance. Because of you, I was able to talk the queen out of a course of action that would have cost a very dear friend of mine her head."

"Then I shall accept your gratitude," Adele replied dryly. "On your *friend*'s behalf, if nothing else."

The way she stressed the word made him focus sharply on her again.

"A friend, Adele. Just that."

She glanced away. "I'm sorry, you know. About the baroness."

Oh, God. She was the last person he'd ever discuss this with. "You hated her."

"That doesn't mean I wished her dead." Adele toyed with her fingers. "I—"

"That's enough." He cut her off sharply, for he could see the guilt within her. Clearly she'd harbored more than a few ill thoughts toward Isabella, and they chastised her even now. "We will not speak of this. I came to say thank you for your assistance."

"Which you have done." She inclined her head regally. "I see you have places to be, judging by the way you keep glancing at the door. Don't worry, Malloryn. I didn't expect any more from you. You've done your duty."

He stared at her a moment longer, frustrated to find himself relieved by the cool expression upon her face.

"Don't expect me in the following days. There's a great deal of trouble to manage."

"Try not to get yourself killed," Adele replied. "I haven't any particular desire to be a widow so soon after my marriage."

"I lied when I said Thomas would cast you out of the house. You'll be provided for in my will, if nothing else." He backed toward the double doors to her bedroom. "You would be free to do whatever you wanted."

Dark lashes obscured her green eyes as she turned to the window. "Am I not free to do as I wish now? I thought we were to maintain separate lives. Indeed, I'm surprised to expect even this small encounter."

The pink silk hung in loose ripples down her narrow spine.

Malloryn hesitated in the doorway.

He knew why he'd come here today.

Isabella's face haunted him every time he closed his eyes. He'd overlooked her feelings—for years possibly—

and now her face would haunt him the same way Catherine's did.

I loved one of them too much.

And the other, not enough.

For all his irritation with his wife's manipulation, her presence in his life was somewhat of a relief. Adele would never expect anything more from him. She filled a role he needed to fill, and he gave her a roof over her head, gold, gems, whatever her mercenary little heart could desire.

She would never give her heart to him.

He would never desire hers.

"Nothing has changed," he replied firmly. "I merely wished to assure myself of your health following our encounter in the Tower."

"Oh, God." A scalded sound echoed in her throat. "Can we not forget it ever happened?"

A burst of relief flushed through him. He would much prefer to.

"An excellent proposition. Good day, Duchess."

"Good day, Your Grace."

And then he turned and walked away, letting thoughts of Adele slip from his mind as he headed for his own bedchamber.

CHAPTER TWENTY-NINE

Gemma had never fancied herself a coward, but there was a lump in her throat thick enough to choke her as she slipped through the back door of the safe house and climbed the stairs to the first level.

Steady now, old girl.

The first person who saw her was Ava. The pale blonde scurried out of the library with her nose in a bio-mechanics book, only glancing up when she saw the hem of Gemma's ragged skirts.

"Gemma?" Ava gasped and dropped the book. "Oh, my goodness! You're alive."

She threw her arms around Gemma and squeezed her so tightly Gemma's shoulder nearly popped out of its socket again. "Ava. My shoulder."

Ava released her. "You're safe. You're truly safe!"

A door opened further down the corridor. Ingrid. "Gemma?"

And then the rest of the Company of Rogues seemed to stream out of every nook and cranny. She'd been expecting a cool welcome, but all their faces lit up in relief, and Gemma's heart lifted.

Kincaid wrapped his arms around her and swung her in the air. "I'd kiss you on the cheek, but you definitely need a bath."

"Maybe two," Ingrid said, and squeezed her for such a long time Gemma didn't think she was going to be allowed to come up for air. "Don't ever go missing again. I cannot cope with another bout of hunting you through the streets, hoping you're alive. No more kidnappings. No more running off with handsome strangers."

"We were nearby," she protested. "You could have found us easily."

Ingrid released a shuddering breath. "I tried to use the tracking device but it remained silent."

"Must have ruined the beacon in the back of Gemma's neck when we shocked her," Byrnes pointed out. "Didn't think of that."

That was when she recognized the lingering tension in the air, and the way several of the others glanced over her shoulder.

Behind her, Obsidian watched them with an aloof expression on his face.

"Obsidian helped me escape from the tower," she whispered, reaching back to take his hand and draw him into the light.

He came, but uneasily, as if still wary of his welcome.

And Gemma slid her arm around his waist somewhat fiercely, as if to defy anyone who might hold a grudge. Obsidian had done more for them than they would ever know.

"Like I told Malloryn," Byrnes muttered, "it would be good to have another *dhampir* on the team."

The breath eased out of her as they all relaxed.

Byrnes was still limping, which caused her instant consternation until he rolled his eyes. "I've had worse wounds from Ingrid. This one time, she bit me on the—"

"Byrnes," Ingrid said sharply.

He grinned and hugged Gemma tight, then passed her on to Charlie, who was shaking his head.

"Remember when you told me I was a fool for jumping off an airship with one of those new gliders? And the lecture you gave me when I thought it would be a good idea to test that new smoke bomb Jack had been working on in my room." Charlie chided. "You broke out of Thorne Tower! Malloryn's in such a lather he's almost frothing at the mouth."

Her heart staggered to a jagged halt. "Malloryn? He's alive?"

She hadn't let herself ask until now.

Charlie's faint smile died, and he hugged her again. "Of course he is. Jesus, Gem. Did you think you'd killed him?"

She had no answer to that. Only a faint choking sound that Charlie clearly felt heaving through her chest, for his hug abruptly tightened.

"Malloryn's like a cockroach," Byrnes drawled. "I don't think anything *can* kill him."

"I heard that," said a familiar voice from behind them all.

The duke.

The Rogues parted, revealing Malloryn stiffly ascending to the top of the stairs with his cane in hand. Herbert lingered at his side as if afraid the duke would topple down the stairs and prepared to catch him.

Dear Herbert, fussing like a mother hen.

Gemma swallowed hard, staring at the way Malloryn leaned on his cane and the bruises mottling his face. "You're alive."

"I'd hug you, Gemma," he said roughly, "but I honestly don't know if I'll fall on my face if I try. You'll have to come here."

He held one arm open as she walked into them, and suddenly her tearless sobs were back. Malloryn curled her against his shirt, and her whole world shattered around her.

"I didn't—"

"I know."

"I nearly killed you—"

"No. You had your chances." He pressed a faint kiss to her hair, and then eased away from her, his gray eyes searching her face. "The fact you didn't means you weren't trying that hard."

"All I could remember was pointing the pistol at the back of your head as you were crawling across the floor—"

"You knocked me out instead."

She froze, the breath locking in her chest as she fought her way through the rush of memories. Trying to find the truth in his words. Had she?

"Trust me. If you wanted me dead, I'd be dead. I think some part of you was still fighting against your commands." He cleared his throat. "And I wasn't crawling. Dukes don't crawl. Even with a shattered kneecap. We tend to... glide, instead."

Gemma couldn't find it in herself to smile. "Is that why you didn't kill me?"

Malloryn glanced away.

He'd always taken risks when it came to her life.

She'd accused him once of not caring enough about the people around him, and pushing and pulling them across the chessboard of life as if they were pawns, but Gemma suddenly realized the truth.

She'd said he wouldn't hesitate to pull that trigger.

She'd been wrong.

He loves you like a sister—one of the last things Isabella had ever said to her.

And oh, God, she could see it now. All those times he'd lectured her. Rolling his eyes at her as he threw a crumpled-up piece of paper at her head. Sending her on easy missions so she wouldn't be hurt, when she'd thought he was dissatisfied with her performance.

She'd spent so many years trying to prove herself to him, only to discover she'd never needed to.

"Gemma." Malloryn's voice roughened as their eyes met. For the first time in her life, she saw him truly speechless.

Help came from an unexpected quarter.

Malloryn likes to pretend he hasn't got a heart," Kincaid muttered, "but he's soft as butter underneath. Of course he couldn't kill you."

"Soft as butter?" Byrnes sounded doubtful. "What? In the middle of the Arctic?"

Ingrid gave him a nudge. "He could have shot *you* the night you were injected with the *dhampir* serum, but he didn't and he didn't even care for you then."

"I'm not sure he cares for me now," Byrnes protested.

"And he saved Kincaid and me from a draining factory last month when it was on fire," Ava broke in. "He's a hero."

Gemma knew what they were doing, and was grateful for it. She swallowed the lump in her throat and found a faint smile.

Before her eyes, Malloryn put himself back together. He pinched the bridge of his nose. "Please. Stop."

"We're embarrassing him," Byrnes said, with an unrepentant grin. "This is the best thing I've seen all year. Are you blushing, Your Grace?"

"I am *not* blushing." It came out as a growl.

"You *are*."

"Carried me out of a burning building over his shoulder," Kincaid continued.

"Hauled Miss Gemma out of a frozen river in the middle of Saint Petersburg," Herbert added, with a coughed *ahem*.

"The next person who opens their mouth will find themselves on desk duty for the rest of their lives," Malloryn said, in an icy voice.

The entire company clamped their mouths shut, but Kincaid and Byrnes snickered under their breaths.

The only one who didn't seem to have relaxed was Obsidian, who was watching the entire affair as if he'd just seen a dog give birth to a two-headed cat.

"You get used to them, sir," Herbert said politely, offering him a glass of blud-wein from the tray he'd brought up the stairs. "It's a little disconcerting at first, and the gentlemen tend to think they're endlessly amusing, but their hearts are in the right place."

Obsidian looked at her with an expression that said, *just what have you gotten me into?* And Gemma couldn't help giving into a soft laugh.

But he took the glass and examined the blud-wein dubiously. "Is there wine in my blood?"

"Enjoy it, Master Obsidian," Herbert called over his shoulder, moving to offer the rest of the company a glass. "It comes from Master Byrnes's private stock."

Byrnes swore, and then everyone was laughing, and Gemma couldn't help herself. She was so exhausted she burst out into a loud laugh that almost turned into a sob when Ava put her arm around her and rested her blonde head on Gemma's shoulder.

"I'm so glad you're back," Ava whispered. "Ingrid was two seconds away from storming the tower, and I was worried the *both* of you would be locked up."

Malloryn overheard her and cleared his throat sharply, gaining everyone's attention. "As much as the jovial mood has lightened the situation, we need to start thinking about what happens next. As grateful as I am to see you alive, Gemma, you broke out of a highly secure prison after you appeared to be trying to assassinate the queen. You look guilty as sin, and I fear it's going to take all my best efforts to resolve this with the council."

The entire company sobered.

"What do we do?" Byrnes asked.

"Who do we have to kill?" Kincaid added promptly.

"It's simple. There's not a great deal any of *us* can do." Malloryn shifted his attention to Obsidian. "I told you once you had a decision to make. An alliance between the pair of us is the last thing I ever expected to be considering, but we have a mutual acquaintance in common whom we are both very fond of. And we are running out of time. The queen and council have listened to what I know about the neural implant, but I don't know enough. I can sense the uncertainty in some of them. I will not put Gemma's life in their hands with even a hint of doubt as to the outcome of this council meeting. So you have a choice. You either flee the country with her, or...."

"That's not an option for Gemma." Obsidian's lashes lowered, masking his eyes. "What else do you have in mind?"

"You stand in council and answer their questions, regardless of what they ask. You give them everything. I won't pretend it will be easy. You will have to betray everything you ever stood for, and I suspect there will be retaliation from your former companions, but if you take this step, I shall do my utmost to protect you. It's your decision. Gemma's life lies in your hands," Malloryn finished simply. "You have one shot to convince the queen my story is true. This is your moment, Obsidian. Them or us."

Gemma held her breath as Obsidian looked at her.

This was more than she'd ever hoped for. If he allied with Malloryn, then perhaps the pair of them had a future.

If *she* had a future....

But Malloryn was demanding everything. Obsidian's loyalty. His soul. His future.

She knew he wasn't fond of the duke, or the council.

The former dukes of Casavian and Caine had been in charge of the Falkirk Asylum project, and two of their offspring were now on the council.

Could he do it? Could he look them in the eye, knowing what their fathers had sentenced him to, and maintain his composure?

Obsidian tilted his head toward her.

"I made my choice the second I kidnapped her. A part of me knew any potential future with my brethren was dwindling. It's always going to be Gemma. And if she is with you, then so am I."

It stole her breath.

Obsidian turned his icy gaze upon the duke. "But you should know, there are people on my side I will not stand against or betray. And I don't take orders well."

"Does it seem as if any of these damned fools take orders well?"

"We listen when it suits us, Your Grace," Byrnes said.

Malloryn ignored him. Standard procedure for dealing with Byrnes. "Come. I want to know everything you know. We need to prepare you for the council meeting."

"Welcome to the Company of Rogues," Charlie said, slapping a hand on his back. "This is really going to upset the ranking."

Obsidian shot him a dangerous look. "Touch me again and you'll lose that hand."

Charlie instinctively hauled it to his chest, his face paling.

"I was jesting," Obsidian said, allowing the faintest of smiles to touch his mouth.

He crossed to her side and offered her his arm, amusement warming his gray eyes.

"Do you think he's really kidding?" Charlie muttered, behind them.

Gemma let out a breath of relief. Oh, he'd fit right in. Eventually.

"According to Gemma, you're a sugarplum, Charlie," Obsidian called over his shoulder. "If I hurt you, Gemma's going to break my fingers. You're safe."

"What?" Charlie sounded aggrieved. "*Gemma!*"

"Your manhood's still intact," she said, rolling her eyes.

"A sugarplum?" Kincaid snickered with malicious delight. "That's brilliant."

"I wouldn't laugh too loudly," Obsidian said. "Unless you want me to repeat what she said about you?"

Kincaid shut up rather abruptly.

"That was somewhat wicked of you," she whispered, and then reached up to brush her lips against Obsidian's cheek. "Thank you."

"For being wicked?"

"For being mine," she replied, and turned her mouth to his to kiss him, right in front of everybody.

"We call it the neural control implant," Obsidian said, staring defiantly back at the seven council members who watched him like hawks. "It was initially developed in Russia, and modified for Lord Balfour's purposes here."

He stood just inside the brass ring set into the floor of the atrium, facing the dais. The atrium was perfectly rounded, columns circling the room. Light spilled through a stained glass window hanging over the dais, casting a luminescent sort of haze over the queen.

A gown of yellow silk draped her small figure, the golden diadem of the realm upon her brow. Eyes the color of warm whiskey locked on him, and her smooth cheeks held no expression. Tension lingered in the way she gripped the arms of her throne, and when she glanced at the ruined remains of the door, he knew why.

He'd barely caught a glimpse of her when Gemma tried to kill her. Merely a crowd of Coldrush Guards settling into place like a shield wall of blue blood bodies around her.

But she'd remember.

"It's a derivative of the device the Blood Court use to control their serfs in Russia. The Russians call it *tsep' razuma*—a chain of the mind—and it was created nearly twenty years ago following the Serf Rebellion. It keeps them docile and forces them to bow to the whims of their blue blood masters. There have been no uprisings since."

The queen's eyelids grew heavy. "They cannot fight it?"

"No."

The entire Council exchanged a look. He recognized Jasper and Rosalind Lynch, the Duke and Duchess of Bleight; Sir Gideon Scott, the head of the humanist faction in London; Aramina Barrons, the Duchess of Casavian, and her consort, Leo Barrons; and Blade, the Devil of Whitechapel. Every single one of them looked ill at ease.

Only Malloryn looked bored, but he'd heard this story several times over.

A faint tinge of horror darkened the queen's eyes. "And it is still in use?"

"The Blood Court is far less evolved than even the prince consort's," Malloryn murmured. "As horrifying as your husband's policies were, our humans were still somewhat protected. In Russia, they are livestock. There are no rules and one of the Blood may take as many lives as he wishes. I have heard of duchesses who fill their baths with blood to keep their skin youthful. Princes who refer to children as 'veal.' When the rebellion was crushed, the Blood chose to make an example of the rebellion's leaders. One in twenty of them were flayed, and their tongues were removed. The rest were crucified. To prevent such a thing from occurring again, most of the Blood forced their serfs and servants to be implanted. Now they cannot even scream when they are bled." Malloryn tipped his head toward Obsidian. "Go on. Tell her about our version of the neural implant."

"It was created by an English scientist named Henry Richter, who worked for Lord Balfour, and was inspired by the Russian version."

The queen flinched when he said Balfour's name.

"Balfour used it for nearly ten years before your own revolution, though it was an imperfect weapon. I believe you are aware of a recent case involving its use. There were rumors of an assassin named the Chameleon who plagued the Echelon and could not be caught. One of the reasons for his elusiveness was because the Chameleon's identity constantly changed. The scions of the Great Houses of the Echelon grew up watching their backs, so it was deemed too difficult to insert an assassin into their households. Instead, Balfour arranged for long-faithful servants or family to be kidnapped off the streets and implanted whilst under anesthesia. They were kept sedated until the procedure was completed, hypnotized, then returned to where they were taken minus their purses or jewelry to plant the seed this was merely a theft. Often they would awaken with no memory of the event, and only a small wound at the back of their skulls, easily explained away as a blow from a blunt object. They would return home and recover, and nobody would be any the wiser, as the neural implant is not activated until required. We called them drones."

"Sleeper agents of the worst kind," Malloryn mused. "The poor bastards didn't even know themselves."

"The Chameleon Protocol originally required a handler with a frequency box to 'flip the switch' so to speak. When the neural implant felt the right frequency vibrating nearby it would activate. Certain instructions were given to them under hypnosis, and the second the frequency blanked their minds they became mindless killing weapons. In some cases, they would not even remember having murdered their target. In others, the frequency destroyed their minds. Some resumed a vegetative state. It wasn't an entirely foolproof plan... until recently.

"Dr. Richter came up with a secondary neural implant which could be initiated purely by stating a certain combination of words. The frequency transmitter is embedded in the neural implant itself, and no handler is required. One can walk past the subject, state the code words, and continue on their way. We used to use a certain passage of music as the code, but there was an incident where one of the drones attended the opera. It didn't end well."

Malloryn looked up sharply. "Wagner's *Die Walkure*?"

"When that man strangled the conductor and shot two members of the audience before turning the pistol on himself?" the Duchess of Bleight asked.

"Yes." Ghost had been livid, and threatened to embed one of the neural implants in the good doctor if he ever heard the strains of the famous opera coming from the doctor's phonograph again.

To this day, Dr. Richter turned pale whenever Silas hummed the opening strains to "Ride of the Valkyries," which was as often as he got the doctor alone.

Silas would have gotten along well with Byrnes.

"How does one know if they've been implanted?" the Duke of Bleight asked.

"Unknown lapses in time, a 'blow' to the head or other unaccounted injury there, a sudden spate of nose bleeds.... The neural implant doesn't always work properly. Some people get a tic in their eyelid, or the muscle of their jaw. Some suffer brain hemorrhages. Indeed, Ghost's preferred victims are usually blue bloods, because the mark of the incision vanishes within an hour of the surgery, and the craving virus often heals any hemorrhages. They are also better assassins, and more difficult to kill."

The entire council shifted.

"Are there any of these 'drones' within the Ivory Tower?" Sir Gideon Scott asked.

"Two, as of my understanding. I gave their names to Malloryn this morning." He hesitated a second. "However, I was not involved in the Chameleon Protocol. It's Ghost's pet project, and I wouldn't be surprised to discover there are more sleeper agents than I'm aware of."

"'Ow the 'ell do we find 'em?" This from Blade.

"You can't," he replied. "The only way to be certain none of the guards or servants are affected is to shock them all, the way I did with Gemma. It shorts the electrics within the neural implant and renders it inert."

"It could also kill some of the human servants," the queen whispered in a horrified voice.

"How close do these handlers need to be to activate their drones?" Lynch asked.

"A hundred yards usually. Dr. Richter's been experimenting with the range."

"They wouldn't get close enough to activate someone within the tower." Lynch rubbed at his mouth. "The outer walls are at least two hundred yards away from the base."

"Therefore, an agent with the right code words would need to be in the building, similar to the situation with Miss Townsend," the Duchess of Casavian mused. "An inside job."

"Unless one keys the code to a certain phrase one expects to be uttered by a certain person," Obsidian countered.

"Such as?"

"And her Majesty, the Queen...." He raised his voice in an effective rendition of the page that had announced her.

The queen's face paled.

Questions poured forth in a sudden flurry as if he'd opened the floodgates, until his mouth grew dry from answering.

No, there was no means to say who was the next intended target for the "Chameleon."

No, he couldn't state where Lord Balfour was now, beyond Russia.

Yes, he could lead Malloryn and a handful of guards upon the *dhampir's* secret base beneath Undertown.

Yes, it was likely there would be retaliation for the botched assassination, as Ghost disliked failure.

Malloryn finally broke the flood of questions, crossing to the middle of the floor to stand next to him. "I know we all have more questions, and I assure you I will extract their answers from Obsidian when I have a chance, but time is growing shorter. We know there is a new threat to the realm, but now we're aware of what it is and which direction it's coming from, we have no time to waste. The queen's safety is at risk every second she stays in the tower. The Coldrush Guards and the servants need to be tested before we can pronounce it safe for the queen to return. And I believe we've all heard enough to pass judgment upon Miss Townsend."

Lynch nodded. "I believe Miss Townsend to be an unwitting tool in the hands of our enemy. All in favor, say aye."

"Aye." Blade.

"Aye." The Duchesses of Bleight and Casavian.

"Aye." Leo Barrons.

A long pause.

Sir Gideon Scott glanced toward the queen. "Unwitting or not, she took down twelve Coldrush Guards and came within inches of assassinating the queen."

Malloryn didn't bother looking at Scott, he merely turned his attention upon the queen—whom, he'd already told Obsidian—was the only one with the power to veto the Council's vote.

A certain sort of look passed between the queen and her spymaster.

"I need her," Malloryn said softly. "She's my best, and we're dealing with the most dangerous conspiracy I've ever had the displeasure of facing. I cannot afford to lose her."

No response from the queen's expression. "You're not usually this sentimental, Malloryn."

Obsidian stepped forward, drawing all eyes. "If Malloryn's argument doesn't sway you, then consider this: my cooperation depends entirely upon Miss Townsend's fate."

"Your fate depends upon my goodwill," she retorted, "for you have worked against this country and its people, and your destiny balances on a knife's edge as it is. Do *not* threaten me—"

"Alexa." A single word from the Duchess of Casavian, but the queen seemed to give it more consideration than any of the others.

"They compromised my throne room."

"It was a fright, I know, but we cannot afford to make emotional decisions. We have learned more today than we have in months." The duchess captured the queen's hand. "With this information we can be prepared for the next assault. We can even set a trap if we will it. Balfour clearly escaped justice once. It cannot be allowed to happen again. I want his head."

The queen pushed to her feet, her skirts sweeping around her ankles as she strode to the edge of the dais. "Very well, Malloryn. I shall grant Miss Townsend a temporary reprieve. You have one week to bring me the head of this Ghost and his compatriots. Someone must pay for this incursion into my bloody throne room. If it is not to be Miss Townsend, then it will be these *dhampir*. Now get out of my sight."

CHAPTER
TWENTY-EIGHT

"The Core's in a former pumping station that was part of Undertown," Obsidian explained. "It's the base of all Balfour's London operations. Years ago, when the Eastern Underground Railway project was disbanded, Balfour took over the pumping station and began fitting it out as a secret facility to train his Falcons. He spent years using treasury funds to make the facility watertight, and when it was finished about fifteen years ago, the tunnels were flooded to prevent any of the local slasher gangs from taking up residence. I suspect they're not the only ones he wanted to hide from."

Malloryn gave a thin, unamused smile. "Right about the time some mysterious unknown agent stole some top-secret documents revealing the names of all his Falcon trainees, and somehow left them on the table in the Council chambers. It derailed his entire Falcon training program. Half of them vanished overnight, particularly those who turned up in the employ of the Dukes of Goethe, Vickers, Morioch, and Bleight. The prince consort was somewhat displeased with his spymaster."

Obsidian looked at Gemma. "How terribly awkward for Balfour. I wonder how someone got their hands on a list of all his student Falcons."

She smiled, just faintly, and sipped her cup of blooded tea. "Balfour must have been careless and left such a list out in plain view. Or in a locked safe, if one is being particular, but who can truly say? And I suppose if he—or his Falcons—had managed to forsake a young trainee's loyalty and cast her to the wolves, she might have taken exception with the circumstances and chosen to do something about it. I'm not saying it was my first mission for Malloryn, but there are certainly revealing coincidences in the timeline of when I defected."

"Hence why she was immediately sent out of the country for several years," Malloryn muttered. "It was a glorious—very dangerous—blow to Balfour. I hear he wanted to see heads roll."

That was his girl. "It seems I was transferred to the Core barely days after you defected from the Falcons. I wonder... what would it have been like if we'd met then?"

How close their paths had come to crossing for years, but it wasn't until he'd been taken to Russia to assist in furthering Balfour's plans there, he'd come across her.

"Kismet," Ingrid murmured.

"Fate," Ava added.

"Good grief," Malloryn said. "Can we focus on planning a highly intense mission into a facility full of killers?"

All three women sighed.

"I'd hoped marriage would soften you," Ingrid said.

"It's romantic," Ava protested.

"It's called pure coincidence," Malloryn replied sarcastically. "And why the hell would marriage soften me?"

"Because I've got fifty quid riding on it," Kincaid said.

Byrnes tried to surreptitiously punch him in the ribs, but the breath exploded from Kincaid and he hunched over.

"Christ. Fuckin'. Jaysus. You keep forgetting your strength these days."

"Sorry," Byrnes said, sounding anything but.

"Fifty quid?" Malloryn's tone turned dangerous as he glanced between both men. His gaze expanded to consider the rest of the room. "I thought we'd finished this nonsense when I married Miss Hamilton?"

Byrnes held his hands up in surrender. "But nobody won. Technically, the bride didn't cry off, and neither did you. Ava was the only one who said you'd get Miss Hamilton to the altar, but she didn't put money on it. So the kitty still stands."

Malloryn's eyes narrowed. "Precisely what are we betting on this time?"

Seven mouths clamped suspiciously shut. Obsidian couldn't resist a faint smile. COR was so different to what he'd known beneath Balfour. He was still growing used to their insolence, and the frustrated way Malloryn seemed to take it all in stride, but he couldn't deny it amused him.

"If we tell you," Gemma admitted, "then it could muddy the waters of the betting pool, because we might be subtly manipulating your decision."

"Herbert?" Malloryn asked coldly.

"I haven't a clue, Your Grace. I am merely the butler."

"Ava?" Malloryn turned on the delicate blonde, as if he knew exactly whom he could break.

"She's as guilty as the rest of us this time," Kincaid said, with a grin, as he settled an arm around his lover's waist. "I'm rubbing off on her."

"Only because I *hope* my bet comes true," Ava told the duke fervently. "It would be lovely to see you happy."

Malloryn pinched the bridge of his nose. "My God. I'm not certain if I *want* to know."

Obsidian tensed, but there was no sign of any fatal eruption coming from the duke.

Merely a pained silence.

Balfour would have given an icy glare and a faint gesture that had one of his Falcons beating the unlucky supplicant who'd spoken half to death.

Ghost would have simply put a bullet in the brain of the first man who thought to jest.

That Malloryn—the duke Balfour cursed under his breath as his most dangerous opponent—merely pressed his lips tightly together in a way that said "I am unamused" left Obsidian unsettled. If there was anything that could convince him the Duke of Malloryn wasn't entirely a cold, manipulative bastard, it was the way he tolerated their banter.

Gemma's hand slipped into his, as if she sensed his unease. "You'll get used to it."

"I hope he doesn't. He's the only one of you who seems to understand what's at stake." Malloryn pressed both hands on the desk. "Is there any chance we could focus on the mission? Any chance at all?" He shot Gemma a look that cut through the laughter. "I thought you wanted to take down the man who put that neural implant in your brain and took over your will?"

This time it was Obsidian's turn to lance the duke with a stare. He pressed his hand to the small of Gemma's back as she abruptly sobered. She'd been trying to forget what happened, and despite his unease with the easy way these people interacted, he knew she needed it.

Gallows humor and all that.

"Of course I do," Gemma replied.

"Have you got paper?" Obsidian asked.

Malloryn snapped his fingers, and Herbert managed to provide paper and a spring-loaded pen.

"What are we to expect?" the duke asked.

There was no way to explain the breadth and scope of the Core. Obsidian began to draw instead, sketching out a map of the internals.

"Munitions factory is here. Training center here. Medical. The lab. These are the cells," he murmured, his pen moving sharply over the paper.

"Munitions factory?" Charlie repeated.

"Cells?" Malloryn's icy gray eyes locked on him.

"Where the newly created *dhampir* are held. Ghost wants them kept separate until their training is completed and they can prove they're in control of the increased blood-lust." It was also where he kept the most dangerous of the *dhampir*. "This cell on the end belongs to X. Avoid this area at all costs. If this cell door is open, evacuate the Core immediately."

"Why?" Charlie asked suspiciously.

"X is one of the original *dhampir*. When we were in Falkirk he started fixating upon one of the nurses. She was kind to him, and he was always... a little unhinged. Dr. Cremorne didn't approve and moved her to another area. X is the one who started the original breakout. He tore his reinforced cell door off and ripped half the building down looking for her. We took advantage of the unrest to escape, but in the fire, Mary died from smoke inhalation. He couldn't understand and he's never been the same. Ghost was forced to insert the neural implant in him to try and control him, but it had an adverse effect upon him. If he gets loose he will kill anything and everything in the Core. If he escapes the Core, he will continue his rampage until it's over. We keep a shock collar on him at all times, and Silas is the only one who can get through to him."

"Excellent." Charlie locked his fingers together and stretched them. "A volatile *dhampir* who makes dangerous *dhampir* assassins sweat. Petition to avoid this entire area completely?"

"Granted," Byrnes said, as if he had the right.

"How many *dhampir* does Ghost have?" Malloryn rested his knuckles on the desk, leaning over the map.

"There are thirty-four *dhampir* recruits in the training center—or there were. A new brand of weapon, conscripted from those of his former Falcons who survived the revolution. Balfour wanted to improve his forces and strip the weakness from them, but only one in three survives the serum transformation. Dr. Richter was forced to replicate Dr. Erasmus Cremorne's *elixir vitae* from our blood samples, and the initial batches proved fatal. Hundreds died until he managed to get the formula to work. Balfour's been searching for Cremorne's diary for years, but one of the former inmates of the asylum said it was destroyed in the fire."

"Thirty-four is more than enough," Malloryn replied through gritted teeth. "His Falcons were more than enough. How the hell are we supposed to deal with over thirty *dhampir*?"

"We're going to need the Nighthawks," Gemma said. "For manpower."

"It gets worse, Your Grace. You're forgetting the rest of us."

"Rest of you?" Byrnes choked out.

"The originals," Gemma murmured. "Those blue bloods who were given over to Falkirk Asylum and survived Dr. Cremorne's experiments. Ghost, Obsidian, Silas, and X."

"Dido is with Balfour in Russia, along with one of the Russian operatives, Jelena. Pray you never meet Jelena. They call her the Ivory Kraken, and she's almost fanatical in her devotion to Balfour. Neither of them were in Falkirk, but created within the Crimson Court." Obsidian strolled around the desk. "X is to be avoided at all costs, and I would prefer to keep Silas out of this if possible—"

"The queen wants the heads of all the *dhampir* arrayed against her," Malloryn pointed out, "or she may take her wrath out upon Gemma."

Obsidian laced his arms across his chest. "I will do anything within my power to protect Gemma. But Silas is my brother. He's the only one I give a damn about."

"He made his choices."

"And I am making mine."

They stared at each other.

"I'm not alone in not having much of a choice," he said softly. "I don't want to redeem myself for actions I couldn't help taking. But I want to reclaim what is left of me. If I let him die without at least trying to sway him, then what does that make me? I told you I wouldn't always obey you. I know where he will be. I only need an hour to warn him before we leave, and you have much to plan before the night is out."

Malloryn's eyes narrowed. "You could risk the entire operation."

"I won't risk Gemma's life. Not even for Silas. But I need to know where his loyalty lies before I completely sunder mine."

"Do you want company?" A muscle ticked in Malloryn's jaw.

"I will deal with Silas by myself. I have... questions for him."

After all, he'd been starting to think about Russia ever since Gemma told him she hadn't set that fire.

He *needed* to know the truth.

And he'd been away from the brotherhood for days now. Who knew what was going on within the ranks?

Silas would know.

"Fine." Malloryn surveyed the rest of the room. "I'll grant you an hour, then I want Ava to prep you for surgery. We need to get that bomb out of your head, or you're useless to me."

"Thank you for caring."

"Don't be late. I'm choosing to grant you a great deal of faith. Gemma and Ingrid, I want you to coordinate the Nighthawks for a dawn strike. Everyone else, begin preparations. I want maps of the area. An assault plan in place. Everybody armored up and carrying as much ammunition as you can possibly handle. You too, Herbert."

Everybody looked at Herbert.

"Yes, Your Grace," the butler said, with a crisp nod, and began to strip out of his superfine coat. "May I bring Molly?"

Gemma grimaced. "This place is located under tons of water, Herbert. One blast through the walls, and we're swimming. I think I'd prefer it if you *didn't* have an explosive shoulder cannon in your armory."

The butler looked somewhat crestfallen.

"Actually, that's why I've invited Herbert. I'm not interested in capturing these *dhampir* or chastising them. I want to cut Balfour's strings out from under him. The plan is to ensure all *dhampir* either killed or captured; and complete and utter destruction of the Core," Malloryn said. "The last of which is right up Herbert's alley."

"I can work with that," Kincaid replied.

"Hear, hear." Byrnes said.

"Let's do this," Charlie said, excitement flashing in his blue eyes.

But Obsidian felt the first stir of doubt through his gut.

Because Ghost had to know his loyalty had shifted by now, and if there was one thing the bastard relished, it was planning a trap.

"Got your note," Silas called, behind him. "Considerin' there's a certain volatile murderous scurf who'd love to get his hands on you right now, what d'you want? It ain't a good idea for either of us to be seen in each other's company."

Obsidian stared out over the city, the wind flapping the hem of his long coat and stirring his hair as he rested one foot on the edge of the guttering of Silas's favorite pub. He couldn't see a single sign of Byrnes, but he knew the other *dhampir* was out there, tracking him. No doubt ensuring he didn't reveal their hand to the enemy.

So much for Malloryn's trust.

"Is Ghost angry?"

Silas snorted. "Spittin' mad. Wants your head on a pike. You know how he gets about betrayal."

"I offered him terms," he said, turning his head to look at his brother. "Gemma's life for my continued loyalty. Considering he put a bloody neural device in her head and sent her to murder the queen, I'll take that as a no. He speaks of betrayal?" His smile held sharp edges. "He's the one who deals it. And in this case, he will reap what he sowed."

"The problem with grantin' you Miss Townsend's life is that your loyalty will always be hers first. He's never liked that. You had to know he'd say no."

"I knew."

But I... hoped.

Silas scratched the back of his head. "Then why the ruttin' hell are you here?"

"Partly to warn you: Malloryn intends to destroy Ghost's operation. I'm going to light the match for him and watch it all burn. Stay out of the way. And then there is another part, the part of me that wants to know the truth. About Russia."

There.

The sudden stillness in Silas's smile. The twitch of his fingers toward his hip, where he kept his pistol. It all played out over Silas's face. *Do I go for the pistol? Or do I try and play this out?*

Obsidian couldn't say he was completely surprised, but it still hurt. Suspicion flavored most of his daily thoughts; he'd hoped, just this once, he'd be proved wrong. He'd told Gemma he trusted two people in this world, and now that figure was halved.

The only one you can trust is Gemma.

She was the light leading him out of his darkness.

"Russia?" Silas's next footfall came a little warily, but he managed to arch a brow. "Seems best to leave all that dead and buried, if you ask me, mate."

"I wasn't asking."

"Fuck me." Silas scrubbed at his mouth. "What d'you want to know? Why now?"

Obsidian began to tug the tips of his leather gloves from his fingers. "I'm starting to recall certain memories. Enough to make me wonder about them. For instance, I've always been able to remember the night Gemma allegedly set fire to my bedroom after drugging me. But, she claims she didn't do it, and I have no recollection of her involvement."

"Of course she'd—"

"I wasn't finished." He dropped the glove, flexing his fingers, and Silas watched the move like a hawk. "I trust her, Silas. But moreover, I trust the fact she had no *reason* to burn me alive. It wasn't Gemma, which means it was someone else. So I started thinking maybe it was Malloryn. I'd seduced his spy and turned her attention from his cause. He would have wanted to remove me, but from what Gemma has told me he didn't *know* I was working for Balfour until the day after the fire.

"Which leaves me with one other suspect. Someone who might have wanted to see Gemma and me parted, no matter what they had to do. Someone who'd made it quite clear he didn't like the attention I paid her. You said it yourself. Ghost doesn't want anyone standing between our loyalty to him. He's a jealous mistress."

"*Don't.*"

"Brotherhood before blood," Obsidian quoted. "Brotherhood before *all* else. Ghost's been meticulous in ensuring our loyalties were never split. He's always demanded our hearts, our souls, and if we started to stray, then he made sure he reeled us back in. Ghost doesn't care for us. He never has. But he demands our loyalty and adoration, and he uses the ties we had—the thought of creating a family when we all lost ours—as a means to chain us to his cause.

"What we have is a mockery. A perversion of family." Especially when he could see the way the Company of Rogues operated. They'd fight for each other. Die for each other. Even Malloryn. "Which brings me to a line of questioning that makes me wonder... I went from a man madly in love with Hollis to someone who was willing to lose all his memories of her and put a bullet in her chest. That's a significant turnaround even I fail to truly believe. I can't fully remember her, but I know how I felt."

I know how I feel.

And it was the first time the Wraith made an appearance.

"You thought she'd tried to burn you alive," Silas said hoarsely.

Obsidian stared through him, seeing the flames again. "I wouldn't have killed her. Not for that." A laugh escaped him. "I *can't* kill her. The second I saw her, I knew she was mine, but I didn't realize some dark piece of me claimed her years ago." Silas came into focus again. "I remember snatches of information about the Chameleon Project. I wouldn't have volunteered for that, no matter how much I thought I wanted to forget her. None of this makes sense to me. So tell the damned truth. *Please.* You owe me that, if nothing else."

"The truth ain't always what you want it to be."

"Do you think I'm afraid of the truth?" He took a menacing step forward, his voice softening. "I always thought you saved me from being burned alive that night. But how did you know there was a fire in my room? The fire started near the bed, and while the bed was ablaze, the rest of the room was only just starting to burn. You had to be close by. Awake. Listening, perhaps. Unless, of course, you set the fire."

All the remaining blood fled Silas's face.

He shook his head, his mouth working, and Obsidian's heart felt like a lump of coal in his chest as suspicion bloomed into understanding.

"I trusted you," he breathed. "I thought you risked your life to save mine. It's the one thing that's kept me going all these years, while he turns my fucking brain to mush. Brotherhood. It meant something *to me*. Why?"

"Because I overheard the pair of you talking one night about runnin' away together. I thought she'd gotten to you. I thought she'd twisted your head, and I told Ghost and.... I screwed up. I botched it. You should have seen the look in his eyes.

"He told me what to do to win you back to our cause, and so I did. I drugged you. Set the fire. Rescued you. It was supposed to be enough but you wouldn't listen. You were worried she'd been in there when that side of the palace went up. You would have burst back in to rescue her, and that was when he took you down with hemlock and sent for Richter. If you wouldn't remain with us of your own accord, then he would ensure you remained out of his."

Silas squeezed his eyes shut in horror. "I didn't *know* what she meant to you 'til it was too late. You were still screamin' for her when they put that fuckin' thing in your head, but when you woke up you were empty. Gave me the shivers just to look at you.

"And Ghost.... He thought it poetic justice to send you after her and put a bullet in her heart. That was the first task he set upon you and it made me ill. But what I hadn't counted on—what I'd never expected—was her feelin's for you." Silas paused, as if seeing it all over again. "I was there as your handler when she ran across that bridge to you. Malloryn was going to kill you, but she threw herself between you." His head bowed low. "I didn't know until then."

"And the explosion?"

The one Gemma believed he'd died in.

Another shudder tore through Silas. "Jelena, I think." He held his hands up as Obsidian took a menacing step toward him. "I don't know. But she wanted you dead. Called you a traitor. And her and Ghost had words afterwards. He had plans for you."

"You son of a bitch."

Silas swallowed. "What are you goin' to do?"

"The same as before. Kill Ghost. Destroy his precious brotherhood. Remind him of what I promised him if he hurt Gemma."

"And me?"

All of this could be laid at Silas's door. Rage burst through him. He'd lost his *mind* because of Silas's treachery, and he wasn't fool enough to think Silas would have confessed if he'd never brought it up.

"I ought to kill you."

Silas turned and darted for the edge of the roof, but Obsidian had been waiting for it. Drawing his dartgun from within his coat, he shot his brother in the neck with a hemlock dart.

Silas took two more steps before his right knee began to weaken beneath him. As Obsidian lowered the dartgun, Silas went down like a marionette with his strings cut. All it would take to end this would be to draw the knife at his side.

He took Gemma from you.

The darkness whispered through him.

A void where the darkest recesses of his soul blinked endless, bottomless eyes back at him. *"Are you ever afraid of what you're capable of?"* Gemma had asked him.

Yes.

Obsidian stalked slowly toward his fallen brother, and there was such an emptiness within him, he didn't know if he could do it or not.

Flames swirled around him again. Fear choking him. Silas coming out of nowhere to rescue him.

He could recall the almost crippling grief he'd felt when he'd thought Gemma betrayed him. The loss of all he'd hoped for between them. His heart had grieved for her. For the lie he'd fallen for.

The relief he'd felt when Silas saved him—an act that proved someone had his back, no matter how easily love had proved to be a lie—was turned on its head.

Silas had never been there for him.

Obsidian closed his eyes.

Time to put more of his pieces back together. But this time, he'd do it properly.

Kneeling down, he flipped Silas over and grabbed him by the throat. Hauling him upwards until the toes of his boots dangled off the ground, Obsidian bared his teeth.

"I could kill you. But I won't," he said, his fingers tightening on Silas's throat. "You are not my brother. You are not my family. You are nothing to me. I've been holding on to the past because of you. I *believed* there was an unbreakable bond between us. I would have risked my life to save you.

"But time and time again, you have proven you value your own skin before mine. *Forged in the fires of Falkirk.* What a joke. Blinded by the smoke of Falkirk, to be honest." He let Silas drop to his knees, and lowered his hand to his side. "There is nothing left for me in the brotherhood. There never was a brotherhood."

As much as the pain of betrayal burned within him, it felt like there was a weight lifted off his shoulders at the words.

He finally knew what mattered.

He knew who he could trust.

Who would be there at his side no matter what. Or throwing herself between him and danger because he mattered to her. His life held value to Gemma, just like all the other Rogues she'd taken into her heart and vowed to protect.

Everything he'd tried to hold on to—family, brotherhood, a sense of belonging, a reason to fight—could be found in his love for Gemma.

And as Silas tried to speak through a paralyzed throat, his fingers twitching, Obsidian stepped back. There was nothing more to say. He finally knew the truth.

He was done.

Or no.... Just one more thing left to do to finally cut all ties.

"You'd be wise to avoid returning to the Core tonight," he murmured, as he walked away. "Consider your life my last gift to you, for all I thought we shared. I hope it gives you cold comfort when you're all alone."

Silas crawled onto his hands and knees long minutes after Obsidian had left, his fingers shaking as he lit his cheroot.

Bloody ruttin' hell. He couldn't help feeling as though he'd stared death in the face and somehow survived.

He should have been kissing the bloody ground beneath him, but there was a hollow pit within him. A horrible, empty feeling, as though he'd done the wrong thing and lost the one person who mattered most to him in this world.

"What the fuck was I s'posed to do?" Smoke spilled from his pursed lips. "They would have killed him."

The second Obsidian set eyes on Hollis Beechworth his brother had begun to wear a target on his back. Ghost didn't believe in betrayal unless he was the one doing it. And they'd all seen the way Obsidian looked at her.

Sooner or later, he would have broken faith with them.

Unless they somehow severed the growing bond between Obsidian and Hollis.

"They would have killed *me* if I didn't do as commanded," he said, but there was an ugly truth there he didn't like to stare in the eye.

"You value your own skin before mine...."

I set the fire.

I set this all into play.

I convinced him he could trust Dr. Richter and the neural device.

I deserve to have him look at me like that.

And now he'd lost the one brother he truly had, and he was in this muck up to his eyeballs with no way out. *Sink or swim*, Silas's mam had always said, but he couldn't even see the shore anymore.

Or could he?

The Core.

Obsidian was going to burn it.

But there was just one thing Obsidian didn't know.

Ghost wasn't alone.

And he'd been expecting the attack.

Fuck.

CHAPTER THIRTY

Dawn silvered the skies.

Gemma felt like a stripped-down version of herself as she primed her weapon on the top of the carriage. Usually she had nerves of steel before a mission, running through her checklist of weapons, and going over and over the mission details and map in her head.

But she kept getting this fluttery feeling in her chest, right beneath her diaphragm.

The Chameleon episode had broken some part of her, and she worried she'd never get it back.

"Are you all right?" Obsidian murmured.

He looked deadly in the formfitting black leather body armor he'd borrowed from the Nighthawks. Strands of ashen brown hair hung to his shoulders. The blond was starting to shine through the dye, like glints of moonlight woven through his hair.

"Are you?"

This was a direct strike at those he'd once considered brothers, after all. She knew how much he longed for family and acceptance, for something to belong to.

No matter whether he'd made the choice to throw his lot in with her and COR, there must still be a part of him that ached for the loss he was facing. Not a single hint of it marred his expression, but then it never did. She was slowly learning to read the minutest ticks of muscle in his jaw and around his eyes. The less emotion he showed, the more he felt, she suspected.

And this morning he was locked down tight, his expression as impenetrable as a vault.

"There's nothing there for me anymore. I don't even know if there ever was. My head's still a mess. I can't work out what's real and what is not." His lashes fluttered. "I saw Silas."

"And?"

Obsidian looked down, giving her hand a faint squeeze. "He set the fire in Russia in order to blame you. It was all a ploy designed to make me distrust you."

That had to hurt.

Gemma stroked his thumb. She understood what he wasn't saying. He'd loved her. And his brothers had seen her as such a threat to his loyalty, they'd engineered a way to fracture his belief in her. It was the missing piece to the puzzle. Everything that happened in Russia had been real. "I must have frightened them a great deal."

He looked up sharply.

"I'm sorry they went to such lengths." She bit her lower lip. "I'm sorry you lost so much because of me—"

"Not because of you," he said instantly, capturing her face with his other hand. "I won't have that. Ghost made his choices. This sits on his head. And I am going to remove it, as payment."

"And Silas?"

It was the one name that made his voice soften, though she wasn't certain if he was aware of it. "He's dead to me."

The same thing he'd said to her once.

"They took everything," he continued. "They took you. They took my memories of my mother. Everything."

"You're getting certain memories back," she said, squeezing his hand. "You can't expect it to happen overnight."

"What if I never get all of them back?"

Gemma scraped her fingers down his chest. There wasn't an inch of fat on him. Only muscle, thick and corded beneath the body armor. Hard. But there was a sense of vulnerability in his voice. "Then we create new ones," she whispered, reaching up and brushing her mouth to his.

Gemma cupped the back of his head and drew him down to her. The kiss felt achingly familiar, and yet somehow unique. Soft. Gentle. All things neither of them had shared with each other before.

She knew sex. She knew pleasure inside out, and exactly how to make a man fall to his knees. But she'd never known this before, not even in Russia.

Vulnerability. Affection. Love.

There were no more secrets between them. No reason not to give herself into his hands. And it was an utterly breathless feeling that made her tremble, despite the barely carnal nature of the kiss.

"Because our story isn't over," she whispered against his lips, as she twined her fingers through his hair. "Its just beginning, *lyubov moya*."

Someone coughed.

"Egad," Kincaid muttered behind them. "Excuse me while I gag."

"I thought it quite touching. Our little Gemma. In love." This from Byrnes. "And if it's any consolation, you and Ava were worse. You kept thinking you were dying. I swear you were begging Malloryn for more time to be with your *kitten* at one point."

"Asshole."

"Prick."

Gemma lowered herself onto her toes, shooting them a rather vexed look.

Byrnes slipped his brass communicator into his ear as he blatantly stared at the pair of them and grinned unrepentantly. Kincaid looked like he'd bitten into a rotten plum.

"I take it all back," she told Obsidian. "Charlie is a sugarplum, and thus to be protected at all costs. But you are quite welcome to thrash either of these two."

The faintest of smiles touched Obsidian's mouth. "Grant me a little credit, my love." He raised his voice. "I'm an assassin. If I want revenge, then nobody would ever see me coming, and it will happen when they least expect it. I'm also fairly imaginative when it comes to paying someone back in kind."

Kincaid actually paled.

Ingrid stalked past, slapping her husband across the back of his head. "Leave them alone and come buckle me up."

"But Ingrid," Byrnes mock moaned, as he followed her, "they were just getting to the gushy part."

Gemma released a deep breath and fixed Obsidian's buckles. "Are you certain you have no regrets? I wouldn't blame you if you did, I must say. You have me now, but unfortunately these fools come with me."

Obsidian stared after Byrnes with a considering look. "You don't know how lucky you are."

The words stalled her. *Lucky?* And then she understood. He'd had no one—the closest ally he'd ever owned had betrayed him.

Gemma kissed him on the cheek. "We'd better join the others. They're about to break into the tunnels."

"Before we go, I have a gift for you," he said, tugging something out of his leather coat. He'd wrapped it in a piece of black silk.

"What is it?"

"Probably not the sort of thing most women hope to get from their lovers." His expression was so serious. So intense. As if he wanted to please her, but wasn't certain this was the right move. "But then, you're not most women."

That stirred her curiosity.

"I adore presents."

"Why does that not surprise me?" His eyes glinted with warm humor.

Gemma unwrapped the package swiftly, revealing a thin steel interlocking necklace that looked somewhat akin to a collar. She could just make out the two small probes jutting out on the side, and a faint frown touched her brow before she realized what they were. Spark conductors.

Her breath caught. "It's a shock collar."

The Coldrush Guards used them on their most dangerous prisoners.

Obsidian tugged the control device out of his pocket. "Range is fifty feet. I flick this switch and you'll go down, a pulse of current running through you."

His earnest gaze met hers, and Gemma was lost for a moment in their arctic depths.

"I know you're nervous the implant might not be destroyed. This will prevent any chance you're a risk to those you love."

Her heart skipped a beat as she reached up to throw her arms around him. Though Ava had managed to get the neural implant out of his head, there'd been no time to deal with hers. "Thank you."

Gemma clicked the collar into place around her throat. "Shock me if this all goes wrong."

"I promise."

And just like that, all the doubt vanished.

Kincaid snorted nearby. "Christ. Fuckin'. Jaysus. Byrnes and I are going to have to sort you out, mate. A shock collar?"

"You wouldn't understand if I tried to explain it," she told him.

"It's done, Gemma," Malloryn said, slipping out of his coat and sliding a shoulder holster over his arms. "Jack said the neural implant was deactivated when he tested it."

Only Obsidian understood. "There are no certainties the neural implant won't reactivate. And until you've lived through it, it's difficult to believe you can trust yourself. I'm Gemma's guarantee she won't lose control again."

She needed that certainty. The fluttery feeling was gone. She *couldn't* hurt anyone if Obsidian held the shock controller. She felt like her old self again.

Grabbing a fistful of his coat, Gemma stretched up on her toes, finding his mouth. The kiss was hungry and desperate. And regrettably, all too short.

"Remind me to thank you later," she breathed, as she lowered herself onto her toes.

His hand slid over her bottom, where he gave her a cheeky pinch. "I'm counting on it."

"Now let's go burn this hellhole to the ground."

Black waters stirred beneath them as Gemma paused on the edge of the Core dock. They'd spent twenty minutes traversing the cold, dark tunnels of Undertown, jumping at every rat that scurried away from them in the darkness.

She couldn't see a damned thing below the water, but Obsidian assured her it was there, and he'd taken out a *dhampir* acolyte on guard in the entrance to Undertown.

One down. Far too many to go.

Byrnes, Herbert, and Ingrid were going to swim into the Core with a handful of Nighthawks, attacking from the rear, thanks to Byrnes drawing the short straw. There was an escape hatch there, Obsidian had explained, which would lead them directly to the munitions factory. Blow the factory and get the hell out, Obsidian had told them, because the training center was nearby and there'd be a dozen good little *dhampir* acolytes in there, vying for Ghost's attention.

Charlie and Kincaid were suited up in a pair of mech suits. Kincaid wore his Achilles II after the first had been crumpled in the draining factory, and Charlie wore a revolution-standard Cyclops that stood about twelve feet tall, his pale face serious behind the single glass slit in his head-mask that gave the Cyclops its name. They were leading a team through the elevation chamber down to a sublevel of the Core, and working their way up.

Which left the air ducts and the cells.

"There's the duct." Obsidian pointed to the enormous steel pipe that clung to the nearby wall. "It will take us directly to the cells."

"Any rousing speeches?" Charlie whispered loudly.

"Don't get killed," Malloryn retorted, tucking his aural communicator into his ear. "Get in, lay your charges, and get out. We've got Ava and Jack on communications, so make sure you touch in with them. Rendezvous point is the safe house at midnight if we lose each other. Watch your backs."

"Aye, Your Grace." Charlie snapped a salute, pistons hissing in the Cyclops suit as he and Kincaid headed for the elevation chamber that led down into the Core. Ten Nighthawks followed them.

"Ready?" Gemma asked, staring at the air duct. An access hole rested several feet above them, the enormous wheel rusted over from the damp tunnels.

"Ladies first?" Obsidian graced her with a smile as she tested the buckles on her harness.

"Heading into a creepy underwater bunker filled with *dhampir*?" Gemma grinned at him. "It's possibly the only occasion where I might insist you go ahead."

Obsidian climbed up to the access hole and used sheer strength to twist the enormous wheel. He popped the cover open and vanished inside, feet first.

Gemma followed, finding herself in a narrow duct that led directly down. Using her hands and feet to hold herself there, she clipped the steel cable that was attached to her harness to an empty rivet hole, took a deep breath, and then dropped down through the duct.

The cable whizzed from the reel at her waist, letting her plummet almost to the bottom. Light spilled through another access hole Obsidian had opened, and she hauled herself up short and slipped through, unclipping herself.

Obsidian knelt beside her, packing away his harness into the small satchel he carried. He drew a pair of wicked-looking knives. "*Ready?*" he mouthed, as Malloryn and several Nighthawks joined them.

Gemma nodded.

The fluttering had gone away, her heart was pounding, and all her senses were on high alert. Drawing the pair of sai strapped to her thighs, she gestured for Obsidian to lead.

Time to kill some *dhampir*.

Working with the Nighthawks held an odd sense of familiarity that comforted Byrnes, even as he stared down into the dark waters.

Until the Guild Master paused beside him.

"Just like old times," Garrett said, flashing a grin at Byrnes. "You. Me. Vampire infested tunnels. Possible mayhem."

"Don't get yourself killed," Byrnes said tightly, as he slipped the breathing apparatus over his head. "My heart's barely recovered from last month. I am *not* going to have to tell your wife some *dhampir* ripped your throat out."

"I already promised Perry nothing's going to happen to me. Apart from punching a *dhampir* or two in the teeth with this." Garrett flexed the steel fingers of his bio-mech arm, and Byrnes couldn't help looking at it.

A member of the Sons of Gilead had tried to shoot Garrett in the heart during a riot, in the hopes the Nighthawks would clash with the human populace. At the very last second, Ava had saved Garrett's life by crying a warning, though he'd had lost his arm in the process.

The craving virus could heal almost everything, but as Byrnes paced outside Garrett's room that day, he'd honestly wondered if Garrett would survive.

It had not been the best moment of his life.

Needless to say, the second Byrnes got a chance to breathe, he was going to go hunting for a certain SOG rifleman. He might even invite Perry. She could always be counted on for a certain spot of murderous revenge.

"Are you ready for this?" he asked Garrett, in a quieter voice.

They'd never exactly seen eye-to-eye, but Garrett was probably one of his first true friends, as much as Byrnes could call anyone a friend. He wasn't... used to feeling like this for other people. Worrying about them. Nervous for the coming fight. All his emotions had been on edge since he'd been forcibly turned into a *dhampir*, and he didn't like it one bit.

Garrett squinted at him in the dark. "Well, I'll be damned. I thought I was talking to Doyle then for a second. He's the one who hovers over me like a nursemaid, not you. Are you sure *you're* all right? I'm not used to this more emotional Byrnes. Ingrid's been a good influence on you."

"Sod off."

Garrett grinned at him. "I'm fine. I promise not to die, or get eaten by a *dhampir*. And when this is all done, you're going to sit down for that arm wrestle you've been promising me for the last month. I know I'm going to beat you, *dhampir* or not." He looked down into the dark waters. "Are you ready?"

Byrnes gave him a thin smile, "Last one in is—"

Garrett shoved him into the water.

The *dhampir* initiates spent most of their lives in their personal quarters or the training center, Obsidian had explained. With the sun rising, a good number of them would be heading to bed.

Which meant they'd be handling the most dangerous section of the facility.

Gemma gestured several of the Nighthawks to fall into place behind her as she pressed her spine to the wall and held her pistol cocked.

Across the hallway from her, Obsidian did the same.

He arched a brow at her. *Ready?*

Gemma nodded.

Holding up three fingers, he slowly counted down. Then they were moving. Rolling into the corridor, she kicked the door of the closest cell open and tossed a smoke bomb inside. A coughing figure emerged, trying to haul his shirt up over his mouth and nose.

Gemma spun and kicked him in the head. As he staggered, she shot him five times. Head and heart. Brutal but efficient. One of the Nighthawks behind her was prepared to cut his heart out as she took point again.

Moving like clockwork, they cleared each cell. Gemma kicked the next door open, coming face to face with a startled *dhampir* who had a knife in hand. He blinked in surprise, and she shot him right between the eyes. His body hit the floor, and she stepped forward and drilled two more bullets into his head, and one into his heart, just in case.

"Clear," she said, as she ducked back out into the corridor.

The Nighthawks were working in pairs.

Malloryn moved with lethal efficiency, but Obsidian was the maestro. Smoke roiled through the cells, brightened only by gunfire. Gemma took another *dhampir* down, and as she emerged, she realized nobody was shooting anymore.

All in all, it probably took them a minute to neutralize the cells, and the final head count was eleven *dhampir* acolytes down and out for good.

Then they were at the end of the hallway, breathing hard.

The last cell door was reinforced heavily, with several iron bars slotted into place.

Obsidian held his finger up to his lips. "X," he mouthed.

An enormous bang suddenly vibrated the door, and Gemma reloaded her pistol, her heart hammering.

"He can't break out, can he?" Malloryn asked quietly.

"These cells can hold a vampire."

Obsidian gestured her past in a hurry, and as they scurried to the main door she could hear that furious pounding behind them. A shiver ran down her spine. Best to get as far away from here as possible.

"Training cells neutralized," Obsidian muttered into the aural communicator he wore. He glanced at the pocket watch in his pocket, and then headed for the door at the end of the hallway.

The floor suddenly shook, dust shaking off nearby shelves. Something shattered in the distance.

Munitions factory. That sounded like Herbert and the others. Right on time.

"We've lost the element of surprise!" Gemma called, as Obsidian started running.

"Time to move fast," Malloryn commanded. "We need to track down Ghost before one of the others finds him first."

The first concussive boom echoed through the Core.

Ghost looked up from the maps he was perusing, listening intently. Gunfire echoed in distant corridors.

"They're here," Dido said, resting her hip against his desk. "They've taken the bait."

He reached for his coat and slipped it on, sliding several pistols into the holster he wore around his chest. "You know what you have to do."

Dido smiled, patting his lapels into place. "Go and be a good little distraction."

Ghost pressed a furious kiss against her lips. "They'll never see you coming, my love. Kill as many of them as you can."

"And the duke?"

"Have fun with Malloryn. Give my regards to Balfour when you see him."

"Don't get yourself killed."

A sneer curled his lip. "By this pathetic bunch? We are gods, Dido. Perfection. No mere blue blood is going to bring me down."

"I'm not worried about the blue bloods," she said.

Obsidian.

He straightened his collar, as another explosion rocked the building. "It's time I buried that rabid dog. Forever."

"Balfour won't like it. We were meant to keep him alive at all costs."

"Unfortunately, Obsidian gave me no choice," he replied, with a tight smile. "If Balfour ever asks, my finger slipped on the trigger."

CHAPTER THIRTY-ONE

"Well, well, well. What have we here?" Kincaid asked, kicking open the door to the medical bay.

Charlie slipped into the room after him, the arm cannon on his Cyclops' arm tracking through the room. Stainless steel benches were covered with an array of instruments. There was a chair in the corner with leather straps hanging from it, and some bizarre sort of helmet that looked like it would lock into place over a man's face....

Did it...? Did it have a needle attached to it? One as thick as the blade on an old-fashioned dirk?

Charlie felt sick. The arm cannon locked on the frantic man shoving files into a battered old travelling case.

"Here. You. Don't move," Charlie snapped.

The man held both hands in the air, his lip quivering. "Don't shoot me! I don't have any weapons. I'm just the doctor."

"Dr. Richter, by any chance?" he asked.

The man glanced between them. "Aye."

Hell. This was the bastard who'd put that device in Obsidian's head. Charlie glanced at the array of paper files strewn on every available bench. "What are you doing?"

Kincaid picked one of the files up, paper spewing from its interior.

"Don't touch that!" The doctor snapped, grabbing for it.

Kincaid drew his pistol and put it directly to the doctor's temples, not taking his eyes off the file. "You ain't in a position to be making demands." He looked up at Charlie. "Look at this."

Pistons hissed in the mechanical legs of the Cyclops he wore as he took several steps closer. Charlie pressed a button and the helmet slid back, so he could see better. "Dido. Zero. Silas…." He paused on the next file. It was thicker than all the others. "Obsidian."

Flipping it open, he glanced at the top page. It looked like a family tree had been torn out of a prayer book of some description, a gilded crest embossed at the top. Charlie turned the paper, reading the last names that had been filled in. *Dmitri Grigoriev. Nikolai Grigoriev. Yekaterina Grigoriev. Irina Grigoriev. Evgeni Grigoriev.*

His gaze zeroed back in on the first name on the list. *Dmitri.*

"Don't have time for this, Charlie," Kincaid warned. "Malloryn wants you to take out the power generator to the entire system. We've got to get moving."

Charlie yanked the doctor's satchel off him, and upended it. He carefully placed the file inside. "I think this is important. Obsidian needs to know what they took from him." He met the doctor's eyes. This wasn't just a family tree. It was a nobleman's bloodlines by the look of it. A Russian nobleman. "He has brothers and sisters he doesn't even know exist."

"If you open that door, you will regret it," the doctor warned. "And they're dead. They're all dead."

"Aye," Kincaid snorted. "And I'd trust a word that comes out of your—"

A sudden scream tore through the stillness of the room.

Bullets started firing.

They'd left several Nighthawks out there in the hallway.

"What was that?" Charlie whispered.

Another Nighthawk screamed, and the dreadful sound of bones breaking echoed as someone was thrown against the steel door. An animalistic bellow sent a chill down his spine.

Dr. Richter sucked in a sharp breath. "We have to get out of here!"

"Why?" Kincaid had his pistol pointed at the door.

"Because X is loose."

Charlie felt the heat drain from his face, as he locked his arm cannon on the door. "Isn't that the crazy *dhampir* we're supposed to stay far, far away from?"

"Fuckin' Jaysus," Kincaid said, shoving the enormous metal chair with its helmet apparatus toward the door to block it. "What are we going to do? We're trapped like rats."

Charlie turned and locked his arm cannon on the far wall. "Block the door. Then stay back."

"There he is!" Malloryn pointed.

A pale figure stepped out into the middle of the munitions factory, accompanied by two of the acolytes.

Thirty feet separated them, but everything in Obsidian went cold. He took a step forward, and saw Ghost still. The world vanished around the pair of them. All he could see was his brother. His master. His nemesis.

You stole my memories.

You sent me to kill her.

You hurt her.

"He's mine," Obsidian said softly, starting toward Ghost.

"I don't think so," Gemma countered, stalking forward at his side. A wicked pair of sai gleamed in her hands, and her breeches were made of tight leather that might have distracted him in better circumstances. "This bastard tore us apart. *He* put that bloody implant in my head."

"Take the left," he told her. "Then you can assist me if you like."

"I've got the right," Malloryn said grimly.

"You treacherous bastard," Ghost spat. "You. You did this."

Obsidian stalked toward him, the knife up his sleeve falling into his hand like an old lover. They'd made him an assassin. Made him the Wraith. Now they could deal with the consequences.

"No," he said, in a chilling voice. "You did this when you stole her from me."

Another explosion rocked the building. Herbert, judging from the sound of it. Malloryn assured him the butler could bury this place in rubble without killing them all in the process.

"So be it. I'll kill you all," Ghost said, drawing both of his knives.

They'd sparred in the past.

He knew every single one of his brother's moves.

But they'd never truly gone head-to-head before.

Flames reflected back off Ghost's dark pupils as he lunged forward, knives flashing in the light. Obsidian ducked and wove, moving faster than lightning.

Ducking under the next blow, Obsidian slammed a fist toward him, his fingers curled around the hilt of his knife. Ghost deflected it, and the pair of them exchanged a ringing pair of blows, hammering at each other with fury. As he spun, the razor-sharp edge of the knife kissed Ghost's cheekbone, raising a thin line of dark blood.

Behind them, Gemma spun low, sweeping Ghost's feet out from under him before turning to drive the sharp prongs of her sai right through the *dhampir's* throat.

Missed.

Ghost hit the floor, then rolled up onto the middle of his back and flipped to his feet. Obsidian drove his clenched fist forward to meet him. Solar plexus. Throat. He spun, kicking up in a blow meant to take Ghost's head off his shoulders. Or give him one hell of a headache in the meantime.

Ghost grabbed his shin, setting his hands in an ankle lock meant to break the joint, but as he dropped his shoulder to follow through, Obsidian threw himself into a spin, his other foot collecting Ghost's face.

The pair of them went down.

He hit the floor, fingers spread. Then he was up and moving with lethal intent, knives winking in the light. Gemma danced behind Ghost, waiting for a chance to strike, which kept Ghost's attention split.

She lunged forward, her sai painting a line of blood across the back of Ghost's hamstring, but Ghost grabbed a fistful of her chignon and hauled her forward, throwing her into Obsidian.

He barely had time to wrap his arms around her and stagger back before Ghost came at them. Shoving her out of the way, Obsidian drove his left knife up, barely countering Ghost's strike.

Then it was his turn to attack.

"I should have killed you when I had the chance," Ghost snarled, deflecting every blow with the steel gauntlets along his forearms.

"You talk too much." Obsidian planted the bottom of his boot into Ghost's chest, and Ghost hit the floor again. Blood dripped from a gash on his forehead as he crouched, his chest heaving. It was almost black in the firelight.

"One on one," Ghost spat. "You know you can't take me."

"I would, but you try convincing Gemma to step aside." He shrugged. "I think she deserves her pound of flesh."

Taking a small device from his pocket, Ghost sneered up at Obsidian. "Let's see how she enjoys this."

Ghost pressed the button.

Obsidian tensed, despite the fact Ava had operated on him last night, removing the second implant in his head.

Nothing happened.

Fire dripped from the ceiling, reflecting back from Ghost's pale eyes. His sneer vanished. He hit the button again. A third time.

His expression fell.

It was glorious.

"Expecting something to happen?" Obsidian let the weight of the knife soften in his palm.

"You deactivated it."

He took a menacing step forward. "One of Malloryn's agents removed it." His voice fell into a soft croon. "Now it's just you and me. No more mind games. No more tricks. Come on. You think you can handle me."

Ghost straightened to his full height.

"Careful," Gemma warned, holding her pistol on Ghost. "I daresay that's not the last of his tricks."

"You're right," Ghost purred, pressing his fingertips to the aural communicator in his ear. "Dido. Did you get a chance to unleash the beast?"

Dido? What the hell was *she* doing here? She was supposed to be in Russia.

And the beast?

His heart started ticking. They had to be speaking of X.

"Shoot him," he told Gemma urgently. The time for revenge was over.

Gemma pulled the trigger, just as Ghost threw himself aside. He scrambled across the stone floors as Gemma's gun retorted.

Bang, bang, bang. It was like the Tower all over again, but this time Ghost was the target.

A pair of bullet holes bloomed in Ghost's back as he fled, but the second she ran out of ammunition, he hissed at them and bolted for the stairs leading up to the factory roof.

"Reload!" Obsidian yelled, as he sprinted after him. "Then get the hell out of here. He's released X."

"Not without you!"

Stubborn bloody woman. "Can you not argue with me just this once?"

"I lost you last time. I'm not doing it again. This is forever, Obsidian. No matter how long or short that forever is."

Ghost hammered up the stairs, the long tail of his coat slapping around his legs.

Obsidian hauled himself after him, the muscles in his thighs aching and his heels ringing on the steel steps. He could hear Gemma on his heels, but all his attention was focused on the *dhampir* in front of him.

You are not going to escape me.

Below them, explosions rocketed the factory, Herbert making judicious use of his shoulder cannon. Heat seared the air, making it hard to breathe. They had to move fast.

Ghost reached the mesh walkway that bisected the factory, and yanked himself around the handrail onto the bridge, half-vanishing into the smoke.

Obsidian followed. He was halfway across the bridge when something blurred out of the shadows above them. An enormous cylinder dropped out of the rafters, and Ghost skidded to a halt ahead of him as it slammed through the other end of the bridge, taking half the walkway with it.

The mesh shuddered. Obsidian's feet nearly went out from under him, and he clung to the rail as the bridge shook and shivered.

Then they were standing there, staring at each other through a falling rain of dripping fire.

This man had stolen his memories.

His will.

His mind.

He'd fucking laughed in Obsidian's face when he sent Gemma to murder the queen.

But now it ended.

"No escape," Obsidian said, twirling his knives in his hands, the well-worn leather of the hilts settling against the calluses there like old friends.

Ghost turned to face him. He stripped his coat off and flung it into the abyss below before drawing his own steel again. "Are you sure you want to do this?"

"I've never been more certain of anything in my life."

"You traitor."

"That seems somewhat hypocritical, coming from your mouth."

Ghost's lip curled. "That cursed bitch ruined you—"

"Gemma only opened my eyes to the truth. I mean nothing to you. This *brotherhood* you preach to us is nothing more than a mockery. You care little for any of us. We are tools to you, nothing more. She set me free."

"As lovely as this little get-together has been," Gemma called behind him, "it's getting a little hot under the collar in here."

Obsidian advanced, and Ghost glanced behind him at the gap in the bridge as if gauging his chances of making it. Smoke billowed around them, stinging his eyes. Ghost smiled at Obsidian and edged closer to give himself room to get a run-up.

Oh no, you don't.

A bullet whizzed past him as Gemma shot at Ghost. The other *dhampir* snarled and threw his hands over his head.

"I'll cut him off," Gemma said, holstering her pistol and swinging under the mesh, so she was hanging above the inferno. He could barely see her through the smoke. "You keep his attention."

"Gemma." One slip, and she'd plunge into the flames below. "We're running out of time."

The entire factory was afire now.

X on the loose.

A thousand tons of water pressing down atop the burning building.

"Well, bloody hurry up and kill him, then we can get the hell out of here," she snapped, crawling along the mesh underneath.

"Apologies," he drawled. "Did you think I wasn't trying?"

Obsidian saw Ghost's gaze flicker down to where Gemma swung like a monkey beneath them.

Like hell.

His threw one of his knives at Ghost, and lunged forward.

They met in a clash of steel, knives whistling through the hot air as both ducked and wove. Grabbing Ghost's wrist, he slammed it upon the rail until Ghost was forced to release one of his blades. In retaliation, an elbow hammered into his teeth, and he staggered back.

Gemma swung beneath them on a small grappling line, and Ghost glanced down. Obsidian slammed Ghost against the rails before he could harm her.

It brought him dangerously within reach and he twisted out of the way like a cat as Ghost knifed him. The kiss of pain was an old friend as blood splashed from his side. Somehow he retaliated, and a thin line of blackened blood sprang up on Ghost's pale cheek as they broke apart.

"You've never beaten me," Ghost snarled.

"I've never really tried."

Over Ghost's shoulder, he saw Gemma haul herself up onto the bridge again like a lithe shadow, her catlike blue eyes locking on Ghost with all the intensity of someone staring between a pair of sights.

She drew her pistol and both of them heard the faint click of the hammer drawing back. No doubt it was aimed directly between Ghost's shoulder blades. Gemma didn't miss.

"It's over," he said.

Ghost raked the burning factory with a hard stare, frustration burning like a hot coal in his eyes. "We could have burned this city to the ground."

"For Balfour?"

"For *us*!" Ghost snapped. "These puling humans don't deserve to rule. They're cattle. Food. And the blue bloods are merely a stepping-stone in our evolutionary path. We could have ushered in a new age and ruled over all. We are gods. Balfour sees that."

"You keep saying *we*. But what you mean is *you*."

"Drop the knife," Gemma told him. "Or I'll shoot you in the back."

A pair of shadows divulged themselves on the other side of the gaping chasm of the bridge. A pale woman materialized in the smoke, her long silvery hair knotted into a chignon as she stalked toward them in an armored corset and a pair of leather trousers.

Obsidian froze.

Behind her, the Duke of Malloryn hauled himself up the last stair.

But it was Dido he focused on.

The gun in her hand, pointed directly at Gemma's back.

A moment of distraction. He saw the glint of silver and felt it slam into his side, right between his ribs. A razor-sharp stab of pain he ignored in the wake of the threat to Gemma.

"Gemma!" he bellowed, trying to warn her.

A pistol retorted, but he couldn't see what had happened to her....

Ghost grabbed him by the chin, slamming him back against the railing as he buried the knife deep and twisted it. "I will always be the better of the two of us. And she will always be your distraction. Your weakness."

Obsidian screamed in pain as the blade ground against his ribs.

Not a weakness, no.

But a reason to win, no matter what the cost.

If she was dead....

He could feel the darkness within him swimming to the surface, bringing with it the primal fury of the other half of his soul.

And for the first time in years, Obsidian gave himself over to it, his teeth elongating.

CHAPTER THIRTY-TWO

"This way!" Charlie screamed, hauling Kincaid along a narrow, poorly lit hallway toward the munitions factory.

He'd caught a glimpse of the monster chasing them as it smashed through the door into the medical bay. X was almost as large as Charlie's entire Cyclops suit, a leather muzzle strapped over his face, and his eyes hazed with broken blood vessels. The second he saw them, those piggish eyes lit up, and then blood was spraying across Charlie's face as X grabbed the doctor and ripped his head clean off.

Charlie had faced vampires and slasher gangs, *dhampir* and enraged blue blood lords in the past few years. Nothing had come closer to making him want to piss himself than the brute bellowing on their heels.

Red gleamed ahead of them.

Fire.

Almost to the factory.

Charlie shot a glance over his shoulder and saw X's broad shoulders backlit by the faint light. He'd paused to rip his mask off and sink his teeth into the doctor's throat, which was probably the only reason they were still alive, but the second they'd bolted he'd given chase.

Kincaid's arm was wrenched from his grasp, and Charlie dropped the satchel he'd somehow still been carrying.

Skidding to a halt, he heard Kincaid scream.

X slammed him against the wall, a single punch driving a dent into the side of Kincaid's Achilles II armor. Solid sheet metal buckled, and Kincaid grunted.

Charlie lunged forward, his steel fingers enclosing around X's throat. He smashed him into the other wall, but X simply bellowed and grabbed hold of his own suit.

Oh, shit.

The *dhampir's* forehead slammed into his, and Charlie lost his grip. A series of blows sent him reeling, as hot breath caressed his face.

"Kincaid!" he screamed.

Teeth raked at the metal collar around his throat, and Charlie scrambled to hold X off. Barely. Then he was staggering back, his feet going out from under him as Kincaid came out of nowhere to tackle X.

Charlie hit the floor with a steely rasp, sliding several feet.

He felt like a frigging turtle on its back, and tried to kick his feet. His legs were strapped inside the Cyclops, and the pistons hissed as the gas-powered joints reacted to his movement. Somehow he rolled onto his side, steel knuckles pushing into the floor as he found his knees.

If he got out of this, then he was going to have to work on the suit's dexterity.

But that was a problem for another time.

Kincaid grappled with the beast, every punch sending him staggering back a step. Fire formed a frame around X, as Kincaid was shoved back against the metal railing of the munitions factory. They had to be several levels above the factory floor.

X peeled the top layer of his chest carapace open and tossed it aside.

"Kincaid!" Charlie yelled, lining them both up. "Get clear!"

Kincaid's eyes locked on him, as Charlie lifted the arm cannon. He grabbed X by the arms and forced the bastard to the side. "Shoot him!"

Charlie pulled the trigger.

The small missile in his arm cannon zoomed toward the enormous monster.

Kincaid managed to get clear at the last second, and X spun, snarling as he tried to snatch at the missile. It exploded as it hit his chest, flinging him over the rail.

And then he was gone.

Charlie's arm shook as he lowered his arm.

Every inch of him started to tremble.

Holy shit.

Had they just survived?

It had all happened so quickly he couldn't quite make heads or tails of it.

Kincaid knelt on one knee, panting. "Mother of Jaysus." Raking a shaky hand through his sweaty hair, he found the blood there and lowered his fingers to rub them together. "That was close."

Charlie managed to push to his feet. He peered over the rail into the inferno. X had vanished. "Do you think he's dead?"

"Surely he couldn't have survived that."

Nothing but silence drifted up through the billowing smoke.

They both looked at each other.

"Time to get out of here?" Charlie suggested. "Just in case?"

"Definitely."

"Let me just fetch the doctor's satchel."

The shot took Gemma high in the shoulder as she tried to drop, alerted by Obsidian's scream.

Gemma's breath was torn from her lungs, pain spasming down her arm. The same bloody arm she'd dislocated. She ground her teeth together and forced her knife into her weaker hand, blocking the pain.

Behind her, separated by a gaping chasm of over ten feet, Malloryn crashed into the *dhampir* woman who'd shot her. The pair of them grappled, the pistol flying from the woman's hand.

Malloryn could handle it.

Gemma's gaze locked on Ghost. He slammed Obsidian against the railing, and the pair of them exchanged ringing blows. Obsidian ducked beneath a wildly swung haymaker and threw a cracking punch that would have taken the head off anyone else's shoulders. Ghost's chin snapped up.

They broke apart, but Ghost lashed out as he danced backward, and Obsidian was still slightly off-balance from that last blow.

The split second slowed down as Gemma watched it all unfold.

It was like Russia all over again.

Dmitri raising the gun.

Pulling the trigger.

The abrupt slam of the bullet, right in the center of her chest.

Inevitable.

A single kick to the chest and Obsidian staggered against the railing, his center of balance too high, his hands flailing as he reached for something. Anything—

He went over, groping for the rails as he fell. The barest edge of his fingertips caught the bottom rung. Gemma scrambled to her knees.

"Dmitri!" she screamed.

Ghost shot her a dark look, then crunched his heel down upon Obsidian's fingers.

And he was gone.

Vanishing into the inferno below, his coat fluttering as he plummeted, like Lucifer falling directly into hell.

Noooo!

Gemma sprinted toward Ghost, sliding to her knees as Ghost lunged for her. The knife in her hand slashed through the back of his knee, effectively hamstringing him as he lunged past. The Falcon within her awoke, the world shutting down to just her and him.

Ghost needed to die.

No hesitation.

Not this time.

She wanted to cut his throat and feel his cold blood splash against her face.

The world vanished into darkness as the hunger roared through her.

Gemma threw herself forward and rolled over her shoulder onto her feet. None too soon. She caught a flash of movement behind her, and drove her boot back as she gained her balance. Her heel smashed into a knee, and Ghost screamed as bone crunched.

"You bitch!"

A blow smashed into her cheek as she spun, sending her staggering against the rail. She lashed behind her with the knife, but another sharp chop to the side of the neck made her head spin, and her right arm was numb from the bullet wedged high.

The world blurred.

Fire. Smoke. Pain.

But pain was an old friend.

A means to sharpen the mind against the brief dulling of her senses.

"Pull the trigger, cadet."

Rage soared through her chest like a phoenix rising from its ashes. This wasn't merely fighting to kill a man who'd hurt Obsidian. No, this was a direct strike at Balfour. Never again would she be used to hurt her friends. Her queen.

Gemma drew on everything she had within her to leap up onto the railing as Ghost lunged toward her.

Launching herself backward into a flip, she plunged her knife down into the thick muscle of his trapezius, driving it as close to the carotid as possible. Ghost fell against the rail with a scream.

She landed on the mesh behind him, head swimming.

Her right hand felt numb, blood slicking her fingers. The bullet wound throbbed. How much blood had she lost?

Too much.

Ghost made an inhuman sound, hauling her knife out of his flesh. Blood welled between his fingers, but not enough to put him down. Gemma hauled the thin wire she carried up her sleeve into both hands and thrust it over his head, yanking it tight as she hauled him back against her. Twisting both ends of the wire, she turned and went down on one knee, bending his larger body over hers as she tried to strangle him.

Go down, damn you.

Ghost choked, kicking furiously.

"Gemma!" Malloryn screamed, but she didn't dare look for him.

Cursing her useless right hand, she twisted into the action, knotting both ends of the wire around her aching hands and setting her teeth against the scream of pain through her shoulder.

Die.

Fingers groped for the bullet wound in her shoulder, digging into it.

The world swam as she screamed, and her hold loosened for one crucial second.

Ghost suddenly kicked against the rail, pushing off. He rolled over her back, taking her arms—and the garrote—with him.

"Gemma, down!"

Malloryn again.

She tried. Honestly, she did.

But the garrote was wrapped too tightly around her hands.

Ghost hauled her toward him, his forehead slamming into hers. She lost a moment. Perhaps too many. Gemma swayed, the world blurring around her in a roar of dark shadows and flames.

And then Ghost hauled her back against his chest and put his knife to her throat as he turned to face Malloryn.

CHAPTER THIRTY-THREE

"Put the pistol down, or I'll cut her throat," Ghost said.

Gemma grabbed his wrist, trying to halt the progress of the knife set against her throat, but it was like gripping steel cables. No give.

She shot Malloryn a nervous look.

There was nothing left of the icy gray of the duke's irises as he stood over the *dhampir* woman he'd felled with his electrode-stimulating device. His dartgun was locked on Ghost, and she knew he was carrying darts laced with Black Vein.

But he froze as he saw her predicament.

"You too," Ghost said, in a dangerously soft voice, wrenching her around just enough to see Obsidian haul himself onto the platform, the silver glint of a grappling hook locked in the mesh.

He'd survived.

Relief burst through her as she realized what must have happened. Obsidian must have flung one of his hooks as he fell, and slowly hauled himself up. She'd been so focused on the fight, she hadn't noticed. She felt like her heart was going to burst right out of her chest.

"Can you not simply die?" Ghost hissed at Obsidian.

"I'm the Wraith. I can't die."

"No? But you can watch her go first."

Gemma squeaked and arched backward as the knife cut her skin. She didn't dare swallow.

"It appears we're at an impasse," Malloryn said coolly. "If you hurt Gemma, then you're a dead man. You cannot escape. There are two of us."

Gemma sucked in a sharp breath, tilting her chin high to try and escape the knife. The shock collar offered no protection.

Her heart pounded in her ears, and she glanced up at Ghost, trying to calculate her trajectory. If she kicked up, she could— No. He had the blasted knife right over her carotid artery.

It might not kill you.

Head or heart, after all. Gemma's heartbeat slowed to a crawl as she considered her options.

"Who said I needed to escape?" Ghost demanded. "As long as it hurts you, Malloryn, then my mission is done. I can't fail. I *won't*." Grabbing her jaw in his fingers, he turned her toward the duke. "It's like déjà vu, isn't it?"

The knife tracked its way lower, and Gemma's eyes rolled as she tried to see where it was going. Its tip pierced the outer layer of her body armor, drawing a bead of blood as he set it to her sternum.

Suddenly she couldn't breathe.

Armored corset or not, if he drove it through her heart, then she'd never survive.

Her frantic gaze met Obsidian's. If this was going to be the end, then the last thing she wanted to see was his face.

"It's like watching Balfour put his pistol to Catherine's temple and pull the trigger, all over again." Ghost mused. "She looks so like Catherine, doesn't she? That's why she was chosen, Malloryn. Sent to kill you, so you'd be the one to put a bullet in her heart. But ah, alas, it was not to be. The little turncoat somehow wrangled her way out of certain death. Or was that you, granting her mercy? She means a lot to you, doesn't she? I suggest you put the gun down. Because while you could kill me, you'll never save her."

The goddamned bastard! Her life was worth more than a means to slight Malloryn.

Gemma's heart fluttered, like a flock of birds taking flight. *"Don't,"* she mouthed at the duke.

The second he dropped his weapon he was vulnerable.

Malloryn remained frozen, his dartgun trained upon them.

"I won't ask again," Ghost spat, and dug the knife in hard enough to cut.

Gemma cried out as blood welled and ran down beneath her corset. It was meant to stop a blow and deflect the edge of a knife. Not to prevent her from being stabbed.

"All right," the duke said softly, bending to place his dartgun on the wire mesh of the bridge.

"Kick it over the edge."

His gaze met hers, as if Malloryn was trying to tell her something.

Then Malloryn kicked his pistol away.

At his feet, Dido slowly crawled to her hands and knees, shooting the duke a merciless look.

"Gemma," Obsidian called in a low voice. "Remember how I took you down in the tower?"

What the hell did he——? She suddenly froze. The shock collar around her throat.

"Do it," she said, reaching up and grabbing Ghost's arm.

Obsidian must have pressed the control device, for current suddenly arced through her.

Gemma screamed, her body jerking and kicking back as Ghost was flung away from her. She hit the mesh, panting hard and the stink of something burning filling her nostrils. Every inch of her body felt like it had been hit with a metal pipe, and her heart gave an erratic squeeze.

She could hear fists striking flesh and someone grunting in the distance, but Obsidian leapt past her.

He kicked Ghost in the ribs as the *dhampir* crawled to his knees, flinging him onto his back.

"This is for Gemma," he said coldly, and drove his knife directly into Ghost's heart.

Blood splashed his face when Obsidian came for her.

"Are you all right?" he demanded, helping her to her feet.

Gemma fell into his arms, wincing as her burned hands came into contact with his chest. They'd heal. Indeed, she could already feel them tingling as the craving virus sought to regenerate her tortured flesh. Her throat was practically on fire. "I'm alive. That's all… that counts. I presume Ghost is no longer with us?"

Obsidian shuddered, wrapping his arms carefully around her and gently pressing her face to his chest. "No. I cut his heart out of his chest."

"We did it."

And they'd both survived.

"I thought I'd lost you," she blurted.

"I thought I'd left you here to die." Obsidian's voice shook as he cupped her face in both hands and kissed her.

She hadn't dared think of the alternative—of what it might be like to truly lose him for good. There hadn't been time.

But it burst through her now, stealing her breath, making her feel ill at the thought of how close they'd come to losing each other forever.

"We need to get out of here," Obsidian said, drawing back from the kiss.

The other half of the mesh walkway was empty.

Gemma froze, her eyes stinging from the overwhelming smoke. She could barely see through it. "Where's Malloryn?"

Obsidian spun around, several large strides taking him to the edge of the broken walkway. "He was just here. I was cutting Ghost's heart out while he put Dido down again."

"Malloryn!" Gemma yelled.

Her voice echoed through the factory, as she started coughing. Her throat felt raw, and her eyes were watering.

There was nothing but static in her aural communicator, as she coughed and hacked. *Damn it.* Gemma sucked in a sharp breath, but it only made her lungs spasm again.

Obsidian stared across the gap where Malloryn had been. "Damn it. Dido must have shaken off the hemlock he hit her with."

Somehow she made her way to his side, covering her mouth with one hand. "What do you mean? Where is he?"

"She's taken him," he rasped.

"Then we need to find him!"

CHAPTER THIRTY-THREE

Blood dripped in a clear trail leading toward the docking bay.

"She won't kill him," Obsidian promised Gemma as they pounded down narrow hallways, heading for the submersibles. His eyes were watering, but at least the air was clearer here. "Balfour's instructions were clear: Malloryn is to survive at all costs. He's supposed to lose everything before Balfour plans to grant him the release of death."

"That's not reassuring!"

He caught a glimpse of the *dhampir* woman ahead of them, dumping the unconscious duke into the open hatch of one of the kraken submersibles in the docking bay.

It was the perfect way to get in and out of London without being seen. The flooded tunnel led directly into the Thames, and from there it was but a brief journey out to sea.

Dido saw them coming and lifted a pistol from her belt.

Obsidian barely had time to note the flare of white recoil before he drove Gemma into the wall. A dart hissed past them.

"What are you doing?" Gemma yelled. "She's going to escape!"

"Dido carries darts laced with Black Vein. If one of them hits us we're dead. She has no need to keep either of us alive."

Another dart buried itself in the wall near his head. Obsidian shoved Gemma's head low and they ran toward the docking bay. There were two submersibles waiting in the bays. Above them a thick glass dome kept the crushing weight of thousands of tons of black water off them.

Dido tugged something from the bag at her belt, and dropped it inside the open hatch of the only other submersible. Then she stepped inside the kraken's belly, reaching up to lower the steel hatch behind her. It clanked shut with a steely rasp as Obsidian leaped on top of it.

He tried to twist the wheel, but it was locked from inside. The submersible suddenly began to tremble beneath his feet, its enormous engines roaring to life.

Foam churned as the kraken's tentacle propellers began whirring behind it.

"Dmitri!" Gemma yelled.

Water bubbled up around his boots as the kraken began to submerge. It hit his knees, and he was forced to leap back onto the dock, where Gemma paced.

"Damn it. Where will she go?"

"We just destroyed their London base. She only has one place to go."

Russia.

"Can we take the other submersible?"

He started toward it, just as an enormous fireball suddenly bloomed within the belly of the beast. The impact launched him off his feet and slammed him into a nearby wall.

When he came to, thick black smoke roiled through the docking bay and flames licked at the timber deck. Gemma knelt beside him, her fingers pressed to his pulse.

"Thank God," she whispered, when his eyes blinked up at her. Slipping an arm under his shoulder, she helped him to his feet. "There goes that plan."

Obsidian looked up. Cracks snaked through the glass above them. Steel shuddered and groaned behind them. Herbert had promised he could bring the Core down if they gave him enough time.

"Gemma." He grabbed her by the shoulders. "Gemma, we have to get out of here. This entire building is about to collapse."

"What about Malloryn?"

The look on her face almost gutted him. "He's gone, Gemma. Dido's taken him with her."

"No!" Gemma shoved away from him, striding toward the ruin of the kraken submersible. She stared at it intently, as if pure determination could resurrect its steel carcass from where it sank into the depths. "I am *not* going to let that bitch get out of here with him!"

An explosion rocketed through the building nearby, flame spewing along the hallway. Obsidian threw himself into her, carrying her to the ground as fire gushed over the top of them.

"We don't have a choice!" he yelled. "We can't rescue him if we're both dead."

Water began hissing through a crack in the wall, spraying across them. Obsidian looked up into the welling darkness above them.

"We're going to have to swim," he yelled, tearing one of the motorized propulsion packs from the wall and slipping it over his shoulders. They'd been hung there for years for precisely this situation. He'd never expected to have to need one of them.

Gemma paled.

And he suddenly remembered her fear of drowning.

"I'll stay with you," he said, slipping the second pack onto her back and strapping it into place. "I promise. We have to escape, Gem, and there's no other way."

"I can do this," she whispered.

"I won't let you go."

Another gush of water suddenly sprang through the wall supports. The groan of the glass above them sounded like some sort of hungry beast. Grabbing the small mouthpiece that was attached to the oxygen canister on the propulsion pack, he settled it over Gemma's mouth, and lashed them together with a small tether.

"There's enough oxygen in there to last three minutes. Are you ready?"

He strapped his mouthpiece into place as Gemma nodded, and held up three fingers, folding them down one at a time.

Three. Two. One.

They both leapt down into the water where Dido had vanished. Kicking hard, he hauled her into the narrow tunnel that led out to sea. The entire world around them was black. Charlie had clearly managed to take out the power grid, so not a single gaslight illuminated the darkness. He was swimming blind.

Flipping the switch on his propulsion pack, he felt the engine kick. None too soon. The world shuddered around them and a wave of water suddenly propelled them forward. He felt Gemma smash into him, and they were buffeted along. The glass dome must have shattered, spilling all its water into the docking bay.

Ears popping with pressure, he tried to hold them steady. The tether between them stretched and pulled, and the mouthpiece was torn from his lips.

A stream of bubbles escaped him.

No air. Bloody hell.

Obsidian's lungs were burning. He had no idea how much further it was, or what condition Gemma was in. All he could do was hope.

Then a light appeared ahead of them.

Daylight.

His ears were ringing as they surged toward it. His lungs began heaving, desperately demanding air.

They were nearly there. A few seconds more....

Both of them surfaced in the Thames with a cough and a gasp. Obsidian sucked in vast lungfuls of sweet oxygen as someone grabbed him by the propulsion pack and turned him around.

"Are you all right?" Gemma called.

Obsidian barely had the strength left to answer her.

The overcast sky seemed so shockingly bright after the darkness. Even as it burned his skin, he'd never seen anything better.

The hollow taste of victory soured Gemma's mouth as COR regathered at the safe house. Everyone else was accounted for, the mission an alleged success, except for one small fact. There'd been no sign of Dido—or Malloryn—as they escaped the burning docking bay. From the flooded underground tunnel, it was a short journey to the Thames, and from there...

Anywhere.

"What do we do about Malloryn?" Gemma whispered, trembling with the cold as Obsidian draped a blanket over her shoulders.

"We don't know where Dido has taken him." Byrnes pinched the bridge of his nose. "We don't even know if he's still alive."

"He's still alive." Obsidian stirred, tugging at the buckles on his damp body armor and trying to pry the hard carapace off his chest. "Dido won't kill him. She wouldn't dare. This was always meant to end with Malloryn watching his world burn. And I know where they're going. It's the only place Dido *can* retreat, with everything having gone horribly wrong."

"Where?" Byrnes demanded.

Gemma squeezed her eyes shut. Obsidian had said it. There was only one place they could go.

"Russia," Obsidian replied. "Saint Petersburg. Dido is taking Malloryn to Balfour."

Ingrid clapped a hand to her lips. "No."

Kincaid thumped a hand on her shoulder. "We'll get him back, Ingrid."

"How?" Ingrid snapped, her eyes flashing with verwulfen bronze as her emotions heated.

The three of them started arguing about the court as Gemma pinched the bridge of her nose. She just needed a moment to think. Time.

Or better yet, Malloryn.

He always had a solution to every problem, and his confidence cut through even the most nervous of dispositions. Vampires rioting through London? *Well, go out there and cut them down, by golly.* A secret organization of blue bloods trying to poison the Echelon's entire blood supply? *Pack your ammunition and haul ass. We're going to stop them.*

But now he was gone, and she had no idea what to do.

Herbert pushed into the study carrying a tray with the tea setting Gemma was so familiar with. Behind him, an 1880 service automaton followed like a duckling scuttling behind its mother, steam hissing through its vents.

"Thought we could all use some refreshment," Herbert said, once more wearing the polite façade of COR's butler, though soot still stained his collar, and his black apron no doubt hide a variety of likeminded sins.

"Unless it's a bottle of brandy, I don't think any of us is going to find it quite refreshing enough," Byrnes grumbled.

"You haven't tried my tea then, Master Byrnes."

Gemma stared at the map on Malloryn's desk, the familiar scent of his office wrapping around her as Herbert fussed over them.

Isabella was gone.

Now Malloryn.

There was no one left to lead them.

She couldn't help thinking Balfour had won this game. Not just won it, but swept them off the map.

Yes, they might have depleted the *dhampir* forces ranged against them. They'd won over Obsidian's loyalty. Stopped the queen's assassination. And yes, they might have blown up a warehouse and the Core, ending the *dhampir* operations in London, but Balfour had been playing the endgame. Every little step they'd taken, he'd been three in front of them.

Without Malloryn, they were just a handful of spies, weren't they?

"What the hell do we do now?" Charlie asked in a quiet voice. "We can't just leave him there."

"It's the Crimson Court," Byrnes said. "Nobody gets out of there alive unless they were invited in in the first place, and I like my head right where it is, thank you very much."

"So we just pretend it didn't happen?" Even Kincaid sounded affronted, and he'd had more reason to hate Malloryn over the years than anyone.

"No." Gemma's voice dropped into the silence like a bomb. "Malloryn's a Rogue, and we don't leave each other behind. No matter what we face."

Attentive faces turned to her, and she suffered a moment of doubt. Could she do this? Could *she* be the one who welded them together in the face of their greatest challenge?

You can do this. Malloryn might have been the brains of the operation, but she had always been the heart and soul of it, his link to the rest of these people.

But there was doubt on every face in the room. Byrnes glanced toward Ingrid, and she knew he saw his wife in danger. Ava's knees went out from under her as she slumped into her chair hopelessly.

"Balfour has had years to build up his alliances there," Byrnes pointed out. "We don't even know what we're walking into."

"Gemma and I know the court," Obsidian said, circling the map. "Our fates were forged there. And I... know of people in the heart of the court who might be sympathetic. There's a possibility I could get in touch with Silas. His allegiances toward the brotherhood aren't watertight. Not anymore." His voice roughened. "And he owes me one."

Heads turned toward him, and Gemma felt a burst of relief when she realized there was someone else to be her rock now.

"That gives us an inside man," Gemma said.

"Perhaps."

Their eyes met.

Pacing back and forth, she pressed a hand to her temples. "What do you know of Balfour's operations there?"

"He married into one of the royal bloodlines; a Grand Duchess by the name of Tatiana Feodorevna. They maintain separate houses, and she's much younger than he is. The marriage is a political alliance only, and there are rumors his wife prefers the company of women, but it affords him a certain type of power. He's not of the Blood, but he's made himself quite useful to several powerful Blood princes."

"Feodorevna? First tier?" she whispered.

"First tier."

The purest of the Blood, related to the Tzarina, and with a direct claim upon the empire's throne should the Tzarina finally greet the long dawn. Of course Balfour would ingratiate himself there. Now, not only was he armed with several ruthless *dhampir* agents, but he would have dozens of political allies, power, money, influence.... How the hell were they going to be able to touch him?

How could they rescue Malloryn?

"We're not actually thinking about infiltrating the Blood court, are we? I'm trying to be the voice of reason here. And this plan sounds positively insane." Byrnes scowled, and scrubbed a hand through his hair.

"I seem to recall Malloryn distracting Zero when she tried to rip your throat out," Charlie pointed out. "He didn't flinch."

"It's not me I'm worried about," Byrnes shot back.

"We've faced vampires, Black Vein, the neural implant, and *dhampir*." Ingrid leveled a steady look upon him. "If you think I'm frightened of the Blood, then you can think again."

"He pulled me out of a burning building," Kincaid said quietly. "Saved my life."

"And he was there to rescue me when that *dhampir* assassin injected me with Black Vein," Ava whispered.

Ingrid simply looked at him. "Caleb."

Byrnes scowled. "Fine. I'm going to enjoy the look on his bloody face when Malloryn sees us. I'm going to remind him he's in our debt every time he gets that constipated look on his face. This will give me years of ammunition against him. This trumps every debt we've ever owed him. Dukes don't crawl? Ha. I'm going to insist upon him kissing my boots."

"I'd like to see that," Kincaid said, pushing to his feet. "How do we do this, Gem? You're in charge."

She met Obsidian's eyes. The tide of the room was shifting. Relief flushed through her. He smiled a little dangerously. Her dark angel.

"Russia is dangerous. But we have a trump card up our sleeve." Gemma straightened, meeting every single eye in the room. "They will never expect us to come for him. Balfour's men know fear, not loyalty. Not love. They don't fight for him or each other. They've been double-crossing each other at every turn, and now we have an insider who can assist us. I won't pretend this will not be a difficult, well-nigh impossible task but we have to try. Who's with me? Who's coming to Russia?"

Every hand in the room rose.

"Can I bring Molly, miss?" Herbert asked.

"You can *definitely* bring Molly. I would like to ram that rocket-launcher right down Balfour's throat."

And Gemma started planning.

"Before I forget," Charlie called, as Obsidian went to run Gemma a bath. "I've got something for you."

Obsidian paused on the stairs. Charlie ran up them as if hadn't just fought a cataclysmic battle, faced a nightmare, and somehow survived.

He handed over a thick file stuffed full of bloodied pages.

"Sorry." Charlie grimaced, trying to wipe some of the blood off. "Your friend, X, came upon us just as we discovered the files. Got a bit mucky for a while. I think most of it is the good doctor's."

His name was on the front. Obsidian frowned. "What is it?"

"All of Dr. Richter's notes about you. Thought you might like to read it. I think there's some mention of where you came from."

His heart skipped a beat as he slowly looked up.

"We didn't look through it," Charlie assured him. "Just enough to ascertain it might be important to you. There's a family tree in the front I think you'll find interesting."

Fingers trembling, Obsidian slowly opened the file. The occasional memory was coming back to him—mostly odd irrelevant flashes that meant little—but nothing solid. He'd long given up on the idea of ever piecing together his past, though the ache of it bothered him.

The second he saw the golden crest at the top, he froze. He recognized that seal, and the family it belonged to.

Grigoriev.

The heat drained out of his face. Dmitri, Nikolai, Yekaterina, Irina and Evgeni. The names stirred something within him. He could see a pair of young children scampering through snowdrifts, their cheeks rosy as they laughed and hurled snowballs at each other.

If this was real, then....

Sergey Grigoriev was his cousin.

The same Sergey who'd allegedly murdered the entire Grigoriev family years ago in a bid to take their power.

The Sergey that Balfour had tasked him to guard.

What did it all mean? How had it happened? Was he truly Dmitri Grigoriev, the eldest son of the former Prince of Tsaritsyn? Who had Marina been?

How had he ended up in London?

How much had Balfour and Dr. Richter taken from him?

"Thank you," he said, slowly. The world reeled around him.

Charlie clapped a hand on his shoulder, gave a wink, and then headed up the stairs. "You're one of us now, Obsidian. Rogues have got to look out for each other."

Gemma was right. The young man truly was a treasure.

He stared down at the file as Charlie disappeared. A damned shame the doctor's throat had been torn out.

Now there was only one man still alive who might know the truth.

It was a good thing he was already planning on heading to Russia.

He was long overdue a certain chat with Lord Balfour.

THE END

COMING 2018

TO CATCH A ROGUE

LONDON STEAMPUNK: THE BLUE BLOOD CONSPIRACY

An impossible heist. A thief and a rogue. But will she steal his heart, instead?

The Company of Rogues finally knows the identity of the mastermind behind a plot against the queen—but their enemy is still one step ahead of them. When he kidnaps one of theirs, the Rogues plan a daring rescue mission that will lead them into the heart of the bloodthirsty Crimson Court.

It's a job for a master thief, and there's nothing Charlie Todd likes more than a challenge. To pull off the impossible, Charlie needs a crew, including the only thief who's ever been able to outfox him.

He broke her heart. But now she must risk it all to save his life...

Lark's spent years trying to forget her past, but the one thing she can't ignore is the way a single smile from Charlie still sets her heart on fire. When he proposes they work together again, it feels just like old times, but she has one rule: this is strictly business.

It's Charlie's last chance to prove he can be trusted with her heart. But Lark's keeping a deadly secret. And as passions are stirred and the stakes mount, it might be the kind of secret that could destroy them all...

Want to know more about To Catch A Rogue? Make sure you sign up to my newsletter at www.becmcmaster.com to be the first to know its release date, read exclusive excerpts, and see cover reveals.

ACKNOWLEDGEMENTS

I owe huge thanks to my editor Olivia from Hot Tree Editing for putting everything it the right place and also her unabashed demands for more Malloryn; to my cover artists from Damonza.com who nailed this cover; and Marisa Wesley and Allyson Gottlieb from Cover Me Darling for the print formatting.

To Kylie Griffin and Jennie Kew, as always, who are the best support team any writer could dream of; and the Central Victorian Writers group for keeping me sane and celebrating the small goals with all those chocolates! And special thanks to my family, and to my other half—my very own beta hero, Byron—who has always been unabashedly proud of this dream of mine, even when I didn't know if I could do it.

Last, not least, to all of my readers who support me on this journey, and have been crazy vocal about their love for the London Steampunk series, and anything else I write!

ABOUT THE AUTHOR

BEC MCMASTER is a writer, a dreamer, and a travel addict. If she's not sitting in front of the computer, she's probably plotting her next overseas trip, and plans to see the whole world, whether it's by paper, plane, or imagination.

Bec grew up on a steady diet of '80s fantasy movies like *Ladyhawke*, *Labyrinth*, and *The Princess Bride*, and loves creating epic, fantasy-based romances with heroes and heroines who must defeat all the odds to have their HEA. She lives in Australia with her very own hero, where she can be found creating the dark and dangerous worlds of the London Steampunk, Dark Arts, Legends of The Storm, or Burned Lands series, where even the darkest hero can find love.

For news on new releases, cover reveals, contests, and special promotions, join her mailing list at www.becmcmaster.com